PENGUIN CLASSICS

THE BOOK OF DISQUIET

'A Modernist touchstone . . . no one has explored alternative selves with Pessoa's mixture of determination and abandon . . . In a time which celebrates fame, success, stupidity, convenience and noise, here is the perfect antidote, a hymn of praise to obscurity, failure, intelligence, difficulty and silence' John Lanchester, *Daily Telegraph*

'His prose masterpiece . . . Richard Zenith has done an heroic job in producing the best English-language version we are likely to see for a long time, if ever' Nicholas Lezard, *Guardian*

'*The Book of Disquiet* was left in a trunk which might never have been opened. The gods must be thanked that it was. I love this strange work of fiction and I love the inventive, hard-drinking, modest man who wrote it in obscurity' Paul Bailey, *Independent*

'Fascinating, even gripping stuff . . . a strangely addictive pleasure' Kevin Jackson, *Sunday Times*

'Must rank as the supreme assault on authorship in modern European literature . . . readers of Zenith's edition will find it supersedes all others in its delicacy of style, rigorous scholarship and sympathy for Pessoa's fractured sensibility . . . the self-revelation of a disoriented and half-disintegrated soul that is all the more compelling because the author himself is an invention . . . Long before postmodernism became an academic industry, Pessoa lived deconstruction' John Gray, *New Statesman*

'Portugal's greatest modern poet . . . deals with the only important question in the world, not less important because it is unanswerable: What am I?' Anthony Burgess, *Observer*

'Pessoa's rapid prose, snatched in flight and restlessly suggestive, remains haunting, often startling, like the touch of a vibrating wire, elusive and persistent like the poetry . . . there is nobody like him' W. S. Merwin, *New York Review of Books*

Fernando Pessoa was born in Lisbon in 1888 and was brought up in Durban, South Africa. In 1905 he returned to Lisbon to enrol at the university, but soon dropped out, preferring to study on his own. He made a modest living translating the foreign correspondence of various commercial firms, and wrote obsessively – in English, Portuguese and French. He self-published several chapbooks of his English poems in 1918 and 1922, and regularly contributed his Portuguese poems to literary journals such as *Orpheu* and *Portugal Futurista*. *Mensagem*, a collection of poems on patriotic themes, won a consolation prize in a national competition in 1934. Pessoa wrote much of his greatest poetry under three main 'heteronyms', Alberto Caeiro, Alvaro de Campos and Ricardo Reis, whose fully fleshed biographies he invented, giving them different writing styles and points of view. He created dozens of other writerly personas, including the assistant bookkeeper Bernardo Soares, fictional author of *The Book of Disquiet*. Although Pessoa was acknowledged as an intellectual and a poet, his literary genius went largely unrecognized until after his death in 1935.

Richard Zenith lives in Lisbon, where he works as a freelance writer, translator and critic. His translations include Galician–Portuguese troubadour poetry, novels by António Lobo Antunes and *Fernando Pesso and Co. – Selected Poems*, which won the 1999 American PEN Award for Poetry in Translation.

FERNANDO PESSOA

The Book of Disquiet

Edited and translated by

RICHARD ZENITH

PENGUIN BOOKS

PENGUIN BOOKS
Published by the Penguin Group
Penguin Group (USA) Inc., 375 Hudson Street, New York, New York 10014, U.S.A.
Penguin Group (Canada), 90 Eglinton Avenue East, Suite 700, Toronto, Ontario, Canada M4P 2Y3 (a division of Pearson Penguin Canada Inc.)
Penguin Books Ltd, 80 Strand, London WC2R 0RL, England
Penguin Ireland, 25 St Stephen's Green, Dublin 2, Ireland (a division of Penguin Books Ltd)
Penguin Group (Australia), 250 Camberwell Road, Camberwell, Victoria 3124, Australia (a division of Pearson Australia Group Pty Ltd)
Penguin Books India Pvt Ltd, 11 Community Centre, Panchsheel Park, New Delhi – 110 017, India
Penguin Group (NZ), 67 Apollo Drive, Rosedale, North Shore 0632, New Zealand (a division of Pearson New Zealand Ltd)
Penguin Books (South Africa) (Pty) Ltd, 24 Sturdee Avenue, Rosebank, Johannesburg 2196, South Africa

Penguin Books Ltd, Registered Offices: 80 Strand, London WC2R 0RL, England

First published in Portugal as *Livro do Desassossego* by Assírio & Alvim 1998
First published in Great Britain by Allen Lane The Penguin Press 2001
Published in Penguin Classics (U.K.) 2002
Published in Penguin Books (U.S.A.) 2003

33

ISBN 978-0-14-118304-6
CIP data available

Printed in the United States of America

Contents

Introduction

I'm astounded whenever I finish something. Astounded and distressed. My perfectionist instinct should inhibit me from finishing; it should inhibit me from even beginning. But I get distracted and start doing something. What I achieve is not the product of an act of my will but of my will's surrender. I begin because I don't have the strength to think; I finish because I don't have the courage to quit. This book is my cowardice. (Text 152)

Fernando António Nogueira Pessoa was born in Lisbon in 1888, died there in 1935, and did not often leave the city as an adult, but he spent nine of his childhood years in the British-governed town of Durban, South Africa, where his stepfather was the Portuguese consul. Pessoa, who was five years old when his natural father died of tuberculosis, developed into a shy and highly imaginative boy, and a brilliant student. Shortly after his seventeenth birthday, he returned to Lisbon to enrol in the university but soon dropped out, preferring to study on his own at the National Library, where he systematically read major works of philosophy, history, sociology and literature (especially Portuguese) in order to complement and extend the traditional English education he had received in South Africa. His production of poetry and prose in English during this period was intense, and by 1910 he was also writing extensively in Portuguese. He published his first essay in literary criticism in 1912, his first piece of creative prose (a passage from *The Book of Disquiet*) in 1913, and his first poems in 1914.

Living sometimes with relatives, sometimes in rented rooms, Pessoa supported himself by doing occasional translations and by drafting letters in English and French for Portuguese firms that did business abroad. Although solitary by nature, with a limited social life and almost no love life, he was an active leader of Portugal's Modernist movement in the 1910s, and he invented several of his own movements, including a Cubist-inspired 'Intersectionism' and a strident, quasi-Futurist 'Sensationism'. Pessoa stood outside the limelight, however, exerting influence through his writings and in his conversations with more conspicuous literary figures. Respected in Lisbon as an intellectual and a poet, he regularly published his work in magazines, several of which he helped to found and run, but his literary genius went largely unrecognized until after his death. Pessoa was convinced of his own genius, however, and he lived for the sake of his writing. Although he was in no hurry to publish, he had grandiose plans for Portuguese and English editions of his complete works, and he seems to have held on to most of what he wrote.

Pessoa's legacy consisted of a large trunk full of poetry, prose, plays, philosophy, criticism, translations, linguistic theory, political writings, horoscopes and assorted other texts, variously typed, handwritten or illegibly scrawled in Portuguese, English and French. He wrote in notebooks, on loose sheets, on the backs of letters, advertisements and handbills, on stationery from the firms he worked for and from the cafés he frequented, on envelopes, on paper scraps, and in the margins of his own earlier texts. To compound the confusion, he wrote under dozens of names, a practice – or compulsion – that began in his childhood. He called his most important personas 'heteronyms', endowing them with their own biographies, physiques, personalities, political views, religious attitudes and literary pursuits (see Table of Heteronyms, pp. 505–9). Some of Pessoa's most memorable work in Portuguese was attributed to the three main poetic heteronyms – Alberto Caeiro, Ricardo Reis and Álvaro de Campos – and to the 'semi-heteronym' called Bernardo Soares, while his vast output of English poetry and prose was in large part credited to heteronyms Alexander Search and Charles Robert Anon, and his writings in French to the lonely Jean Seul. The many other alter egos included translators, short-story writers, an English literary critic, an astrologer, a philosopher and an unhappy nobleman who committed suicide. There was even a female persona: the hunchbacked and helplessly lovesick Maria José. At the turn of the century, sixty-five years after Pessoa's death, his vast written world had still not been completely charted by researchers, and a significant part of his writings was still waiting to be published.

'Fernando Pessoa, strictly speaking, doesn't exist.' So claimed Álvaro de Campos, one of the characters invented by Pessoa to spare himself the trouble of living real life. And to spare himself the trouble of organizing and publishing the richest part of his prose, Pessoa invented *The Book of Disquiet*, which never existed, strictly speaking, and can never exist. What we have here isn't a book but its subversion and negation: the ingredients for a book whose recipe is to keep sifting, the mutant germ of a book and its weirdly lush ramifications, the rooms and windows to build a book but no floor plan and no floor, a compendium of many potential books and many others already in ruins. What we have in these pages is an anti-literature, a kind of primitive, verbal CAT scan of one man's anguished soul.

Long before the deconstructionists began to apply their sledgehammers to the conceptual edifice that sheltered our Cartesian sense of personal identity, Pessoa had already self-deconstructed, and without any hammer. Pessoa never set out to destroy himself or anything else. He didn't attack, like Derrida, the assumption that language has the power to mean, and he didn't take apart history and our systems of thought, in the manner of Foucault. He just looked squarely at himself in the mirror, and saw us all:

> Each of us is several, is many, is a profusion of selves. So that the self who disdains his surroundings is not the same as the self who suffers or takes joy in them. In the vast colony of our being there are many species of people who think and feel in different ways. (Text 396)

The problem with *Cogito, ergo sum*, for Pessoa, wasn't in the philosophical principle but in the grammatical subject. 'Be what I think? But I think of being so many things!' cried heteronym Álvaro de Campos in 'The Tobacco Shop', and those myriad thoughts and potential selves suggested anything but a unified I. Much more than a literary ploy, heteronymy was how Pessoa – in the absence of a stable and centred ego – could exist. 'We think, therefore we are' is what, in effect, he says. And even this form of self-affirmation is chancy, for in his moments of greatest doubt and detachment, Pessoa looks within and whispers, with horror: 'They think, therefore they are.'

Doubt and hesitation are the absurd twin energies that powered Pessoa's inner universe and informed *The Book of Disquiet*, which was its piecemeal map. He explained his trouble and that of his book to a poet friend, Armando Cortes-Rodrigues, in a letter dated 19 November 1914: 'My state of mind compels me to work hard, against my will, on *The Book of Disquiet*. But it's all fragments, fragments, fragments.' And in a letter written the previous month to the same friend, he spoke of a 'deep and calm depression' that allowed him to write only 'little things' and 'broken, disconnected pieces of *The Book of Disquiet*'. In this respect, that of perpetual fragmentation, the author and his *Book* were forever faithful to their principles. If Pessoa split himself into dozens of literary characters who contradicted each other and even themselves, *The Book of Disquiet* likewise multiplied without ceasing, being first one book and then another, told by this voice then that voice, then another, still others, all swirling and uncertain, like the cigarette smoke through which Pessoa, sitting in a café or next to his window, watched life go by.

Pessoa's three major poetic heteronyms – the Zennish shepherd called Alberto Caeiro, the classicist Ricardo Reis, and world traveller Álvaro de Campos – burst on to the stage of Pessoa's life together, in 1914. *The Book of Disquiet* was born one year before that, with the publication of Pessoa's first piece of creative writing, called 'In the Forest of Estrangement', where the '[h]alf awake and half asleep' narrator, stagnating 'in a lucid, heavily immaterial torpor, in a dream that is a shadow of dreaming', reports on his imaginary stroll with his unreal female double:

> And what a refreshing and happy horror that there was nobody there! Not even we, who walked there, were there... For we were nobody. We were nothing at all... We had no life for Death to have to kill. We were so tenuous and slight that the wind's passing left us prostrate, and time's passage caressed us like a breeze grazing the top of a palm.

Written under his own name, this long and languid prose text was presented in a literary magazine as an excerpt 'from *The Book of Disquiet*, in preparation'. Pessoa worked on this book for the rest of his life, but the more he 'prepared' it, the more unfinished it became. Unfinished and unfinishable. Without a plot or plan to follow, but as disquiet as a literary work can be, it kept growing even as its borders became ever more indefinite and its existence as a book ever less viable – like the existence of Fernando Pessoa as a citizen in this world.

By the early part of the 1920s the directionless *Book* seems to have drifted into the doldrums, but at the end of that decade – when little more was to be heard from Alberto Caeiro (or from his ghost, since the shepherd supposedly died of TB in 1915) and nothing at all novel from Ricardo Reis (stuck in his role as a 'Greek Horace who writes in Portuguese') – Pessoa brought new life to the work in the person of Bernardo Soares, its ultimate fictional author. Over half of *The Book of Disquiet* was written in the last six years of Pessoa's life, competing for his attention, and we may even say affection, with the irrepressible Álvaro de Campos, the poet-persona who grew old with Pessoa and held a privileged place in his inventor's heart. Soares the assistant bookkeeper and Campos the naval engineer never met in the pen-and-paper drama of Pessoa's heteronyms, who were frequently pitted against one another, but the two writer-characters were spiritual brothers, even if their worldly occupations were at odds. Campos wrote prose as well as poetry, and much of it reads as if it came, so to speak, from the hand of Soares. Pessoa was often unsure who was writing when he wrote, and it's curious that the very first item among the more than 25,000 pieces that make up his archives in the National Library of Lisbon bears the heading *A. de C. (?) or B. of D. (or something else)*.

Bernardo Soares was so close to Pessoa – closer even than Campos – that he couldn't be considered an autonomous heteronym. 'He's a semi-heteronym,' Pessoa wrote in the last year of his life, 'because his personality, although not my own, doesn't differ from my own but is a mere mutilation of it.' Many of Soares's aesthetic and existential reflections would no doubt be part of Pessoa's autobiography, had he written one, but we shouldn't confound the creature with his creator. Soares was not a replica of Pessoa, not even in miniature, but a mutilated Pessoa, with missing parts. Soares had irony but not much of a sense of humour; Pessoa was endowed with large measures of both. Though shy and withdrawn, Pessoa wouldn't say he felt 'like one of those damp rags used for house-cleaning that are taken to the window to dry but are forgotten, balled up, on the sill where they slowly leave a stain' (Text 29). Like his semi-heteronym, Pessoa was an office worker in the Baixa, Lisbon's old commercial district, and for a time he regularly dined at a restaurant on the Rua dos Douradores, the site of Soares's rented room and of Vasques & Co., the firm where he worked. But whereas Soares was condemned to the drudgery of filling in ledgers with the prices and quantities of fabric sold, Pessoa had a comparatively prestigious job writing business letters in English and French, for firms that did business abroad. He came and went pretty much as he wanted, never being obliged to work set hours.

As for their respective inner lives, Soares takes his progenitor's as a model: 'I've created various personalities within. . . I've so externalized myself on the inside that I don't exist there except externally. I'm the empty stage where various actors act out various plays' (Text 299). Coming from Soares, this is a strange declaration. Are we supposed to believe that the assistant bookkeeper, one of the actors who played on the stage of Pessoa's life, had his own troupe of heteronyms? If so, should we then suppose that these subheteronyms had sub-subheteronyms? The notion of an endless heteronymic lineage might have amused Pessoa, but the reason for his alter egos was to explain and express himself, and perhaps to provide a bit of reflective company. Soares, in the passage cited, is describing Pessoa's own dramatic method of survival. And whatever he may be saying about himself, Soares is clearly speaking for Pessoa in the passage that begins 'Only once was I truly loved' (Text 235), written in the 1930s, not long after Pessoa broke up with Ophelia Queiroz, his one and only paramour. Surely it is Pessoa who believes, or wants to believe, that 'Literature is the most agreeable way of ignoring life' (Text 116). And isn't it he, after all, who one day happened to look at his neighbour's window and identified with a crumpled rag left on the sill?

Soares had no inner life of his own, and the full-fledged heteronyms hardly had more. A novelist's characters are often based on friends or family members, but all of Pessoa's characters were carved out of his own soul – of what he really was (in the case of Soares) or of what he wanted to be (in the case of the early, adventurous Campos) – and they each received only a piece of him. When we read Soares or Campos, we get lost in their universes and forget about their author, but they *are* Pessoa, or parts of Pessoa, who made himself into nothing so that he could become everything, and everyone. Pessoa was the first one to forget Pessoa.

If Bernardo Soares does not measure up to the full Pessoa, neither are his reflections and reveries the sum total of *The Book of Disquiet*, to which he was after all a Johnny-come-lately. The book went through various permutations before the bookkeeper arrived with his well-wrought but emotionally direct style of prose, and even the word 'disquiet' changed meaning over time.

In its early days *The Book of Disquiet*, attributed to Pessoa himself, consisted largely of post-Symbolist texts cast in the rarefied register of 'In the Forest of Estrangement' but usually without the shimmery finish, and some of them weren't finished at all. This did not necessarily make them less beautiful, but it was an understandable frustration for their author. 'Fragments, fragments, fragments,' Pessoa wrote to his friend Cortes-Rodrigues, because certain texts abounded in blank spaces for words or phrases or whole paragraphs to be inserted later (but they rarely were), while other 'texts' were no more than sketches or notations for prose pieces that never materialized. *The Book of Disquiet* always remained – as if this were a condition for its existence – a work that was still waiting to happen, that needed to be written in large part, rewritten in other parts, then articulated and fine-tuned, or was it time to rethink the whole project? Pessoa was never sure.

The initial idea was a book of texts with titles, for which he left various lists. Certain titles, such as 'Dolorous Interlude' and 'Rainy Landscape', became generic designations, applied to various texts that shared the announced theme or atmosphere but remained autonomous. Other titles, such as 'Our Lady of Silence', denoted ambitious works in progress, made up of passages written at different times and varying in length from a few scribbled sentences to several pages crammed with tiny letters. And there are titles for which no texts have been found, perhaps because they were never written. (Pessoa's archives contain dozens of lists with titles for non-existent poems, stories, treatises and entire books. Had he even halfway realized all his literary projects, the tomes would fill up a respectable library. *The Book of Disquiet*, a non-book in the non-library, is emblematic of the capricious author's difficulty.) These early texts attempted to elucidate a psychic state or mood via a deliberately archaic use of gothic and romantic themes. Lush descriptions of court life, of sexless women, of strange weather and unreal landscapes prevail. The underlying psyche belongs to Pessoa but is abstracted. The writing is impersonal and the narrative voice ethereal, with the things and the words that name things all seeming to hover in a yellowish space. The word 'disquiet' refers not so much to an existential trouble in man as to the restlessness and uncertainty everywhere present and now distilled in the rhetorical narrator. But other forms of disquiet start to impinge on the work, which takes unexpected turns.

Not so unexpected, perhaps, was the theoretical and pedagogical dimension that emerged here as it did almost everywhere in Pessoa's *œuvre*. It was only natural, even inevitable, that the oneiric texts of *Disquiet* would lead to expository texts that set forth the why and how of dreams, with the four passages titled 'The Art of Effective Dreaming' constituting a veritable manual for dreamers at all levels, from beginner to advanced. 'Sentimental Education', in much the same way, serves as a kind of primer to accompany the many 'Sensationist' texts.

It was likewise in this didactic spirit, but with a rather bizarre result, that Pessoa wrote his 'Advice to Unhappily Married Women', in which he teaches dissatisfied wives how to cheat on their husbands by 'imagining an orgasm with man A while copulating with man B', a practice that yields best results 'in the days immediately preceding menstruation'.

Pessoa's sexual abstinence (it is probable, though not provable, that he died a virgin) was by his own account a conscious choice, which he apparently sought to justify in *The Book of Disquiet*, with passages insisting on the impossibility of possessing another body, on the superiority of love in two dimensions (enjoyed by couples that inhabit paintings, stained-glass windows and Chinese teacups), and on the virtues of renunciation and asceticism. *The Book*, indeed, is rife with religious vocabulary, although the mysticism preached by Pessoa hallowed no god, except perhaps himself ('God is me,' he concludes in 'The Art of Effective Dreaming for Metaphysical Minds').

But more than anything else, it was existential concerns – operating on both a general and personal level – that subverted the initial project of *The Book of Disquiet*. On a general level, since *The Book*'s author belonged 'to a generation that inherited disbelief in the Christian faith and created in itself a disbelief in all other faiths'. And since 'we were left, each man to himself, in the desolation of feeling ourselves live', the generational sense of lostness quickly became a personal struggle for identity and meaning (Text 306). Pessoa's inner life – registered in 'Fragments of an Autobiography', 'Apocalyptic Feeling' and similar texts, with and without titles – invaded the pages of what had begun as a very different kind of book. Pessoa realized that the project had slipped out of his hand (if in fact he'd ever firmly grasped it), for in yet another letter to Cortes-Rodrigues he wrote that *The Book of Disquiet*, 'that pathological production', was going 'complexly and tortuously forward', as if of its own accord.

And so Pessoa let the book go, scribbling *B. of D.* at the head of all sorts of texts, sometimes as an afterthought, or with a question mark indicating doubt. *The Book of Disquiet* – forever tentative, indefinite and in transition – is one of those rare works in which *forme* and *fond* perfectly reflect each other. Always with the intention of revising and assembling the variously handwritten and typed passages, but never with the courage or patience to take up the task, Pessoa kept adding material, and the parameters of the already unwieldy work kept expanding. Besides his post-Symbolist flights and diary-like musings, Pessoa included maxims, sociological observations, aesthetic credos, theological reflections and cultural analyses. He even put the *B. of D.* trademark on the copy of a letter to his mother (in Appendix II).

Though Pessoa hatched dozens of publication plans for his works, he saw only one real book, *Mensagem* (*Message*), make it into print, the year before he died. (He self-published several chap-books of his English poems.) Pessoa was so addicted to writing and scheming – and the schemes included unlikely business ventures as well as the publication of his *œuvre* – that he had no time or energy left over to get that *œuvre* into publishable shape. Or perhaps it was just too tedious to think about. Nothing better illustrates the problem than *The Book of Disquiet*, a micro-chaos within the larger chaos of Pessoa's written universe. But that consummate disorder is what gives *The Book* its peculiar greatness. It is like a treasure chest of both polished and uncut gems, which can be arranged and rearranged in infinite combinations, thanks precisely to the lack of a pre-established order.

No other work of Pessoa interacted so intensely with the rest of his universe. If Bernardo Soares says that his heart 'drains out... like a broken bucket' (Text 154) or that his mental life is 'a bucket that got knocked over' (Text 442), Álvaro de Campos declares 'My heart is a poured-out bucket' (in 'The Tobacco Shop') and compares his thinking to 'an overturned bucket' (in a poem dated 16 August 1934). If Soares thinks that 'Nothing is more oppressive than the affection of others' (Text 348), a Ricardo Reis ode (dated 1 November 1930) maintains that 'The same love by which we're loved/Oppresses us with its wanting.' And when the assistant bookkeeper longs to 'notice everything for the first time... as direct manifestations of Reality', we can't help but think of Alberto Caeiro, whose verses are a continual hymn to the direct, unmediated vision of things.

We can leaf through *The Book of Disquiet* as through a lifelong sketchbook revealing the artist in all his heteronymic variety. Or we may read it as a travel journal, a 'book of random impressions' (Text 442), Pessoa's faithful companion throughout his literary odyssey that never left Lisbon. Or we may see it as the 'factless autobiography' (Text 12) of a man who dedicated his life to not living, who cultivated 'hatred of action like a greenhouse flower' (Text 103).

The Book of Disquiet, which took different forms, also knew different authors. As long as *The Book* was just one book, consisting of post-Symbolist texts with titles, the announced author was Fernando Pessoa, but when it mutated to accommodate diaristic passages, inevitably more intimate and revealing, Pessoa followed his usual custom of hiding behind other names, the first of which was Vicente Guedes. In fact Guedes was initially responsible only for the diary (or diaries) that pushed its (or their) way into *The Book of Disquiet*. The 'autobiography of a man who never existed' is how Pessoa, in a passage intended for a Preface, described Guedes's 'gentle book', which is referred to in another passage as the *Diary*, as if this were its actual title. Pessoa, in his publication plans, began to cite Vicente Guedes as the fictional author of *The Book of Disquiet*, which suggests that it and the 'gentle' *Diary* were one and the same book. On the other hand, the archives contain a fragmentary passage from a 'Diary of Vicente Guedes', dated 22 August 1914, which pokes fun at a second-rate Portuguese writer and surely does not belong in *Disquiet*. Diaries usually have dates, but almost no dated material entered *The Book of Disquiet* until 1929, when Vicente Guedes had already been given his walking papers. Whatever intentions Pessoa may have one day had, the early *Book of Disquiet* never boiled down to a diary, though it did encompass a 'Random Diary' and a 'Lucid Diary' – or single entries from projected diaries with these names – as well as the aforecited 'Fragments of an Autobiography', all of which date (according to manuscript and stylistic evidence) from 1915 to 1920, when Guedes was active.

Vicente Guedes was one of Pessoa's busiest and most versatile collaborators in the 1910s. Besides his diary writings, Guedes translated, or was supposed to translate, plays and poems by the likes of Aeschylus, Shelley and Byron, as well as 'A Very Original Dinner', a mystery story penned by Alexander Search, the most prolific of the English-language heteronyms. Though he shirked his duties as a translator, Guedes 'really' wrote a few poems, a number of short stories and several mystical tales. In one of these tales, 'The Ascetic', the title character tells his interlocutor that paradises and nirvanas are 'illusions inside other illusions. If you dream you're dreaming, is the dream you dream less real than the dream you dream you're dreaming?' This sort of musing is vaguely reminiscent of *Disquiet* in its formative phase, which may be why Pessoa decided to entrust it to Guedes, whose wide-ranging literary talents made him a potentially excellent author-administrator of such a capacious work.

The manuscript identifying Vicente Guedes as the author of a *Diary* that was supposed to be part (or perhaps all) of the early *Book of Disquiet* also includes a passage titled 'Games of Solitaire' (Text 351), which evokes the evenings that the narrator spent as a child with his elderly aunts in a country house. The passage is preceded by this notation:

> *B. of D.*
> A section entitled: *Games of Solitaire*
> (include *In the Forest of Estrangement*?)

In its language and tone, 'Forest of Estrangement' has absolutely nothing in common with the passage about old aunts playing solitaire while their sleepy maid brews tea. Perhaps this was conceived as a mere port of entry to the section that would have the same name and whose 'games of solitaire' would be exercises in daydreamy prose such as 'Estrangement', written by Pessoa for the same reason we play cards: to pass the time. Whatever the case, *The Book* was in trouble. Pessoa didn't know what to do with the early texts that wafted in the misty atmosphere of the strange forest, and perhaps he considered excluding them altogether. What place could they have in a diary? Or even next to a diary?

More than ten years later, Bernardo Soares would reformulate the games of solitaire (Text 12):

> I make landscapes out of what I feel. I make holidays of my sensations... My elderly aunt would play solitaire throughout the endless evening. These confessions of what I feel are my solitaire. I don't interpret them like those who read cards to tell the future. I don't probe them, because in solitaire the cards don't have any special significance.

In the same passage, Soares compares his mental and literary activity to another domestic pastime, crochet, as Álvaro de Campos also does in a poem dated 9 August 1934:

> I also have my crochet.
> It dates from when I began to think.
> Stitch on stitch forming a whole without a whole...
> A cloth, and I don't know if it's for a garment or for nothing.
> A soul, and I don't know if it's for feeling or living.

What's highly significant about the assistant bookkeeper's crochet is that 'between one and another plunge' of the hooked needle, 'all enchanted princes can stroll in their parks'. This observation would seem odd or just plain weird, were it not for the royal dreams and reveries that filled up many pages of *Disquiet* in its early days. In

Soares, as we shall see, Pessoa managed to conciliate (though never to his full satisfaction) the sumptuous, imperial dreams of *The Book*'s first phase with the concerns of a modest, twentieth-century office clerk. Vicente Guedes, who was also an assistant bookkeeper, seems to have been groomed for the same conciliatory role, but in spite of his several mystical tales, Guedes was too coldly rational in his diary entries to be believable as a writer of wispy post-Symbolist texts, and Pessoa never directly named him as their author. But Guedes held the title of general author of *The Book of Disquiet* for at least five years and perhaps as long as ten, for whatever it's worth, since the manuscript evidence suggests that most of the 1920s was (as indicated earlier) a fallow period for *The Book*.

It was probably in 1928 that Pessoa, now wearing the mask of Bernardo Soares, returned to *The Book of Disquiet*, which became a resolutely confirmed diary, as acutely personal as it was objective – as if the world around and inside the diarist were all the same film that he stared at intently, sometimes listened to, but never touched. Many of the passages were dated, though this practice was never systematic and seems to have been only gradually adopted. It's curious that the first passage from this period with a date, 22 March 1929 (Text 19), is post-Symbolist in flavour, with drums, bugles and 'princesses from other people's dreams' but with no mention of the assistant bookkeeper, whose fiction was perhaps still hazy and needed to be fleshed out. It was only in 1930 that Pessoa began to date a large number of the passages destined for *The Book of Disquiet*, which had finally found its street: the Rua dos Douradores, where Soares worked in an office and where he also lived, in a humble rented room, writing in his spare time. And so Art, notes Soares, resides 'on the very same street as Life, but in a different place. . . Yes, for me the Rua dos Douradores contains the meaning of everything and the answer to all riddles, except for the riddle of why riddles exist, which can never be answered' (Text 9).

We know almost nothing about Bernardo Soares before he moved to the Rua dos Douradores. His name heads a list of ten stories in one of Pessoa's notebooks, where we also find a rather extensive publication programme for Pessoa's *œuvre*, with Soares identified only as a short-story writer. *The Book of Disquiet*, listed in the same programme, isn't attributed to any author. Had Vicente Guedes already been sacked? Perhaps not yet. But once Soares assumed *The Book*'s authorship, he also assumed, more or less, the old author's biography. More accurately, Vicente Guedes, who died young (it was Pessoa who was to publish and present his manuscript to the public), was apparently reincarnated in Bernardo Soares, who had the very same profession, who also lived in a fourth-floor room in Lisbon's Baixa district (only the name of the street changed), and who was also a highly motivated diarist. To judge by his elderly aunt who spent long evenings playing solitaire, Soares even inherited Guedes's childhood.

Though not identical to Guedes, Soares came to replace him, and since Pessoa could move his pawns forwards and backwards, this replacement was able to have retroactive effect. The eleven excerpts from *Disquiet* published in magazines between 1929 and 1934 were naturally attributed to Bernardo Soares, but Pessoa also credited him (in a typed inventory of Soares's literary production) with the only previously published excerpt, namely 'Forest of Estrangement', dating from long before Soares was ever conceived. In Pessoa's notes and extensive correspondence from the 1930s, in which he discussed in detail the heteronymic enterprise, Guedes never merits the slightest reference, and the three *Disquiet* passages from the teens that mention him by name were left out of the large envelope in which Pessoa, some time before his death, gathered material for the book. That same envelope includes a typed 'note' (in Appendix III) explaining that the earlier passages would have to be revised to conform with the 'true psychology' of Bernardo Soares. It may be argued that since Pessoa never actually brought off this revision, the early passages retain Vicente Guedes's style and tone – more analytical, less emotionally impressionable than Soares – and therefore his authorship. But this is to take the game even further than Pessoa did. What is actually happening? The narrator – whether his name is Guedes or Soares – ages as the creating and informing spirit of Pessoa ages, and so the voice naturally changes, but not as strikingly as the voice of Álvaro de Campos, whose short and melancholy poems of the 1930s were vastly different from the loud 'Sensationist' odes of the 1910s.

Yet another disquieted persona, the Baron of Teive, was vaguely or potentially connected to *The Book of Disquiet*, not as its author but as a contributor. Pessoa gave birth to aristocratic Teive in 1928, probably the same year that Bernardo Soares went from being a minor short-story writer to the author of Pessoa's major prose work. Like Soares, Teive also suffered from tedium (one of the most oft-occurring words in *The Book*), also found life stupidly meaningless, and was also sceptical to the point of no return, no salvation. His 'only manuscript', written on the eve of his suicide and titled *The Education of the Stoic*, was found in the drawer of a hotel room, presumably by Pessoa, who compared the Baron with the bookkeeper in a fragmentary Preface (see Appendix III). Their Portuguese, wrote Pessoa, is the same, but whereas the aristocrat 'thinks clearly, writes clearly, and controls his emotions, though not his feelings, the bookkeeper controls neither emotions nor feelings, and what he thinks depends on what he feels'. Pessoa himself was not always certain of this subtle distinction, for he labelled one passage (Text 207) *B. of D. (or Teive?)*, and there were a handful of other passages clearly labelled *Teive* that he subsequently placed in the large envelope with *Disquiet* material. Was he thinking of pillaging parts of the Baron's 'only manuscript' for the benefit of Bernardo Soares? Quite possibly so, since Teive's opus, contrary to what its 'only' designation suggests, was a hodgepodge of unassembled and fragmentary pieces that Pessoa had perhaps despaired of ever pulling together and cleaning up. *The Book of Disquiet*, much vaster, was that much more unorganized, but Pessoa loved it too dearly to ever dream of giving up on it.

Besides threatening the Baron's intellectual property, the ostensibly unassuming bookkeeper almost took over a large chunk of poetry signed by Pessoa himself. The above-mentioned inventory of Bernardo Soares's literary output includes not only the poetic prose texts of *The Book*'s inaugural period but also 'Slanting Rain' (written in 1914, published in 1915), 'Stations of the Cross' (written in 1914–15, published in 1916) and other poems by Pessoa founded on 'ultra-Sensationist experiences'. These poems are nearly contemporaneous with 'Forest of Estrangement' and drink from the same post-Symbolist waters, so Pessoa thought – for a moment – that they might as well live under the same roof, on the Rua dos Douradores, which is cited at the top of the inventory. In fact the inventory is probably both a c.v. for Soares *and* a Table of Contents for *The Book of Disquiet*. And at the bottom of the page we find this strange observation: 'Soares is not a poet. In his poetry he falls short; it isn't sustained like his prose. His poems are the refuse of his prose, the sawdust of his first-rate work.'

Pessoa, in the late 1920s, felt ambivalent about the Intersectionist and ultra-Sensationist poems he had written under his own name almost fifteen years previous. Reassigning them to *The Book of Disquiet* would not only save Pessoa's name from the momentary embarrassment he may have felt for being their author; it could also help redeem them, by providing an enhancing context. But it was a short-lived idea. In a follow-up note (see Appendix III) written on the same typewriter as the inventory, we read:

> Collect later on, in a separate book, the various poems I had mistakenly thought to include in *The Book of Disquiet*; this book of poems should have a title indicating that it contains something like refuse or marginalia – something suggestive of detachment.

Pessoa, forever indecisive, just like his semi-heteronym, had gone back to his original plan: a book of prose, in elegant and even poetic Portuguese, but still and always prose. What had ever given him the idea of bringing poetry into it?

The Book of Disquiet had become one of Pessoa's pet projects, and he desperately, if somewhat ineptly, tried to make its disparate parts cohere. The prose that had made its way into *The Book* was so heterogeneous that its new agent of cohesion, Bernardo Soares, would have to be much more than a diarist. To make Soares a believable author of such a multifaceted work, Pessoa decided to widen his literary horizons in a big way, making him even a poet. If Álvaro de Campos and Ricardo Reis, fundamentally poets, also wrote prose, why shouldn't Bernardo Soares write verses? But no: this would have only complicated matters. Pessoa realized this and backed down, repossessing the poems he had passed on to Soares, as we can deduce from a letter, written in 1935, which cites 'Slanting Rain' as an 'orthonymic' work (attributed to Pessoa himself). Soares retained possession of the poetic prose he had inherited, however, and he legitimated that inheritance by his own practice, admirably demonstrated in the excerpt (Text 386) he wrote on 28 November 1932, an obvious sequel to 'In the Forest of Estrangement'. And in another text (420), Soares ingeniously brings the 'Funeral March of Ludwig II, King of Bavaria' to the Rua dos Douradores. Fighting his incurable tendency to creative and intellectual entropy, Pessoa sought at least a relative unity for his *Book of Disquiet*, 'without giving up the dreaminess and logical disjointedness of its intimate expression' (from the cited 'note' in Appendix III).

In Bernardo Soares – a prose writer who poetizes, a dreamer who thinks, a mystic who doesn't believe, a decadent who doesn't indulge – Pessoa invented the best author possible (and who was just a mutilated copy of himself) to provide unity to a book which, by nature, couldn't have one. The semi-fiction called Soares, more than a justification or handy solution for this scattered *Book*, is an implied model for whoever has difficulty adapting to real, normal, everyday life. The only way to survive in this world is by keeping alive our dream, without ever fulfilling it, since the fulfilment never measures up to what we imagine – this was the closest thing to a message that Pessoa left, and he gave us Bernardo Soares to show us how it's done.

How is it done? By not doing. By dreaming insistently. By performing our daily duties but *living*, simultaneously, in the imagination. Travelling far and wide, in the geography of our minds. Conquering like Caesar, amid the blaring trumpets of our reverie. Experiencing intense sexual pleasure, in the privacy of our fantasy. Feeling everything in every way, not in the flesh, which always tires, but in the imagination.

> To dream, for example, that I'm simultaneously, separately, severally the man and the woman on a stroll that a man and woman are taking along the river. To see myself – at the same time, in the same way, with equal precision and without overlap, being equally but separately integrated into both things – as a conscious ship in a South Sea and a printed page from an old book. How absurd this seems! But everything is absurd, and dreaming least of all. (Text 157)

To dream one's life and to live one's dreams, feeling what's dreamed and what's lived with an intensity so extreme it makes the distinction between the two meaningless – this credo echoed in nearly every reach of Pessoa's universe, but Soares was its most practical example. While the other heteronymic stars *talk* about dreaming and feeling everything, Bernardo Soares actually has vivid, splendorous dreams and feels each tiny circumstance of his workaday life on the Rua dos Douradores. The post-Symbolist texts with misty forests, lakes, kings and palaces are crucial, for they are the imaginary substance, the very dreams of Soares, put into words. And the various 'Rainy Landscapes', with their excruciating descriptions of storms and winds, are illustrations of how to really *feel* the weather and, by extension, all of nature and the life that surrounds us.

Pessoa was keenly aware that 'Nature is parts without a whole' (from Caeiro's *The Keeper of Sheep*, XLVII) and that the notion of unity is always an illusion. Well, not quite. A relative, provisional, fleeting unity, a unity which doesn't pretend to be smooth and absolute or even unambiguously singular, which is built around an imagination, a fiction, a writing instrument – this was the unity that Fernando Pessoa, in Bernardo Soares, was betting on. And he won his bet. *The Book of Disquiet*, whose ultimate ambition was to reflect the jagged thoughts and fractured emotions that can inhabit one man, achieved this modest but genuine unity. There was perhaps, in the twentieth century, no other book as honest as this *Book*, which can hardly claim to be one.

Honesty. It went unmentioned until now, and it's what most distinguishes *The Book of Disquiet*. It is probably fair to call honesty the pre-eminent virtue of great writers, for whom the most personal things become, through the alchemy of truth, universal. Strangely or not, it was precisely in his faking, in his self-othering – a profoundly personal process – that Pessoa was astonishingly true and honest to himself. By being so who he was, and so very Portuguese, he succeeded in being the most foreign and universal of writers. 'My nation is the Portuguese language,' he declared through Bernardo Soares (Text 259), but he also said: 'I don't write in Portuguese. I write my own self.' And immediately before these words he exclaims: 'What Hells and Purgatories and Heavens I have inside me! But who sees me do anything that disagrees with life – me, so calm and peaceful?' (Text 443).

In the lucidly felt prose of Bernardo Soares, Pessoa wrote himself, wrote his century, and wrote us – down to the hells and heavens we harbour, even if we're unbelievers, like Pessoa. Soares called this implausible book his 'confessions', but they have nothing to do with the religious or literary variety. In these pages there is no hope or even desire for remission or salvation. There is also no self-pity, and no attempt to aestheticize the narrator's irremediably human condition. Bernardo Soares doesn't confess except in the sense of 'recognize', and the object of that recognition is of no great consequence. He describes his own self, because it is the landscape that is closest and most real, the one he can describe best. And what was flesh became word. Here is the assistant bookkeeper's confession:

> I am, in large measure, the selfsame prose I write. . . I've made myself into the character of a book, a life one reads. Whatever I feel is felt (against my will) so that I can write that I felt it. Whatever I think is promptly put into words, mixed with images that undo it, cast into rhythms that are something else altogether. From so much self-revising, I've destroyed myself. From so much self-thinking, I'm now my thoughts and not I. I plumbed myself and dropped the plumb; I spend my life wondering if I'm deep or not, with no remaining plumb except my gaze that shows me – blackly vivid in the mirror at the bottom of the well – my own face that observes me observing it.
>
> (Text 193, dated 2 September 1931)

No other writer ever achieved such a direct transference of self to paper. *The Book of Disquiet* is the world's strangest photograph, made out of words, the only material capable of capturing the recesses of the soul it exposes.

Richard Zenith, 2001

NOTES

It is in his *Notes for the Memory of my Master Caeiro* that Álvaro de Campos apprises us of Pessoa's non-existence. Reis was described as 'a Greek Horace who writes in Portuguese' in a letter Pessoa wrote to an Englishman on 31 October 1924. The fragmentary passage titled 'Diary of Vicente Guedes' was transcribed by Teresa Rita Lopes for her *Pessoa por Conhecer* (Lisbon: Estampa, 1990), where a list specifying Guedes's translating duties was also published. Guedes's unpublished 'O Asceta' ('The Ascetic') is catalogued in the Pessoa Archives under the number $27^{20}V^{3}/1$. The translated excerpt of the Campos poem dated 9 August 1934 is taken from *Fernando Pessoa & Co. – Selected Poems* (New York: Grove Press, 1998). The list of ten short stories attributed to Bernardo Soares is catalogued under 144G/29, the publication programme that identifies Soares as a short-story writer under 144G/38. The typed inventory of Soares's literary production, on the Rua dos Douradores, is reproduced in my Introduction to the *Livro do Desassossego*. The Afterword to my edition of Teive's *A Educação do Estóico* (*The Education of the Stoic*) (Lisbon: Assírio & Alvim, 1999) undertakes a thorough comparison of the Baron and Bernardo Soares.

Notes on the Text and Translation

Had Pessoa prepared his *Livro do Desassossego* (*The Book of Disquiet*) for publication, it would have been a smaller book. He planned to make a 'rigorous' selection from among all the texts he had written, to adapt the older ones to the 'true psychology' of Bernardo Soares, and to undertake 'an overall revision of the style' (see the 'note' in Appendix III). This operation would have resulted in a smooth, polished book with perhaps half as many pages, and perhaps half as much genius. Purged of whatever was fragmentary and incomplete, the book would have gained novelistic virtues such as plot and dramatic tension, but it would have run the risk of becoming just another book, instead of what it remains: a monument as wondrous as it is impossible.

Pessoa published twelve excerpts from *The Book of Disquiet* in literary magazines and left, in the famous trunk that contained his extravagant written life, about 450 additional texts marked *L. do D.* and/or included in a large envelope labelled *Livro do Desassossego*. Most of this material was incorporated in the first edition of the work, published only in 1982, forty-seven years after Pessoa's death. It was a heroic effort, since Pessoa's archives are notoriously labyrinthine and his handwriting often virtually illegible, and it was doomed – for these very reasons – to be seriously flawed. A new edition, published in 1990–91 (the first volume of which was republished, with extensive revisions, in 1997), presented improved readings and over one hundred previously unpublished texts, most of which were not explicitly identified with *The Book of Disquiet*, although the majority of them could have been penned or typed with Bernardo Soares in mind.

My own edition of the *Livro do Desassossego* (Lisbon: Assírio & Alvim, 1998) – which is the source text for this translation – makes further improvements in the readings, filling in most of the remaining lacunas and correcting several hundred errors in previous transcriptions. I was more cautious about embracing material not specifically marked or set aside by Pessoa for inclusion. The borders of this work are fuzzy, but they exist. They exclude, for instance, the reams of political theory written by Pessoa. Nor is there a place for his writings in pure philosophy and literary criticism. But there are a number of stray and unidentified texts – my edition includes about fifty – that do seem to belong here. Seem to me, that is. It is impossible to avoid subjectivity when editing and publishing such a fragmentary *œuvre* as Pessoa's.

This subjectivity tends to sheer arbitrariness when it comes to organizing this book, whose passages were scattered across the years and pages of Pessoa's adult life. Chronological order? About a hundred passages written between 1929 and 1934 are dated, but only five during the first sixteen years of *Disquiet*'s existence. To attempt a chronology for the undated texts on the basis of stylistic or thematic affinities is treacherous or even foolhardy, as we can understand by looking at several dated texts, such as the aforementioned 'sequel' to 'In the Forest of Estrangement', which we would confidently situate in 1913 or 1914, if we didn't know it was written on 28 November 1932. Text 429, conversely, is dated 18 September 1917 but reads exactly like Soares from the 1930s. An exhaustive analysis of paper and ink types and of Pessoa's handwriting would probably yield a reasonably chronological order, but would that be a good way to publish the material? Pessoa had a few ideas on how to organize *The Book*, but chronological order wasn't one he ever mentioned. It is true that many passages from the final phase were dated, but even then not the majority, and Pessoa never suggested that these be published as a group apart, separately from the older material.

What Pessoa did suggest shows only what a loss he was at to organize his *Book*. 'Alternate passages like this with the long ones?' he asked himself at the top of a passage (Text 201) that isn't particularly short. Another passage (Text 124) carries the heading (written in English) *Chapter on Indifference or something like that*, suggesting a thematic organization. In the 'note' already cited, Pessoa mulled over whether it was better to publish 'Funeral March for Ludwig II' in a separate book, with other 'Large Texts' that had titles, or to leave it 'as it is'.

And how was it? Mixed up with hundreds of other texts, large and small, like pieces of a jigsaw puzzle without a discernible picture or pattern. Perhaps this would be the best way to go: an edition of loose pieces, orderable according to each reader's fancy, or according to how they happen to fall.

Since a loose-leaf edition is impractical, and since every established order is the wrong order, the mere circumstance of publication entails a kind of original sin. Every editor of this *Book*, automatically guilty, should (and I hereby do) (1) apologize for tampering with the original non-order, (2) emphasize that the order presented can claim no special validity, and (3) recommend that readers invent their own order or, better yet, read the work's many parts in absolutely random order.

In this edition, the dated passages from the last phase (1929–34) serve as a skeleton – an infallibly Soaresian skeleton – for articulating the body of the text. The hope is that the older passages, interspersed among the later ones, will be at least superficially coloured by the 'true psychology' of Bernardo Soares. I saw no reason to disrupt the chronological order of the passages forming the skeleton, as this makes for a certain objectivity in this otherwise subjective arrangement, but I relegated the dates to the Notes, lest readers who skip this paragraph suppose that the passages falling between the dated ones are contemporaneous. Some of them are, but others go back to the 1910s. As explained in the opening essay, the post-Symbolist texts (mostly from the teens) are the evidence – the visible, *dreamed* dreams – that the dreamer talks about in his 'confessions', and so it makes sense for the two kinds of texts to rub shoulders. They complement each other.

But the 'Large Texts', as Pessoa denominated the early prose pieces that weren't always that long but were large in their ambitions and sometimes had 'grandiose titles', have been placed in a separate section, called 'A Disquiet Anthology'. Pessoa himself recognized that they did not easily fit into Soares's 'Factless Autobiography' (one of various self-descriptive epithets found in the assistant bookkeeper's scattered journal of thoughts), which is why he considered taking the even more radical step of removing them to a separate book.

For no other reason than to facilitate consultation and referral, I have assigned numbers to the passages in the first section (most of which are untitled), and arranged the texts from the second section by their titles, alphabetically. Pessoa left over six hundred alternate words or phrasings in the margins and between the lines of the manuscripts that constitute *The Book of Disquiet*. For the purposes of this translation, I have usually preferred the first word or phrasing. Only those few alternate wordings that might interest a general reader are recorded in the Notes, which also provide archival references, composition and publication dates, and explanations of the cultural, historical and literary references. My edition of the original text, *Livro do Desassossego*, offers more detailed information about the editorial procedures followed (with regard to the transcriptions, for example) and includes, in an Appendix, some fragmentary material not found here.

Many of the manuscripts that Pessoa labelled for inclusion in *The Book of Disquiet* were really just notes or sketches for longer, polished pieces that he never finally wrote. This is especially evident in passages where the paragraphs are separated by spaces, as in Text 14 or Text 18. Even fluent, well-articulated passages are sometimes pocked, as it were, by blank spaces for words or phrases that Pessoa never got around to supplying. Often these lacunas correspond to a missing adjective or non-essential connective and could be smoothed over in a translation – made to disappear, that is – without being unfaithful to the meaning of the original sentence. But this 'smoothing' would entail an unfaithfulness to the book's general spirit of fragmentation and disconnectedness. The text presented here reflects the blips and roughness of the original but aims, at the same time, to be reader-friendly. This explains the presence of two different symbols to indicate lacunas left by the author in the original manuscripts; the five-dot ellipsis is the 'friendlier', less obtrusive symbol, but is used only where it will not induce the reader to make a false bridge between the words that precede and follow it, as if it stood for a mere rhythmic pause. In a few cases, where the basic sense of the missing word(s) seems obvious to the point of being inevitable, a word (or two) with that sense has been inserted in square brackets.

Verbal repetition is part of Pessoa's style and has been respected, except where the effect seems too mannered for English to bear. The translation is also generally faithful to the use (or not) of capital letters in the original. This usage is noticeably erratic when it comes to the 'gods' or 'Gods', with the two forms sometimes coexisting in the same passage, as in Text 87.

The translated edition of this work that I published in 1991 as *The Book of Disquietude* (Carcanet Press) informs important aspects of the Portuguese edition I produced in 1998 and of this revised, reorganized and expanded English edition. Some of the discrepancies between this and other English translations (including my first effort) are due to the rather different source text that has emerged as I and other researchers have re-examined the original manuscripts.

SYMBOLS USED IN THE TEXT

□ – blank space left by the author for one or more words within a sentence
. . . . . – place where a sentence breaks off, space left for an unwritten sentence or paragraph, or blank space inside a sentence where the hiatus does not interrupt a phrasal unit
[?] – translation based on a conjectural reading of the author's handwriting
[. . .] – illegible word or phrase
[ ] – word(s) added by translator
* – find note at the back of the volume, under the appropriate Text number or title.

Acknowledgements

I'm grateful to Maria Aliete Galhoz for having broken the ground, with her patient work in the Pessoa archives; to José Blanco for his enthusiasm, support and friendship; to Michael Schmidt for believing in Pessoa when few had heard of him; to Hermínio Monteiro and Lúcia Pinho e Melo for their good work and encouragement; to Jennifer Hengen and Simon Winder for having, in a certain way, gone out on a limb; to Ellah Allfrey and Sarah Coward for their inspired suggestions; and to the staff workers at the National Library of Lisbon and the Casa Fernando Pessoa for their gracious assistance.

I especially thank Teresa Rita Lopes and Manuela Parreira da Silva for their generous help in deciphering the original manuscripts; Manuela Neves and Manuela Rocha for their similar generosity in helping me interpret difficult passages; and Martin Earl for his insightful critique of my Introduction.

The Book of Disquiet

by Bernardo Soares,
assistant bookkeeper in the city of Lisbon

Preface

FERNANDO PESSOA

Lisbon has a certain number of eating establishments in which, on top of a respectable-looking tavern, there's a regular dining room with the solid and homey air of a restaurant in a small trainless town. In these first-floor dining rooms, fairly empty except on Sundays, one often comes across odd sorts, unremarkable faces, a series of asides in life.

There was a time in my life when a limited budget and the desire for quiet made me a regular patron of one of these first-floor restaurants. And it happened that whenever I ate dinner there around seven o'clock, I nearly always saw a certain man who didn't interest me at first, but then began to.

Fairly tall and thin, he must have been about thirty years old. He hunched over terribly when sitting down but less so standing up, and he dressed with a carelessness that wasn't entirely careless. In his pale, uninteresting face there was a look of suffering that didn't add any interest, and it was difficult to say just what kind of suffering this look suggested. It seemed to suggest various kinds: hardships, anxieties, and the suffering born of the indifference that comes from having already suffered a lot.

He always ate a small dinner, followed by cigarettes that he rolled himself. He conspicuously observed the other patrons, not suspiciously but with more than ordinary interest. He didn't observe them with a spirit of scrutiny but seemed interested in them without caring to analyse their outward behaviour or to register their physical appearance. It was this peculiar trait that first got me interested in him.

I began to look at him more closely. I noticed that a certain air of intelligence animated his features in a certain uncertain way. But dejection – the stagnation of cold anguish – so consistently covered his face that it was hard to discern any of his other traits.

I happened to learn from a waiter in the restaurant that the man worked in an office near by.

One day there was an incident in the street down below – a fist fight between two men. Everyone in the first-floor restaurant ran to the windows, including me and the man I've been describing. I made a casual remark to him and he replied in like manner. His voice was hesitant and colourless, as in those who hope for nothing because it's perfectly useless to hope. But perhaps it was absurd to see this in my supper-time peer.

I don't know why, but from that day on we always greeted each other. And then one day, perhaps drawn together by the stupid coincidence that we both arrived for dinner at nine-thirty, we struck up a conversation. At a certain point he asked me if I wrote. I said that I did. I told him about the literary review Orpheu,* *which had just recently come out. He praised it, he praised it highly, and I was taken aback. I told him I was surprised, for the art of those who write in* Orpheu *speaks only to a few. He said that perhaps he was one of the few. Furthermore, he added, this art wasn't exactly a novelty for him, and he shyly observed that, having nowhere to go and nothing to do, nor friends to visit, nor any interest in reading books, he usually spent his nights at home, in his rented room, likewise writing.*

◆

He had furnished his two rooms with a semblance of luxury, no doubt at the expense of certain basic items. He had taken particular pains with the armchairs, which were soft and well-padded, and with the drapes and rugs. He explained that with this kind of an interior he could 'maintain the dignity of tedium'. In rooms decorated in the modern style, tedium becomes a discomfort, a physical distress.

Nothing had ever obliged him to do anything. He had spent his childhood alone. He never joined any group. He never pursued a course of study. He never belonged to a crowd. The circumstances of his life were marked by that strange but rather common phenomenon – perhaps, in fact, it's true for all lives – of being tailored to the image and likeness of his instincts, which tended towards inertia and withdrawal.

He never had to face the demands of society or of the state. He even evaded the demands of his own instincts. Nothing ever prompted him to have friends or lovers. I was the only one who was in some way his intimate. But even if I always felt that I was relating to an assumed personality and that he didn't really consider me his friend, I realized from the beginning that he needed someone to whom he could leave the book that he left. This troubled me at first, but I'm glad to say that I was able to see the matter from a psychologist's point of view, and I remained just as much his friend, devoted to the end for which he'd drawn me to himself – the publication of this book.

Even in this respect circumstances were strangely favourable to him, for they brought him somebody of my character, who could be of use to him.

A Factless Autobiography

In these random impressions, and with no desire to be other than random, I indifferently narrate my factless autobiography, my lifeless history. These are my Confessions, and if in them I say nothing, it's because I have nothing to say.

– Text 12

I

I was born in a time when the majority of young people had lost faith in God, for the same reason their elders had had it – without knowing why. And since the human spirit naturally tends to make judgements based on feeling instead of reason, most of these young people chose Humanity to replace God. I, however, am the sort of person who is always on the fringe of what he belongs to, seeing not only the multitude he's a part of but also the wide-open spaces around it. That's why I didn't give up God as completely as they did, and I never accepted Humanity. I reasoned that God, while improbable, might exist, in which case he should be worshipped; whereas Humanity, being a mere biological idea and signifying nothing more than the animal species we belong to, was no more deserving of worship than any other animal species. The cult of Humanity, with its rites of Freedom and Equality, always struck me as a revival of those ancient cults in which gods were like animals or had animal heads.

And so, not knowing how to believe in God and unable to believe in an aggregate of animals, I, along with other people on the fringe, kept a distance from things, a distance commonly called Decadence. Decadence is the total loss of unconsciousness, which is the very basis of life. Could it think, the heart would stop beating.

For those few like me who live without knowing how to have life, what's left but renunciation as our way and contemplation as our destiny? Not knowing nor able to know what religious life is, since faith isn't acquired through reason, and unable to have faith in or even react to the abstract notion of man, we're left with the aesthetic contemplation of life as our reason for having a soul. Impassive to the solemnity of any and all worlds, indifferent to the divine, and disdainers of what is human, we uselessly surrender ourselves to pointless sensation, cultivated in a refined Epicureanism, as befits our cerebral nerves.

Retaining from science only its fundamental precept – that everything is subject to fatal laws, which we cannot freely react to since the laws themselves determine all reactions – and seeing how this precept concurs with the more ancient one of the divine fatality of things, we abdicate from every effort like the weak-bodied from athletic endeavours, and we hunch over the book of sensations like scrupulous scholars of feeling.

Taking nothing seriously and recognizing our sensations as the only reality we have for certain, we take refuge there, exploring them like large unknown countries. And if we apply ourselves diligently not only to aesthetic contemplation but also to the expression of its methods and results, it's because the poetry or prose we write – devoid of any desire to move anyone else's will or to mould anyone's understanding – is merely like when a reader reads out loud to fully objectify the subjective pleasure of reading.

We're well aware that every creative work is imperfect and that our most dubious aesthetic contemplation will be the one whose object is what we write. But everything is imperfect. There's no sunset so lovely it couldn't be yet lovelier, no gentle breeze bringing us sleep that couldn't bring a yet sounder sleep. And so, contemplators of statues and mountains alike, enjoying both books and the passing days, and dreaming all things so as to transform them into our own substance, we will also write down descriptions and analyses which, when they're finished, will become extraneous things that we can enjoy as if they happened along one day.

This isn't the viewpoint of pessimists like Vigny,* for whom life was a prison in which he wove straw to keep busy and forget. To be a pessimist is to see everything tragically, an attitude that's both excessive and uncomfortable. While it's true that we ascribe no value to the work we produce and that we produce it to keep busy, we're not like the prisoner who busily weaves straw to forget about his fate; we're like the girl who embroiders pillows for no other reason than to keep busy.

I see life as a roadside inn where I have to stay until the coach from the abyss pulls up. I don't know where it will take me, because I don't know anything. I could see this inn as a prison, for I'm compelled to wait in it; I could see it as a social centre, for it's here that I meet others. But I'm neither impatient nor common. I leave who will to stay shut up in their rooms, sprawled out on beds where they sleeplessly wait, and I leave who will to chat in the parlours, from where their songs and voices conveniently drift out here to me. I'm sitting at the door, feasting my eyes and ears on the colours and sounds of the landscape, and I softly sing – for myself alone – wispy songs I compose while waiting.

Night will fall on us all and the coach will pull up. I enjoy the breeze I'm given and the soul I was given to enjoy it with, and I no longer question or seek. If what I write in the book of travellers can, when read by others at some future date, also entertain them on their journey, then fine. If they don't read it, or are not entertained, that's fine too.

2

I have to choose what I detest – either dreaming, which my intelligence hates, or action, which my sensibility loathes; either action, for which I wasn't born, or dreaming, for which no one was born.

Detesting both, I choose neither; but since I must on occasion either dream or act, I mix the two things together.

3

I love the stillness of early summer evenings downtown, and especially the stillness made more still by contrast, on the streets that seethe with activity by day. Rua do Arsenal, Rua da Alfândega, the sad streets extending eastward from where the Rua da Alfândega ends, the entire stretch along the quiet docks – all of this comforts me with sadness when on these evenings I enter the solitude of their ensemble. I slip into an era prior to the one I'm living in; I enjoy feeling that I'm a contemporary of Cesário Verde,* and that in me I have, not verses like his, but the identical substance of the verses that were his.

Walking on these streets, until the night falls, my life feels to me like the life they have. By day they're full of meaningless activity; by night they're full of a meaningless lack of it. By day I am nothing, and by night I am I. There is no difference between me and these streets, save they being streets and I a soul, which perhaps is irrelevant when we consider the essence of things. There is an equal, abstract destiny for men and for things; both have an equally indifferent designation in the algebra of the world's mystery.

But there's something else. . . In these languid and empty hours, a sadness felt by my entire being rises from my soul to my mind – a bitter awareness that everything is a sensation of mine and at the same time something external, something not in my power to change. Ah, how often my own dreams have raised up before me as things, not to replace reality but to declare themselves its equals, in so far as I scorn them and they exist apart from me, like the tram now turning the corner at the end of the street, or like the voice of an evening crier, crying I don't know what but with a sound that stands out – an Arabian chant like the sudden patter of a fountain – against the monotony of twilight!

Future married couples pass by, chatting seamstresses pass by, young men in a hurry for pleasure pass by, those who have retired from everything smoke on their habitual stroll, and at one or another doorway a shopkeeper stands like an idle vagabond, hardly noticing a thing. Army recruits – some of them brawny, others slight – slowly drift along in noisy and worse-than-noisy clusters. Occasionally someone quite ordinary goes by. Cars at that time of day are rare, and their noise is musical. In my heart there's a peaceful anguish, and my calm is made of resignation.

All of this passes, and none of it means anything to me. It's all foreign to my fate, and even to fate as a whole. It's just unconsciousness, curses of protest when chance hurls stones, echoes of unknown voices – a collective mishmash of life.

4

. . . and from the majestic heights of my dreams, I return to being an assistant bookkeeper in the city of Lisbon.

But the contrast doesn't overwhelm me, it frees me. And its irony is my blood. What should theoretically humiliate me is what I unfurl as my flag; and the laughter I should be using to laugh at myself is a bugle I blow to herald – and to create – a dawn into which I'm transformed.

The nocturnal glory of being great without being anything! The sombre majesty of splendours no one knows. . . And I suddenly experience the sublime feeling of a monk in the wilderness or of a hermit in his retreat, acquainted with the substance of Christ in the sands and in the caves of withdrawal from the world.

And at this table in my absurd room, I, a pathetic and anonymous office clerk, write words as if they were the soul's salvation, and I gild myself with the impossible sunset of high and vast hills in the distance, with the statue I received in exchange for life's pleasures, and with the ring of renunciation on my evangelical finger, the stagnant jewel of my ecstatic disdain.

5

I have before me, on the slanted surface of the old desk, the two large pages of the ledger, from which I lift my tired eyes and an even more tired soul. Beyond the nothing that this represents, there's the warehouse with its uniform rows of shelves, uniform employees, human order, and tranquil banality – all the way to the wall that fronts the Rua dos Douradores. Through the window the sound of another reality arrives, and the sound is banal, like the tranquillity around the shelves.

I lower new eyes to the two white pages, on which my careful numbers have entered the firm's results. And smiling to myself I remember that life, which contains these pages with fabric types, prices and sales, blank spaces, letters and ruled lines, also includes the great navigators, the great saints, and the poets of every age, not one of whom enters the books – a vast progeny banished from those who determine the world's worth.

In the very act of entering the name of an unfamiliar cloth, the doors of the Indus and of Samarkand open up, and Persian poetry (which is from yet another place), with its quatrains whose third lines don't rhyme, is a distant anchor for me in my disquiet. But I make no mistake: I write, I add, and the bookkeeping goes on, performed as usual by an employee of this office.

6

I asked for very little from life, and even this little was denied me. A nearby field, a ray of sunlight, a little bit of calm along with a bit of bread, not to feel oppressed by the knowledge that I exist, not to demand anything from others, and not to have others demand anything from me – this was denied me, like the spare change we might deny a beggar not because we're mean-hearted but because we don't feel like unbuttoning our coat.

Sadly I write in my quiet room, alone as I have always been, alone as I will always be. And I wonder if my apparently negligible voice might not embody the essence of thousands of voices, the longing for self-expression of thousands of lives, the patience of millions of souls resigned like my own to their daily lot, their useless dreams, and their hopeless hopes. In these moments my heart beats faster because I'm conscious of it. I live more because I live on high. I feel a religious force within me, a species of prayer, a kind of public outcry. But my mind quickly puts me in my place. . . I remember that I'm on the fourth floor of the Rua dos Douradores, and I take a drowsy look at myself. I glance up from this half-written page at life, futile and without beauty, and at the cheap cigarette I'm about to extinguish in the ashtray beyond the fraying blotter. Me in this fourth-floor room, interrogating life!, saying what souls feel!, writing prose like a genius or a famous author! Me, here, a genius!. . .

7

Today, in one of the pointless and worthless daydreams that constitute a large part of my inner life, I imagined being forever free from the Rua dos Douradores, from Vasques my boss, from Moreira the head bookkeeper, from all the employees, from the delivery boy, the office boy and the cat. In my dream I experienced freedom, as if the South Seas had offered me marvellous islands to be discovered. It would all be repose, artistic achievement, the intellectual fulfilment of my being.

But even as I was imagining this, during my miniature midday holiday in a café, an unpleasant thought assaulted my dream: I realized I would feel regret. Yes, I say it as if confronted by the actual circumstance: I would feel regret. Vasques my boss, Moreira the head bookkeeper, Borges the cashier, all the young men, the cheerful boy who takes letters to the post office, the boy who makes deliveries, the gentle cat – all this has become part of my life. And I wouldn't be able to leave it without crying, without feeling that – like it or not – it was a part of me which would remain with all of them, and that to separate myself from them would be a partial death.

Besides, if tomorrow I were to bid them all farewell and take off my Rua dos Douradores suit, what other activity would I end up doing (for I would have to do something), or what other suit would I end up wearing (for I would have to wear some other suit)?

We all have a Vasques who's the boss – visible for some of us, invisible for others. My Vasques goes by that very name, and he's a hale and pleasant man, occasionally short-tempered but never two-faced, self-interested but basically fair, with a sense of justice that's lacking in many great geniuses and human marvels of civilization, right and left. Other people answer to vanity, or to the lure of wealth, glory, immortality. For my boss I prefer the man named Vasques, who in difficult moments is easier to deal with than all the abstract bosses in the world.

Deeming that I earn too little, a friend of mine who's a partner in a successful firm that does a lot of business with the government said the other day: 'You're being exploited, Soares.' And I remembered that indeed I am. But since in life we must all be exploited, I wonder if it's any worse to be exploited by Vasques and his fabrics than by vanity, by glory, by resentment, by envy or by the impossible.

Some are exploited by God himself, and they are prophets and saints in this vacuous world.

And in the same way that others return to their homes, I retreat to my non-home: the large office on the Rua dos Douradores. I arrive at my desk as at a bulwark against life. I have a tender spot – tender to the point of tears – for my ledgers in which I keep other people's accounts, for the old inkstand I use, for the hunched back of Sérgio, who draws up invoices a little beyond where I sit. I love all this, perhaps because I have nothing else to love, and perhaps also because nothing is worth a human soul's love, and so it's all the same – should we feel the urge to give it – whether the recipient be the diminutive form of my inkstand or the vast indifference of the stars.

8

Vasques – the boss. At times I'm inexplicably hypnotized by Senhor Vasques. What is this man to me besides an occasional obstacle, as the owner of my time, in the daylight hours of my life? He treats me well and is polite when he talks to me, except on his grumpy days, when he's fretting about something and isn't polite to anyone. But why does he occupy my thoughts? Is he a symbol? A cause? What is he?

Vasques – the boss. I already remember him in the future with the nostalgia I know I'm bound to feel. I'll be peacefully ensconced in a small house on the outskirts of somewhere or other, enjoying a tranquillity in which I won't write the works I don't write now, and to keep on not writing them I'll come up with even better excuses than the ones I use today to elude myself. Or I'll be in an institution for paupers, happy in my utter defeat, mixed up with the rabble of would-be geniuses who were no more than beggars with dreams, thrown in with the anonymous throng of those who didn't have strength enough to conquer nor renunciation enough to conquer by not competing. Wherever I may be, I'll miss Senhor Vasques and the office on the Rua dos Douradores, and the monotony of my daily life will be like the remembrance of the loves that never came my way and the triumphs that weren't to be mine.

Vasques – the boss. I see him today from that future as I see him today from right here: medium height, stocky, a bit coarse but affectionate, frank and savvy, brusque and affable, a boss not only in his handling of money but also in his unhurried hands, in their thick hair and veins that look like small coloured muscles, in his full but not fat neck, and in his ruddy and taut cheeks with their dark, always close-shaven whiskers. I see him, I see his energetically deliberate gestures, his eyes thinking within about things outside. It displeases me when I've somehow displeased him, and my soul rejoices when he smiles, with his broad and human smile, like an applauding crowd.

Perhaps the lack of some more distinguished figure in my immediate world explains why Senor Vasques, a common and even brutish man, sometimes gets so enmeshed in my thoughts that I forget myself. I believe there's a symbol here. I believe or almost believe that somewhere, in a remote life, this man was something much more important to me than he is today.

9

Ah, I understand! Vasques my boss is Life – monotonous and necessary, imperious and inscrutable Life. This banal man represents the banality of Life. For me he is everything, externally speaking, because for me Life is whatever is external.

And if the office on the Rua dos Douradores represents life for me, the fourth-floor room* where I live, on this same Rua dos Douradores, represents Art for me. Yes, Art, residing on the very same street as Life, but in a different place. Art, which gives me relief from life without relieving me of living, being as monotonous as life itself, only in a different place. Yes, for me the Rua dos Douradores contains the meaning of everything and the answer to all riddles, except for the riddle of why riddles exist, which can never be answered.

10

Futile and sensitive, I'm capable of violent and consuming impulses – both good and bad, noble and vile – but never of a sentiment that endures, never of an emotion that continues, entering into the substance of my soul. Everything in me tends to go on to become something else. My soul is impatient with itself, as with a bothersome child; its restlessness keeps growing and is forever the same. Everything interests me, but nothing holds me. I attend to everything, dreaming all the while. I note the slightest facial movements of the person I'm talking with, I record the subtlest inflections of his utterances; but I hear without listening, I'm thinking of something else, and what I least catch in the conversation is the sense of what was said, by me or by him. And so I often repeat to someone what I've already repeated, or ask him again what he's already answered. But I'm able to describe, in four photographic words, the facial muscles he used to say what I don't recall, or the way he listened with his eyes to the words I don't remember telling him. I'm two, and both keep their distance – Siamese twins that aren't attached.

11

Litany

We never know self-realization.

We are two abysses – a well staring at the sky.

12

I envy – but I'm not sure that I envy – those for whom a biography could be written, or who could write their own. In these random impressions, and with no desire to be other than random, I indifferently narrate my factless autobiography, my lifeless history. These are my Confessions, and if in them I say nothing, it's because I have nothing to say.

What is there to confess that's worthwhile or useful? What has happened to us has happened to everyone or only to us; if to everyone, then it's no novelty, and if only to us, then it won't be understood. If I write what I feel, it's to reduce the fever of feeling. What I confess is unimportant, because everything is unimportant. I make landscapes out of what I feel. I make holidays of my sensations. I can easily understand women who embroider out of sorrow or who crochet because life exists. My elderly aunt would play solitaire throughout the endless evening. These confessions of what I feel are my solitaire. I don't interpret them like those who read cards to tell the future. I don't probe them, because in solitaire the cards don't have any special significance. I unwind myself like a multicoloured skein, or I make string figures of myself, like those woven on spread fingers and passed from child to child. I take care only that my thumb not miss its loop. Then I turn over my hand and the figure changes. And I start over.

To live is to crochet according to a pattern we were given. But while doing it the mind is at liberty, and all enchanted princes can stroll in their parks between one and another plunge of the hooked ivory needle. Needlework of things. . . Intervals. . . Nothing. . .

Besides, what can I expect from myself? My sensations in all their horrible acuity, and a profound awareness of feeling. . . A sharp mind that only destroys me, and an unusual capacity for dreaming to keep me entertained. . . A dead will and a reflection that cradles it, like a living child. . . Yes, crochet. . .

13

My deplorable condition isn't in the least affected by these words I join together to form, little by little, my haphazard book of musings. My worthless self lives on at the bottom of every expression, like an indissoluble residue at the bottom of a glass from which only water was drunk. I write my literature as I write my ledger entries – carefully and indifferently. Next to the vast starry sky and the enigma of so many souls, the night of the unknown abyss and the chaos of nothing making sense – next to all this, what I write in the ledger and what I write on this paper that tells my soul are equally confined to the Rua dos Douradores, woefully little in the face of the universe's millionaire expanses.

All of this is dream and phantasmagoria, and it matters little whether the dream be of ledger entries or of well-crafted prose. Does dreaming of princesses serve a better purpose than dreaming of the front door to the office? All that we know is our own impression, and all that we are is an exterior impression, a melodrama in which we, the self-aware actors, are also our own spectators, our own gods by permission of some department or other at City Hall.

14

We may know that the work we continue to put off doing will be bad. Worse, however, is the work we never do. A work that's finished is at least finished. It may be poor, but it exists, like the miserable plant in the lone flowerpot of my neighbour who's crippled. That plant is her happiness, and sometimes it's even mine. What I write, bad as it is, may provide some hurt or sad soul a few moments of distraction from something worse. That's enough for me, or it isn't enough, but it serves some purpose, and so it is with all of life.

A tedium that includes the expectation of nothing but more tedium; a regret, right now, for the regret I'll have tomorrow for having felt regret today – huge confusions with no point and no truth, huge confusions...

...where, curled up on a bench in a railway station, my contempt dozes in the cloak of my discouragement...

...the world of dreamed images which are the sum of my knowledge as well as of my life...

To heed the present moment isn't a great or lasting concern of mine. I crave time in all its duration, and I want to be myself unconditionally.

15

Inch by inch I conquered the inner terrain I was born with. Bit by bit I reclaimed the swamp in which I'd languished. I gave birth to my infinite being, but I had to wrench myself out of me with forceps.

16

I daydream between Cascais* and Lisbon. I went to Cascais to pay a property tax for my boss, Senhor Vasques, on a house he owns in Estoril.* I took anticipated pleasure in the trip, an hour each way in which to enjoy the forever changing views of the wide river and its Atlantic estuary. But on actually going out there, I lost myself in abstract contemplations, seeing but not seeing the riverscapes I'd looked forward to seeing, while on the way back I lost myself in mentally nailing down those sensations. I wouldn't be able to describe the slightest detail of the trip, the slightest scrap of what there was to see. What I got out of it are these pages, the fruit of contradiction and forgetting. I don't know if this is better or worse than the contrary, nor do I know what the contrary is.

The train slows down, we're at Cais do Sodré.* I've arrived at Lisbon, but not at a conclusion.

17

Perhaps it's finally time for me to make this one effort: to take a good look at my life. I see myself in the midst of a vast desert. I tell what I literarily was yesterday, and I try to explain to myself how I got here.

18

With merely a kind of smile in my soul, I passively consider the definitive confinement of my life to the Rua dos Douradores, to this office, to the people who surround me. An income sufficient for food and drink, a roof over my head, and a little free time in which to dream and write, to sleep – what more can I ask of the Gods or expect from Destiny?

I've had great ambitions and boundless dreams, but so has the delivery boy* or the seamstress, because everyone has dreams. What distinguishes certain of us is our capacity for fulfilling them, or our destiny that they be fulfilled.

In dreams I am equal to the delivery boy and the seamstress. I differ from them only in knowing how to write. Yes, writing is an act, a personal circumstance that distinguishes me from them. But in my soul I'm their equal.

I realize that there are islands to the South and great cosmopolitan attractions and . . . . .

If I had the world in my hand, I'm quite sure I would trade it for a ticket to Rua dos Douradores.

Perhaps my destiny is to remain forever a bookkeeper, with poetry or literature as a butterfly that alights on my head, making me look ridiculous to the extent it looks beautiful.

I'll miss Moreira, but what's that next to a glorious promotion?

I know that the day I become head bookkeeper of Vasques & Co. will be one of the great days of my life. I know it with foretasted bitterness and irony, but also with the intellectual advantage of certainty.

19

In the cove on the seashore, among the woods and meadows that fronted the beach, the fickleness of inflamed desire rose out of the uncertainty of the blank abyss. To choose the wheat or to choose the many [*sic*] was all the same, and the distance kept going, through cypress trees.

The magic power of words in isolation, or joined together on the basis of sound, with inner reverberations and divergent meanings even as they converge, the splendour of phrases inserted between the meanings of other phrases, the virulence of vestiges, the hope of the woods, and the absolute peacefulness of the ponds on the farms of my childhood of ruses. . . And so, within the high walls of absurd audacity, in the rows of trees and in the startled tremors of what withers, someone other than me would hear from sad lips the confession denied to more insistent parties. Never again, not even if the knights were to come back on the road that was visible from the top of the wall, would there be peace in the Castle of the Last Souls, where lances jangled in the unseen courtyard, nor would any other name on this side of the road be remembered but the one which at night would enchant, like the Moorish ladies of folklore,* the child who later died to life and to wonder.

Over the furrows in the grass, like remembrances of what was to come, the treading of the last lost men sounded ever so lightly, their dragging steps opening nothings in the restless greenery. Those who would come were bound to be old, and only the young would never arrive. The drums rumbled on the roadside, and the bugles hung uselessly from exhausted arms that would have dropped them if they still had strength enough to drop something.

But when the illusion was over, the dead clamour sounded yet again, and the dogs could be seen nervously hesitating on the tree-lined paths. It was all absurd, like mourning the dead, and princesses from other people's dreams strolled about freely and indefinitely.

20

Whenever I've tried to free my life from a set of the circumstances that continuously oppress it, I've been instantly surrounded by other circumstances of the same order, as if the inscrutable web of creation were irrevocably at odds with me. I yank from my neck a hand that was choking me, and I see that my own hand is tied to a noose that fell around my neck when I freed it from the stranger's hand. When I gingerly remove the noose, it's with my own hands that I nearly strangle myself.

21

Whether or not they exist, we're slaves to the gods.

22

The image of myself I saw in mirrors is the same one I hold against the bosom of my soul. I could never be anything but frail and hunched over, even in my thoughts.

Everything about me belongs to a glossy prince pasted, along with other decals, in the old album of a little boy who died long ago.

To love myself is to feel sorry for myself. Perhaps one day, towards the end of the future, someone will write a poem about me, and I'll begin to reign in my Kingdom.

God is the fact that we exist and that's not all.

23

Absurdity

Let's act like sphinxes, however falsely, until we reach the point of no longer knowing who we are. For we are, in fact, false sphinxes, with no idea of what we are in reality. The only way to be in agreement with life is to disagree with ourselves. Absurdity is divine.

Let's develop theories, patiently and honestly thinking them out, in order to promptly act against them – acting and justifying our actions with new theories that condemn them. Let's cut a path in life and then go immediately against that path. Let's adopt all the poses and gestures of something we aren't and don't wish to be, and don't even wish to be taken for being.

Let's buy books so as not to read them; let's go to concerts without caring to hear the music or to see who's there; let's take long walks because we're sick of walking; and let's spend whole days in the country, just because it bores us.

24

Today, feeling almost physically ill because of that age-old anxiety which sometimes wells up, I ate and drank rather less than usual in the first-floor dining room of the restaurant responsible for perpetuating my existence. And as I was leaving, the waiter, having noted that the bottle of wine was still half full, turned to me and said: 'So long, Senhor Soares, and I hope you feel better.'

The trumpet blast of this simple phrase relieved my soul like a sudden wind clearing the sky of clouds. And I realized something I had never really thought about: with these café and restaurant waiters, with barbers and with the delivery boys on street corners I enjoy a natural, spontaneous rapport that I can't say I have with those I supposedly know more intimately.

Camaraderie has its subtleties.

Some govern the world, others are the world. Between an American millionaire, a Caesar or Napoleon, or Lenin, and the Socialist leader of a small town, there's a difference in quantity but not of quality. Below them there's us, the unnoticed: the reckless playwright William Shakespeare, John Milton the schoolteacher, Dante Alighieri the tramp, the delivery boy who ran an errand for me yesterday, the barber who tells me jokes, and the waiter who just now demonstrated his camaraderie by wishing me well, after noticing I'd drunk only half the wine.

25

It's a hopelessly bad lithograph. I stare at it without knowing if I see it. It's one among others in the shop window – in the middle of the window under the steps.

She holds Spring against her breast and stares at me with sad eyes. Her smile shines, because the paper's glossy, and her cheeks are red. The sky behind her is the colour of light blue cloth. She has a sculpted, almost tiny mouth, and above its postcard expression her eyes keep staring at me with an enormous sorrow. The arm holding the flowers reminds me of someone else's. Her dress or blouse has a low neck that reveals one shoulder. Her eyes are genuinely sad: they stare at me from the depth of the lithographic reality with a truth of some sort. She came with Spring. Her eyes are large, but that's not what makes them sad. I tear myself from the window with violent steps. I cross the street and turn around with impotent indignation. She still holds the Spring she was given, and her eyes are sad like all the things in life I've missed out on. Seen from a distance, the lithograph turns out to be more colourful. The figure's hair is tied at the top by a pinker than pink ribbon; I hadn't noticed. In human eyes, even in lithographic ones, there's something terrible: the inevitable warning of consciousness, the silent shout that there's a soul there. With a huge effort I pull out of the sleep in which I was steeped, and like a dog I shake off the drops of dark fog. Oblivious to my departure, as if bidding farewell to something else, those sad eyes of the whole of life – of this metaphysical lithograph that we observe from a distance – stare at me as if I knew something of God. The print, which has a calendar at the bottom, is framed above and below by two flatly curved, badly painted black strips. Within these upper and lower limits, above 1929 and an outmoded calligraphic vignette adorning the inevitable 1st of January, the sad eyes ironically smile at me.

Funny where I knew that figure from. In the corner at the back of the office there's an identical calendar which I've seen countless times, but due to some lithographic mystery, or some mystery of my own, the eyes of the office copy express no sorrow. It's just a lithograph. (Printed on glossy paper, it sleeps away its subdued life above the head of left-handed Alves.)

All of this makes me want to smile, but I feel a profound anxiety. I feel the chill of a sudden sickness in my soul. I don't have the strength to balk at this absurdity. What window overlooking what secret of God am I confronting against my will? Where does the window under the stairs lead to? What eyes stared at me from out of the lithograph? I'm practically trembling. I involuntarily raise my eyes to the far corner of the office where the real lithograph is. I keep raising my eyes to that corner of the office where the real lithograph is. I keep raising my eyes to that corner.

26

To give each emotion a personality, a heart to each state of the heart!

The girls came around the bend in a large group. They sang as they walked, and the sound of their voices was happy. I don't know who or what they might be. I listened to them for a time from afar, without a feeling of my own, but a feeling of sorrow for them impressed itself on my heart.

For their future? For their unconsciousness?

Not directly for them, and perhaps, after all, only for me.

27

Literature – which is art married to thought, and realization untainted by reality – seems to me the end towards which all human effort would have to strive, if it were truly human and not just a welling up of our animal self. To express something is to conserve its virtue and take away its terror. Fields are greener in their description than in their actual greenness. Flowers, if described with phrases that define them in the air of the imagination, will have colours with a durability not found in cellular life.

What moves lives. What is said endures. There's nothing in life that's less real for having been well described. Small-minded critics point out that such-and-such poem, with its protracted cadences, in the end says merely that it's a nice day. But to say it's a nice day is difficult, and the nice day itself passes on. It's up to us to conserve the nice day in a wordy, florid memory, sprinkling new flowers and new stars over the fields and skies of the empty, fleeting outer world.

Everything is what we are, and everything will be, for those who come after us in the diversity of time, what we will have intensely imagined – what we, that is, by embodying our imagination, will have actually been. The grand, tarnished panorama of History amounts, as I see it, to a flow of interpretations, a confused consensus of unreliable eyewitness accounts. The novelist is all of us, and we narrate whenever we see, because seeing is complex like everything.

Right now I have so many fundamental thoughts, so many truly metaphysical things to say that I suddenly feel tired, and I've decided to write no more, think no more. I'll let the fever of saying put me to sleep instead, and with closed eyes I'll stroke, as if petting a cat, all that I might have said.

28

A breath of music or of a dream, of something that would make me almost feel, something that would make me not think.

29

After the last drops of rain began to fall more slowly from the rooftops and the sky's blue began to spread over the street's paving-stones, then the vehicles sang a different song, louder and happier, and windows could be heard opening up to the no longer forgetful sun. From the narrow street at the end of the next block came the loud invitation of the first seller of lottery tickets, and nails being nailed into crates in the shop opposite reverberated in the limpid space.

It was an ambiguous holiday, official but not strictly observed. Work and repose coexisted, and I had nothing to do. I'd woken up early, and I took a long time getting ready to exist. I paced from one side of the room to the other, dreaming out loud incoherent and impossible things – deeds I'd forgotten to do, hopeless ambitions haphazardly realized, fluid and lively conversations which, were they to be, would already have been. And in this reverie without grandeur or calm, in this hopeless and endless dallying, I paced away my free morning, and my words – said out loud in a low voice – multiplied in the echoing cloister of my inglorious isolation.

Seen from the outside, my human figure was ridiculous like everything human in its intimacy. Over the pyjamas of my abandoned sleep I'd put on an old overcoat, habitually employed for these morning vigils. My old slippers were falling apart, especially the left one. And with my hands in the pockets of my posthumous coat, I strolled down the avenue of my small room in broad and decisive steps, playing out in my useless reverie a dream no different from anybody else's.

Through the open coolness of my only window, thick drops of leftover rain could still be heard falling from the rooftops. It was still somewhat moist and cool from having rained. The sky, however, was triumphantly blue, and the clouds that remained from the defeated or tired rain retreated behind the Castle, surrendering to the sky its rightful paths.

It was an occasion to be happy. But something weighed on me, some inscrutable yearning, an indefinable and perhaps even noble desire. Perhaps it was just taking me a long time to feel alive. And when I leaned out my high window, looking down at the street I couldn't see,

I suddenly felt like one of those damp rags used for house-cleaning that are taken to the window to dry but are forgotten, balled up, on the sill where they slowly leave a stain.

30

Sadly, or perhaps not, I recognize that I have an arid heart. An adjective matters more to me than the real weeping of a human soul. My master Vieira* .....

But sometimes I'm different. Sometimes I have the warm tears of those who don't have and never had a mother; and the eyes that burn with these dead tears burn inside my heart.

I don't remember my mother. She died when I was one year old. My distracted and callous sensibility comes from the lack of that warmth and from my useless longing after kisses I don't remember. I'm artificial. It was always against strange breasts that I woke up, cuddled as if by proxy.

Ah, it's my longing for whom I might have been that distracts and torments me! Who would I be now if I'd received the affection that comes from the womb and is placed, through kisses, on a baby's face?

Perhaps my regret for having never been a son plays a large role in my emotional indifference. Whoever held me as a child against her face couldn't hold me against her heart. Only she who was far away, in a tomb, could have done that – she who would have belonged to me, had Fate willed it.

They told me later on that my mother was pretty, and they say that, when they told me, I made no comment. I was already fit in body and soul, but ignorant about emotions, and people's speech was not yet news from other, hard-to-imagine pages.

My father, who lived far away, killed himself when I was three, and so I never met him. I still don't know why he lived far away. I never cared to find out. I remember his death as a grave silence during the first meals we ate after learning about it. I remember that the others would occasionally look at me. And I would look back, dumbly comprehending. Then I'd eat with more concentration, since they might, when I wasn't looking, still be looking at me.

I'm all of these things, like it or not, in the confused depths of my fatal sensibility.

31

The clock in the back of the deserted house (everyone's sleeping) slowly lets the clear quadruple sound of four o'clock in the morning fall. I still haven't fallen asleep, and I don't expect to. There's nothing on my mind to keep me from sleeping and no physical pain to prevent me from relaxing, but the dull silence of my strange body just lies there in the darkness, made even more desolate by the feeble moonlight of the street lamps. I'm so sleepy I can't even think, so sleepless I can't feel.

Everything around me is the naked, abstract universe, consisting of nocturnal negations. Divided between tired and restless, I succeed in touching – with the awareness of my body – a metaphysical knowledge of the mystery of things. Sometimes my soul starts fading, and then the random details of daily life float on the surface of consciousness, and I find myself entering amounts while floundering in sleeplessness. At other times I wake up from the half-sleep I'd fallen into, and hazy images with poetical and unpredictable colours play out their silent show to my inattention. My eyes aren't completely closed. My faint vision is fringed by a light from far away; it's from the street lamps that border the deserted street down below.

To cease, to sleep, to replace this intermittent consciousness with better, melancholy things, whispered in secret to someone who doesn't know me!. . . To cease, to be the ebb and flow of a vast sea, fluidly skirting real shores, on a night in which one really sleeps!. . . To cease, to be unknown and external, a swaying of branches in distant rows of trees, a gentle falling of leaves, their sound noted more than their fall, the ocean spray of far-off fountains, and all the uncertainty of parks at night, lost in endless tangles, natural labyrinths of darkness!. . . To cease, to end at last, but surviving as something else: the page of a book, a tuft of dishevelled hair, the quiver of the creeping plant next to a half-open window, the irrelevant footsteps in the gravel of the bend, the last smoke to rise from the village going to sleep, the wagoner's whip left on the early morning roadside... Absurdity, confusion, oblivion – everything that isn't life...

In my own way I sleep, without slumber or repose, this vegetative life of imagining, and the distant reflection of the silent street lamps, like the quiet foam of a dirty sea, hovers behind my restless eyebrows.

I sleep and unsleep.

Behind me, on the other side of where I'm lying down, the silence of the house touches infinity. I hear time fall, drop by drop, and not one drop that falls can be heard. My physical heart is physically oppressed by the almost forgotten memory of all that has been or that I've been. I feel my head materially supported by the pillow in which it makes a valley. My skin and the skin of the pillowcase are like two people touching in the shadows. Even the ear on which I'm lying mathematically engraves itself on my brain. I blink with fatigue, and my eyelashes make an infinitesimal, inaudible sound against the felt whiteness of the pillow's slope. I breathe, sighing, and my breathing happens – it isn't mine. I suffer without feeling or thinking. The house's clock, definitely located in the midst of the infinite, strikes the half hour, dry and void. Everything is so full, so deep, so black and so cold!

I pass times, I pass silences; formless worlds pass by me.

Like a child of Mystery, a cock suddenly crows, unaware that it's night-time. I can sleep, for it's morning in me. And I feel my mouth smile, slightly displacing the soft pleats of the pillowcase pressed against my face. I can surrender to life, I can sleep, I can forget myself... And as incipient slumber wraps me in darkness, either I remember the cock that crowed, or it is the cock itself that crows a second time.

32

Symphony of a Restless Night

Everything was sleeping as if the universe were a mistake. The wind, blowing uncertainly, was a formless flag unfurled over a non-existent army post. High, strong gusts ripped through nothing at all, and the window-frames shook their panes to make the edges rattle. Underlying everything, the hushed night was the tomb of God* (and my soul felt sorry for God).

Suddenly a new order of universal things acted on the city, the wind whistled in its lulls, and there was a slumbering awareness of countless agitations on high. Then the night closed like a trapdoor, and a vast calm made me wish I'd been sleeping.

33

During the first days of Autumn when nightfall arrives suddenly, as if prematurely, and it seems we took longer to do our day's work, I enjoy, while still working, the thought of not working which the darkness brings, for the darkness is night, and night means sleep, home, freedom. When the lights come on, dispelling darkness from the large office, and we continue our day's work in the beginning of night, I feel a comfort that's absurd, like a remembrance belonging to someone else, and I'm at peace with the numbers I write, as if I were reading while waiting to fall asleep.

We're all slaves of external circumstances. A sunny day transports us from a café on a narrow side street to wide-open fields; an overcast sky in the country makes us close up, taking shelter as best we can in the house without doors of our own self; the onset of night, even in the midst of daytime activities, enlarges – like a slowly opening fan – our awareness that we ought to rest.

But the work doesn't slow down; it gets livelier. We no longer work; we amuse ourselves with the labour to which we're condemned. And all of a sudden, across the huge columned sheet of my numerary destiny, the old house of my elderly aunts, shut off from the world, shelters the drowsy ten o'clock tea, and the kerosene lamp of my lost childhood, glowing only on the linen-covered table, blinds me to the sight of Moreira, illuminated by a black electricity infinities away from me. The maid, who is even older than my aunts, brings in the tea, along with the vestiges of her interrupted nap and the affectionately patient grumpiness of old-time servants, and across all my dead past I enter items and totals without a single mistake. I retreat into myself, get lost in myself, forget myself in far-away nights uncontaminated by duty and the world, undefiled by mystery and the future.

And so gentle is the sensation that estranges me from debits and credits that if by chance I'm asked a question, I answer in a soft voice, as if my being were hollow, as if it were nothing more than a typewriter I carry around with me – portable, opened and ready. It doesn't faze me when my dreams are interrupted; they're so gentle that I keep dreaming them as I speak, write, answer, or even discuss. And through it all the long-lost tea finishes, the office is going to close... From the ledger which I slowly shut I raise my eyes, sore from the tears they didn't shed, and with confused feelings I accept, because I must, that with the closing of my office my dream also closes; that as my hand shuts the ledger it also pulls a veil over my irretrievable past; that I'm going to life's bed wide awake, unaccompanied and without peace, in the ebb and flow of my confused consciousness, like two tides in the black night where the destinies of nostalgia and desolation meet.

34

Sometimes I think I'll never leave the Rua dos Douradores. And having written this, it seems to me eternity.

Not pleasure, not glory, not power... Freedom, only freedom.

To go from the phantoms of faith to the ghosts of reason is merely to change cells. Art, if it frees us from the abstract idols of old, should also free us from magnanimous ideas and social concerns, which are likewise idols.

To find our personality by losing it – faith itself endorses this destiny.

35

. . . and a deep and weary disdain for all those who work for mankind, for all those who fight for their country and give their lives so that civilization may continue. . .

. . . a disdain full of disgust for those who don't realize that the only reality is each man's soul, and that everything else – the exterior world and other people – is but an unaesthetic nightmare, like the result, in dreams, of a mental indigestion.

My aversion to effort becomes an almost writhing horror before all forms of violent effort. War, energetic and productive labour, helping others – all this strikes me as the product of an impertinence . . . . .

Everything useful and external tastes frivolous and trivial in the light of my soul's supreme reality and next to the pure sovereign splendour of my more original and frequent dreams. These, for me, are more real.

36

It's not the cracked walls of my rented room, nor the shabby desks in the office where I work, nor the poverty of the same old downtown streets in between, which I've crossed and recrossed so many times they seem to have assumed the immobility of the irreparable – none of that is responsible for my frequent feeling of nausea over the squalor of daily life. It's the people who habitually surround me, the souls who know me through conversation and daily contact without knowing me at all – they're the ones who cause a salivary knot of physical disgust to form in my throat. It's the sordid monotony of their lives, outwardly parallel to my own, and their keen awareness that I'm their fellow man – that is what dresses me in a convict's clothes, places me in a jail cell, and makes me apocryphal and beggarly.

There are times when each detail of the ordinary interests me for its own sake, and I feel a fondness for things, because I can read them clearly. Then I see – as Vieira* said that Sousa,* in his descriptions, saw – the ordinary in its singularity, and I have the poetic soul that inspired the intellectual age of poetry among the Greeks. But there are also moments, such as the one that oppresses me now, when I feel my own self far more than I feel external things, and everything transforms into a night of rain and mud where, lost in the solitude of an out-of-the-way station, I wait interminably for the next third-class train.

Yes, my particular virtue of being very often objective, and thus sidetracked from thinking about myself, suffers lapses of affirmation, as do all virtues and even all vices. And I start to wonder how I'm able to go on, how I dare have the faint-heartedness to be here among these people, exactly like them, in true conformity to their shoddy illusion. Like flashes from a distant lighthouse, I see all the solutions offered by the imagination's female side: flight, suicide, renunciation, grandiose acts of our aristocratic self-awareness, the swashbuckling novel of existences without balconies.

But the ideal Juliet of the best possible reality closed the high window of the literary encounter on the fictitious Romeo of my blood. She obeys her father; he obeys his. The feud between the Montagues and the Capulets continues, the curtain falls on what didn't happen, and I go on home – to my rented room where I loathe the landlady who isn't home, her children I hardly ever see, and the people from the office that I'll see only tomorrow – with the collar of a clerk's coat turned up without astonishment over the neck of a poet, with my boots (always purchased in the same shop) automatically avoiding the puddles of cold rain, and with a bit of mixed concern, for having once more forgotten my umbrella and the dignity of my soul.*

37

Dolorous Interlude

An object tossed into a corner, a rag that fell on to the road, my contemptible being feigns to the world.

38

I envy all people, because I'm not them. Since this always seemed to me like the most impossible of all impossibilities, it's what I yearned for every day, and despaired of in every sad moment.

A dull blast of grim sunlight burned my eyes' physical sensation of seeing. A hot yellow languished in the black green of the trees. The torpor . . . . .

39

All of a sudden, as if a surgical hand of destiny had operated on a long-standing blindness with immediate and sensational results, I lift my gaze from my anonymous life to the clear recognition of how I live. And I see that everything I've done, thought or been is a species of delusion or madness. I'm amazed by what I managed not to see. I marvel at all that I was and that I now see I'm not.

I look at my past life as at a field lit up by the sun when it breaks through the clouds, and I note with metaphysical astonishment how my most deliberate acts, my clearest ideas and my most logical intentions were after all no more than congenital drunkenness, inherent madness and huge ignorance. I didn't even act anything out. I was the role that got acted. At most, I was the actor's motions.

All that I've done, thought or been is a series of submissions, either to a false self that I assumed belonged to me because I expressed myself through it to the outside, or to a weight of circumstances that I supposed was the air I breathed. In this moment of seeing, I suddenly find myself isolated, an exile where I'd always thought I was a citizen. At the heart of my thoughts I wasn't I.

I'm dazed by a sarcastic terror of life, a despondency that exceeds the limits of my conscious being. I realize that I was all error and deviation, that I never lived, that I existed only in so far as I filled time with consciousness and thought. I feel, in this moment, like a man who wakes up after a slumber full of real dreams, or like a man freed by an earthquake from the dim light of the prison he'd grown used to.

This sudden awareness of my true being, of this being that has always sleepily wandered between what it feels and what it sees, weighs on me like an untold sentence to serve.

It's so hard to describe what I feel when I feel I really exist and my soul is a real entity that I don't know what human words could define it. I don't know if I have a fever, as I feel I do, or if I've stopped having the fever of sleeping through life. Yes, I repeat, I'm like a traveller who suddenly finds himself in a strange town, without knowing how he got there, which makes me think of those who lose their memory and for a long time are not themselves but someone else. I was someone else for a long time – since birth and consciousness – and suddenly I've woken up in the middle of a bridge, leaning over the river and knowing that I exist more solidly than the person I was up till now. But the city is unknown to me, the streets are new, and the trouble has no cure. And so, leaning over the bridge, I wait for the truth to go away and let me return to being fictitious and non-existent, intelligent and natural.

It was just a brief moment, and it's already over. Once more I see the furniture all around me, the pattern on the old wallpaper, and the sun through the dusty panes. I saw the truth for a moment. For a moment I was consciously what great men are their entire lives. I recall their words and deeds and wonder if they were also successfully tempted by the Demon of Reality. To know nothing about yourself is to live. To know yourself badly is to think. To know yourself in a flash, as I did in this moment, is to have a fleeting notion of the intimate monad, the soul's magic word. But that sudden light scorches everything, consumes everything. It strips us naked of even ourselves.

It was just a moment, and I saw myself. I can no longer even say what I was. And now I'm sleepy, because I think – I don't know why – that the meaning of it all is to sleep.

40

Sometimes I feel, I'm not sure why, a touch of foretold death... Perhaps it's an indefinite sickness which, because it doesn't materialize in pain, tends to become spiritualized in nothingness, the end. Or perhaps it's a weariness that needs a slumber far deeper than sleeping affords. All I know is that I feel like a sick man who has been getting steadily worse, until at last he calmly and without regret extends his feeble hands over the bedspread he had been clutching.

And then I wonder what this thing is that we call death. I don't mean the mystery of death, which I can't begin to fathom, but the physical sensation of ceasing to live. Humanity is afraid of death, but indecisively. The normal man makes a good soldier in combat; the normal man, when sick or old, rarely looks with horror at the abyss of nothing, though he admits its nothingness. This is because he lacks imagination. And nothing is less worthy of a thinking man than to see death as a slumber. Why a slumber, if death doesn't resemble sleep? Basic to sleep is the fact we wake up from it, as we presumably do not from death. If death resembles sleep, we should suppose that we wake up from it, but this is not what the normal man imagines; he imagines death as a slumber no one wakes up from, which means nothing. Death doesn't resemble slumber, I said, since in slumber one is alive and sleeping, and I don't know how death can resemble anything at all for us, since we have no experience of it, nor anything to compare it to.

Whenever I see a dead body, death seems to me a departure. The corpse looks to me like a suit that was left behind. Someone went away and didn't need to take the one and only outfit he'd worn.

41

Silence emerges from the sound of the rain and spreads in a crescendo of grey monotony over the narrow street I contemplate. I'm sleeping while awake, standing by the window, leaning against it as against everything. I search in myself for the sensations I feel before these falling threads of darkly luminous water that stand out from the grimy building façades and especially from the open windows. And I don't know what I feel or what I want to feel. I don't know what to think or what I am.

All the pent-up bitterness of my life removes, before my sensationless eyes, the suit of natural happiness it wears in the random events that fill up each day. I realize that, while often happy and often cheerful, I'm always sad. And the part of me that realizes this is behind me, as if bent over my leaning self at the window, as if looking over my shoulder or even over my head to contemplate, with eyes more intimate than my own, the slow and now wavy rain which filigrees the grey and inclement air.

To shrug off all duties, even those not assigned to us, to repudiate all homes, even those that weren't ours, to live off vestiges and the ill-defined, in grand purple robes of madness and in counterfeit laces of dreamed majesties... To be something, anything, that doesn't feel the weight of the rain outside, nor the anguish of inner emptiness... To wander without thought or soul – sensation without sensation – along mountain roads and through valleys hidden between steep slopes, into the far distance, irrevocably immersed... To be lost in landscapes like paintings... A coloured non-existence in the background...

A light gust of wind, which I can't feel on this side of the window, breaks the even fall of rain into aerial discrepancies. A part of the sky hidden from view is clearing. I notice this because I can now make out the calendar on the wall through the less than clean window that faces my own.

I forget. I don't see. I don't think.

The rain stops, and for a moment a fine dust of miniature diamonds hangs in the air, like tiny crumbs from an enormous tablecloth bluely shaken on high. I can feel that part of the sky has cleared. I can see more distinctly the calendar through the window opposite. It has a woman's face, and the rest is easy because I remember it, and the toothpaste is the brand everyone knows.

But what was I thinking about before I got lost in seeing? I don't know. Effort? Will? Life? A huge onslaught of light reveals a now almost entirely blue sky. But there is no peace – ah, there will never be! – at the bottom of my heart, an old well in a corner of the farm that was sold, a dust-coated memory of childhood shut up in the attic of someone else's house. I have no peace, nor even – alas! – the desire to have it. . .

42

Only as a lack of personal hygiene can I understand my wallowing in this flat, invariable life I lead, this dust or filth stuck on the surface of never changing.*

We should wash our destiny the way we wash our body, and change life the way we change clothes – not to preserve life, as when we eat and sleep, but out of objective respect for ourselves, which is what personal hygiene is all about.

There are many people whose lack of hygiene is not a chosen condition but a shrugging of the intellect's shoulders. And there are many whose dullness and sameness of life is not what they wanted for their life, nor the result of not having wanted any life, but just a dulling of their own self-awareness, a spontaneous irony of the intellect.

There are pigs repelled by their own filth that don't draw away from it because the feeling of repulsion is so strong it paralyses, as when a frightened man freezes instead of fleeing the danger. There are pigs like me that wallow in their destiny, not drawing away from the banality of daily life because they're enthralled by their own impotence. They're like birds captivated by the thought of the snake, like flies that hover around branches without seeing a thing, until they're within the sticky reach of the chameleon's tongue.

In a similar sort of way, I promenade my conscious unconsciousness along my tree branch of the usual. I promenade my destiny that goes forward, though I don't go anywhere, and my time that advances, though I stay put. And the only thing that alleviates my monotony are these brief commentaries I make with respect to it. I'm grateful that my cell has windows inside the bars, and on the dust of the necessary that covers the panes I write my name in capital letters, my daily signature on my covenant with death.

With death? No, not even with death. Whoever lives like me doesn't die: he terminates, wilts, devegetates. The place where he was remains without him being there; the street where he walked remains without him being seen on it; the house where he lived is inhabited by not-him. That's all, and we call it nothing; but not even this tragedy of negation can be staged to applause, for we don't even know for sure if it's nothing, we, these vegetable manifestations of both truth and life, dust on both the outside and the inside of the panes, grandchildren of Destiny and stepchildren of God, who married Eternal Night when she was widowed by the Chaos that fathered us.

To depart from the Rua dos Douradores for the Impossible... To leave my desk for the Unknown... But with this journey intersected by Reason – the Great Book that says we existed.

43

The abstract intelligence produces a fatigue that's the worst of all fatigues. It doesn't weigh on us like bodily fatigue, nor disconcert like the fatigue of emotional experience. It's the weight of our consciousness of the world, a shortness of breath in our soul.

Then, as if they were wind-blown clouds, all of the ideas in which we've felt life and all the ambitions and plans on which we've based our hopes for the future tear apart and scatter like ashes of fog, tatters of what wasn't nor could ever be. And behind this disastrous rout, the black and implacable solitude of the desolate starry sky appears.

The mystery of life distresses and frightens us in many ways. Sometimes it comes upon us like a formless phantom, and the soul trembles with the worst of fears – that of the monstrous incarnation of non-being. At other times it's behind us, visible only as long as we don't turn around to look at it, and it's the truth in its profound horror of our never being able to know it.

But the horror that's destroying me today is less noble and more corrosive. It's a longing to be free of wanting to have thoughts, a desire to never have been anything, a conscious despair in every cell of my body and soul. It's the sudden feeling of being imprisoned in an infinite cell. Where can one think of fleeing, if the cell is everything?

And then I feel an overwhelming, absurd desire for a kind of Satanism before Satan, a desire that one day – a day without time or substance – an escape leading outside of God will be discovered, and our deepest selves will somehow cease participating in being and non-being.

44

There's a sleepiness of our conscious attention that I can't explain but that often attacks me, if something so hazy can be said to attack. I'll be walking down a street as if I were sitting down, and my attention, although alert to everything, will have the inertia of a body completely at rest. I would be incapable of deliberately stepping aside for an approaching passer-by. I would be incapable of responding with words, or even with thoughts inside my mind, to a question asked me by a random stranger who happened to cross paths with my random presence. I would be incapable of having a desire, a hope, or anything at all representing a movement of my general will or even – if I may so speak – of the partial will belonging to each of my component parts. I would be incapable of thinking, of feeling, of wanting. And I walk, I roam, I keep going. Nothing in my movements (I notice by what others don't notice) transmits my state of stagnation to the observable plane. And this spiritless state, which would be natural and therefore comfortable in someone lying down or reclining, is singularly uncomfortable, even painful, in a man walking down the street.

It's like being intoxicated with inertia, drunk but with no enjoyment in the drinking or in the drunkenness. It's a sickness with no hope of recovery. It's a lively death.

45

To live a dispassionate and cultured life in the open air of ideas, reading, dreaming and thinking of writing – a life so slow it constantly verges on tedium, but pondered enough never to find itself there. To live this life far from emotions and thought, living it only in the thought of emotions and in the emotion of thoughts. To goldenly stagnate in the sun, like a murky pond surrounded by flowers. To possess, in the shade, that nobility of spirit that makes no demands on life. To be in the whirl of the worlds like dust of flowers, sailing through the afternoon air on an unknown wind and falling, in the torpor of dusk, wherever it falls, lost among larger things. To be this with a sure understanding, neither happy nor sad, grateful to the sun for its brilliance and to the stars for their remoteness. To be no more, have no more, want no more... The music of the hungry beggar, the song of the blind man, the relic of the unknown wayfarer, the tracks in the desert of the camel without burden or destination...

46

I experience a feeling of inspiration and liberation as I passively reread those simple lines by Caeiro* that tell what naturally results from the smallness of his village. Since it is small, he says, there one can see more of the world than in the city, and so his village is larger than the city...

Because I'm the size of what I see
And not the size of my stature.

Lines like these, which seem to spring into being on their own, independently of whoever says them, cleanse me of all the metaphysics that I automatically tack on to life. After reading them, I step over to my window overlooking the narrow street, I look at the immense sky and the countless stars, and I'm free, with a winged splendour whose fluttering sends a shiver throughout my body.

'I'm the size of what I see!' Each time I think on this phrase with all my nerves, the more it seems destined to redesign the whole starry universe. 'I'm the size of what I see!' How large are the mind's riches, ranging from the well of profound emotions to the distant stars that are reflected in it and so in some sense are there!

And since now I know I can see, I look upon the vast objective metaphysics of all the heavens with a certainty that makes me want to die singing. 'I'm the size of what I see!' And the vague moonlight, entirely mine, begins to mar with vagueness the blackish blue horizon.

I want to raise my arms and shout wild and strange things, to speak to the lofty mysteries, to affirm a new and vast personality to the boundless expanses of empty matter.

But I control myself and calm down. 'I'm the size of what I see!' And the phrase becomes my entire soul, I rest all my emotions on it, and over me, on the inside, as over the city on the outside, there descends an indecipherable peace from the hard moonlight that broadly begins to shine as the night falls.

47

. . . in the sad disarray of my confused emotions. . .

A twilight sadness made of fatigue and false renunciations, a tedium of feeling anything at all, a pain as of a choked sob or a discovered truth. . . A landscape of abdications unfolds in my oblivious soul: walkways lined by abandoned gestures, high flower beds of dreams that weren't even well dreamed, incongruities like hedges separating deserted paths, suppositions like old pools whose fountains are broken. It all gets entangled and squalidly looms in the sad disarray of my confused sensations.

48

To understand, I destroyed myself. To understand is to forget about loving. I know nothing more simultaneously false and telling than the statement by Leonardo da Vinci that we cannot love or hate something until we've understood it.

Solitude devastates me; company oppresses me. The presence of another person derails my thoughts; I dream of the other's presence with a strange absent-mindedness that no amount of my analytical scrutiny can define.

49

Isolation has carved me in its image and likeness. The presence of another person – of any person whatsoever – instantly slows down my thinking, and while for a normal man contact with others is a stimulus to spoken expression and wit, for me it is a counterstimulus, if this compound word be linguistically permissible. When all by myself, I can think of all kinds of clever remarks, quick comebacks to what no one said, and flashes of witty sociability with nobody. But all of this vanishes when I face someone in the flesh: I lose my intelligence, I can no longer speak, and after half an hour I just feel tired. Yes, talking to people makes me feel like sleeping. Only my ghostly and imaginary friends, only the conversations I have in my dreams, are genuinely real and substantial, and in them intelligence gleams like an image in a mirror.

The mere thought of having to enter into contact with someone else makes me nervous. A simple invitation to have dinner with a friend produces an anguish in me that's hard to define. The idea of any social obligation whatsoever – attending a funeral, dealing with someone about an office matter, going to the station to wait for someone I know or don't know – the very idea disturbs my thoughts for an entire day, and sometimes I even start worrying the night before, so that I sleep badly. When it takes place, the dreaded encounter is utterly insignificant, justifying none of my anxiety, but the next time is no different: I never learn to learn.

'My habits are of solitude, not of men.' I don't know if it was Rousseau or Senancour who said this. But it was some mind of my species, it being perhaps too much to say of my race.

50

A firefly flashes forward at regular intervals. Around me the dark countryside is a huge lack of sound that almost smells pleasant. The peace of all this is painful and oppressive. An amorphous tedium smothers me.

I rarely go to the country, and almost never for a whole day or to spend the night. But since the friend in whose house I'm staying wouldn't let me turn down his invitation, today I came out here, feeling all embarrassed, like a bashful person going to a big party. I arrived here in good spirits, I've enjoyed the fresh air and wide-open landscape, I ate a good lunch and supper, and now, late at night, in my unlit room, the uncertain surroundings fill me with anxiety.

The window of the room where I'm to sleep looks out on to the open field, on to an indefinite field that is all fields, on to the vast and vaguely starry night, in which a breeze that cannot be heard is felt. Sitting next to the window, I contemplate with my senses the nothingness of the universal life outside. There is, at this hour, a disquieting harmony, extending from the visible invisibility of everything to the slightly rough wood of the white sill, where my left hand rests sideways on the old, cracked paint.

And yet how often I've longingly envisioned this peace that I would almost flee, if I could do so easily and gracefully! How often back home, among the tall buildings and narrow streets, I've supposed that peace, prose and definitive reality would be here among natural things rather than there, where the tablecloth of civilization makes us forget the already painted pine it covers! And now that I'm here, feeling healthy and tired after a good long day, I'm restless, I feel trapped, I'm homesick.

I don't know if it happens only to me or to everyone who, through civilization, has been born a second time. But for me, and perhaps for other people like me, it seems that what's artificial has become natural, and what's natural is now strange. Or rather, it's not that what's artificial has become natural; it's simply that what's natural has changed. I have no use for motor vehicles. I have no use for the products of science – telephones, telegraphs – which make life easy, nor for its fanciful by-products – phonographs, radios – which make life amusing for those who are amused by such things.

None of that interests me, none of it appeals. But I love the Tagus because of the big city along its shore. I delight in the sky because I see it from the fourth floor on a downtown street. Nothing nature or the country can give me compares with the jagged majesty of the tranquil, moonlit city as seen from Graça or São Pedro de Alcântara.* There are no flowers for me like the variegated colouring of Lisbon on a sunny day.

The beauty of a naked body is only appreciated by cultures that use clothing. Modesty is important for sensuality like resistance for energy.

Artificiality is the best way to enjoy what's natural. Whatever I've enjoyed in these vast fields I've enjoyed because I don't live here. One who has never lived under constraints doesn't know what freedom is.

Civilization is an education in nature. Artificiality is the path for appreciating what's natural. We should never, however, take the artificial for the natural.

It's the harmony between the natural and the artificial that constitutes the natural state of the superior human soul.

51

The black sky to the south of the Tagus was an evil-looking black in contrast to the vividly white wings of the gulls that flew around restlessly. But the storm had passed. The huge dark mass that threatened rain had moved to the far shore, and the downtown, still damp from the drizzle that had fallen, smiled from the ground to a sky whose northern reaches began to be blue instead of white. The cool spring air felt almost cold.

At empty and imponderable times like this, I like to employ my thoughts in a meditation that's nothing at all but that captures, in its void transparency, something of the desolate chill in the cleared-up day, with the black sky in the background, and certain intuitions – like seagulls – which evoke by way of contrast the mystery of everything shrouded in darkness.

But suddenly, and contrary to my literary intention, the black depths of the southern sky – by a true or false recollection – evoke for me another sky, perhaps seen in another life, in a North traversed by a smaller river, with sad rushes and no city. I don't know how, but a landscape made for wild ducks unrolls across my imagination, and with the graphic clarity of a bizarre dream I feel I'm right next to the scene I imagine.

A landscape for hunters and anxieties, with rushes growing along rivers whose jagged banks jut like miniature muddy capes into the lead-yellow waters, then re-enter to form slimy bays for toy-like boats, swampy recesses where water glistens over the sludge that's hidden between the black-green stalks of rushes too thick to walk through. . .

The desolation is of a lifeless grey sky, here and there crumpled into clouds with more black in their grey. I don't feel the wind but it's there, and the opposite shore turns out to be a long island behind which – great and abandoned river! – the true shore can be glimpsed, lying in the depthless distance.

No one has been there or will ever go there. Even if I could go backwards in time and space, fleeing the world for that landscape, no one would ever join me there. I would wait in vain for what I didn't know I was waiting for, and in the end there would be nothing but a slow falling of night, with the whole of space gradually turning the colour of the darkest clouds, which little by little would vanish into the abolished mass of sky.

And suddenly, here, I feel the cold from over there. It comes from my bones and makes my flesh shiver. I gasp and wake up. The man who passes me under the arcade by the Stock Exchange stares at me warily, without knowing why. And the black sky, closing in, pressed even lower over the southern shore.

52

The wind was rising... First it was like the voice of a vacuum, a sucking of space into a hole, an absence in the air's silence. Then there was a sobbing, a sobbing from the world's depths, the realization that the panes were rattling and that it really was the wind. Then it sounded louder, a deafening howl, a disembodied weeping before the deepening night, a screeching of things, a falling of fragments, an atom from the end of the world.

And then it seemed . . . . .

53

When Christianity passed over souls like a storm that rages all night until morning, the havoc it had invisibly wreaked could be felt, but only after it had passed did the actual damage become clear. Some thought that the damage resulted from Christianity's departure, but this was just what revealed the damage, not what caused it.

And so our world of souls was left with this visible damage, this glaring affliction, without the darkness to cloak it with its false affection. Souls were seen for what they were.

In recent times, souls contracted a sickness known as Romanticism, which is Christianity without illusions or myths, stripped to its withered and diseased essence.

The fundamental error of Romanticism is to confuse what we need with what we desire. We all need certain basic things for life's preservation and continuance; we all desire a more perfect life, complete happiness, the fulfilment of our dreams and . . . . .

It's human to want what we need, and it's human to desire what we don't need but find desirable. Sickness occurs when we desire what we need and what's desirable with equal intensity, suffering our lack of perfection as if we were suffering for lack of bread. The Romantic malady is to want the moon as if it could actually be obtained.

'You can't have your cake and eat it too.'

Whether in the base realm of politics or in the private sanctuary of each man's soul, the malady is the same.

The pagan didn't know, in the real world, this sickly dimension of things and of himself. Being human, he also desired the impossible, but he didn't *crave* it. His religion was □ and only in the inner sanctum of mystery, only to the initiated, far from the common people and the □, was it given to know the transcendental things of religions that fill the soul with the world's emptiness.

54

In my dreams I've sometimes tried to be the unique and imposing individual that the Romantics envisaged in themselves, and I always end up laughing out loud at the very idea. The ultimate man exists in the dreams of all ordinary men, and Romanticism is merely the turning inside out of the empire we normally carry around inside us. Nearly all men dream, deep down, of their own mighty imperialism: the subjection of all men, the surrender of all women, the adoration of all peoples and – for the noblest dreamers – of all eras. Few men devoted, like me, to dreaming are lucid enough to laugh at the aesthetic possibility of dreaming of themselves in this way.

The gravest accusation against Romanticism has still not been made: that it plays out the inner truth of human nature. Its excesses, its absurdities and its ability to seduce and move hearts all come from its being the outer representation of what's deepest in the soul – a concrete, visible representation that would even be possible, if human possibility depended on something besides Fate.

Even I, who laugh at these seductions that play on the mind, very often catch myself thinking how nice it would be to be famous, how pleasant to be doted on, how colourful to be triumphant! But I'm unable to envision myself in these lofty roles without a hearty snicker from the other I that's always near by, like a downtown street. See myself famous? What I see is a famous bookkeeper. Feel myself raised to the thrones of renown? It happens in the office on the Rua dos Douradores, and my colleagues ruin the scene. Hear myself cheered by swarming crowds? The cheering reaches me in my rented room on the fourth floor and collides with the shabby furniture and the banality that humiliates me from the kitchen to my dreams. I didn't even have castles in Spain, like the Spanish grandees of all illusions. My castles were made of old, grubby playing cards from an incomplete deck that could never be used to play anything; they didn't even fall but had to be knocked down by the impatient hand of the old maid, who wanted to put back the tablecloth that had been pulled to one side, because the hour for tea had struck like a curse from Fate. But even this vision is flawed, for I have neither the house in the country nor the elderly aunts, at whose table I might sip a relaxing cup of tea at the end of an evening with the family. My dream even failed in its metaphors and depictions. My empire didn't even happen among the old playing cards. My march of triumph didn't get as far as a teapot or an old cat. I'll die as I've lived, amid all the junk on the outskirts, sold by weight among the postscripts of the broken.

May I at least carry, to the boundless possibility contained in the abyss of everything, the glory of my disillusion like that of a great dream, and the splendour of not believing like a banner of defeat: a banner in feeble hands, but still and all a banner, dragged through mud and the blood of the weak but raised high for who knows what reason – whether in defiance, or as a challenge, or in mere desperation – as we vanish into quicksand. No one knows for what reason, because no one knows anything, and the sand swallows those with banners as it swallows those without. And the sand covers everything: my life, my prose, my eternity.

I carry my awareness of defeat like a banner of victory.

55

However much my soul may be descended from the Romantics, I can find no peace of mind except in reading classical authors. The very sparseness by which their clarity is expressed comforts me in some strange way. From them I get a joyful sense of expansive life that contemplates large open spaces without actually travelling through them. Even the pagan gods take a rest from the unknown.

The obsessive analysis of our sensations (sometimes of merely imagined sensations), the identification of our heart with the landscape, the anatomic exposure of all our nerves, the substitution of desire for the will and of longing for thinking – all these things are far too familiar to be of interest to me or to give me peace when expressed by another. Whenever I feel them, and precisely because I feel them, I wish I were feeling something else. And when I read a classical author, that something else is given to me.

I frankly and unblushingly admit it: there's not a passage of Chateaubriand or a canto of Lamartine – passages that often seem to be the voice of my own thoughts, cantos that often seem to have been written for me to know myself – that transports and uplifts me like a passage of Vieira's prose,* or like certain odes by one of our few classical writers who truly followed Horace.

I read and am liberated. I acquire objectivity. I cease being myself and so scattered. And what I read, instead of being like a nearly invisible suit that sometimes oppresses me, is the external world's tremendous and remarkable clarity, the sun that sees everyone, the moon that splotches the still earth with shadows, the wide expanses that end in the sea, the blackly solid trees whose tops greenly wave, the steady peace of ponds on farms, the terraced slopes with their paths overgrown by grape-vines.

I read as one who abdicates. And since the royal crown and robe are never as grand as when the departing king leaves them on the ground, I lay all my trophies of tedium and dreaming on the tiled floor of my antechambers, then climb the staircase with no other nobility but that of seeing.

I read as one who's passing through. And it's in classical writers, in the calm-spirited, in those who if they suffer don't mention it, that I feel like a holy transient, an anointed pilgrim, a contemplator for no reason of a world with no purpose, Prince of the Great Exile, who as he was leaving gave the last beggar the ultimate alms of his desolation.

56

The firm's monied partner, chronically afflicted by a vague illness, decided on a whim during one of his healthy respites to have a group portrait made of the office personnel. And so the day before yesterday a cheerful photographer lined us all up against the grimy white partition, made of flimsy wood, that divides the main office from the private one of Senhor Vasques. In the middle was Vasques himself; flanking him in a definite, then indefinite, ranking by category were the other human souls that daily come together here as one body to accomplish small tasks whose ultimate objective is the secret of the Gods.

Today when I arrived at the office, a little late and having quite forgotten the static event of the twice-taken photograph, I found Moreira (unusually early for him) and one of the sales representatives furtively leaning over some blackish sheets, which I recognized with a start as the first proofs of the photographs. In fact they were two proofs of the same shot, the one that had turned out better.

I suffered the truth on seeing myself there, since my face was of course the first one I looked for. I've never had a flattering notion of my physical appearance, but I never felt it to be more insignificant than there, next to the familiar faces of my colleagues, in that line-up of daily expressions. I look like a nondescript Jesuit. My gaunt and inexpressive face has no intelligence or intensity or anything else to raise it out of that lifeless tide of faces. Lifeless, no. There are some truly expressive physiognomies there. Senhor Vasques looks just like himself – broad, cheerful face with hard features and a steady gaze, completed by his stiff moustache. The man's shrewdness and energy – banal enough, and recurring in thousands of men throughout the world – are nevertheless inscribed on that photograph as on a psychological passport. The two travelling salesmen look sharp, and the local sales representative turned out well, though he's half hidden by Moreira's shoulder. And Moreira! Moreira, my supervisor, the epitome of monotonous constancy, looks much more alive than I! Even the office boy (and here I'm unable to repress a feeling that I tell myself isn't envy) has a forthrightness of expression that is smiles away from my blank effacement, reminiscent of a sphinx from the stationer's.*

What does this mean? What is this truth that film doesn't mistake? What is this certainty that a cold lens documents? Who am I, that I should look like that? Anyway... And the insult of the whole ensemble?

'You came out really well,' Moreira said suddenly. And then, turning to the sales representative: 'It's his spitting image – don't you think?' And the sales representative agreed with a happy affability that tossed me into the rubbish bin.

57

And today, thinking about what my life has been, I feel like some sort of animal that's being carried in a basket under a curved arm between two suburban train stations. The image is stupid, but the life it defines is even more stupid. These baskets usually have two lids, like half ovals, that lift up at one end or the other should the animal squirm. But the arm of the one carrying it, resting a bit on the hinges in the middle, won't allow such a weak thing to do more than slightly and uselessly raise the lids, like tired wings of a butterfly.

I forgot that I was talking about me in the description of the basket. I clearly see it, along with the fat, sunburned arm of the maid carrying it. I can't see any more of the maid than her arm and its down. I can't get comfortable unless – All of a sudden a breezy coolness [passes through] those white rods and strips which baskets are made of and inside of which I squirm, an animal aware that it's going from one station to another. I'm resting on what seems to be a long seat, and I hear people talking outside my basket. All is calm and so I sleep, until I'm lifted up again at the station.

58

The environment is the soul of things. Each thing has its own expression and this expression comes from outside it. Each thing is the intersection of three lines, and these three lines form the thing: a certain quantity of material, the way in which we interpret it, and the environment it's in. This table on which I'm writing is a block of wood, it's the table, and it's a piece of furniture among others in the room. My impression of this table, if I wish to transcribe it, will be composed of the notions that it is made of wood, that I call it a table and attribute certain uses to it, and that it receives, reflects and is transformed by the objects placed on top of it, in whose juxtaposition it has an external soul. And its very colour, the fading of that colour, its spots and cracks – all came from outside it, and this (more than its wooden essence) is what gives it its soul. And the core of that soul, its being a table, also came from the outside, which is its personality.

I consider it neither a human nor a literary error to attribute a soul to the things we call inanimate. To be a thing is to be the object of an attribution. It may be erroneous to say that a tree feels, that a river runs, that a sunset is sad or that the calm ocean (blue from the sky it doesn't have) smiles (from the sun outside it). But it's every bit as erroneous to attribute beauty to things. It's every bit as erroneous to say that things possess colour, form, perhaps even being. This ocean is saltwater. This sunset is the initial diminishing of sunlight in this particular latitude and longitude. This little boy playing next to me is an intellectual mass of cells – better yet, he's a clockwork of subatomic movements, a strange electrical conglomeration of millions of solar systems in miniature.

Everything comes from outside, and the human soul itself may be no more than the ray of sunlight that shines and isolates from the soil the pile of dung that's the body.

In these considerations there may be an entire philosophy for someone with the strength to draw conclusions. It won't be me. Lucid vague thoughts and logical possibilities occur to me, but they all dim in the vision of a ray of sunlight that gilds a pile of dung like wetly squished dark straw, on the almost black soil next to a stone wall.

That's how I am. When I want to think, I look. When I want to descend into my soul, I suddenly freeze, oblivious, at the top of the long spiral staircase, looking through the upper-storey window at the sun that bathes the sprawling mass of rooftops in a tawny farewell.

59

Whenever my ambition, influenced by my dreams, raised up above the everyday level of my life, so that for a moment I seemed to soar, like a child on a swing, I always – like the child – had to come down to the public garden and face my defeat, with no flags to wave in battle and no sword I was strong enough to unsheathe.

I suppose that most of the people I chance to pass in the street also feel – I notice it in their silently moving lips and in their eyes' vague uncertainty, or in the sometimes raised voice of their joint mumbling – like a flagless army fighting a hopeless war. And probably all of them – I turn around to see their slumping, defeated-looking shoulders – share with me this sense of salesmanly squalor, of being no more than humiliatingly vanquished stragglers amid reeds and scum, with no moonlight over the shores or poetry in the marshes.

Like me, they have an exalted and sad heart. I know them all. Some are shop assistants, others are office workers, and still others are small businessmen. Then there are the conquerors from the bars and cafés, unwittingly sublime in the ecstasy of their self-centred chatter, or content to remain self-centredly silent, with no need to defend what they're too stingy to say. But they're all poets, poor devils, who drag past my eyes, as I drag past theirs, the same sorry sight of our common incongruity. They all have, like me, their future in the past.

At this very moment, idle and alone in the office, because everyone else went to lunch, I'm staring through the grimy window at an old man who's slowly teetering down the other side of the street. He's not drunk; he's dreaming. He's attentive to what doesn't exist. Perhaps he still hopes. If there's any justice in the Gods' injustice, then may they let us keep our dreams, even when they're impossible, and may our dreams be happy, even when they're trivial. Today, because I'm still young, I can dream of South Sea islands and impossible Indias. Tomorrow perhaps the same Gods will make me dream of owning a small tobacco shop, or of retiring to a house in the suburbs. Every dream is the same dream, for they're all dreams. Let the Gods change my dreams, but not my gift for dreaming.

While thinking about this, I forgot about the old man. Now I don't see him. I open the window to get a better look, but he's not there. He left. For me he had the visual mission of a symbol; having finished his mission, he turned the corner. If I were told that he'd turned the absolute corner and was never here, I would accept it with the same gesture I'm about to employ to close the window.

Succeed?. . .

Poor salesmanly demigods who conquer empires with lofty words and intentions but need to scrounge up money for food and the rent! They're like the troops of a disbanded army whose commanders had a glorious dream, which in them – now trudging through the scum of marshes – has been reduced to a vague notion of grandeur, the consciousness of having belonged to an army, and the vacuity of not even knowing what the commander they never saw had ever done.

Each of them, for a moment, has dreamed he's the commander of the army whose rear guard he deserted. Each of them, from the sludge of streams, has hailed the victory which no one could win and which left only crumbs on the stained tablecloth that nobody remembered to shake.

They fill in the cracks of daily activity like dust in the cracks of badly dusted furniture. In normal, ordinary daylight they shine like grey worms against the reddish mahogany. They can be removed with a thin nail, but no one has the patience to bother.

My hapless peers with their lofty dreams – how I envy and despise them! I'm with the others, with the even more hapless, who have no one but themselves to whom they can tell their dreams and show what would be verses if they wrote them. I'm with these poor slobs who have no books to show, who have no literature besides their own soul, and who are suffocating to death due to the fact they exist without having taken that mysterious, transcendental exam that makes one eligible to live.

Some are heroes who flattened five men on a street corner just yesterday. Others are seducers to whom even non-existent women have surrendered. They believe these things when they tell them, and perhaps they tell them so as to believe. Others . . . . . For them the world's conquerors, whoever they may be, are everyday people.

And like eels in a wooden tub, they slither under and over each other, without ever leaving the tub. Sometimes they're mentioned in the newspapers. Some of them are mentioned rather often. But they never become famous.

These people are happy, for they've been given the enchanted dream of stupidity. But those, like me, who've been given dreams without illusions . . . . .

60

Dolorous Interlude

Should you ask me if I'm happy, I'll answer that I'm not.

61

It's noble to be timid, illustrious to fail to act, sublime to be inept at living.

Only Tedium, which is a withdrawal, and Art, which is a disdain, gild with a semblance of contentment our . . . . .

The will-o'-the-wisps generated by our rotting lives are at least a light in our darkness.

Only unhappiness is elevating, and only the tedium that comes from unhappiness is heraldic like the descendants of ancient heroes.

I'm a well of gestures that haven't even all been traced in my mind, of words I haven't even thought to form on my lips, of dreams I forgot to dream to the end.

I'm the ruins of buildings that were never more than ruins, whose builder, halfway through, got tired of thinking about what he was building.

Let's not forget to hate those who enjoy, just because they enjoy, and to despise those who are happy, because we didn't know how to be happy like them. This false disdain and feeble hatred are merely the plinth – rough-hewn and dirtied by the soil where it stands – for the unique and haughty statue of our Tedium, a dark figure whose inscrutable smile gives its face a vague aura of mystery.

Blessed are those who entrust their lives to no one.

62

I'm physically nauseated by commonplace humanity, which is the only kind there is. And sometimes I wilfully aggravate the nausea, like someone who induces vomiting to be relieved of the urge to vomit.

One of my favourite strolls, on mornings when I dread the banality of the approaching day as if I were dreading jail, is to walk slowly past the still unopened shops and stores, listening to the scraps of conversation that groups of young women or young men, or women with men, let fall – like ironic alms – in the invisible school of my open-air meditation.

And it's always the same succession of the same old phrases. . . 'And then she said. . . ,' and the tone foreshadows the intrigue to follow. 'If it wasn't him, it was you. . . ,' and the voice that answers bristles in a protest already out of my hearing range. 'You said it, yes sir, I heard you. . . ,' and the seamstress's shrill voice declares 'My mother says she's not interested. . .' 'Me?', and the astonishment of the fellow carrying a lunch wrapped in white paper doesn't convince me, and probably not the dirty blonde either. 'It must have been. . . ,' and the giggling of three of the four girls drowns out the obscenity that . . . . . 'And then I walked straight up to the guy, and right in his face, but I mean right in his face, José, just imagine. . . ,' and the poor devil is lying, because the office supervisor – I can tell by the voice that the other contender was the supervisor of the office in question – wouldn't receive the straw gladiator's challenge in the arena surrounded by desks. 'And then I went and smoked in the bathroom. . .' laughs the little boy with dark patches on his trouser-seat.

Others, passing by singly or together, don't speak, or they speak and I don't hear, but I can discern their voices, transparent to my penetrating intuition. I dare not say – not even to myself in writing, even though I could rip it up instantly – what I have seen in casually glancing eyes, in their involuntary lowering, in their sordid shifting. I dare not say, because when vomiting is induced, one heave is enough.

'The guy was so soused he couldn't even see the stairs.' I raise my head. At least this young man describes. These people are more bearable when they describe, since in describing they forget themselves. My nausea subsides. I see the guy. I see him photographically. Even the innocuous slang heartens me. Blessed breeze across my forehead – the guy so soused he couldn't see the steps of the staircase – perhaps the staircase where humanity stumbles, gropes and shoves its way up the corrugated illusion which only a wall separates from the sharp drop behind the building.

Intrigue, gossip, the loud boasting over what one didn't have the guts to do, the contentment of each miserable creature dressed in the unconscious consciousness of his own soul, sweaty and smelly sexuality, the jokes they tell like monkeys tickling each other, their appalling ignorance of their utter unimportance. . . All of this leaves me with the impression of a monstrous and vile animal created in the chaos of dreams, out of desires' soggy crusts, out of sensations' chewed-up leftovers.

63

The entire life of the human soul is mere motions in the shadows. We live in a twilight of consciousness, never in accord with whom we are or think we are. Everyone harbours some kind of vanity, and there's an error whose degree we can't determine. We're something that goes on during the show's intermission; sometimes, through certain doors, we catch a glimpse of what may be no more than scenery. The world is one big confusion, like voices in the night.

I've just reread these pages on which I write with a lucidity that endures only in them, and I ask myself: What is this, and what good is it? Who am I when I feel? What in me dies when I am?

Like someone on a hill who tries to make out the people in the valley, I look down at myself from on high, and I'm a hazy and confused landscape, along with everything else.

In these times when an abyss opens up in my soul, the tiniest detail distresses me like a letter of farewell. I feel as if I'm always on the verge of waking up. I'm oppressed by the very self that encases me, asphyxiated by conclusions, and I'd gladly scream if my voice could reach somewhere. But there's this heavy slumber that moves from one group of my sensations to another, like drifting clouds that make the half-shaded grass of sprawling fields turn various colours of sun and green.

I'm like someone searching at random, not knowing what object he's looking for nor where it was hidden. We play hide-and-seek with no one. There's a transcendent trick in all of this, a fluid divinity we can only hear.

Yes, I reread these pages that represent worthless hours, brief illusions or moments of calm, large hopes channelled into the landscape, sorrows like closed rooms, certain voices, a huge weariness, the unwritten gospel.

We all have our vanity, and that vanity is our way of forgetting that there are other people with a soul like our own. My vanity consists of a few pages, passages, doubts. . .

I reread? A lie! I don't dare reread. I can't reread. What good would it do me to reread? The person in the writing is someone else. I no longer understand a thing. . .

64

I weep over my imperfect pages, but if future generations read them, they will be more touched by my weeping than by any perfection I might have achieved, since perfection would have kept me from weeping and, therefore, from writing. Perfection never materializes. The saint weeps, and is human. God is silent. That is why we can love the saint but cannot love God.

65

That noble and divine timidity which guards □ the soul's treasures and regalia. . .

How I'd love to infect at least one soul with some kind of poison, worry or disquiet! This would console me a little for my chronic failure to take action. My life's purpose would be to pervert. But do my words ring in anyone else's soul? Does anyone hear them besides me?

66

WITH A SHRUG

We generally colour our ideas of the unknown with our notions of the known. If we call death a sleep, it's because it seems like sleep on the outside; if we call death a new life, it's because it seems like something different from life. With slight misconceptions of reality we fabricate our hopes and beliefs, and we live off crusts that we call cakes, like poor children who make believe they're happy.

But that's how all life is, or at least that particular system of life generally known as civilization. Civilization consists in giving something a name that doesn't belong to it and then dreaming over the result. And the false name joined to the true dream does create a new reality. The object does change into something else, because we make it change. We manufacture realities. The raw material remains the same, but our art gives it a form that makes it into something not the same. A pinewood table is still pinewood, but it's also a table. We sit at the table, not at the pinewood. Although love is a sexual instinct, it's not with sexual instinct that we love but with the conjecture of some other feeling. And that conjecture is already some other feeling.

I don't know what subtle effect of light, or vague noise, or memory of a fragrance or melody, intoned by some inscrutable external influence, prompted these divagations when I was walking down the street and which now, seated in a café, I leisurely and distractedly record. I don't know where I was going with my thoughts, nor where I would wish to go. Today there's a light, warm and humid fog, sad with no threats, monotonous for no reason. I'm grieved by a feeling that I can't place; I'm lacking an argument apropos I don't know what; I have no willpower in my nerves. Beneath my consciousness I'm sad. And I write these carelessly written lines not to say this and not to say anything, but to give my distraction something to do. I slowly cover, with the soft strokes of a dull pencil (I'm not sentimental enough to sharpen it), the white sandwich paper that they gave me in this café, for it suits me just fine, as would any other paper, as long as it was white. And I feel satisfied. I lean back. The afternoon comes to a monotonous and rainless close, in an uncertain and despondent tone of light. And I stop writing because I stop writing.

67

Often enough the surface and illusion catch me, their prey, and I feel like a man. Then I'm happy to be in the world, and my life is transparent. I float. And it gives me pleasure to get my pay-cheque and go home. I feel the weather without seeing it, and there's some organic sensation that pleases me. If I contemplate, I don't think. On these days I'm particularly fond of gardens.

There's something strange and pathetic in the very substance of public gardens that I'm only really aware of when I'm not very aware of myself. A garden is a synopsis of civilization – an anonymous modification of nature. There are plants there, but also streets – yes, streets. Trees grow, but there are benches beneath their shade. On the broad walkways facing the four sides of the city, the benches are larger and are almost always occupied.

I don't mind seeing flowers in orderly rows, but I hate the public use of flowers. If the rows of flowers were in closed parks, if the trees shaded feudal retreats, if the benches were vacant, then my useless contemplation of gardens could console me. But gardens in cities, useful as well as ordered, are for me like cages, in which the coloured spontaneities of the trees and flowers have only enough room to have one, space enough not to escape, and beauty all alone, without the life that belongs to beauty.

But there are days when this is the landscape that belongs to me, and I enter it like an actor in a tragicomedy. On these days I'm in error, but at least in a certain way I'm happier. When I'm distracted, I start imagining that I really have a house or home to return to. When I forget, I become a normal man, reserved for some purpose, and I brush down another suit and read the newspaper from front to back.

But the illusion never lasts long, partly because it doesn't last and partly because night arrives. And the colours of the flowers, the shade of the trees, the geometry of streets and flower beds – it all fades and shrinks. Above this error in which I feel like a man, the enormous stage setting of stars suddenly appears, as if daylight had been a curtain hiding it from view. And then my eyes forget the amorphous audience, and I wait for the first performers with the excitement of a child at the circus.

I'm liberated and lost.

I feel. I shiver with fever. I'm I.

68

The weariness caused by all illusions and all that they entail – our losing them, the uselessness of our having them, the pre-weariness of having to have them in order to lose them, the regret of having had them, the intellectual chagrin of having had them while knowing full well they would end.

The consciousness of life's unconsciousness is the oldest tax levied on the intelligence. There are unconscious forms of intelligence – flashes of wit, waves of understanding, mysteries and philosophies – that are like bodily reflexes, that operate as automatically as the liver or kidneys handle their secretions.

69

It's raining hard, harder, still harder. . . It's as if something were going to collapse in the blackness outside. . .

The city's uneven, mountainous mass looks to me today like a plain, a plain covered by rain. All around, as far as my gaze reaches, everything is the pale black colour of rain.

I'm full of odd sensations, all of them cold. Right now it seems to me that the landscape is all a fog, and that the buildings are the fog that hides it.

A pre-neurosis born of what I'll be when I no longer am grips my body and soul. An absurd remembrance of my future death sends a shiver down my spine. In the fog of my intuition, I feel like dead matter fallen in the rain and mourned by the howling wind. And the chill of what I won't feel gnaws at my present heart.

70

If I have no other virtue, I at least have the permanent novelty of free, uninhibited sensation.

Today, walking down the Rua Nova do Almada, I happened to gaze at the back of the man walking ahead of me. It was the ordinary back of an ordinary man, a simple sports coat on the shoulders of an incidental pedestrian. He carried an old briefcase under his left arm, and his right hand held the curved handle of a rolled-up umbrella, which he tapped on the ground to the rhythm of his walking.

I suddenly felt something like tenderness for that man. I felt the tenderness one feels for common human banality, for the daily routine of the family breadwinner going to work, for his humble and happy home, for the happy and sad pleasures that necessarily make up his life, for the innocence of living without analysing, for the animal naturalness of that coat-covered back.

My eyes returned to the man's back, the window through which I saw these thoughts.

I had the same sensation as when we watch someone sleep. When asleep we all become children again. Perhaps because in the state of slumber we can do no wrong and are unconscious of life, the greatest criminal and the most self-absorbed egotist are holy, by a natural magic, as long as they're sleeping. For me there's no discernible difference between killing a child and killing a sleeping man.

This man's back is sleeping. His entire person, walking ahead of me at the very same speed, is sleeping. He walks unconsciously, lives unconsciously. He sleeps, for we all sleep. All life is a dream. No one knows what he's doing, no one knows what he wants, no one knows what he knows. We sleep our lives, eternal children of Destiny. That's why, whenever this sensation rules my thoughts, I feel an enormous tenderness that encompasses the whole of childish humanity, the whole of sleeping society, everyone, everything.

It's an immediate humanitarianism, without aims or conclusions, that overwhelms me right now. I feel a tenderness as if I were seeing with the eyes of a god. I see everyone as if moved by the compassion of the world's only conscious being. Poor hapless men, poor hapless humanity! What are they all doing here?

I see all the actions and goals of life, from the simple life of lungs to the building of cities and the marking off of empires, as a drowsiness, as involuntary dreams or respites in the gap between one reality and another, between one and another day of the Absolute. And like an abstractly maternal being, I lean at night over both the good and bad children, equal when they sleep and are mine. I feel for them with an infinite capacity for tenderness.

I tear my gaze from the back of the man ahead of me and look at all the other people walking down this street, and I embrace each and every one of them with the same cold, absurd tenderness that came to me from the back of the unconscious man I'm following. The whole lot is just like him: the girls chatting on their way to the workshop, the young men laughing on their way to the office, the big-bosomed maids returning with their heavy purchases, the delivery boys running their first errands – all of this is one and the same unconsciousness, diversified among different faces and bodies, like marionettes moved by strings leading to the same fingers of an invisible hand. They go on their way with all the manners and gestures that define consciousness, and they're conscious of nothing, for they're not conscious of being conscious. Whether clever or stupid, they're all equally stupid. Whether old or young, they're all the same age. Whether men or women, all are of the same sex that doesn't exist.

71

The cause of my profound sense of incompatibility with others is, I believe, that most people think with their feelings, whereas I feel with my thoughts.

For the ordinary man, to feel is to live, and to think is to know how to live. For me, to think is to live, and to feel is merely food for thought.

It's curious that what little capacity I have for enthusiasm is aroused by those most unlike me in temperament. I admire no one in literature more than the classical writers, who are the ones I least resemble. Forced to choose between reading only Chateaubriand or Vieira,* I would choose Vieira without a moment's hesitation.

The more a man differs from me, the more real he seems, for he depends that much less on my subjectivity. And that's why the object of my close and constant study is the same common humanity that I loathe and stay away from. I love it because I hate it. I like to look at it because I hate to feel it. The landscape, admirable as a picture, rarely makes a comfortable bed.

72

Amiel* said that a landscape is a state of emotion, but the phrase is a flawed gem of a feeble dreamer. As soon as the landscape is a landscape, it ceases to be a state of emotion. To objectify is to create, and no one would say that a finished poem is a state of thinking about writing one. Seeing is perhaps a form of dreaming, but if we call it seeing instead of dreaming, it's so we can distinguish between the two.

But what good are these speculations in linguistic psychology? Independently of me the grass grows, the rain falls on the grass that grows, and the sun shines on the patch of grass that grew or will grow; the hills have been there for ages, and the wind blows in the same way as when Homer heard it, even if he didn't exist. It would be better to say that a state of emotion is a landscape, for the phrase would contain not the lie of a theory but the truth of a metaphor.

These incidental words were dictated to me by the panorama of the city as seen from the look-out of São Pedro de Alcântara,* under the universal light of the sun. Every time I contemplate a wide panorama, forgetting the five feet six inches of height and the one hundred and thirty-five pounds in which I physically consist, I smile a supremely metaphysical smile for those who dream that dreaming is a dream, and I love the truth of the absolutely external with a noble purity of understanding.

The Tagus in the background is a blue lake, and the hills of the far shore are a flattened Switzerland. A small ship – a black cargo steamer – departs from Poço do Bispo* in the direction of the estuary, which I can't see. May the Gods all preserve for me (until my present form ceases) this clear and sunlit view of external reality, the instinctive awareness of my unimportance, the cosiness of being small, and the solace of being able to imagine myself happy.

73

On arriving at the solitary summits of natural elevations, we experience a feeling of privilege; with our own added height, we're higher than the summits themselves. Nature's utmost, at least in that place, is beneath our own two feet. Our position makes us kings of the visible world. Everything around us is lower: life is a descending slope or a low-lying plain next to the elevation and pinnacle we've become.

Everything we are is due to chance and trickery, and this height we boast isn't ours; we're no taller on the summit than our normal height. The hill on which we tread elevates us; it's the height we're at that makes us higher.

A rich man breathes easier; a famous man is freer; a title of nobility is itself a small hill. Everything is artifice, but not even the artifice is ours. We climb it, or were brought to it, or we were born in the house on the hill.

Great, however, is the man who realizes that the difference in distance from the valley to the sky and from the hill to the sky makes no difference. Should the flood waters rise, we're better off in the hills. But when God curses us as Jupiter, with lightning bolts, or as Aeolus, with high winds, then the best cover will be to have remained in the valley, and the best defence to lie low.

Wise is the man who has the potential for height in his muscles but who renounces climbing in his consciousness. By virtue of his gaze, he has all hills, and by virtue of his position, all valleys. The sun that gilds the summits will gild them more for him than for someone at the top who must endure the bright light; and the palace perched high in the woods will be more beautiful for those who see it from the valley than for those who, imprisoned in its rooms, forget it.

I take comfort in these reflections, since I can't take comfort in life. And the symbol merges with reality when, as a transient body and soul in these low-lying streets that lead to the Tagus, I see the luminous heights of the city glowing, like a glory from beyond, with the various lights of a sun that has already set.

74

THUNDERSTORM

The blue of the sky showing between the still clouds was smudged with transparent white.

The boy at the back of the office suspended for a moment the cord going round the eternal package.

'I can only remember one other like this,' he statistically remarked.

A cold silence. The sounds from the street seemed to be cut by a knife. Then there was a long, cosmically held breath, a kind of generalized dread. The entire universe had stopped dead. Moments, moments, moments. . . Silence blackened the darkness.

All of a sudden, live steel . . . . .

How human the metallic peal of the trams! How happy the landscape of simple rain falling on the street resurrected from the chasm!

Oh Lisbon, my home!

75

I don't need fast cars or express trains to feel the delight and terror of speed. All I require is a tram and my gift for abstraction, which I've developed to an astonishing degree.

On a tram in motion I'm able, through my constant and instantaneous analysis, to separate the idea of the tram from the idea of speed, separating them so completely that they're distinct things-in-reality. Then I can feel myself riding not inside the tram but inside its Mere Speed. And should I get bored and want the delirium of excessive speed, I can transfer the idea to the Pure Imitation of Speed, increasing or decreasing it at will, extending it beyond the fastest possible speeds of trains.

I abhor running real risks, but it's not because I'm afraid of feeling too intensely. It's because they break my perfect focus on my sensations, and this disturbs and depersonalizes me.

I never go where there's risk. I fear the tedium of dangers.

A sunset is an intellectual phenomenon.

76

I sometimes enjoy (in split fashion) thinking about the possibility of a future geography of our self-awareness. I believe that the future historian of his own sensations may be able to make a precise science out of the attitude he takes towards his self-awareness. We're only in the beginnings of this difficult art – at this point just an art: the chemistry of sensations in its as yet alchemical stage. This scientist of tomorrow will pay special attention to his own inner life, subjecting it to analysis with a precision instrument created out of himself. I see no inherent obstacle to making, out of steels and bronzes of thought, a precision instrument for self-analysis. I mean steels and bronzes that are really steels and bronzes, but of the mind. Perhaps that's the only way it can be made. Perhaps it will be necessary to formulate the idea of a precision instrument, concretely visualizing it, in order to undertake a rigorous inner analysis. And it will surely be necessary to reduce the mind to some kind of real matter with a space for it to exist in. All of this depends on an extreme refinement of our inner sensations, which, when taken as far as they can go, will doubtless reveal or create in us a space just as real as the space that's occupied by material things and that, come to think of it, has no reality.

For all I know, this inner space may just be a new dimension of the other one. Perhaps scientific research will eventually discover that everything is dimensions of the same space, which is neither physical nor spiritual, so that in one dimension we live as bodies, and in another as souls. And perhaps there are other dimensions where we live other, equally real facets of ourselves. Sometimes I enjoy getting lost in the useless meditation of just how far this research might take us.

Perhaps it will be discovered that what we call God, so obviously on a plane beyond logic and space-time reality, is one of our modes of existence, a sensation of ourselves in another dimension of being.

This seems to me perfectly possible. Perhaps dreams are yet another dimension in which we live, or perhaps they're a cross between two dimensions. As our body lives in length, in breadth and in height, it may be that our dreams live in the ideal, in the ego and in space – in space through their visible representation, in the ideal through their non-material essence, and in the ego through their personal dimension as something intimately ours. The ego itself, the I in each one of us, is perhaps a divine dimension. All of this is complex and will no doubt be determined in its time. Today's dreamers are perhaps the great precursors of the ultimate science of the future. Of course I don't believe in an ultimate science of the future, but that's beside the point.

I periodically formulate metaphysics such as these, with the serious concentration of someone who's truly at work to forge science. And it's possible I may actually be forging it. I have to be careful not to take too much pride in this, since pride can undermine the strict impartiality of scientific objectivity.

77

There's no pastime like the use of science, or things that smack of science, for futile ends, and so I often pass the time by intently studying my psyche as others see it. The pleasure I get from this sterile artifice is sometimes sad, sometimes painful.

I carefully study the overall impression I make on others, from which I then draw conclusions. I'm a fellow most people like, and they even have a vague and curious respect for me. But I don't arouse ardent emotions. No one will ever passionately be my friend. That's why so many are able to respect me.

78

Certain sensations are slumbers that fill up our mind like a fog and prevent us from thinking, from acting, from clearly and simply being. As if we hadn't slept, something of our undreamed dreams lingers in us, and the torpor of the new day's sun warms the stagnant surface of our senses. We're drunk on not being anything, and our will is a bucket poured out on to the yard by the listless movement of a passing foot.

We look but don't see. The long street bustling with clothed animals is like a flat-lying signboard whose letters move around and make no sense. The buildings are just buildings. We're no longer able to give meaning to what we see, though we see perfectly well what's there.

The banging of the crate-maker's hammer reverberates close by, yet remotely. Each blow makes a distinctly separate sound, with an echo and without any point. The wagons creak as they do on days when storms threaten. Voices emerge from the air, not from throats. The river in the background is tired.

It's not tedium that we feel. Nor is it grief. It's a desire to sleep with another personality, to be able to forget everything with a pay increase. We feel nothing, unless maybe an automatism down below, which makes the legs we possess strike the feet inside our shoes against the ground, in the oblivious act of walking. Perhaps we don't even feel that. There's a squeezing in our head around the eyes, and as if fingers were plugging our ears.

It's like a head-cold of the soul. And this literary image of being sick makes us wish that life were a convalescence, obliging us to stay off our feet. And the idea of convalescence makes us think of villas on the outskirts of town – not the gardens that surround them but their cosy interiors, far from the road and the turning wheels. No, we don't feel anything. We consciously pass through the door we have to enter, and the fact we have to enter it is enough to put us to sleep. We pass through everything. Where's your tambourine, O bear that just stands there?

79

Faint, like something just beginning, the low-tide smell wafted over the Tagus and putridly spread over the streets near the shore. The stench was crisply nauseating, with a cold torpor of lukewarm sea. I felt life in my stomach, and my sense of smell shifted to behind my eyes. Tall, sparse bundles of clouds alighted on nothing, their greyness disintegrating into a pseudo-white. A cowardly sky threatened the atmosphere, as if with inaudible thunder, made only of air.

There was even stagnation in the flight of the gulls; they seemed to be lighter than air, left there by someone. Nothing oppressed. The late afternoon disquiet was my own; a cool breeze intermittently blew.

My ill-starred hopes, born of the life I've been forced to live! They're like this hour and this air, fogless fogs, unravelled basting of a false storm. I feel like screaming, to put an end to this landscape and my meditation. But the stench of ocean imbues my intent, and the low tide inside me has exposed the sludgy blackness that's somewhere out there, though I can see it only by its smell.

All this stupid insistence on being self-sufficient! All this cynical awareness of pretended sensations! All this imbroglio of my soul with these sensations, of my thoughts with the air and the river – all just to say that life smells bad and hurts me in my consciousness. All for not knowing how to say, as in that simple and all-embracing phrase from the Book of Job, 'My soul is weary of my life!'

80

Dolorous Interlude

Everything wearies me, including what doesn't weary me. My happiness is as painful as my pain.

If only I could be a child sailing paper boats in a cistern on the farm, with a rustic canopy of criss-crossing trellis vines projecting chequers of sunlight and green shade on the shiny dark surface of the shallow water.

There's a thin sheet of glass between me and life. However clearly I see and understand life, I can't touch it.

Rationalize my sadness? What for, if rationalization takes effort? Sad people can't make an effort.

I can't even renounce those banal acts of life that I so abhor. To renounce is an effort, and I don't have it in me to make any effort.

How often I regret not being the driver of that car or the coachman of that carriage! Or any imaginary banal Other whose life, because it's not mine, deliciously fills me with desire for it and fills me with its otherness! If I were one of them, I wouldn't dread life like a Thing, and the thought of life as a Whole wouldn't crush the shoulders of my thinking.

My dreams are a stupid shelter, like an umbrella against lightning.

I'm so listless, so pathetic, so short on gestures and acts.

However deeply I delve into myself, all of my dreams' paths lead to clearings of anxiety.

There are times when dreaming eludes even me, an obsessive dreamer, and then I see things in vivid detail. The mist in which I take refuge dissipates. And every visible edge cuts the skin of my soul. Every harsh thing I see wounds the part of me that recognizes its harshness. Every object's visible weight weighs heavy inside my soul.

It's as if my life amounted to being thrashed by it.

81

The carts in the street purr slow, distinct sounds in seeming accord with my drowsiness. It's lunchtime but I've stayed in the office. It's a warm day, a bit overcast. And the sounds, for some reason, which might be my drowsiness, are exactly like the day.

82

The fitful evening breeze blows I don't know what vague caress (and the less it's a caress, the gentler it is) across my forehead and my understanding. I know only that the tedium I suffer shifts and gives me a moment's relief, as when a piece of clothing stops rubbing against a sore.

Pathetic sensibility that depends on a slight movement of air to achieve what little tranquillity it knows! But so is all human sensibility, and I doubt that the arrival of unexpected cash or an unexpected smile counts any more for other people than a briefly passing breeze counts for me.

I can think about sleeping. I can dream of dreaming. I see more clearly the objectivity of everything. The outer feeling of life is more agreeable to me. And all of this because a slight shift in the breeze delights the surface of my skin as I approach the street corner.

All that we love or lose – things, human beings, meanings – rubs our skin and so reaches the soul, and in the eyes of God the event is no more than this breeze that brought me nothing besides an imaginary relief, the propitious moment, and the wherewithal to lose everything splendidly.

83

Whirls, whirlpools, in life's fluid futility! In this large downtown square, the soberly multicoloured flow of people passes by, changes course, forms pools, divides into streams, converges into brooks. While my eyes distractedly watch, I inwardly fashion this aquatic image which is more suitable than any other (in part because I thought it would rain) for this random movements.

As I wrote this last sentence, which for me says exactly what it means, I thought it might be useful to put at the end of my book, when I finally publish it, a few 'Non-Errata' after the 'Errata', and to note: *the phrase 'this random movements' on page so-and-so, is correct as is, with the noun in the plural and the demonstrative in the singular.* But what does this have to do with what I was thinking? Nothing, which is why I let myself think it.

Around the square the streetcars grumble and clang. They look like giant yellow mobile matchboxes, in which a child stuck a slanted used match to serve as a mast. When jerking into motion, they loudly and ironly screech. Around the statue in the middle, the pigeons are like black crumbs that flit about as if they were being scattered by the wind. The plump creatures take tiny steps with their tiny feet.

And they are shadows, shadows. . .

Seen from up close, people are monotonously diverse. Vieira* said that Frei Luís de Sousa* wrote about 'the common with singularity'. These people are singular with commonality, contrary to the style of *The Life of the Archbishop*. It seems to me a pity, though I'm indifferent to it all. I ended up here for no reason, like everything in life.

Towards the east, only partially visible, the city rises almost straight up in a static assault on the Castle. The pallid sun, hidden from view by the sudden outcrop of houses, bathes them in a blurry halo. The sky is a damply whitish blue. Perhaps a gentler version of yesterday's rain will return today. The wind seems to be easterly, perhaps because it smells vaguely ripe and green, like the adjacent market. There are more out-of-towners on the eastern than the western side of the square. With a racket like carpeted gun reports, the corrugated metal blinds of the market lower upwards; I don't know why, but that's the motion the sound suggests to me – perhaps because they usually make this sound when lowered, but now they're being raised. Everything has an explanation.

Suddenly I'm all alone in the world. I see all this from the summit of a mental rooftop. I'm alone in the world. To see is to be distant. To see clearly is to halt. To analyse is to be foreign. No one who passes by touches me. Around me there is only air. I'm so isolated I can feel the distance between me and my suit. I'm a child in a nightshirt carrying a dimly lit candle and traversing a huge empty house. Living shadows surround me – only shadows, offspring of the stiff furniture* and of the light I carry. Here in the sunlight they surround me but are people.

84

Today, during a break from feeling, I reflected on the style of my prose. Exactly how do I write? I had, like many others, the perverted desire to adopt a system and a norm. It's true that I wrote before having the norm and the system, but so did everyone else.

Analysing myself this afternoon, I've discovered that my stylistic system is based on two principles, and in the best tradition of the best classical writers I immediately uphold these two principles as general foundations of all good style: 1) to express what one feels exactly as it is felt – clearly, if it is clear; obscurely, if obscure; confusedly, if confused – and 2) to understand that grammar is an instrument and not a law.

Let's suppose there's a girl with masculine gestures. An ordinary human creature will say, 'That girl acts like a boy.' Another ordinary human creature, with some awareness that to speak is to tell, will say, 'That girl is a boy.' Yet another, equally aware of the duties of expression, but inspired by a fondness for concision (which is the sensual delight of thought), will say, 'That boy.' I'll say, 'She's a boy', violating one of the basic rules of grammar – that pronouns must agree in gender and number with the nouns they refer to. And I'll have spoken correctly; I'll have spoken absolutely, photographically, outside the norm, the accepted, the insipid. I won't have spoken, I'll have told.

In establishing usage, grammar makes valid and invalid divisions. For example, it divides verbs into transitive and intransitive. But a man who knows how to say what he says must sometimes make a transitive verb intransitive so as to photograph what he feels instead of seeing it in the dark, like the common lot of human animals. If I want to say I exist, I'll say, 'I am.' If I want to say I exist as a separate entity, I'll say, 'I am myself.' But if I want to say I exist as an entity that addresses and acts on itself, exercising the divine function of self-creation, then I'll make *to be* into a transitive verb. Triumphantly and anti-grammatically supreme, I'll speak of 'amming myself'. I'll have stated a philosophy in just two words. Isn't this infinitely preferable to saying nothing in forty sentences? What more can we demand from philosophy and diction?

Let grammar rule the man who doesn't know how to think what he feels. Let it serve those who are in command when they express themselves. It is told of Sigismund, King of Rome,* that when someone pointed out a grammatical mistake he had made in a speech, he answered, 'I am King of Rome, and above all grammar.' And he went down in history as Sigismund *super-grammaticam*. A marvellous symbol! Every man who knows how to say what he has to say is, in his way, King of Rome. The title is royal, and the reason for it is imperial.*

85

When I consider all the people I know or have heard of who write prolifically or who at least produce lengthy and finished works, I feel an ambivalent envy, a disdainful admiration, an incoherent mixture of mixed feelings.

The creation of something complete and whole, be it good or bad – and if it's never entirely good, it's very often not all bad – yes, the creation of something complete seems to stir in me above all a feeling of envy. A completed thing is like a child; although imperfect like everything human, it belongs to us like our own children.

And I, whose self-critical spirit allows me only to see my lapses and defects, I, who dare write only passages, fragments, excerpts of the non-existent, I myself – in the little that I write – am also imperfect.

Better either the complete work, which is in any case a work, even if it's bad, or the absence of words, the unbroken silence of the soul that knows it is incapable of acting.

86

Perhaps everything in life is the degeneration of something else. Perhaps existence is always an approximation – an advent, or surroundings.

Just as Christianity was but the prophetic degeneration of a debased

Neo-Platonism, the Romanization of Hellenism through Judaism,* so our age – senile and carcinogenic* – is the multiple deviation of all great goals, concordant or conflicting, whose defeat gave rise to all the negations we use to affirm ourselves.*

We live an intermission with band music.

But what do I, in this fourth-floor room, have to do with sociologies such as these?* They are all a dream to me, like Babylonian princesses, and to occupy ourselves with humanity is a futile enterprise – an archaeology of the present.

I'll disappear in the fog as a foreigner to all life, as a human island detached from the dream of the sea, as a uselessly existing ship that floats on the surface of everything.

87

Metaphysics has always struck me as a prolonged form of latent insanity. If we knew the truth, we'd see it; everything else is systems and approximations. The inscrutability of the universe is quite enough for us to think about; to want to actually understand it is to be less than human, since to be human is to realize it can't be understood.

I'm handed faith like a sealed package on a strange-looking platter and am expected to accept it without opening it. I'm handed science, like a knife on a plate, to cut the folios of a book whose pages are blank. I'm handed doubt, like dust inside a box – but why give me a box if all it contains is dust?

I write because I don't know, and I use whatever abstract and lofty term for Truth a given emotion requires. If the emotion is clear and decisive, then I naturally speak of the gods, thereby framing it in a consciousness of the world's multiplicity. If the emotion is profound, then I naturally speak of God, thereby placing it in a unified consciousness. If the emotion is a thought, I naturally speak of Fate, thereby shoving it up against the wall.*

Sometimes the mere rhythm of a sentence will require God instead of the Gods; at other times the two syllables of 'the Gods' will be necessary, and I'll verbally change universe; on still other occasions what will matter is an internal rhyme, a metrical displacement, or a burst of emotion, and polytheism or monotheism will prevail accordingly. The Gods are contingent on style.

88

Where is God, even if he doesn't exist? I want to pray and to weep, to repent of crimes I didn't commit, to enjoy the feeling of forgiveness like a caress that's more than maternal.

A lap in which to weep, but a huge and shapeless lap, spacious like a summer evening, and yet cosy, warm, feminine, next to a fireplace... To be able to weep in that lap over inconceivable things, failures I can't remember, poignant things that don't exist, and huge shuddering doubts concerning I don't know what future...

A second childhood, an old nursemaid like I used to have, and a tiny bed where I'd be lulled to sleep by tales of adventure that my flagging attention would hardly even follow – stories that once ran through infant hair as blond as wheat... And all of this enormous and eternal, guaranteed for ever and having God's lofty stature, there in the sad, drowsy depths of the ultimate reality of Things...

A lap or a cradle or a warm arm around my neck... A softly singing voice that seems to want to make me cry... A fire crackling in the fireplace... Heat in the winter... My consciousness listlessly wandering... And then a peaceful, soundless dream in a huge space, like a moon whirling among the stars...

When I put away my artifices and lovingly arrange in a corner all my toys, words, images and phrases, so dear to me I feel like kissing them, then I become so small and innocuous, so alone in a room so large and sad, so profoundly sad!

Who am I, finally, when I'm not playing? A poor orphan left out in the cold among sensations, shivering on the street corners of Reality, forced to sleep on the steps of Sadness and to eat the bread offered by

Fantasy. I was told that my father, whom I never knew, is called God, but the name means nothing to me. Sometimes at night, when I'm feeling lonely, I call out to him with tears and form an idea of him I can love. But then it occurs to me that I don't know him, that perhaps he's not how I imagine, that perhaps this figure has never been the father of my soul...

When will all this end – these streets where I drag my misery, these steps where I coldly crouch and feel the night running its hands through my tatters? If only God would one day come and take me to his house and give me warmth and affection... Sometimes I think about this and weep with joy just because I can think about it. But the wind blows down the street, and the leaves fall on the pavement. I lift my eyes and look at the stars, which make no sense at all. And all that remains of this is I, a poor abandoned child that no Love wanted as its adopted son and no Friendship accepted as its playmate.

I'm so cold, so weary in my abandonment. Go and find my Mother, O Wind. Take me in the Night to the house I never knew. Give me back my nursemaid, O vast Silence, and my crib and the lullaby that used to put me to sleep.

89

The only attitude worthy of a superior man is to persist in an activity he recognizes is useless, to observe a discipline he knows is sterile, and to apply certain norms of philosophical and metaphysical thought that he considers utterly inconsequential.

90

To recognize reality as a form of illusion and illusion as a form of reality is equally necessary and equally useless. The contemplative life, to exist at all, must see real-life accidents as the scattered premises of an unattainable conclusion, but it must also consider the contingencies of dreams as in some sense worthy of the attention we give them, since this attention is what makes us contemplatives.

Anything and everything, depending on how one sees it, is a marvel or a hindrance, an all or a nothing, a path or a problem. To see something in constantly new ways is to renew and multiply it. That is why the contemplative person, without ever leaving his village, will nevertheless have the whole universe at his disposal. There's infinity in a cell or a desert. One can sleep cosmically against a rock.

But there are times in our meditation – and they come to all who meditate – when everything is suddenly worn-out, old, seen and reseen, even though we have yet to see it. Because no matter how much we meditate on something, and through meditation transform it, whatever we transform it into can only be the substance of meditation. At a certain point we are overwhelmed by a yearning for life, by a desire to know without the intellect, to meditate with only our senses, to think in a tactile or sensory mode, from inside the object of our thought, as if it were a sponge and we were water. And so we also have our night, and the profound weariness produced by emotions becomes even more profound, since in this case the emotions come from thought. But it's a night without slumber or moon or stars, a night as if all had been turned inside out – infinity internalized and ready to burst, and the day converted into the black lining of an unfamiliar suit.

Yes, it's always better to be the human slug that loves what it doesn't know, the leech that's unaware of how repugnant it is. To ignore so as to live! To feel in order to forget! Ah, and all the events lost in the green-white wake of age-old ships, like a cold spit off the tall rudder that served as a nose under the eyes of the ancient cabins!

91

A glimpse of open country above a stone wall on the outskirts of town is more liberating for me than an entire journey would be for someone else. Every point of view is the apex of an inverted pyramid, whose base is indeterminate.

There was a time when I was irritated by certain things that today make me smile. And one of those things, which I'm reminded of nearly every day, is the way men who are active in day-to-day life smile at poets and artists. They don't always do it, as the intellectuals who write in newspapers suppose, with an air of superiority. Often they do it with affection. But it's as if they were showing affection to a child, someone with no notion of life's certainty and exactness.

This used to irritate me, because I naïvely assumed that this outward smile directed at dreaming and self-expression sprang from an inner conviction of superiority. In fact it's only a reaction to something that's different. While I once took this smile as an insult, because it seemed to imply a superior attitude, today I see it as the sign of an unconscious doubt. Just as adults often recognize in children a quick-wittedness they don't have, so the smilers recognize in us, who are devoted to dreaming and expressing, something different that makes them suspicious, just because it's unfamiliar. I like to think that the smartest among them sometimes detect our superiority, and then smile in a superior way to hide the fact.

But our superiority is not the kind that many dreamers have imagined we have. The dreamer isn't superior to the active man because dreaming is superior to reality. The dreamer's superiority is due to the fact that dreaming is much more practical than living, and the dreamer gets far greater and more varied pleasure out of life than the man of action. In other and plainer words, the dreamer is the true man of action.

Life being fundamentally a mental state, and all that we do or think valid to the extent we consider it valid, the valuation depends on us. The dreamer is an issuer of banknotes, and the notes he issues circulate in the city of his mind just like real notes in the world outside. Why should I care if the currency of my soul will never be convertible to gold, when there is no gold in life's factitious alchemy? After us all comes the deluge, but only after us all. Better and happier those who, recognizing that everything is fictitious, write the novel before someone writes it for them and, like Machiavelli, don courtly garments to write in secret.

92

I've never done anything but dream. This, and this alone, has been the meaning of my life. My only real concern has been my inner life.* My worst sorrows have evaporated when I've opened the window on to the street of my dreams* and forgotten myself in what I saw there.

I've never aspired to be more than a dreamer. I paid no attention to those who spoke to me of living. I've always belonged to what isn't where I am and to what I could never be. Whatever isn't mine, no matter how base, has always had poetry for me. The only thing I've loved is nothing at all. The only thing I've desired is what I couldn't even imagine. All I asked of life is that it go on by without my feeling it. All I demanded of love is that it never stop being a distant dream. In my own inner landscapes, all of them unreal, I've always been attracted to what's in the distance, and the hazy aqueducts – almost out of sight in my dreamed landscapes – had a dreamy sweetness in relation to the rest of the landscape, a sweetness that enabled me to love them.

I am still obsessed with creating a false world, and will be until I die. Today I don't line up spools of thread and chess pawns (with an occasional bishop or knight sticking out) in the drawers of my chest, but I regret that I don't, and in my imagination I line up the characters – so alive and dependable! – who occupy my inner life, and this makes me feel cosy, like sitting by a warm fire in winter. I have a world of friends inside me, with their own real, individual, imperfect lives.

Some of them are full of problems, while others live the humble and picturesque life of bohemians. Others are travelling salesmen. (To be able to imagine myself as a travelling salesman has always been one of my great ambitions – unattainable, alas!) Others live in the rural towns and villages of a Portugal inside me; they come to the city, where I sometimes run into them, and I open wide my arms with emotion. And when I dream this, pacing in my room, talking out loud, gesticulating – when I dream this and picture myself running into them, then I rejoice, I'm fulfilled, I jump up and down, my eyes water, I throw open my arms and feel a genuine, enormous happiness.

Ah, no nostalgia hurts as much as nostalgia for things that never existed! The longing I feel when I think of the past I've lived in real time, when I weep over the corpse of my childhood life – this can't compare to the fervour of my trembling grief as I weep over the non-reality of my dreams' humble characters, even the minor ones I recall having seen just once in my pseudo-life, while turning a corner in my envisioned world, or while passing through a doorway on a street that I walked up and down in the same dream.

My bitterness over nostalgia's impotence to revive and resurrect becomes a tearful rage against God, who created impossibilities, when I think about how the friends of my dreams – with whom I've shared so much in a make-believe life and with whom I've had so many stimulating conversations in imaginary cafés – have never had a space of their own where they could truly exist, independent of my consciousness of them!

Oh, the dead past that survives in me and that has never been anywhere but in me! The flowers from the garden of the little country house that never existed except in me! The pine grove, orchards and vegetable plots of the farm that was only a dream of mine! My imaginary excursions, my outings in a countryside that never existed! The trees along the roadside, the pathways, the stones, the rural folk passing by – all of this, which was never more than a dream, is recorded in my memory, where it hurts, and I, who spent so many hours dreaming these things, now spend hours remembering having dreamed them, and it's a genuine nostalgia that I feel, an actual past that I mourn, a real-life corpse that I stare at, lying there solemnly in its coffin.

Then there are the landscapes and lives that weren't exclusively internal. Certain paintings without great artistic merit and certain prints on walls I saw every day became realities in me. My sensation in these cases was different – sadder and more poignant. It grieved me that I couldn't be there too, whether or not the scenes were real. That I couldn't at least be an inconspicuous figure drawn in at the foot of those moonlit woods I saw on a small print in a room where I once slept – and this was after my childhood was quite finished! That I couldn't imagine being hidden there, in the woods next to the river, bathed by the eternal (though poorly rendered) moonlight, watching the man going by in a boat beneath the branches of a willow tree. In these cases I was grieved by my inability to dream completely. My nostalgia exhibited other features. The gestures of my despair were different. The impossibility that tortured me resulted in a different kind of anxiety. Ah, if all of this at least had a meaning in God, a fulfilment in accord with the tenor of my desires, fulfilled I don't know where, in a vertical time, consubstantial with the direction of my nostalgias and reveries! If there could at least be a paradise made of all this, even if only for me! If I could at least meet the friends I've dreamed of, walk along the streets I've created, wake up amid the racket of roosters and hens and the early morning rustling in the country house where I pictured myself – and all of this more perfectly arranged by God, placed in the right order for it to exist, in the form needed for me to possess it, which is something not even my dreams can achieve, for there's always at least one dimension missing in the inward space that harbours these hapless realities.

I raise my head from the sheet of paper where I'm writing. . . It's early still. It's just past noon on a Sunday. Life's basic malady, that of being conscious, begins with my body and discomfits me. To have no islands where those of us who are uncomfortable could go, no ancient garden paths reserved for those who've retreated into dreaming! To have to live and to act, however little; to have to physically touch because there are other, equally real people in life! To have to be here writing this, because my soul needs it, and not to be able to just dream it all, to express it without words, without so much as consciousness, through a construction of myself in music and diffuseness, such that tears would well in my eyes as soon as I felt like expressing myself, and I would flow like an enchanted river across gentle slopes of my own self, ever further into unconsciousness and the Far-away, to no end but God.

93

The intensity of my sensations has always been less than the intensity of my awareness of them. I've always suffered more from my consciousness that I was suffering than from the suffering of which I was conscious.

The life of my emotions moved early on to the chambers of thought, and that's where I've most fully lived my emotional experience of life.

And since thought, when it shelters emotion, is more demanding than emotion by itself, the regime of consciousness in which I began to live what I felt made how I felt more down-to-earth, more physical, more titillating.

By thinking so much, I became echo and abyss. By delving within, I made myself into many. The slightest incident – a change in the light, the tumbling of a dry leaf, the faded petal that falls from a flower, the voice speaking on the other side of the stone wall, the steps of the speaker next to those of the listener, the half-open gate of the old country estate, the courtyard with an arch and houses clustered around it in the moonlight – all these things, although not mine, grab hold of my sensory attention with the chains of longing and emotional resonance. In each of these sensations I am someone else, painfully renewed in each indefinite impression.

I live off impressions that aren't mine. I'm a squanderer of renunciations, someone else in the way I'm I.

94

To live is to be other. It's not even possible to feel, if one feels today what he felt yesterday. To feel today what one felt yesterday isn't to feel – it's to remember today what was felt yesterday, to be today's living corpse of what yesterday was lived and lost.

To erase everything from the slate from one day to the next, to be new with each new morning, in a perpetual revival of our emotional virginity – this, and only this, is worth being or having, to be or have what we imperfectly are.

This dawn is the first dawn of the world. Never did this pink colour yellowing to a warm white so tinge, towards the west, the face of the buildings whose windowpane eyes gaze upon the silence brought by the growing light. There was never this hour, nor this light, nor this person that's me. What will be tomorrow will be something else, and what I see will be seen by reconstituted eyes, full of a new vision.

High city hills! Great marvels of architecture that the steep slopes secure and make even greater, motley chaos of heaped up buildings that the daylight weaves together with bright spots and shadows – you are today, you are me, because I see you, you are what [I'll be] tomorrow, and I love you from the deck rail as when two ships pass, and there's a mysterious longing and regret in their passing.

95

I lived inscrutable hours, a succession of disconnected moments, in my night-time walk to the lonely shore of the sea. All the thoughts that have made men live and all their emotions that have died passed through my mind, like a dark summary of history, in my meditation that went to the seashore.

I suffered in me, with me, the aspirations of all eras, and every disquietude of every age walked with me to the whispering shore of the sea. What men wanted and didn't achieve, what they killed in order to achieve, and all that souls have secretly been – all of this filled the feeling soul with which I walked to the seashore. What lovers found strange in those they love, what the wife never revealed to her husband, what the mother imagines about the son she didn't have, what only had form in a smile or opportunity, in a time that wasn't the right time or in an emotion that was missing – all of this went to the seashore with me and with me returned, and the waves grandly churned their music that made me live it all in slumber.

We are who we're not, and life is quick and sad. The sound of the waves at night is a sound of the night, and how many have heard it in their own soul, like the perpetual hope that dissolves in the darkness with a faint plash of distant foam! What tears were shed by those who achieved, what tears lost by those who succeeded! And all this, in my walk to the seashore, was a secret told me by the night and the abyss. How many we are! How many of us fool ourselves! What seas crash in us, in the night when we exist, along the beaches that we feel ourselves to be, inundated by emotion! All that was lost, all that should have been sought, all that was obtained and fulfilled by mistake, all that we loved and lost and then, after losing it and loving it for having lost it, realized we never loved; all that we believed we were thinking when we were feeling; all the memories we took for emotions; and the entire ocean, noisy and cool, rolling in from the depths of the vast night to ripple over the beach, during my nocturnal walk to the seashore. . .

Who even knows what he thinks or wants? Who knows what he is to himself? How many things music suggests, and we're glad they can never be! How many things the night recalls, and we weep, and they never even were! As if a long, horizontal peace had raised its voice, the risen wave crashes and then calms, and a dribbling can be heard up and down the invisible beach.

How much I die if I feel for everything! How much I feel if I meander this way, bodiless and human, with my heart as still as a beach, and the entire sea of all things beating loud and derisive, then becoming calm, on the night that we live, on my eternal nocturnal walk to the seashore.

96

I see dreamed landscapes as plainly as real ones. If I lean out over my dreams, I'm leaning out over something. If I see life go by, my dream is of something.

Somebody said about somebody else that for him the figures of dreams had the same shape and substance as the figures of life. Although I can see why somebody might say the same thing about me, I wouldn't agree. For me, the figures of dreams aren't identical to those of life. They're parallel. Each life – that of dreams and that of the world – has a reality all its own that's just as valid as the other, but different. Like things near versus things far away. The figures of dreams are nearer to me, but . . . . .

97

The truly wise man is the one who can keep external events from changing him in any way. To do this, he covers himself with an armour of realities closer to him than the world's facts and through which the facts, modified accordingly, reach him.

98

Today I woke up very early, with a sudden and confused start, and I slowly got out of bed, suffocating from an inexplicable tedium. No dream had caused it; no reality could have created it. It was a complete and absolute tedium, but founded on something. The obscure depths of my soul had been the battleground where unknown forces had invisibly waged war, and I shook all over from the hidden conflict. A physical nausea, prompted by all of life, was born in the moment I woke up. A horror at the prospect of having to live got up with me out of bed. Everything seemed hollow, and I had the chilling impression that there is no solution for whatever the problem may be.

An extreme nervousness made my slightest gestures tremble. I was afraid I might go mad – not from insanity but from simply being there. My body was a latent shout. My heart pounded as if it were talking.

Taking wide, false steps that I vainly tried to take differently, I walked barefoot across the short length of the room and diagonally through the emptiness of the inner room, where in a corner there's a door to the hallway. With jerky and incoherent movements I hit the brushes on top of the dresser, I knocked a chair out of place, and at a certain point my swinging hand struck one of the hard iron posts of my English bed. I lit a cigarette, which I smoked subconsciously, and only when I saw that ashes had fallen on the headboard – how, if I hadn't leaned against it? – did I understand that I was possessed, or something of the sort, in fact if not in name, and that my normal, everyday self-awareness had intermingled with the abyss.

I received the announcement of morning – the cold faint light that confers a vague whitish blue on the unveiled horizon – like a grateful kiss from creation. Because this light, this true day, freed me – freed me from I don't know what. It gave an arm to my as-yet-unrevealed old age, it cuddled my false childhood, it helped my overwrought sensibility find the repose it was desperately begging for.

Ah, what a morning this is, awakening me to life's stupidity, and to its great tenderness! I almost cry when I see the old narrow street come into view down below, and when the shutters of the corner grocer reveal their dirty brown in the slowly growing light, my heart is soothed, as if by a real-life fairy tale, and it begins to have the security of not feeling itself.

What a morning this grief is! And what shadows are retreating? What mysteries have taken place? None. There's just the sound of the first tram, like a match to light up the soul's darkness, and the loud steps of my first pedestrian, which are concrete reality telling me in a friendly voice not to be this way.

99

There are times when everything wearies us, including what we would normally find restful. Wearisome things weary us by definition, restful things by the wearying thought of procuring them. There are dejections of the soul past all anxiety and all pain; I believe they're known only by those who elude human pains and anxieties and are sufficiently diplomatic with themselves to avoid even tedium. Reduced, in this way, to beings armoured against the world, it's no wonder that at a certain point in their self-awareness the whole set of armour should suddenly weigh on them and life become an inverted anxiety, a pain not suffered.

I am at one of those points, and I write these lines as if to prove that I'm at least alive. All day long I've worked as if in a half-sleep, doing my sums the way things are done in dreams, writing left to right across my torpor. All day long I've felt life weighing on my eyes and against my temples – sleep in my eyes, pressure from inside my temples, the consciousness of all this in my stomach, nausea, despondency.

To live strikes me as a metaphysical mistake of matter, a dereliction of inaction. I refuse to look at the day to find out what it can offer that might distract me and that, being recorded here in writing, might cover up the empty cup of my not wanting myself. I refuse to look at the day, and with my shoulders hunched forward I ignore whether the sun is present or absent outside in the subjectively sad street, in the deserted street where the sound of people passes by. I ignore everything, and my chest hurts. I've stopped working and don't feel like budging. I'm looking at the grimy white blotting paper, tacked down at the corners and spread out over the advanced age of the slanted desk top. I examine the crossed out scribbles of concentration and distraction. There are various instances of my signature, upside down and turned around. A few numbers here and there, wherever. A few confused sketches, sketched by my absent-mindedness. I look at all this as if I'd never seen a blotter, like a fascinated bumpkin looking at some newfangled thing, while my entire brain lies idle behind the cerebral centres that control vision.

I feel more inner fatigue than will fit in me. And there's nothing I want, nothing I prefer, nothing to flee.

100

I always live in the present. I don't know the future and no longer have the past. The former oppresses me as the possibility of everything, the latter as the reality of nothing. I have no hopes and no nostalgia. Knowing what my life has been up till now – so often and so completely the opposite of what I wanted –, what can I assume about my life tomorrow, except that it will be what I don't assume, what I don't want, what happens to me from the outside, reaching me even via my will? There's nothing from my past that I recall with the futile wish to repeat it. I was never more than my own vestige or simulacrum. My past is everything I failed to be. I don't even miss the feelings I had back then, because what is felt requires the present moment – once this has passed, there's a turning of the page and the story continues, but with a different text.

Brief dark shadow of a downtown tree, light sound of water falling into the sad pool, green of the trimmed lawn – public garden shortly before twilight: you are in this moment the whole universe for me, for you are the full content of my conscious sensation. All I want from life is to feel it being lost in these unexpected evenings, to the sound of strange children playing in gardens like this one, fenced in by the melancholy of the surrounding streets and topped, beyond the trees' tallest branches, by the old sky where the stars are again coming out.

101

If our life were an eternal standing by the window, if we could remain there for ever, like hovering smoke, with the same moment of twilight forever paining the curve of the hills... If we could remain that way for beyond for ever! If at least on this side of the impossible we could thus continue, without committing an action, without our pallid lips sinning another word!

Look how it's getting dark!... The positive quietude of everything fills me with rage, with something that's a bitterness in the air I breathe. My soul aches... A slow wisp of smoke rises and dissipates in the distance... A restless tedium makes me think no more of you...

All so superfluous! We and the world and the mystery of both.

102

Life is whatever we conceive it to be. For the farmer who considers his field to be everything, the field is an empire. For a Caesar whose empire is still not enough, the empire is a field. The poor man possesses an empire, the great man a field. All that we truly possess are our own sensations; it is in them, rather than in what they sense, that we must base our life's reality.

This has nothing to do with anything.

I've dreamed a great deal. I'm tired from having dreamed but not tired of dreaming. No one tires of dreaming, because dreaming is forgetting, and forgetting doesn't weigh a thing; it's a dreamless sleep in which we're awake. In dreams I've done everything. I've also woken up, but so what? How many Caesars I've been! And the great men of history – how mean-spirited! Caesar, after his life was spared by a merciful pirate, ordered a search to find the pirate, who was then crucified. Napoleon, in the will he wrote in Saint Helena, made a bequest to a common criminal who tried to assassinate Wellington. O greatness of spirit no greater than that of the squint-eyed neighbour lady! O great men of another world's cook! How many Caesars I've been and still dream of being.

How many Caesars I've been, but not the real ones. I've been truly imperial while dreaming, and that's why I've never been anything. My armies were defeated, but the defeat was fluffy, and no one died. I lost no flags. My dream didn't get as far as the army; my flags never turned the corner into full dreamed view. How many Caesars I've been, right here, on the Rua dos Douradores. And the Caesars I've been still live in my imagination; but the Caesars that were are dead, and the Rua dos Douradores – Reality, that is – cannot know them.

I throw an empty matchbox towards the abyss that's the street beyond the sill of my high window without balcony. I sit up in my chair and listen. Distinctly, as if it meant something, the empty matchbox resounds on the street, declaring to me its desertedness. Not another sound can be heard, except the sounds of the whole city. Yes, the sounds of the city on this long Sunday – so many, all at odds, and all of them right.

How little, from the real world, forms the support of the best reflections: the fact of arriving late for lunch, of running out of matches, of personally, individually throwing the matchbox out the window, of feeling out of sorts for having eaten late, the fact it's Sunday virtually guaranteeing a lousy sunset, the fact I'm nobody in the world, and all metaphysics.

But how many Caesars I've been!

103

I cultivate hatred of action like a greenhouse flower. I dissent from life and am proud of it.

104

No intelligent idea can gain general acceptance unless some stupidity is mixed in with it. Collective thought is stupid because it's collective. Nothing passes into the realm of the collective without leaving at the border – like a toll – most of the intelligence it contained.

In youth we're twofold. Our innate intelligence, which may be considerable, coexists with the stupidity of our inexperience, which forms a second, lesser intelligence. Only later on do the two unite. That's why youth always blunders – not because of its inexperience, but because of its non-unity.

Today the only course left for the man of superior intelligence is abdication.

105

Aesthetics of Abdication

To conform is to submit, and to conquer is to conform, to be conquered. Thus every victory is a debasement. The conqueror inevitably loses all the virtues born of frustration with the *status quo* that led him to the fight that brought victory. He becomes satisfied, and only those who conform – who lack the conqueror's mentality – are satisfied. Only the man who never achieves his goal conquers. Only the man who is forever discouraged is strong. The best and most regal course is to abdicate. The supreme empire belongs to the emperor who abdicates from all normal life and from other men, for the preservation of his supremacy won't weigh on him like a load of jewels.

106

Sometimes, when I lift my dazed head from the books where I record other people's accounts and the absence of a life I can call my own, I feel a physical nausea, which might be from hunching over, but which transcends the numbers and my disillusion. I find life distasteful, like a useless medicine. And that's when I feel, and can clearly picture, how easy it would be to get rid of this tedium, if I had the simple strength of will to really want to get rid of it.

We live by action – by acting on desire. Those of us who don't know how to want – whether geniuses or beggars – are related by impotence. What's the point of calling myself a genius, if I'm after all an assistant bookkeeper? When Cesário Verde* made sure the doctor knew that he was not Senhor Verde, an office worker, but Cesário Verde the poet, he used one of those self-important terms that reek of vanity. What he always was, poor man, was Senhor Verde, an office worker. The poet was born after he died, for it was only then that he was appreciated as a poet.

To act – that is true wisdom. I can be what I want to be, but I have to want whatever it is. Success consists in being successful, not in having the potential for success. Any wide piece of ground is the potential site of a palace, but there's no palace until it's built.

My pride was stoned by blind men, my disillusion trampled on by beggars.

'I want you only to dream of you,' they tell the beloved woman in verses they never send – they who dare not tell her anything. This 'I want you only to dream of you' is a verse from an old poem of mine. I record the memory with a smile, and don't even comment on the smile.

107

I'm one of those souls women say they love but never recognize when they meet us – one of those souls that they would never recognize, even if they recognized us. I endure the sensitivity of my feelings with an attitude of disdain. I have all the qualities for which romantic poets are admired, and even the lack of those qualities, which makes one a true romantic poet. I find myself partially described in novels as the protagonist of various plots, but the essence of my life and soul is never to be a protagonist.

I don't have any idea of myself, not even the kind that consists in the lack of an idea of myself. I'm a nomad in my self-awareness. The herds of my inner riches scattered during the first watch.

The only tragedy is not being able to conceive of ourselves as tragic. I've always clearly seen that I coexist with the world. I've never clearly felt that I needed to coexist with it. That's why I've never been normal.

To act is to rest.

All problems are insoluble. The essence of there being a problem is that there's no solution. To go looking for a fact means the fact doesn't exist. To think is to not know how to be.

Sometimes I spend hours at the Terreiro do Paço,* next to the river, meditating in vain. My impatience keeps trying to tear me away from that peace, and my inertia keeps holding me there. And in this state of bodily torpor that suggests sensuality only in the way the wind's whispering recalls voices, I meditate on the eternal insatiability of my vague desires, on the permanent fickleness of my impossible yearnings. I suffer mainly from the malady of being able to suffer. I'm missing something I don't really want, and I suffer because this isn't true suffering.

The wharf, the afternoon and the smell of ocean all enter, together, into the composition of my anxiety. The flutes of impossible shepherds are no sweeter than the absence of flutes that right now reminds me of them. The distant idylls alongside streams grieve me in this inwardly analogous moment . . . . .

108

It's possible to feel life as a sickness in the stomach, the very existence of one's soul as a muscular discomfort. Desolation of spirit, when sharply felt, stirs distant tides in the body, where it suffers pain by proxy.

I'm conscious of myself on a day when the pain of being conscious is, as the poet* says,

> *lassitude, nausea,*
> *and agonizing desire.*

109

(storm)

Dark silence lividly teems. Above the occasional creaking of a fast-moving cart, a nearby truck produces a thundering sound – a ridiculous mechanical echo of what's really happening in the closely distant skies.

Again, without warning, magnetic light gushes forth, flickering. My heart beats with a gulp. A glass dome shatters on high into large bits. A new sheet of ruthless rain strikes the sound of the ground.

(Senhor Vasques) His wan face is an unnatural and befuddled green. I watch him take his laboured breaths with the kinship of knowing I'll be no different.

110

After I've slept many dreams, I go out to the street with eyes wide open but still with the aura and assurance of my dreams. And I'm astonished by my automatism, which prevents others from really knowing me. For I go through daily life still holding the hand of my astral nursemaid; my steps are in perfect accord with the obscure designs of my sleeping mind. And I walk in the right direction; I don't stagger; I react well; I exist.

But in the respites when I don't have to watch where I'm going to avoid vehicles or oncoming pedestrians, when I don't have to speak to anyone or enter a door up ahead, then I launch once more like a paper boat on to the waters of sleep, and once more I return to the fading illusion that cuddles my hazy consciousness of the morning now emerging amid the sounds of the vegetable carts.

And it is then, in the middle of life's bustle, that my dream becomes a marvellous film. I walk along an unreal downtown street, and the reality of its non-existent lives affectionately wraps my head in a white cloth of false memories. I'm a navigator engaged in unknowing myself. I've overcome everything where I've never been. And this somnolence that allows me to walk, bent forward in a march over the impossible, feels like a fresh breeze.

Everyone has his alcohol. To exist is alcohol enough for me. Drunk from feeling, I wander as I walk straight ahead. When it's time, I show up at the office like everyone else. When it's not time, I go to the river to gaze at the river, like everyone else. I'm no different. And behind all this, O sky my sky, I secretly constellate and have my infinity.

111

Every man of today, unless his moral stature and intellectual level are that of a pygmy or a churl, loves with romantic love when he loves. Romantic love is a rarefied product of century after century of Christian influence, and everything about its substance and development can be explained to the unenlightened by comparing it to a suit fashioned by the soul or the imagination and used to clothe those whom the mind thinks it fits, when they happen to come along.

But every suit, since it isn't eternal, lasts as long as it lasts; and soon, under the fraying clothes of the ideal we've formed, the real body of the person we dressed it in shows through.

Romantic love is thus a path to disillusion, unless this disillusion, accepted from the start, decides to vary the ideal constantly, constantly sewing new suits in the soul's workshops so as to constantly renew the appearance of the person they clothe.

112

We never love anyone. What we love is the idea we have of someone. It's our own concept – our own selves – that we love.

This is true in the whole gamut of love. In sexual love we seek our own pleasure via another body. In non-sexual love, we seek our own pleasure via our own idea. The masturbator may be abject, but in point of fact he's the perfect logical expression of the lover. He's the only one who doesn't feign and doesn't fool himself.

The relations between one soul and another, expressed through such uncertain and variable things as shared words and proffered gestures, are deceptively complex. The very act of meeting each other is a non-meeting. Two people say 'I love you' or mutually think it and feel it, and each has in mind a different idea, a different life, perhaps even a different colour or fragrance, in the abstract sum of impressions that constitute the soul's activity.

Today I'm lucid as if I didn't exist. My thinking is as naked as a skeleton, without the fleshly tatters of the illusion of expression. And these considerations that I forge and abandon weren't born from anything – at least not from anything in the front rows of my consciousness. Perhaps it was the sales representative's disillusion with his girlfriend, perhaps a sentence I read in one of the romantic tales that our newspapers reprint from the foreign press, or perhaps just a vague nausea for which I can think of no physical cause. . .

The scholiast who annotated Virgil was wrong. Understanding is what wearies us most of all. To live is to not think.

113

Two or three days like the beginning of love. . .

The value of this for the aesthete is in the feelings it produces. To go further would be to enter the realm of jealousy, suffering and anxiety. In this antechamber of emotion there's all the sweetness of love – hints of pleasure, whiffs of passion – without any of its depth. If this means giving up the grandeur of tragic love, we must remember that tragedies, for the aesthete, are interesting to observe but unpleasant to experience. The cultivation of life hinders that of the imagination. It is the aloof, uncommon man who rules.

No doubt this theory would satisfy me, if I could convince myself that it's not what it is: a complicated jabber to fill the ears of my intelligence, to make it almost forget that at heart I'm just timid, with no aptitude for life.

114

Aesthetics of Artificiality

Life hinders the expression of life. If I actually lived a great love, I would never be able to describe it.

Not even I know if this I that I'm disclosing to you, in these meandering pages, actually exists or is but a fictitious, aesthetic concept I've made of myself. Yes, that's right. I live aesthetically as someone else. I've sculpted my life like a statue made of matter that's foreign to my being. Having employed my self-awareness in such a purely artistic way, and having become so completely external to myself, I sometimes no longer recognize myself. Who am I behind this unreality? I don't know. I must be someone. And if I avoid living, acting and feeling, then believe me, it's so as not to tamper with the contours of my invented personality. I want to be exactly like what I wanted to be and am not. If I were to give in to life, I'd be destroyed. I want to be a work of art, at least in my soul, since I can't be one in my body. That's why I've sculpted myself in quiet isolation and have placed myself in a hothouse, cut off from fresh air and direct light – where the absurd flower of my artificiality can blossom in secluded beauty.

Sometimes I muse about how wonderful it would be if I could string all my dreams together into one continuous life, a life consisting of entire days full of imaginary companions and created people, a false life which I could live and suffer and enjoy. Misfortune would sometimes strike me there, and there I would also experience great joys. And nothing about me would be real. But everything would have a sublime logic; it would all pulse to a rhythm of sensual falseness, taking place in a city built out of my soul and extending all the way to the platform next to an idle train, far away in the distance within me... And it would all be vivid and inevitable, as in the outer life, but with an aesthetics of the Dying Sun.

115

To organize our life in such a way that it becomes a mystery to others, that those who are closest to us will only be closer to not knowing us. That is how I've shaped my life, almost without thinking about it, but I did it with so much instinctive art that even to myself I've become a not entirely clear and definite individual.

116

To write is to forget. Literature is the most agreeable way of ignoring life. Music soothes, the visual arts exhilarate, and the performing arts (such as acting and dance) entertain. Literature, however, retreats from life by turning it into a slumber. The other arts make no such retreat – some because they use visible and hence vital formulas, others because they live from human life itself.

This isn't the case with literature. Literature simulates life. A novel is a story of what never was, and a play is a novel without narration. A poem is the expression of ideas or feelings in a language no one uses, because no one talks in verse.

117

Most people are afflicted by an inability to say what they see or think. They say there's nothing more difficult than to define a spiral in words; they claim it's necessary to use the unliterary hand, twirling it in a steadily upward direction, so that human eyes will perceive the abstract figure immanent in a wire spring and a certain type of staircase. But if we remember that to say is to renew, we will have no trouble defining a spiral: it's a circle that rises without ever closing. I realize that most people would never dare define it this way, for they suppose that defining is to say what others want us to say rather than what's required for the definition. I'll say it more accurately: a spiral is a potential circle that winds round as it rises, without ever completing itself. But no, the definition is still abstract. I'll resort to the concrete, and all will become clear: a spiral is a snake without a snake, vertically wound around nothing.

All literature is an attempt to make life real. As all of us know, even when we don't act on what we know, life is absolutely unreal in its directly real form; the country, the city and our ideas are all absolutely fictitious things, the offspring of our complex sensation of our own selves. Impressions are incommunicable unless we make them literary.

Children are particularly literary, for they say what they feel and not what someone has taught them to feel. Once I heard a child, who wished to say that he was on the verge of tears, say not 'I feel like crying,' which is what an adult, i.e. an idiot, would say, but rather, 'I feel like tears.' And this phrase – so literary it would seem affected in a well-known poet, if he could ever invent it – decisively refers to the warm presence of tears about to burst from eyelids that feel the liquid bitterness. 'I feel like tears'! That small child aptly defined his spiral.

To say! To know how to say! To know how to exist via the written voice and the intellectual image! This is all that matters in life; the rest is men and women, imagined loves and factitious vanities, the wiles of our digestion and forgetfulness, people squirming – like worms when a rock is lifted – under the huge abstract boulder of the meaningless blue sky.

118

Why should I care that no one reads what I write? I write to forget about life, and I publish because that's one of the rules of the game. If tomorrow all my writings were lost, I'd be sorry, but I doubt I'd be violently and frantically sorry, as one might expect, given that with my writings would go my entire life. I would probably be like the mother who loses her son but is back to normal in a few months' time. The great earth that cares for the hills would also, in a less motherly fashion, take care of the pages I've written. Nothing matters, and I'm sure there have been people who, looking at life, didn't have much patience for this child that was still awake, when all they wanted was the peace that would come once the child went to bed.

119

It has always disappointed me to read the allusions in Amiel's diary* to the fact that he published books. That's where he falls down. How great he would be otherwise!

Amiel's diary has always grieved me on my own account. When I came to the passage where he says that Scherer* described the fruit of the mind as 'the consciousness of consciousness', I felt it as a direct reference to my soul.

120

That obscure and almost imponderable malice that gladdens every human heart when confronted by the pain and discomfort of others has been redirected, in me, to my own pains, so that I can actually take pleasure in feeling ridiculous or contemptible, as if it were someone else in my place. By a strange and fantastic transformation of sentiments, I don't feel that malicious and all-too-human gladness when faced with other people's pain and embarrassment. When others are in difficulty, what I feel isn't sorrow but an aesthetic discomfort and a sinuous irritation. This isn't due to compassion but to the fact that whoever looks ridiculous looks that way to others and not just to me, and it irritates me when someone looks ridiculous to others; it grieves me that any animal of the human species should laugh at the expense of another when he has no right to. I don't care if others laugh at my expense, for I have the advantage of an armoured contempt towards whatever's outside me.

I've surrounded the garden of my being with high iron gratings – more imposing than any stone wall – in such a way that I can perfectly see others while perfectly excluding them, keeping them in their place as others.

To discover ways of not acting has been my main concern in life.

I refuse to submit to the state or to men; I passively resist. The state can only want me for some sort of action. As long as I don't act, there's nothing it can get from me. Since capital punishment has been abolished, the most it can do is harass me; were this to occur, I would have to armour my soul even more, and live even deeper inside my dreams. But this hasn't happened yet. The state has never bothered me. Fate, it seems, has looked out for me.

121

Like all men endowed with great mental mobility, I have an irrevocable, organic love of settledness. I abhor new ways of life and unfamiliar places.

122

The idea of travelling nauseates me.

I've already seen what I've never seen.

I've already seen what I have yet to see.

The tedium of the forever new, the tedium of discovering – behind the specious differences of things and ideas – the unrelenting sameness of everything, the absolute similarity of a mosque and a temple and a church, the exact equivalence of a cabin and a castle, the same physical body for a king in robes and for a naked savage, the eternal concordance of life with itself, the stagnation of everything I live, all of it equally condemned to change*...

Landscapes are repetitions. On a simple train ride I uselessly and restlessly waver between my inattention to the landscape and my inattention to the book that would amuse me if I were someone else. Life makes me feel a vague nausea, and any kind of movement aggravates it.

Only landscapes that don't exist and books I'll never read aren't tedious. Life, for me, is a drowsiness that never reaches the brain. This I keep free, so that I can be sad there.

Ah, let those who don't exist travel! For someone who isn't anything, like a river, forward motion is no doubt life. But for those who are alert, who think and feel, the horrendous hysteria of trains, cars and ships makes it impossible to sleep or to wake up.

From any trip, even a short one, I return as from a slumber full of dreams – in a dazed confusion, with one sensation stuck to another, feeling drunk from what I saw.

I can't rest for lack of good health in my soul. I can't move because of something lacking between my body and soul; it's not movement that I'm missing, but the very desire to move.

Often enough I've wanted to cross the river – those ten minutes from the Terreiro do Paço to Cacilhas.* And I've always felt intimidated by so many people, by myself, and by my intention. Once or twice I've made the trip, nervous the whole way, setting my foot on dry land only after I'd returned.

When one feels too intensely, the Tagus is an endless Atlantic, and Cacilhas another continent, or even another universe.

123

Renunciation is liberation. Not wanting is power.

What can China give me that my soul hasn't already given me? And if my soul can't give it to me, how will China give it to me? For it's with my soul that I'll see China, if I ever see it. I could go and seek riches in the Orient, but not the riches of the soul, because I am my soul's riches, and I am where I am, with or without the Orient.

Travel is for those who cannot feel. That's why travel books are always so unsatisfying as books of experience. They're worth only as much as the imagination of the one who writes them, and if the writer has imagination, he can as easily enchant us with the detailed, photographic description – down to each tiny coloured pennant – of scenes he imagined as he can with the necessarily less detailed description of the scenes he thought he saw. All of us are near-sighted, except on the inside. Only the eyes we use for dreaming truly see.

There are basically only two things in our earthly experience: the universal and the particular. To describe the universal is to describe what is common to all human souls and to all human experience – the broad sky, with day and night occurring in it and by it; the flowing of rivers, all with the same fresh and nunnish water; the vast waving mountains known as oceans, which hold the majesty of height in the secret of their depths; the fields, the seasons, houses, faces, gestures; clothes and smiles; love and wars; gods both finite and infinite; the formless Night, mother of the world's origin; Fate, the intellectual monster that is everything. . . Describing these or any other universals, my soul speaks the primitive and divine language, the Adamic tongue that everyone understands. But what splintered, Babelish language would I use to describe the Santa Justa Lift,* the Reims Cathedral, the breeches worn by the Zouaves, or the way Portuguese is pronounced in the province of Trás-os-Montes? These are surface differences, the ground's unevenness, which we can feel by walking but not by our abstract feeling. What's universal in the Santa Justa Lift is the mechanical technology that makes life easier. What's true in the Reims Cathedral is neither Reims nor the Cathedral but the religious splendour of buildings dedicated to understanding the human soul's depths. What's eternal in the Zouaves' breeches is the colourful fiction of clothes, a human language whose social simplicity is, in a certain way, a new nakedness. What's universal in local accents is the homely tone of voice in those who live spontaneously, the diversity within groups, the multicoloured parade of customs, the differences between peoples, and the immense variety of nations.

Eternal tourists of ourselves, there is no landscape but what we are. We possess nothing, for we don't even possess ourselves. We have nothing because we are nothing. What hand will I reach out, and to what universe? The universe isn't mine: it's me.

124

(Chapter on Indifference or something like that)

Every soul worthy of itself desires to live life in the Extreme. To be satisfied with what one is given is for slaves. To ask for more is for children. To conquer more is for madmen, because every conquest is . . . . .

To live life in the Extreme means to live it to the limit, but there are three ways of doing this, and it's up to the superior soul to choose one of the ways. The first way to live life in the extreme is by possessing it to an extreme degree, via a Ulyssean journey through all experiential sensations, through all forms of externalized energy. Few people, however, in all the ages of the world, have been able to shut their eyes with a fatigue that's the sum of all fatigues, having possessed everything in every way.

Indeed few can get life to yield to them completely, body and soul, making them so sure of its love that jealous thoughts become impossible. But this must surely be the desire of every superior, strong-willed soul. When this soul, however, realizes that it can never accomplish such a feat, that it lacks the strength to conquer all parts of the Whole, then there are two other roads it can follow. One is total renunciation, formal and complete abstention, whereby it transfers to the sensible sphere whatever cannot be wholly possessed in the sphere of activity and energy; better to supremely not act than to act spottily, inadequately and in vain, like the superfluous, inane, vast majority of men. The other road is that of perfect equilibrium, the search for the Limit in Absolute Proportion, whereby the longing for the Extreme passes from the will and emotion to the Intelligence, one's entire ambition being not to live all life or to feel all life but to organize all life, to consummate it in intelligent Harmony and Coordination.

The longing to understand, which in noble souls often replaces the longing to act, belongs to the sphere of sensibility. To replace energy with the Intelligence, to break the link between will and emotion, stripping the material life's gestures of any and all interest – this, if achieved, is worth more than life, which is so hard to possess in its entirety and so sad when possessed only in part.

The argonauts said* that it wasn't necessary to live, only to sail. We, argonauts of our pathological sensibility, say that it's not necessary to live, only to feel.

125

Your ships, Lord, didn't make a greater voyage than the one made by my thought, in the disaster of this book. They rounded no cape and sighted no far-flung beach – beyond what daring men had dared and what minds had dreamed – to equal the capes I rounded with my imagination and the beaches where I landed with my . . . . .

Thanks to your initiative, Lord, the Real World was discovered. The Intellectual World will be discovered thanks to mine.

Your argonauts* grappled with monsters and fears. In the voyage of my thought, I also had monsters and fears to contend with. On the path to the abstract chasm that lies in the depths of things there are horrors that the world's men don't imagine and fears to endure that human experience doesn't know. The cape of the common sea beyond which all is mystery is perhaps more human than the abstract path to the world's void.

Separated from their native soil, banished from the path leading back to their homes, forever widowed from the tranquillity of life being the same, your emissaries finally arrived, when you were already dead, at the oceanic end of the Earth. They saw, materially, a new sky and new earth.

I, far away from the paths to myself, blind to the vision of the life I love, ... I too have finally arrived at the vacant end of things, at the imponderable edge of creation's limit, at the port-in-no-place of the World's abstract chasm.

I have entered, Lord, that Port. I have wandered, Lord, over that sea. I have gazed, Lord, at that invisible chasm.

I dedicate this work of supreme Discovery to the memory of your Portuguese name, creator of argonauts.

126

I have times of great stagnation. It's not, as happens to everyone, that I let days and days go by without sending a postcard in response to the urgent letter I received. It's not, as happens to no one, that I indefinitely postpone what's easy and would be useful, or what's useful and would be pleasurable. There's more subtlety in my self-contradiction. I stagnate in my very soul. My will, emotions and thought stop functioning, and this suspension lasts for days on end; only the vegetative life of my soul – words, gestures, habits – expresses me to others and, through them, to myself.

In these periods of shadowy subsistence, I'm unable to think, feel or want. I can't write more than numbers and scribbles. I don't feel, and the death of a loved one would strike me as having happened in a foreign language. I'm helpless. It's as if I were sleeping and my gestures, words and deliberate acts were no more than a peripheral respiration, the rhythmic instinct of some organism.

Thus the days keep passing, and if I added them all up, who knows how much of my life they would amount to? It sometimes occurs to me, when I shake off this state of suspension, that perhaps I'm not as naked as I suppose, that perhaps there are still intangible clothes covering the eternal absence of my true soul. It occurs to me that thinking, feeling and wanting can also be stagnations, on the threshold of a more intimate thinking, a feeling that's more mine, a will lost somewhere in the labyrinth of who I really am.

However it may be, I'll let it be. And to whatever god or gods that be, I'll let go of who I am, according as luck and chance determine, faithful to a forgotten pledge.

127

I don't get indignant, because indignation is for the strong; I'm not resigned, because resignation is for the noble; I don't hold my peace, because silence is for the great. And I'm neither strong, nor noble, nor great. I suffer and I dream. I complain because I'm weak. And since I'm an artist, I amuse myself by making my complaints musical and by arranging my dreams according to my idea of what makes them beautiful.

I only regret not being a child, since then I could believe in my dreams, and not being a madman, since then I could keep everyone around me from getting close to my soul . . . . .

Taking dreams for reality, living too intensely what I dream, has given this thorn to the false rose of my dreamed life: that not even dreams cheer me, because I see their defects.

Not even by colourfully painting my window can I block out the noise of the life outside, which doesn't know I'm observing it.

Happy the creators of pessimistic systems! Besides taking refuge in the fact of having made something, they can exult in their explanation of universal suffering, and include themselves in it.

I don't complain about the world. I don't protest in the name of the universe. I'm not a pessimist. I suffer and complain, but I don't know if suffering is the norm, nor do I know if it's human to suffer. Why should I care to know?

I suffer, without knowing if I deserve to. (A hunted doe.)

I'm not a pessimist. I'm sad.

128

I've always rejected being understood. To be understood is to prostitute oneself. I prefer to be taken seriously for what I'm not, remaining humanly unknown, with naturalness and all due respect.

Nothing would bother me more than if they found me strange at the office. I like to revel in the irony that they don't find me at all strange. I like the hair shirt of being regarded by them as their equal. I like the crucifixion of being considered no different. There are martyrdoms more subtle than those recorded for the saints and hermits. There are torments of our mental awareness as there are of the body and of desire. And in the former, as in the latter, there's a certain sensuality . . . . .

129

The office boy was tying up the day's packages in the twilight coolness of the empty office. 'What a thunderclap!' the cruel bandit said to no one, in the loud voice of a 'Good morning!' My heart started beating again. The apocalypse had passed. There was a respite.

And with what relief – a flashing light, a pause, the hard clap – did this now near, then retreating thunder relieve us of what had been. God had ceased. My lungs breathed heavily. I realized it was stuffy in the office. I noticed that there were other people besides the office boy. They had all been silent. I heard something crisp and tremulous: it was one of the Ledger's large and heavy pages that Moreira, checking something, had abruptly turned.

130

I often wonder what I would be like if, shielded from the winds of fate by the screen of wealth, I'd never been brought by the dutiful hand of my uncle to an office in Lisbon, nor risen from it to other offices, all the way up to this paltry pinnacle as a competent assistant bookkeeper, with a job that's like a siesta and a salary that I can live on.

I realize that if I'd had this imagined past, I wouldn't now be able to write these pages, which are at least something, and therefore better than all the pages I would only have dreamed of writing in better circumstances. For banality is a form of intelligence, and reality –

especially if stupid or crude – is a natural complement of the soul.

My job as a bookkeeper is responsible for a large part of what I'm able to feel and think, since this occurs as a denial and evasion of that selfsame job.

If I had to list, in the blank space of a questionnaire, the main literary influences on my intellectual development, I would immediately jot down the name of Cesário Verde,* but I would also write in the names of Senhor Vasques my boss, of Moreira the head bookkeeper, of Vieira the local sales representative, and of António the office boy. And as the crucial address of them all I would write LISBON in big letters.

The fact is that not only Cesário Verde, but also my co-workers, have served as correction coefficients for my vision of the world. I think that's the term (whose exact meaning I obviously don't know) for the treatment given by engineers to mathematics so that it can be applied to life. If it is the right term, then that's what I meant. If it isn't, then let's imagine it could be, the intention substituting for the failed metaphor.

And if I think, with all the lucidity I can muster, about what my life has apparently been, I see it as a coloured thing – a chocolate wrapper or a cigar band – swept from the dirty tablecloth by the brisk brush of the housemaid (who's listening overhead) and landing in the dustpan with the crumbs and the crusts of reality proper. It stands out from other things with a similar destiny by its privilege of getting to ride in the dustpan as well. And above the maid's brushing the gods continue their conversation, indifferent to the affairs of the world's servants.

Yes, if I'd been wealthy, shielded, spruce, ornamental, I wouldn't even have been this brief episode of pretty paper among crumbs; I would have remained on a lucky dish – 'Thank you but no' – and have retreated to the sideboard to grow old. This way, rejected after my useful substance has been eaten, I go to the rubbish bin with the dust of what's left of Christ's body, and I can't imagine what will follow and among what stars, but something – inevitably – will follow.

131

Since I have nothing to do and nothing to think about doing, I'm going to describe my ideal on this sheet of paper –

Note

The sensibility of Mallarmé in the style of Vieira;* to dream like Verlaine in the body of Horace; to be Homer in the moonlight.

To feel everything in every way; to be able to think with the emotions and feel with the mind; not to desire much except with the imagination; to suffer with haughtiness; to see clearly so as to write accurately; to know oneself through diplomacy and dissimulation; to become naturalized as a different person, with all the necessary documents; in short, to use all sensations but only on the inside, peeling them all down to God and then wrapping everything up again and putting it back in the shop window like the sales assistant I can see from here with the small tins of a new brand of shoe polish.

All these ideals, possible or impossible, now end. Now I face reality, which isn't even the sales assistant (whom I don't see), only his hand, the absurd tentacle of a soul with a family and a fate, and it twists like a spider without a web while putting back tins of polish in the window.

And one of the tins fell, like the Fate of us all.*

132

The more I contemplate the spectacle of the world and the ever-changing state of things, the more profoundly I'm convinced of the inherent fiction of everything, of the false importance exhibited by all realities. And in this contemplation (which has occurred to all thinking souls at one time or another), the colourful parade of customs and fashions, the complex path of civilizations and progress, the grandiose commotion of empires and cultures – all of this strikes me as a myth and a fiction, dreamed among shadows and ruins. But I'm not sure whether the supreme resolution of all these dead intentions – dead even when achieved – lies in the ecstatic resignation of the Buddha, who, once he understood the emptiness of things, stood up from his ecstasy saying, 'Now I know everything', or in the jaded indifference of the emperor Severus: 'Omnia fui, nihil expedit – I've been everything, nothing's worth the trouble.'

133

. . . the world – a dunghill of instinctive forces that nevertheless shines in the sun with pale shades of light and dark gold.

The way I see it, plagues, storms and wars are products of the same blind force, sometimes operating through unconscious microbes, sometimes through unconscious waters and thunderbolts, and sometimes through unconscious men. For me, the difference between an earthquake and a massacre is like the difference between murdering with a knife and murdering with a dagger. The monster immanent in things, for the sake of his own good or his own evil, which are apparently indifferent to him, is equally served by the shifting of a rock on a hilltop or by the stirring of envy or greed in a heart. The rock falls and kills a man; greed or envy prompts an arm, and the arm kills a man. Such is the world – a dunghill of instinctive forces that nevertheless shines in the sun with pale shades of light and dark gold.

To oppose the brutal indifference that constitutes the manifest essence of things, the mystics discovered it was best to renounce. To deny the world, to turn our backs on it as on a swamp at whose edge we suddenly find ourselves standing. To deny, like the Buddha, its absolute reality; to deny, like Christ, its relative reality; to deny . . . . .

All I asked of life is that it ask nothing of me. At the door of the cottage I never had, I sat in the sunlight that never fell there, and I enjoyed the future old age of my tired reality (glad that I hadn't arrived there yet). To still not have died is enough for life's wretches, and to still have hope . . . . .

. . . . . satisfied with dreams only when I'm not dreaming, satisfied with the world only when I'm dreaming far away from it. A swinging pendulum, back and forth, forever moving to arrive nowhere, eternally captive to the twin fatality of a centre and a useless motion.

134

I seek and don't find myself. I belong to chrysanthemum hours, neatly lined up in flowerpots. God made my soul to be a decorative object.

I don't know what overly pompous and selective details define my temperament. If I love the ornamental, it must be because I sense something there that's identical to the substance of my soul.

135

The simplest, truly simplest things, which nothing can make semi-simple, become complex when I live them. To wish someone a good day sometimes intimidates me. My voice gets caught, as if there were a strange audacity in saying these words out loud. It's a kind of squeamishness about existing – there's no other way to put it!

The constant analysis of our sensations creates a new way of feeling, which seems artificial to those who only analyse with the intellect, and not with sensation itself.

All my life I've been metaphysically glib, serious at playing around. I haven't done anything seriously, however much I may have wanted to. A mischievous Destiny had fun with me.

To have emotions made of chintz, or of silk, or of brocade! To have emotions that could be described like that! To have describable emotions!

I feel in my soul a divine regret for everything, a choked and sobbing grief for the condemnation of dreams in the flesh of those who dreamed them. And I hate without hatred all the poets who wrote verses, all the idealists who saw their ideals take shape, all those who obtained what they wanted.

I haphazardly roam the calm streets, walking until my body is as tired as my soul, grieved to the point of that old and familiar grief that likes to be felt, pitying itself with an indefinable, maternal compassion set to music.

Sleep! To fall asleep! To have peace! To be an abstract consciousness that's conscious only of breathing peacefully, without a world, without heavens, without a soul – a dead sea of emotion reflecting an absence of stars!

136

The burden of feeling! The burden of having to feel!

137

. . . the hypersensitivity of my feelings, or perhaps merely of their expression, or perhaps, more accurately, of the intelligence which lies between the former and the latter and which forms, from my wish to express, the fictitious emotion that exists only to be expressed. (Perhaps it's just the machine in me that reveals who I'm not.)

138

There's an erudition of acquired knowledge, which is erudition in the narrowest sense, and there's an erudition of understanding, which we call culture. But there's also an erudition of the sensibility.

Erudition of the sensibility has nothing to do with the experience of life. The experience of life teaches nothing, just as history teaches nothing. True experience comes from restricting our contract with reality while increasing our analysis of that contact. In this way our sensibility becomes broader and deeper, because everything is in us – all we need to do is look for it and know how to look.

What's travel and what good is it? Any sunset is the sunset; one doesn't have to go to Constantinople to see it. The sensation of freedom that travel brings? I can have it by going from Lisbon to Benfica,* and have it more intensely than one who goes from Lisbon to China, because if the freedom isn't in me, then I won't have it no matter where I go. 'Any road,' said Carlyle,* 'this simple Entepfuhl road, will lead you to the end of the World.' But the Entepfuhl road, if it is followed all the way to the end, returns to Entepfuhl; so that Entepfuhl, where we already were, is the same end of the world we set out to find.

Condillac begins his celebrated book* with: 'No matter how high we climb or how low we descend, we never escape our sensations.' We never disembark from ourselves. We never attain another existence unless we other ourselves by actively, vividly imagining who we are. The true landscapes are those that we ourselves create since, being their gods, we see them as they truly are, which is however we created them. None of the four corners of the world is the one that interests me and that I can truly see; it's the fifth corner that I travel in, and it belongs to me.

Whoever has crossed all the seas has crossed only the monotony of himself. I've crossed more seas than anyone. I've seen more mountains than there are on earth. I've passed through more cities than exist, and the great rivers of non-worlds have flown sovereignly under my watching eyes. If I were to travel, I'd find a poor copy of what I've already seen without taking one step.

In the countries that others go to, they go as anonymous foreigners. In the countries I've visited, I've been not only the secret pleasure of the unknown traveller, but also the majesty of the reigning king, the indigenous people and their culture, and the entire history of the nation and its neighbours. I saw every landscape and every house because they were me, made in God from the substance of my imagination.

139

For a long time now I haven't written. Months have gone by in which I haven't lived, just endured, between the office and physiology, in an inward stagnation of thinking and feeling. Unfortunately, this isn't even restful, since in rotting there's fermentation.

For a long time now I haven't written and haven't even existed. I hardly even seem to be dreaming. The streets for me are just streets. I do my office work conscious only of it, though I can't say without distraction: in the back of my mind I'm sleeping instead of meditating (which is what I usually do), but I still have a different existence behind my work.

For a long time now I haven't existed. I'm utterly calm. No one distinguishes me from who I am. I just felt myself breathe as if I'd done something new, or done it late. I'm beginning to be conscious of being conscious. Perhaps tomorrow I'll wake up to myself and resume the course of my own existence. I don't know if that will make me more happy or less. I don't know anything. I lift my pedestrian's head and see that, on the hill of the Castle, the sunset's reflection is burning in dozens of windows, in a lofty brilliance of cold fire. Around these hard-flamed eyes, the entire hillside has the softness of day's end. I'm able at least to feel sad, and to be conscious that my sadness was just now crossed – I saw it with my ears – by the sudden sound of a passing tram, by the casual voices of young people, and by the forgotten murmur of the living city.

For a long time now I haven't been I.

140

It sometimes happens, more or less suddenly, that in the midst of my sensations I'm overwhelmed by such a terrible weariness of life that I can't even conceive of any act that might relieve it. Suicide seems a dubious remedy, and natural death – even assuming it brings unconsciousness – an insufficient one. Rather than the cessation of my existence, which may or may not be possible, this weariness makes me long for something far more horrifying and profound: never to have existed at all, which is definitely impossible.

Now and then I seem to discern, in the generally confused speculations of the Indians, something of this longing that's even more negative than nothingness. But either they lack the keenness of sensation to communicate what they think, or they lack the acuity of thought to really feel what they feel. The fact is that what I discern in them I don't clearly see. The fact is that I think I'm the first to express in words the sinister absurdity of this incurable sensation.

And yet I do cure it, by writing about it. Yes, for every truly profound desolation, one that's not pure feeling but has some intelligence mixed in with it, there's always the ironic remedy of expressing it. If literature has no other usefulness, it at least has this one, though it serves only a few.

The ailments of our intelligence unfortunately hurt less than those of our feelings, and those of our feelings unfortunately less than those of the body. I say 'unfortunately' because human dignity would require it to be the other way around. There is no mental anguish *vis-à-vis* the unknown that can hurt us like love or jealousy or nostalgia, that can overwhelm us like intense physical fear, or that can transform us like anger or ambition. But neither can any pain that ravishes the soul be as genuinely painful as a toothache, a stomach-ache, or the pain (I imagine) of childbirth.

We're made in such a way that the same intelligence that ennobles certain emotions or sensations, elevating them above others, also humbles them, when it extends its analysis to a comparison among them all.

I write as if sleeping, and my entire life is an unsigned receipt.

Inside the coop where he'll stay until he's killed, the rooster sings anthems to liberty because he was given two roosts.

141

Rainy Landscape

Each drop of rain is my failed life weeping in nature. There's something of my disquiet in the endless drizzle, then shower, then drizzle, then shower, through which the day's sorrow uselessly pours itself out over the earth.

It rains and keeps raining. My soul is damp from hearing it. So much rain. . . My flesh is watery around my physical sensation of it.

An anguished cold holds my poor heart in its icy hands. The grey □ hours get longer, flattening out in time; the moments drag.

So much rain!

The gutters spew out little torrents of sudden water. A troubling noise of falling rain falls through my awareness that there are downspouts. The rain groans as it listlessly batters the panes . . . . .

A cold hand squeezes my throat and prevents me from breathing life.

Everything is dying in me, even the knowledge that I can dream! I can't get physically comfortable. Every soft thing I lean against hurts my soul with sharp edges. All eyes I gaze into are terribly dark in this impoverished daylight, propitious for dying without pain.

142

The most contemptible thing about dreams is that everyone has them. The delivery boy who dozes against the lamppost in between deliveries is thinking about something in his darkened mind. I know what he's thinking about: the very same things into which I plummet, between one and another ledger entry, in the summer tedium of the stock-still office.

143

I pity those who dream the probable, the reasonable and the accessible more than those who fantasize about the extraordinary and remote. Those who have grandiose dreams are either lunatics who believe in what they dream and are happy, or they're mere daydreamers whose reveries are like the soul's music, lulling them and meaning nothing. But those who dream the possible will, very possibly, suffer real disillusion. I can't be too disappointed over not having become a Roman emperor, but I can sorely regret never once having spoken to the seamstress who at the street corner turns right at about nine o'clock every morning. The dream that promises us the impossible denies us access to it from the start, but the dream that promises the possible interferes with our normal life, relying on it for its fulfilment. The one kind of dream lives by itself, independently, while the other is contingent on what may or may not happen.

That's why I love impossible landscapes and the vast empty stretches of plains I'll never see. The historical ages of the past are sheer wonder, because I know from the outset that I can't be part of them. I sleep when I dream of what doesn't exist; dreaming of what might exist wakes me up.

It's midday in the deserted office, and I lean out one of the balcony windows overlooking the street down below. My distraction, aware of the movement of people in my eyes, is too steeped in its meditation to see them. I sleep on my elbows propped painfully on the railing and feel a great promise in knowing nothing. With mental detachment I look at the arrested street full of hurrying people, and I make out the details: the crates piled up on a cart, the sacks at the door of the other warehouse, and, in the farthest window of the grocery on the corner, the glint of those bottles of Port wine that I imagine no one can afford to buy. My spirit abandons the material dimension. I investigate with my imagination. The people passing by on the street are always the same ones who passed by a while ago, always a group of floating figures, patches of motion, uncertain voices, things that pass by and never quite happen.

To take note, not with my senses, but with the awareness of my senses. . . The possibility of other things. . . And suddenly, from behind me, I hear the metaphysically abrupt arrival of the office boy. I feel like I could kill him for barging in on what I wasn't thinking. I turn around and look at him with a silence full of hatred, tense with latent homicide, my mind already hearing the voice he'll use to tell me something or other. He smiles from the other side of the room and says 'Good afternoon' in a loud voice. I hate him like the universe. My eyes are sore from imagining.

144

After many days of rain, the sky brings back its hidden blue to the vast expanses on high. Between the streets, whose puddles sleep like country ponds, and the clear and chilly gladness overhead, there's a contrast that makes the dirty streets congenial and the dreary winter sky spring-like. It's Sunday and I have nothing to do. It's such a nice day that I don't even feel like dreaming. I enjoy it with all the sincerity of my senses, to which my intelligence bows. I walk like a liberated shop assistant. I feel old, just so I can have the pleasure of feeling myself being rejuvenated.

In the large Sunday square there's a solemn flurry of a different sort of day. People are coming out of Mass at the church of São Domingos, and another one is about to begin. I see those who are leaving and those who still haven't entered, because they're waiting for people who aren't there watching who's coming out.

None of these things are important. They are, like everything in the ordinary world, a slumber of mysteries and battlements, and like a herald who has just arrived, I gaze at the open plain of my meditation.

When I was a child, I used to go to this Mass, or perhaps another one, but I think it was this one. I wore my only good suit, out of respect, and enjoyed every minute, even when there was nothing special to enjoy. I lived externally, and the suit was clean and new. What more can one want, when he's going to die and doesn't know it, led by a mother's hand?

I used to enjoy all of this, but only now do I realize how much I enjoyed it. I would enter Mass as into a great mystery, and come out at the end as into a clearing. And that's how it really was, and how it still really is. It's only the self who no longer believes and is now an adult, with a soul that remembers and weeps – only this self is fiction and confusion, anguish and the grave.

Yes, what I am would be unbearable if I couldn't remember what I've been. And this crowd of strangers who are still leaving Mass, and the beginning of the potential crowd arriving for the next Mass, are like boats passing by on a slow river, beneath the open windows of my house on the bank.

Memories, Sundays, Masses, the pleasure of having been, the miracle of time having remained because it already went by, and since it was mine it will never be forgotten. . . Absurd diagonal of my normal sensations, sudden sound of an old carriage around the square, creaking its wheels in the depths of the cars' noisy silences and somehow or other, by a maternal paradox of time, subsisting today, right here, between what I am and what I've lost, in my backward gaze that is me. . .

145

The higher a man rises, the more things he must do without. There's no room on the pinnacle except for the man himself. The more perfect he is, the more complete; and the more complete, the less other.

These thoughts occurred to me after reading a newspaper article about the great and multifaceted life of a celebrity – an American millionaire who had been everything. He had achieved all that he'd aspired to – money, love, friendship, recognition, travels, collections. Money can't buy everything, but the personal magnetism that enables a man to make lots of money can, indeed, obtain most things.

As I laid the paper down on the restaurant table, I was already thinking how a similar article, narrowing the focus, could have been written about the firm's sales representative, more or less my acquaintance, who's eating lunch at the table in the back corner, as he does every day. All that the millionaire had, this man has – in smaller measure, to be sure, but abundantly for his stature. Both men have had equal success, and there isn't even a difference in their fame, for here too we must see each man in his particular context. There's no one in the world who doesn't know the name of the American millionaire, but there's no one in Lisbon's commercial district who doesn't know the name of the man eating lunch in the corner.

These men obtained all that their hand could grasp within arm's reach. What varied in them was the length of their arm; they were identical in other respects. I've never been able to envy this sort of person. I've always felt that virtue lay in obtaining what was out of one's reach, in living where one isn't, in being more alive after death than during life, in achieving something impossible, something absurd, in overcoming – like an obstacle – the world's very reality.

Should someone point out that the pleasure of enduring is nil after one ceases to exist, I would first of all respond that I'm not sure if it is, because I don't know the truth about human survival. Secondly, the pleasure of future fame is a present pleasure – the fame is what's future. And it's the pleasure of feeling proud, equal to no pleasure that material wealth can bring. It may be illusory, but it is in any case far greater than the pleasure of enjoying only what's here. The American millionaire can't believe that posterity will appreciate his poems, given that he didn't write any. The sales representative can't imagine that the future will admire his pictures, since he never painted any.

I, however, who in this transitory life am nothing, can enjoy the thought of the future reading this very page, since I do actually write it; I can take pride – like a father in his son – in the fame I will have, since at least I have something that could bring me fame. And as I think this, rising from the table, my invisible and inwardly majestic stature rises above Detroit, Michigan, and over all the commercial district of Lisbon.

It was not, however, with these reflections that I began to reflect. What I initially thought about was how little a man must be in this life in order to live beyond it. One reflection is as good as another, for they are the same. Glory isn't a medal but a coin: on one side the head, on the other a stated value. For the larger values there are no coins, just paper, whose value is never much.

With metaphysical psychologies such as these, humble people like me console themselves.

146

Some have a great dream in life that they never accomplish. Others have no dream, and likewise never accomplish it.

147

Every struggle, no matter what its goal, is forced by life to make adjustments; it becomes a different struggle, serves different ends, and sometimes accomplishes the very opposite of what it set out to do. Only slight goals are worth pursuing, because only a slight goal can be entirely fulfilled. If I struggle to make a fortune, I can make it in a certain way; the goal is slight, like all quantitative goals, personal or otherwise, and it's attainable, verifiable. But how shall I fulfil the intention of serving my country, or of enriching human culture, or of improving humanity? I can't be certain of the right course of action, nor verify whether the goals have been achieved . . . . .

148

The perfect man, for the pagans, was the perfection of the man that exists; for Christians, the perfection of the man that does not exist; and for Buddhists, the perfection of no man existing.

Nature is the difference between the soul and God.

Everything stated or expressed by man is a note in the margin of a completely erased text. From what's in the note we can extract the gist of what must have been in the text, but there's always a doubt, and the possible meanings are many.

149

Many people have defined man, and in general they've defined him in contrast with animals. That's why definitions of man often take the form, 'Man is a such-and-such animal', or 'Man is an animal that...', and then we're told what. 'Man is a sick animal,' said Rousseau, and that's partly true. 'Man is a rational animal,' says the Church, and that's partly true. 'Man is a tool-using animal,' says Carlyle, and that's partly true. But these definitions, and others like them, are always somewhat off the mark. And the reason is quite simple: it's not easy to distinguish man from animals, for there's no reliable criterion for making the distinction. Human lives run their course with the same inherent unconsciousness as animal lives. The same fundamental laws that rule animal instincts likewise rule human intelligence, which appears to be no more than an instinct in the formative stage, as unconscious as any instinct, and less perfect since still not fully formed.

'All that exists comes from unreason,' says The Greek Anthology. And everything, indeed, comes from unreason. Since it deals only with dead numbers and empty formulas, mathematics can be perfectly logical, but the rest of science is no more than child's play at dusk, an attempt to catch birds' shadows and to stop the shadows of wind-blown grass.

The funny thing is that, while it's difficult to formulate a definition that truly distinguishes man from animals, it's easy to differentiate between the superior man and the common man.

I've never forgotten that phrase from Haeckel,* the biologist, whom I read in the childhood of my intelligence, that period when we're attracted to popular science and writings that attack religion. The phrase is more or less the following: The distance between the superior man (a Kant or a Goethe, I believe he says) and the common man is much greater than the distance between the common man and the ape. I've never forgotten the phrase, because it's true. Between me, whose rank is low among thinking men, and a farmer from Loures,* there is undoubtedly a greater distance than between the farmer and, I won't say a monkey, but a cat or dog. None of us, from the cat on up to me, is really in charge of the life imposed on us or of the destiny we've been given; we are all equally derived from no one knows what; we're shadows of gestures performed by someone else, embodied effects, consequences that feel. But between me and the farmer there's a difference of quality, due to the presence in me of abstract thought and disinterested emotion; whereas between him and the cat, intellectually and psychologically, there is only a difference of degree.

The superior man differs from the inferior man and his animal brothers by the simple trait of irony. Irony is the first sign that our consciousness has become conscious, and it passes through two stages: the one represented by Socrates, when he says, 'All I know is that I know nothing,' and the other represented by Sanches,* when he says, 'I don't even know if I know nothing.' In the first stage we dogmatically doubt ourselves, and every superior man arrives there. In the second stage we come to doubt not only ourselves but also our own doubt, and few men have reached that point in the already so long yet short span of time that the human race has beheld the sun and night over the earth's variegated surface.

To know oneself is to err, and the oracle that said 'Know thyself' proposed a task more difficult than the labours of Hercules and a riddle murkier than the Sphinx's. To consciously not know ourselves – that's the way! And to conscientiously not know ourselves is the active task of irony. I know nothing greater, nor more worthy of the truly great man, than the patient and expressive analysis of the ways in which we don't know ourselves, the conscious recording of the unconsciousness of our conscious states, the metaphysics of autonomous shadows, the poetry of the twilight of disillusion.

But something always eludes us, some analysis or other always gets muddled, and the truth – even if false – is always beyond the next corner. And this is what tires us even more than life (when life tires us) and more than the knowledge and contemplation of life (which always tire us).

I stand up from the chair where, propped distractedly against the table, I've entertained myself with the narration of these strange impressions. I stand up, propping my body on itself, and walk to the window, higher than the surrounding rooftops, and I watch the city going to sleep in a slow beginning of silence. The large and whitely white moon sadly clarifies the terraced differences in the buildings opposite. The moonlight seems to illuminate icily all the world's mystery. It seems to reveal everything, and everything is shadows with admixtures of faint light, false and unevenly absurd gaps, inconsistencies of the visible. There's no breeze, and the mystery seems to loom larger. I feel queasy in my abstract thought. I'll never write a page that sheds light on me or that sheds light on anything. A wispy cloud hovers hazily over the moon, like a coverture. I'm ignorant, like these rooftops. I've failed, like all of nature.

150

The persistence of instinctive life in the guise of human intelligence is one of my most constant and profound contemplations. The artificial disguise of consciousness only highlights for me the unconsciousness it doesn't succeed in disguising.

From birth to death, man is the slave of the same external dimension that rules animals. Throughout his life he doesn't live, he vegetatively thrives, with greater intensity and complexity than an animal. He's guided by norms without knowing that they guide him or even that they exist, and all his ideas, feelings and acts are unconscious – not because there's no consciousness in them but because there aren't two consciousnesses.

Flashes of awareness that we live an illusion – that, and no more, is what distinguishes the greatest of men.

With a wandering mind I consider the common history of common men. I see how in everything they are slaves of a subconscious temperament, of extraneous circumstances, and of the social and anti-social impulses in which, with which and over which they clash like petty objects.

How often I've heard people say the same old phrase that symbolizes all the absurdity, all the nothingness, all the verbalized ignorance of their lives. It's the phrase they use in reference to any material pleasure: 'This is what we take away from life. . .' Take where? take how? take why? It would be sad to wake them out of their darkness with questions like that. . . Only a materialist can utter such a phrase, because everyone who utters such a phrase is, whether he knows it or not, a materialist. What does he plan to take from life, and how? Where will he take his pork chops and red wine and lady friend? To what heaven that he doesn't believe in? To what earth, where he'll take only the rottenness that was the latent essence of his whole life? I can think of no phrase that's more tragic, or that reveals more about human humanity. That's what plants would say if they could know that they enjoy the sun. That's what animals would say about their somnambulant pleasures, were their power of self-expression not inferior to man's. And perhaps even I, while writing these words with a vague impression that they might endure, imagine that my memory of having written them is what I 'take away from life'. And just as a common corpse is lowered into the common ground, so the equally useless corpse of the prose I wrote while waiting will be lowered into common oblivion. A man's pork chops, his wine, his lady friend – who am I to make fun of them?

Brothers in our common ignorance, different expressions of the same blood, diverse forms of the same heredity – which of us can deny the other? A wife can be denied, but not mother, not father, not brother.

151

Outside, in the slow moonlit night, the wind slowly shakes things that cast fluttering shadows. Perhaps it's just hanging laundry from the floor above, but the shadows don't know they're from shirts, and they impalpably flutter in hushed harmony with everything else.

I left the shutters open so as to wake up early, but so far I haven't succeeded in falling asleep or even in staying wide awake, and the night's already so old that not a sound can be heard. There's moonlight beyond the shadows of my room, but it doesn't come through the window. It exists like a day of hollow silver, and the roof of the building opposite, which I can see from my bed, is liquid with a blackish whiteness. In the moon's hard light there's a sad peace, like lofty congratulations to someone who can't hear them.

And without seeing, without thinking, my eyes now closed on my non-existent slumber, I meditate on what words can truly describe moonlight. The ancients would say that it is silvery or white. But this supposed whiteness actually consists of many colours. Were I to get out of bed and look past the cold panes, I know I would see that in the high lonely air the moonlight is greyish white, blued by a subdued yellow; that over the various, unequally dark rooftops it bathes the submissive buildings with a black white and floods the red brown of the highest clay tiles with a colourless colour. At the end of the street – a placid abyss where the naked cobblestones are unevenly rounded – it has no colour other than a blue which perhaps comes from the grey of the stones. In the depths of the horizon it must be almost dark blue, different from the black blue in the depths of the sky. On the windows where it strikes, the moonlight is a black yellow.

From here in my bed, if I open my eyes, heavy with the sleep I cannot find, it looks like snow turned into colour, with floating threads of warm nacre. And if I think with what I feel, it's a tedium turned into white shadow, darkening as if eyes were closing on this hazy whiteness.

152

I'm astounded whenever I finish something. Astounded and distressed. My perfectionist instinct should inhibit me from finishing; it should inhibit me from even beginning. But I get distracted and start doing something. What I achieve is not the product of an act of my will but of my will's surrender. I begin because I don't have the strength to think; I finish because I don't have the courage to quit. This book is my cowardice.

If I often interrupt a thought with a scenic description that in some way fits into the real or imagined scheme of my impressions, it's because the scenery is a door through which I flee from my awareness of my creative impotence. In the middle of the conversations with myself that form the words of this book, I'll feel the sudden need to talk to someone else, and so I'll address the light which hovers, as now, over rooftops that glow as if they were damp, or I'll turn to the urban hillside with its tall and gently swaying trees that seem strangely close and on the verge of silently collapsing, or to the steep houses that overlap like posters, with windows for letters, and the dying sun gilding their moist glue.

Why do I write, if I can't write any better? But what would become of me if I didn't write what I can, however inferior it may be to what I am? In my ambitions I'm a plebeian, because I try to achieve; like someone afraid of a dark room, I'm afraid to be silent. I'm like those who prize the medal more than the struggle to get it, and savour glory in a fur-lined cape.

For me, to write is self-deprecating, and yet I can't quit doing it. Writing is like the drug I abhor and keep taking, the addiction I despise and depend on. There are necessary poisons, and some are extremely subtle, composed of ingredients from the soul, herbs collected from among the ruins of dreams, black poppies found next to the graves of our intentions, the long leaves of obscene trees whose branches sway on the echoing banks of the soul's infernal rivers.

To write is to lose myself, yes, but everyone loses himself, because everything gets lost. I, however, lose myself without any joy – not like the river flowing into the sea for which it was secretly born, but like the puddle left on the beach by the high tide, its stranded water never returning to the ocean but merely sinking into the sand.

153

I stand up from my chair with a monstrous effort, but I have the impression that I carry it with me and that it's heavier, for it's the chair of subjectivity.

154

Who am I to myself? Just one of my sensations.

My heart drains out helplessly, like a broken bucket. Think? Feel? How everything wearies when it's defined!

155

Just as some people work because they're bored, I sometimes write because I have nothing to say. Daydreaming, which occurs naturally to people when they're not thinking, in me takes written form, for I know how to dream in prose. And there are many sincere feelings and much genuine emotion that I extract from not feeling.

There are moments when the emptiness of feeling oneself live attains the consistency of a positive thing. In the great men of action, namely the saints, who act with all of their emotion and not just part of it, this sense of life's nothingness leads to the infinite. They crown themselves with night and the stars, and anoint themselves with silence and solitude. In the great men of inaction, to whose number I humbly belong, the same feeling leads to the infinitesimal; sensations are stretched, like rubber bands, to reveal the pores of their slack, false continuity.

And in these moments both types of men love sleep, as much as the common man who doesn't act and doesn't not act, being a mere reflection of the generic existence of the human species. Sleep is fusion with God, Nirvana, however it be called. Sleep is the slow analysis of sensations, whether used as an atomic science of the soul or left to doze like a music of our will, a slow anagram of monotony.

In my writing I linger over the words, as before shop windows I don't really look at, and what remains are half-meanings and quasi-expressions, like the colours of fabrics that I didn't actually see, harmonious displays composed of I don't know what objects. In writing I rock myself, like a crazed mother her dead child.

One day, I don't know which, I found myself in this world, having lived unfeelingly from the time I was evidently born until then. When I asked where I was, everyone misled me, and they contradicted each other. When I asked them to tell me what I should do, they all spoke falsely, and each one said something different. When in bewilderment I stopped on the road, everyone was shocked that I didn't keep going to no one knew where, or else turn back – I, who'd woken up at the crossroads and didn't know where I'd come from. I saw that I was on stage and didn't know the part that everyone else recited straight off, also without knowing it. I saw that I was dressed as a page, but they didn't give me the queen, and blamed me for not having her. I saw that I had a message in my hand to deliver, and when I told them that the sheet of paper was blank, they laughed at me. And I still don't know if they laughed because all sheets are blank, or because all messages are to be guessed.

Finally I sat down on the rock at the crossroads as before the fireplace I never had. And I began, all by myself, to make paper boats with the lie they'd given me. No one would believe in me, not even as a liar, and there was no lake where I could try out my truth.

Lost and idle words, random metaphors, chained to shadows by a vague anxiety... Remnants of better times, spent on I don't know what garden paths... Extinguished lamp whose gold gleams in the dark, in memory of the dead light... Words tossed not to the wind but to the ground, dropped from limp fingers, like dried leaves that had fallen on them from an invisibly infinite tree... Nostalgia for the pools of unknown farms... Heartfelt affection for what never happened...

To live! To live! And at least the hope that I might sleep soundly in Proserpina's bed.

156

What imperious queen, standing by her ponds, holds on to the memory of my broken life? I was the pageboy of tree-lined paths that weren't enough for the soaring moments of my blue peace. Ships in the distance completed the sea that lapped my terraces, and in the clouds towards the south I lost my soul, like an oar dropped in the water.

157

To create in myself a nation with its own politics, parties and revolutions, and to be all of it, everything, to be God in the real pantheism of this people-I, to be the substance and movement of their bodies and their souls, of the very ground they tread and the acts they perform! To be everything, to be them and not them! Ah, this is one of the dreams I'm still far from realizing. And if I realized it, perhaps I would die. I'm not sure why, but it seems one couldn't live after committing such a great sacrilege against God, after usurping the divine power of being everything.

What pleasure it would give me to create a Jesuitry of sensations!

There are metaphors more real than the people who walk in the street. There are images tucked away in books that live more vividly than many men and women. There are phrases from literary works that have a positively human personality. There are passages from my own writings that chill me with fright, so distinctly do I feel them as people, so sharply outlined do they appear against the walls of my room, at night, in the shadows . . . . . I've written sentences whose sound, read out loud or silently (impossible to hide their sound), can only be of something that has acquired absolute exteriority and a full-fledged soul.

Why do I sometimes set forth contradictory and irreconcilable methods of dreaming and of learning to dream? Probably because I'm so used to feeling what's false as true, and what I dream as vividly as what I see, that I've lost the human distinction – false, I believe – between truth and falsehood.

For me it's enough to perceive something clearly, with my eyesight or my hearing or any of my other senses, in order to feel that it's real. It can even happen that I simultaneously feel two things that can't logically coexist. No matter.

There are people who spend long hours suffering because they can't be a figure in a painting or in one of the suits from a deck of cards. There are souls who suffer not being able to live today in the Middle Ages as if this were a divine curse. I used to experience this kind of suffering, but no longer. I've moved beyond that level. But it does sadden me that I can't dream of myself as, say, two kings in different kingdoms that belong to universes with different kinds of space and time. Not to be able to achieve this truly makes me grieve. It smacks to me of going hungry.

To visualize the inconceivable in dreams is one of the great triumphs that I, as advanced a dreamer as I am, only rarely attain. To dream, for example, that I'm simultaneously, separately, severally the man and the woman on a stroll that a man and woman are taking along the river. To see myself – at the same time, in the same way, with equal precision and without overlap, being equally but separately integrated into both things – as a conscious ship in a South Sea and a printed page from an old book. How absurd this seems! But everything is absurd, and dreaming least of all.

158

For a man who has ravished Proserpina like Dis, even if only in his dreams, how can the love of an earthly woman be anything but a dream?

Like Shelley, I loved Antigone before time was; temporal loves were flat to my taste, all reminding me of what I'd lost.

159

Twice in my adolescence – which I feel so remotely it seems like someone else's story that I read or was told – I enjoyed the humiliating grief of being in love. From my present vantage point, looking back to that past which I can no longer designate as 'long ago' or 'recent', I think it was good that this experience of disillusion happened to me so early.

Nothing happened, except in what I felt. Outwardly speaking, legions of men have suffered the same inner torments. But . . . . .

Through an experience that simultaneously involved my sensibility and intelligence, I realized early on that the imaginative life, however morbid it might seem, is the one that suits temperaments like mine. The fictions of my imagination (as it later developed) may weary me, but they don't hurt or humiliate. Impossible lovers can't possibly cheat on us, or smile at us falsely, or be calculating in their caresses. They never forsake us, and they don't die or disappear.

Our soul's great anxieties are always cosmic cataclysms, upsetting the stars all around us and making the sun veer off course. In all souls that feel, Fate sooner or later plays out an apocalypse of anxiety, with all heavens and worlds raining down over their disconsolation.

To feel that you're superior and to be treated by Fate as supremely and incurably inferior – who in such a plight can boast about being a man?

Were I ever granted a flash of expressive power so great that it concentrated all art in me, I would write a eulogy to sleep. I know no greater pleasure in life than that of being able to sleep. The total snuffing out of life and the soul, the complete banishment of all beings and people, the night without memory or illusion, the absence of past and future . . . . .

160

The entire day, in all the desolation of its scattered and dull clouds, was filled with the news of revolution. Such reports, true or false, always fill me with a peculiar discomfort, a mixture of disdain and physical nausea. It galls my intelligence when someone imagines that things will change by shaking them up. Violence of whatever sort has always been, for me, a flagrant form of human stupidity. All revolutionaries, for that matter, are stupid, as are all reformers to a lesser extent – lesser because they're less troublesome.

Revolutionary or reformer – the error is the same. Unable to dominate and reform his own attitude towards life, which is everything, or his own being, which is almost everything, he flees, devoting himself to modifying others and the outside world. Every revolutionary and reformer is a fugitive. To fight for change is to be incapable of changing oneself. To reform is to be beyond repair.*

A sensitive and honest-minded man, if he's concerned about evil and injustice in the world, will naturally begin his campaign against them by eliminating them at their nearest source: his own person. This task will take his entire life.

Everything, for us, is in our concept of the world. To modify our concept of the world is to modify the world for us, or simply to modify the world, since it will never be, for us, anything but what it is for us. That inner justice we summon to write a fluent and beautiful page, that true reformation of enlivening our dead sensibility – these things are the truth, our truth, the only truth. Everything else in the world is scenery, picture frames for our feelings, book bindings for our thoughts. And this is true whether it be the colourful scenery of beings and things – fields, houses, posters, clothes – or the colourless scenery of monotonous souls that periodically rise to the surface with hackneyed words and gestures, then sink back down into the fundamental stupidity of human expression.

Revolution? Change? What I really want, with all my heart, is for the atonic clouds to stop greyly lathering the sky. What I want is to see the blue emerge, a truth that is clear and sure because it is nothing and wants nothing.

161

Nothing irks me more than the vocabulary of social responsibility. The very word 'duty' is unpleasant to me, like an unwanted guest. But the terms 'civic duty', 'solidarity', 'humanitarianism' and others of the same ilk disgust me like rubbish dumped out of a window right on top of me. I'm offended by the implicit assumption that these expressions pertain to me, that I should find them worthwhile and even meaningful.

I recently saw in a toy-shop window some objects that reminded me exactly of what these expressions are: make-believe dishes filled with make-believe tidbits for the miniature table of a doll. For the real, sensual, vain and selfish man, the friend of others because he has the gift of speech and the enemy of others because he has the gift of life, what is there to gain from playing with the dolls of hollow and meaningless words?

Government is based on two things: restraint and deception. The problem with those glittering expressions is that they neither restrain nor deceive. At most they intoxicate, which is something else again.

If there's one thing I hate, it's a reformer. A reformer is a man who sees the world's superficial ills and sets out to cure them by aggravating the more basic ills. A doctor tries to bring a sick body into conformity with a normal, healthy body, but we don't know what's healthy or sick in the social sphere.

I see humanity as merely one of Nature's latest schools of decorative painting. I don't distinguish in any fundamental way between a man and a tree, and I naturally prefer whichever is more decorative, whichever interests my thinking eyes. If the tree is more interesting to me than the man, I'm sorrier to see the tree felled than to see the man die. There are departing sunsets that grieve me more than the deaths of children. I keep my own feelings out of everything, in order to be able to feel.

I almost reproach myself for writing these sketchy reflections in this moment when a light breeze, rising from the afternoon's depths, begins to take on colour. In fact it's not the breeze that takes on colour but the air through which it hesitantly glides. I feel, however, as if the breeze were being coloured, so that's what I say, for I have to say what I feel, given that I'm I.

162

All of life's unpleasant experiences – when we make fools of ourselves, act thoughtlessly, or lapse in our observance of some virtue – should be regarded as mere external accidents which can't affect the substance of our soul. We should see them as toothaches or calluses of life, as things that bother us but remain outside us (even though they're ours), or that only our organic existence need consider and our vital functions worry about.

When we achieve this attitude, which in essence is that of the mystics, we're protected not only from the world but also from ourselves, for we've conquered what is foreign in us, contrary and external to us, and therefore our enemy.

Horace said* that the just man will remain undaunted, even if the world crumbles all around him. Although the image is absurd, the point is valid. Even if what we pretend to be (because we coexist with others) crumbles around us, we should remain undaunted – not because we're just, but because we're ourselves, and to be ourselves means having nothing to do with external things that crumble, even if they crumble right on top of what for them we are.

For superior men, life should be a dream that spurns confrontations.

163

Direct experience is an evasion, or hiding place, for those without any imagination. Reading about the risks incurred by a man who hunts tigers, I feel all the risks worth feeling, save the actual physical risk, which wasn't really worth feeling, for it vanished without a trace.

Men of action are the involuntary slaves of the men of reason. The worth of things depends on their interpretation. Certain men make things which other men invest with meaning, bringing them to life. To narrate is to create, while to live is merely to be lived.

164

Inaction makes up for everything. Not acting gives us everything. To imagine is everything, as long as it doesn't tend towards action. No one can be king of the world except in dreams. And every one of us who really knows himself wants to be king of the world.

To imagine, without being, is the throne. To desire, without wanting, is the crown. We have what we renounce, for we conserve it eternally intact in our dreams, by the light of the sun that isn't, or of the moon that cannot be.

165

Whether I like it or not, everything that isn't my soul is no more for me than scenery and decoration. Through rational thought I can recognize that a man is a living being just like me, but for my true, involuntary self he has always had less importance than a tree, if the tree is more beautiful. That's why I've always seen human events – the great collective tragedies of history or of what we make of history – as colourful friezes, with no soul in the figures that appear there. I've never thought twice about anything tragic that has happened in China. It's just scenery in the distance, even if painted with blood and disease.

With ironic sadness I remember a workers' demonstration, carried out with I don't know how much sincerity (for I find it hard to admit sincerity in collective endeavours, given that the individual, all by himself, is the only entity capable of feeling). It was a teeming and rowdy group of animated idiots, who passed by my outsider's indifference shouting various things. I instantly felt disgusted. They weren't even sufficiently dirty. Those who truly suffer don't form a group or go around as a mob. Those who suffer, suffer alone.

What a pathetic group! What a lack of humanity and true pain! They were real and therefore unbelievable. No one could ever use them for the scene of a novel or a descriptive backdrop. They went by like rubbish in a river, in the river of life, and to see them go by made me sick to my stomach and profoundly sleepy.

166

If I carefully consider the life men lead, I find nothing to distinguish it from the life of animals. Both man and animal are hurled unconsciously through things and the world; both have their leisure moments; both complete the same organic cycle day after day; both think nothing beyond what they think, nor live beyond what they live. A cat wallows in the sun and goes to sleep. Man wallows in life, with all of its complexities, and goes to sleep. Neither one escapes the fatal law of being what he is. Neither one tries to shake off the weight of being. The greatest among men love glory, but not the glory of a personal immortality, just an abstract immortality, in which they don't necessarily participate.

These considerations, which occur to me frequently, prompt an admiration in me for a kind of person that by nature I abhor. I mean the mystics and ascetics – the recluses of all Tibets, the Simeon Stylites of all columns. These men, albeit by absurd means, do indeed try to escape the animal law. These men, although they act madly, do indeed reject the law of life by which others wallow in the sun and wait for death without thinking about it. They really seek, even if on top of a column; they yearn, even if in an unlit cell; they long for what they don't know, even if in the suffering and martyrdom they're condemned to.

The rest of us, living animal lives of varying complexity, 'cross the stage as walk-ons who don't speak, satisfied by the pompous solemnity of the crossing. Dogs and men, cats and heroes, fleas and geniuses – we all play at existing without thinking about it (the most advanced of us thinking only about thinking) under the vast stillness of the stars. The others – the mystics of pain and sacrifice – at least feel, in their body and their daily lives, the magic presence of mystery. They have escaped, for they reject the visible sun; they know plenitude, for they've emptied themselves of the world's nothingness.

Speaking about them, I almost feel like a mystic myself, though I know I could never be more than these words written whenever the whim hits me. I will always belong to the Rua dos Douradores, like all of humanity. I will always be, in verse or prose, an office employee.

I will always be, with or without mysticism, local and submissive, a servant of my feelings and of the moments when they occur. I will always be, under the large blue canopy of the silent sky, a pageboy in an unintelligible rite, dressed in life for the occasion, executing steps, gestures, stances and expressions without knowing why, until the feast – or my role in it – ends and I can treat myself to tidbits in the large tents I've been told are down below, at the back of the garden.

167

It's one of those days when the monotony of everything oppresses me like being thrown into jail. The monotony of everything is merely the monotony of myself, however. Each face, even if seen just yesterday, is different today, because today isn't yesterday. Each day is the day it is, and there was never another one like it in the world. Only our soul makes the identification – a genuinely felt but erroneous identification – by which everything becomes similar and simplified. The world is a set of distinct things with varied edges, but if we're near-sighted, it's a continual and indecipherable fog.

I feel like fleeing. Like fleeing from what I know, fleeing from what's mine, fleeing from what I love. I want to depart, not for impossible Indias or for the great islands south of everything, but for any place at all – village or wilderness – that isn't this place. I want to stop seeing these unchanging faces, this routine, these days. I want to rest, far removed, from my inveterate feigning. I want to feel sleep come to me as life, not as rest. A cabin on the seashore or even a cave in a rocky mountainside could give me this, but my will, unfortunately, cannot.

Slavery is the law of life, and it is the only law, for it must be observed: there is no revolt possible, no way to escape it. Some are born slaves, others become slaves, and still others are forced to accept slavery. Our faint-hearted love of freedom – which, if we had it, we would all reject, unable to get used to it – is proof of how ingrained our slavery is. I myself, having just said that I'd like a cabin or a cave where I could be free from the monotony of everything, which is the monotony of me – would I dare set out for this cabin or cave, knowing from experience that the monotony, since it stems from me, will always be with me? I myself, suffocating from where I am and because I am – where would I breathe easier, if the sickness is in my lungs rather than in the things that surround me? I myself, who long for pure sunlight and open country, for the ocean in plain view and the unbroken horizon – could I get used to my new bed, the food, not having to descend eight flights of stairs to the street, not entering the tobacco shop on the corner, not saying good-morning to the barber standing outside his shop?

Everything that surrounds us becomes part of us, infiltrating our physical sensations and our feeling of life, and like spittle of the great Spider it subtly binds us to whatever is close, tucking us into a soft bed of slow death which is rocked by the wind. Everything is us, and we are everything, but what good is this, if everything is nothing? A ray of sunlight, a cloud whose shadow tells us it is passing, a breeze that rises, the silence that follows when it ceases, one or another face, a few voices, the incidental laughter of the girls who are talking, and then night with the meaningless, fractured hieroglyphs of the stars.

168

. . . And I, who timidly hate life, fear death with fascination.* I fear this nothingness that could be something else, and I fear it as nothing and as something else simultaneously, as if gross horror and non-existence could coincide there, as if my coffin could entrap the eternal breathing of a bodily soul, as if immortality could be tormented by confinement. The idea of hell, which only a satanic soul could have invented, seems to me to have derived from this sort of confusion – a mixture of two different fears that contradict and contaminate each other.

169

Page by page I slowly and lucidly reread everything I've written, and I find that it's all worthless and should have been left unwritten. The things we achieve, whether empires or sentences, have (because they've been achieved) the worst aspect of real things: the fact they're perishable. But that's not what worries or grieves me about these pages as I reread them now, in these idle moments. What grieves me is that it wasn't worth my trouble to write them, and the time I spent doing it earned me nothing but the illusion, now shattered, that it was worth doing.

Whatever we pursue, we pursue for the sake of an ambition, but either we never realize the ambition, and we're poor, or we think we've realized it, and we're rich fools.

What grieves me is that my best is no good, and that another whom I dream of, if he existed, would have done it better. Everything we do, in art or in life, is the imperfect copy of what we thought of doing. It belies the notion of inner as well as of outer perfection; it falls short not only of the standard it should meet but also of the standard we thought it could meet. We're hollow on the inside as well as on the outside, pariahs in our expectations and in our realizations.

With what power of the solitary human soul I produced page after reclusive page, living syllable by syllable the false magic, not of what I wrote, but of what I thought I was writing! As if under an ironic sorcerer's spell, I imagined myself the poet of my prose, in the winged moments when it welled up in me – swifter than the strokes of my pen – like an illusory revenge against the insults of life! And today, rereading, I see my dolls bursting, the straw coming out of their torn seams, eviscerated without ever having been...

170

After the last rains went south, leaving only the wind that had chased them away, then the gladness of the sure sun returned to the city's hills, and hanging white laundry began to appear, flapping on the cords stretched across sticks outside the high windows of buildings of all colours.

I also felt happy, because I exist. I left my rented room with a great goal in mind, which was simply to get to the office on time. But on this particular day the compulsion to live participated in that other good compulsion which makes the sun come up at the times shown in the almanac, according to the latitude and longitude of each place on earth. I felt happy because I couldn't feel unhappy. I walked down the street without a care, full of certainty, because the office I work at and the people who work with me are, after all, certainties. It's no wonder that I felt free, without knowing from what. In the baskets along the pavement of the Rua da Prata, the bananas for sale were tremendously yellow in the sunlight.

It really takes very little to satisfy me: the rain having stopped, there being a bright sun in this happy South, bananas that are yellower for having black splotches, the voices of the people who sell them, the pavement of the Rua da Prata, the Tagus at the end of it, blue with a green-gold tint, this entire familiar corner of the universe.

The day will come when I see no more of this, when I'll be survived by the bananas lining the pavement, by the voices of the shrewd saleswomen, and by the daily papers that the boy has set out on the opposite corner of the street. I'm well aware that the bananas will be others, that the saleswomen will be others, and that the newspapers will show – to those who bend down to look at them – a different date from today's. But they, because they don't live, endure, although as others. I, because I live, pass on, although the same.

I could easily memorialize this moment by buying bananas, for the whole of today's sun seems to be focused on them like a searchlight without a source. But I'm embarrassed by rituals, by symbols, by buying in the street. They might not wrap the bananas the right way. They might not sell them to me as they should be sold, since I don't know how to buy them as they should be bought. They might find my voice strange when I ask the price. Better to write than to dare live, even if living means merely to buy bananas in the sunlight, as long as the sun lasts and there are bananas for sale.

Later, perhaps... Yes, later... Another, perhaps... Or perhaps not...

171

Only one thing astonishes me more than the stupidity with which most people live their lives, and that's the intelligence of this stupidity.

On the face of it, the monotony of ordinary lives is horrifying. In this simple restaurant where I'm eating lunch, I look at the figure of the cook behind the counter and at the old waiter, near my table, who serves me and who I believe has been a waiter here for thirty years. What kind of lives do these men lead? For forty years that figure of a man has spent most of every day in a kitchen; he doesn't get much time off; he sleeps relatively little; he occasionally goes to his home town, returning without hesitation or regret; he slowly saves his slowly earned money, which he has no plans to spend; he would get ill if he had to retire for good from his kitchen to the piece of land he bought in Galicia; he has been in Lisbon for forty years and has never yet gone to the Rotunda* or to a theatre, and just once to the circus at the Coliseum, whose clowns still inhabit his life's inner vestiges. He married – I don't know how or why – and has four sons and a daughter, and his smile, as he leans over the counter in my direction, expresses a tremendous, solemn, satisfied happiness. And he's not pretending, nor would he have reason to pretend. If he feels happy, it's because he really is.

And what of the old waiter who serves me and who has just set before me what must be the millionth coffee he's set on a customer's table? He has the same life as the cook, the only difference being the fifteen or twenty feet between the dining area and the kitchen, where they carry out their respective functions. As for the rest, the waiter has only two sons, goes more often to Galicia, has seen more of Lisbon than the cook, knows Oporto, where he spent four years, and is equally happy.

It shocks me to consider the panorama of these lives, but before I can feel horror, pity and indignation on their account, it occurs to me that those who feel no horror or pity or indignation are the very ones who would have every right to – namely, the people who live these lives. It's the central error of the literary imagination: to suppose that others are like us and must feel as we do. Fortunately for humanity, each man is just who he is, it being given only to the genius to be a few others as well.

What's given, in fact, always depends on the person or thing it's given to. A minor incident in the street brings the cook to the door and entertains him more than I would be entertained by contemplating the most original idea, by reading the greatest book, or by having the most gratifying of useless dreams. If life is basically monotony, he has escaped it more than I. And he escapes it more easily than I. The truth isn't with him or with me, because it isn't with anyone, but happiness does belong to him.

Wise is the man who monotonizes his existence, for then each minor incident seems a marvel. A hunter of lions feels no adventure after the third lion. For my monotonous cook, a fist-fight on the street always has something of a modest apocalypse. One who has never been outside Lisbon travels to the infinite in the tram to Benfica,* and should he ever go to Sintra,* he'll feel as though he's been to Mars. The man who has journeyed all over the world can't find any novelty in five thousand miles, for he finds only new things – yet another novelty, the old routine of the forever new – while his abstract concept of novelty got lost at sea after the second new thing he saw.

A man of true wisdom, with nothing but his senses and a soul that's never sad, can enjoy the entire spectacle of the world from a chair, without knowing how to read and without talking to anyone.

Monotonizing existence, so that it won't be monotonous. Making daily life anodyne, so that the littlest thing will amuse. My days at the office, where I always do the very same dull and useless work, are punctuated by visions of me escaping, by dreamed remnants of faraway islands, by feasts in the promenades of parks from other eras, by other landscapes, other feelings, another I. But I realize, between two ledger entries, that if I had all this, none of it would be mine. Better, after all, to have Vasques my boss than the kings of my dreams; better, after all, the office on Rua dos Douradores than the grand promenades of impossible parks. Having Vasques as my boss, I can enjoy dreaming of kings; having the office on Rua dos Douradores, I can enjoy the inner vision of non-existent landscapes. But if I had the kings of my dreams, what would I have left to dream? If I had impossible landscapes, what other impossibilities would remain for me to imagine?

Give me monotony – the dull repetition of the same old days, today an exact copy of yesterday – while my observant soul enjoys the fly that flits past my eyes and distracts me, the laughter that drifts up from I'm not sure which street, the liberation I feel when it's time to close the office, and the infinite repose of a day off.

I can imagine that I'm everything, because I'm nothing. If I were something, I wouldn't be able to imagine. An assistant bookkeeper can dream he is the Roman emperor, but the King of England cannot, for in his dreams the King of England is precluded from being any king other than the one he is. His reality won't let him feel.*

172

The slope leads to the mill, but effort leads to nothing.

It was an early autumn afternoon, when the sky has a cold, dead warmth, and clouds smother the light with blankets of moisture.

Destiny gave me only two things: accounting ledgers and a talent for dreaming.

173

Dreaming is the worst of drugs, because it's the most natural of all. It works its way into our habits like no other drug can. We take it unawares, like a poison slipped in a drink. It doesn't hurt, doesn't make you pale, and won't knock you out, but the soul that takes it can't be cured, for it can never let go of its poison, which is its very own self.

Like a pageant in the mist . . . . .

In dreams I learned to crown the □ foreheads of the ordinary with images; to say the banal with mystery and the simple with meanders; to gild, with the sun of artifice, the dark corners and forgotten furniture; and, whenever I write, to give music (as if lulling myself) to the fluid phrases of my fixation.

174

After a bad night's sleep, nobody likes us. The sleep which deserted us took with it something that made us human. We feel a latent irritation that even seems to imbue the inorganic air around us. It's we, after all, who deserted ourselves; it's between us and us that the silent battle of diplomacy is fought.

Today I've dragged my feet and heavy fatigue through the streets. My soul has been reduced to a tied-up ball of thread, and what I am and have been, which is me, forgot its name. I don't know if I'll have a tomorrow. All I know is that I didn't sleep, and the confusion I feel at certain moments imposes long silences on my internal speech.

Ah, the huge parks enjoyed by others, the gardens familiar to so many, the tree-lined paths where people who will never know me walk! I stagnate between sleepless nights, as one who never dared to be superficial, and my meditation is startled awake like a dream when it ends.

I'm a widowed house, cloistered in itself, haunted by shy and furtive ghosts. I'm always in the next room, or they are, and trees loudly rustle all around me. I wander and find; I find because I wander. Ah, it's you, my childhood days, dressed up in pinafores!

And during all of this I walk down the street, a wandering sleepyhead, a stray leaf. Some slow wind has swept me off the ground and I drift, like the end of twilight, among the details of the landscape. My eyelids weigh heavy on my dragging feet. Because I'm walking I feel like sleeping. My mouth is shut as if to seal my lips. I walk the way a ship sinks.

No, I didn't sleep, but I'm more myself when I haven't slept and still can't sleep. I'm truly I in the incidental and symbolic eternity of this half-souled state in which I delude myself. One or two people look at me as if they knew me and found me strange. I'm vaguely aware of looking back at them, with eyes I can feel under the eyelids that rub against their surface, but I'd rather not know about the world's existence.

I'm sleepy, very sleepy, totally sleepy!

175

The generation I belong to was born into a world where those with a brain as well as a heart couldn't find any support. The destructive work of previous generations left us a world that offered no security in the religious sphere, no guidance in the moral sphere, and no tranquillity in the political sphere. We were born into the midst of metaphysical anguish, moral anxiety and political disquiet. Inebriated with objective formulas, with the mere methods of reason and science, the generations that preceded us did away with the foundations of the Christian faith, for their biblical criticism – progressing from textual to mythological criticism – reduced the gospels and the earlier scriptures of the Jews to a doubtful heap of myths, legends and mere literature, while their scientific criticism gradually revealed the mistakes and ingenuous notions of the gospels' primitive 'science'. At the same time, the spirit of free inquiry brought all metaphysical problems out into the open, and with them all the religious problems that had to do with metaphysics. Drunk with a hazy notion they called 'positivism', these generations criticized all morality and scrutinized all rules of life, and all that remained from the clash of doctrines was the certainty of none of them and the grief over there being no certainty. A society so undisciplined in its cultural foundations could obviously not help but be a victim, politically, of its own chaos, and so we woke up to a world eager for social innovations, a world that gleefully pursued a freedom it didn't grasp and a progress it had never defined.

But while the sloppy criticism of our fathers bequeathed us the impossibility of being Christians, it didn't bequeath us an acceptance of the impossibility; while it bequeathed us a disbelief in established moral codes, it didn't bequeath us an indifference to morality and the rules for peaceful human coexistence; while it left the thorny problem of politics in doubt, it didn't leave our minds unconcerned about how to solve it. Our fathers blithely wreaked destruction, for they lived in a time that was still informed by the solidity of the past. The very thing they destroyed was what gave strength to society and enabled them to destroy without noticing that the building was cracking. We inherited the destruction and its aftermath.

Today the world belongs only to the stupid, the insensitive and the agitated. Today the right to live and triumph is awarded on virtually the same basis as admission into an insane asylum: an inability to think, amorality, and nervous excitability.

176

The Inn of Reason

On the road halfway between faith and criticism stands the inn of reason. Reason is faith in what can be understood without faith, but it's still a faith, since to understand presupposes that there's something understandable.

177

Metaphysical theories that can give us the momentary illusion that we've explained the unexplainable; moral theories that can fool us for an hour into thinking we finally know which of all the closed doors leads to virtue; political theories that convince us for a day that we've solved some problem, when there are no solvable problems except in mathematics. . . May our attitude towards life be summed up in this consciously futile activity, in this preoccupation that gives no pleasure but at least keeps us from feeling the presence of pain.

There's no better sign that a civilization has reached its height than the awareness, in its members, of the futility of all effort, given that we're ruled by implacable laws, which nothing can repeal or obstruct. We may be slaves shackled to the whim of gods who are stronger than us, but they're not any better, being subject – like us – to the iron hand of an abstract Fate, which is superior to justice and kindness, indifferent to good and evil.

178

We are death. What we call life is the slumber of our real life, the death of what we really are. The dead are born, they don't die. The worlds are switched around in our eyes. We're dead when we think we're living; we start living when we die.

The relation that exists between sleep and life is the same that exists between what we call life and what we call death. We're sleeping, and this life is a dream, not in a metaphorical or poetic sense, but in a very real sense.

Everything in our activities that we hold to be superior participates in death and is death. What are ideals but an admission that life is worthless? What is art but the negation of life? A statue is a dead body, chiselled to capture death in incorruptible matter. Pleasure itself, which seems to be an immersion in life, is in fact an immersion in ourselves, a destruction of the relations between us and life, an excited shadow of death.

The very act of living means dying, since with each day we live, we have one less day of life remaining.

We inhabit dreams, we are shadows roaming through impossible forests, in which the trees are houses, customs, ideas, ideals and philosophies.

Never finding God, and never even knowing if God exists! Passing from world to world, from incarnation to incarnation, forever coddled by illusion, forever caressed by error...

Never arriving at Truth, and never resting! Never reaching union with God! Never completely at peace but always with a hint of peace, always with a longing for it!

179

There's a childish instinct in humanity that makes the proudest among us, if he's a man and not crazy, long – Blessed Father! – for the paternal hand that would guide us, in whatever shape or form as long as it guides us, through the world's mystery and confusion. Each of us is a speck of dust that the wind of life lifts up and then drops. We have to depend on a stronger force, to place our small hand in another hand, for today is always uncertain, the sky always far, and life always alien.

Those of us who have risen highest merely have a deeper awareness of how uncertain and empty everything is.

Perhaps we're guided by an illusion; we're surely not guided by consciousness.

180

If one day I become financially secure, so that I can freely write and publish, I know I'll miss this precarious life in which I hardly write and don't publish at all. I'll miss it not only because it will be a life, however mediocre, that I'll never have again, but also because every sort of life has a special quality and particular pleasure, and when we take up another life, even a better one, that particular pleasure isn't as good, that special quality is less special, until they fade away, and there's something missing.

If one day I succeed in carrying the cross of my intention to the good Calvary, I'll find another calvary on that good Calvary, and I'll miss the time when I was futile, mediocre and imperfect. I will in some sense be less.

I'm tired. I had a long day full of idiotic work in this almost deserted office. Two employees are out sick and the others aren't here. I'm alone, except for the office boy in the back. I miss the future when I'll be able to look back and miss all of this, however absurdly.

I'm tempted to ask whatever gods there be to keep me here, as if in a strong-box, safe from life's sorrows as well as its joys.

181

In the faint shadows cast by the last light before evening gives way to night, I like to roam unthinkingly through what the city is changing into, and I walk as if nothing had a cure. I carry with me a vague sadness that's pleasant to my imagination, less so to my senses. As my feet wander I inwardly skim, without reading, a book of text interspersed with swift images, from which I leisurely form an idea that's never completed.

There are those who read as swiftly as they see, and they finish without having taken it all in. So I, from the book skimmed in my soul, glean a hazy story, remembrances of another wanderer, snatches of descriptions of twilights or moonlights, with garden paths in the middle, and various silk figures passing by, passing by. . .

I don't discriminate between one and another tedium. I move along in the street, in the evening and in my dreamed reading all at the same time, and the roads are really travelled. I emigrate and rest, as if aboard a ship that's already on the high sea.

Suddenly the dead street lamps light up in unison on the two extensions of the long curved street. My sadness increases, as if with a thud. The book has finished. In the viscous air of the abstract street there is only an external thread of feeling, like the slobber of an idiot Destiny, dripping on my soul's consciousness.

Another life, of the city at nightfall. Another soul, of one who watches the night. I walk uncertainly and allegorically, unreally sentient. I'm like a story that someone told, and so well was it told that I took on just a hint of flesh at the beginning of one of the chapters of this novel that's the world: 'At that moment a man could be seen walking slowly down So-and-so Street.'

What do I have to do with life?

182

Interlude

I bowed out of life before it began, for not even in dreams did I find it attractive. Dreams themselves wearied me, and this brought me a false, external sensation, as of having come to the end of an infinite road. I overflowed from myself to end up I don't know where, and that's where I've uselessly stagnated. I'm something that I used to be. I'm never where I feel I am, and if I seek myself, I don't know who's seeking me. My boredom with everything has numbed me. I feel banished from my soul.

I observe myself. I'm my own spectator. My sensations pass, like external things, before I don't know what gaze of mine. I bore myself no matter what I do. All things, down to their roots in mystery, have the colour of my boredom.

The flowers Time gave me were already wilted. The only thing I can do is pluck their petals slowly. And this is so fraught with old age!

The slightest action weighs on me like a heroic deed. The mere idea of a gesture wearies me, as if it were something I actually thought of doing.

I aspire to nothing. Life hurts me. I'm not well where I am nor anywhere else I can think of being.

What would be ideal is to have no more action than the false action of a fountain – to go up so as to fall down in the same place, pointlessly shimmering in the sun and making sound in the silence of the night so that whoever dreams would think of rivers in his dream and smile forgetfully.

183

Since the dull beginning of the hot, deceitful day, dark clouds with jagged edges had been ranging over the oppressed city. Towards the estuary they were grimly piled one on top the other, and as they spread, so did a forewarning of tragedy, in the streets' vague rancour against the altered sun.

At midday, when we left for lunch, a dire expectation hung in the pallid atmosphere. Shreds of tattered clouds were growing blacker in the foreground. Towards the Castle the sky was clear but with something ominous in its blue. The sun was out but it wasn't enticing.

When we returned to the office, at half-past one, the sky seemed clearer, but only over one of the older parts of town, towards the estuary, where there was indeed more visibility. On the city's northern side, the clouds slowly coalesced into just one cloud, black and implacable, creeping forward with blunted grey-white claws at the ends of its black arms. Soon it would reach the sun, and the usual city noises seemed to hush, as if waiting. Towards the east the sky was somewhat clearer, or seemed so, but the heat had become even more unpleasant. We sweated in the shadows of the large office. 'A huge thunderstorm is on its way,' said Moreira, and he turned the page of the ledger.

By three o'clock the sun had ceased being functional. It was necessary to switch on the lights (which was depressing, for it was summer), first at the back of the office, where goods were being wrapped for shipping, and then in the middle, where it was getting hard to fill out the delivery notes and to mark down the numbers of the railroad vouchers. Finally, close to four o'clock, even those of us privileged to have windows could no longer see well enough to work. The whole office was electrically lit up. Senhor Vasques threw open the door to his private office and said, 'Moreira, I was supposed to go to Benfica,* but there's no way – it's going to pour.' 'And it's coming from that direction,' answered Moreira, who lived near the Avenida.* The noises from the street, suddenly loud and clear, were somewhat altered. And I don't know why, but the bells from the trams one block over sounded sad.

184

Before summer ends and autumn arrives, in the warm interim when the air weighs heavy and the colours dim, the late afternoons wear an almost tangible robe of imitation glory. They're comparable to those tricks of the imagination, when it makes nostalgia out of nothing, and they go on indefinitely, like the wakes of ships that form never-ending snakes.

These late afternoons fill me, like a sea at high tide, with a feeling worse than tedium but for which there's no other name. It's a feeling of desolation I'm unable to pinpoint, a shipwreck of my entire soul. I feel as if I'd lost a benevolent God, as if the Substance of everything had died. And the physical universe is like a corpse that I loved when it was life, but it has all dissolved to nothing in the still warm light of the last coloured clouds.

My tedium takes on an air of horror, and my boredom is a fear. My sweat isn't cold, but my awareness of it is. I'm not physically ill, but my soul's anxiety is so intense that it passes through my pores and chills my body.

So great is this tedium, so sovereign my horror of being alive, that I can't conceive of anything that might serve as a palliative, antidote, balsam or distraction for it. Sleeping horrifies me the way everything does. Dying is as horrifying as everything else. Going and stopping are the same impossible thing. Hope and doubt are equally cold and grey. I'm a shelf of empty jars.

And yet what nostalgia for the future* if I let my ordinary eyes receive the dead salutation of the declining day! How grand is hope's burial, advancing in the still golden hush of the stagnant skies! What a procession of voids and nothings extends over the reddish blue that will pale in the vast expanses of crystalline space!

I don't know what I want or don't want. I've stopped wanting, stopped knowing how to want, stopped knowing the emotions or thoughts by which people generally recognize that they want something or want to want it. I don't know who I am or what I am. Like someone buried under a collapsed wall, I lie under the toppled vacuity of the entire universe. And so I go on, in the wake of myself, until the night sets in and a little of the comfort of being different wafts, like a breeze, over my incipient self-unawareness.*

Ah, the high and larger moon of these placid nights, torpid with anguish and disquiet! Sinister peace of the heavens' beauty, cold irony of the warm air, blue blackness misted by moonlight and reticent to reveal stars.

185

INTERLUDE

This dreadful hour when I shrink to being possible or rise to mortality.

If only the morning wouldn't dawn. If only I and this alcove and its interior atmosphere where I belong could all be spiritualized into Night, absolutized into Darkness, so that not so much as a shadow of me would remain that could taint, with my memory, whatever lived on.

186

Would to the gods, sad heart of mine, that Fate had a meaning! Would to Fate, rather, that the gods had one!

Sometimes, when I wake up at night, I feel invisible hands weaving my destiny.

Here lies my life. Nothing in me disturbs a thing.

187

My life's central tragedy is, like all tragedies, an irony of Fate. I reject real life for being a condemnation; I reject dreaming for being an easy way out. But my real life couldn't be more banal and contemptible, and my dream life couldn't be more constant and intense. I'm like a slave who gets drunk during siesta – two degradations in one body.

Yes, I distinctly see – with the clarity of reason when it flashes in the blackness of life and isolates the objects around us that make it up – all that is shoddy, worn-out, neglected and spurious in this street called Douradores which is my entire life: this office that's sordid down to the marrow of its employees, this monthly rented room where nothing transpires but a dead man's life, this corner grocery whose owner I know in the way people know each other, these young men at the door of the old tavern, this toilsome uselessness of the unchanging days, these same characters repeating their same old lines, like a drama consisting only of secrecy, and with the scenery turned inside out...

But I also realize that to flee this would mean to overcome it or repudiate it, and I'll never overcome it, because I don't go beyond it in reality, and I'll never repudiate it, because no matter what I dream, I always remain where I am.

And my dreaming! The disgrace of escaping into myself, the cowardice of reducing my life to that refuse of the soul which others experience only in their sleep, in the posture of death as they snore, in that stillness when they look like highly developed vegetables!

I can't make one noble gesture that's not confined to my own soul, nor have one useless desire that's not truly, utterly useless!

Caesar aptly defined what ambition is all about when he said: 'Better to be first in the village than the second in Rome!' I'm nothing in the village and nothing in any Rome. The corner grocer is at least respected from the Rua da Assunção to the Rua da Vitória; he's the Caesar of a square city block. Me superior to him? In what, if nothingness admits neither superiority nor inferiority, nor even comparison?

He is Caesar of an entire square block, and it's only right that all the women like him.

And so I drag myself to do what I don't want and to dream what I can't have, my life . . . . . , as meaningless as a broken public clock.

My hazy but constant sensibility and my long but conscious dream ☐ which together form my privilege of a life in the shadows.

188

The ordinary man, however hard his life may be, at least has the pleasure of not thinking about it. To take life as it comes, living it externally like a cat or a dog – that is how people in general live, and that is how life should be lived, if we would have the contentment of the cat or dog.

To think is to destroy. Thought itself is destroyed in the process of thinking, because to think is to decompose. If men knew how to meditate on the mystery of life, if they knew how to feel the thousand complexities which spy on the soul in every single detail of action, then they would never act – they wouldn't even live. They would kill themselves from fright, like those who commit suicide to avoid being guillotined the next day.

189

Rainy Day

The air is a veiled yellow, like a pale yellow seen through a dirty white. There's scarcely any yellow in the grey air, but the paleness of the grey has a yellow in its sadness.

190

Any change in one's usual routine is always received by the spirit as a chilly novelty, a slightly uncomfortable pleasure. Anyone who leaves the office at five o'clock when he's in the habit of leaving at six is bound to experience a mental holiday, and a feeling like regret for not knowing what to do with himself.

Yesterday I left the office at four, as I had to take care of some business far away, and by five o'clock I was through with it. I'm not used to being out on the streets at that hour, and I found that I was in a different city. The soft light on the usual façades was uselessly tranquil, and the usual pedestrians passed by in the city next to me, like sailors who'd disembarked from last night's ship.

I returned to the office, which was still open, and my colleagues were naturally astonished, as I'd already bid farewell for the day. What? You're back? Yes, I'm back. There, all alone with those familiar faces who don't exist for me spiritually, I was free from having to feel. It was in a certain sense home – the place, that is, where one doesn't feel.

191

It sometimes occurs to me, with sad delight, that if one day (in a future to which I won't belong) the sentences I write are read and admired, then at last I'll have my own kin, people who 'understand' me, my true family in which to be born and loved. But far from being born into it, I'll have already died long ago. I'll be understood only in effigy, when affection can no longer compensate for the indifference that was the dead man's lot in life.

Perhaps one day they'll understand that I fulfilled, like no one else, my instinctive duty to interpret a portion of our century; and when they've understood that, they'll write that in my time I was misunderstood, that the people around me were unfortunately indifferent and insensitive to my work, and that it was a pity this happened to me. And whoever writes this will fail to understand my literary counterpart in that future time, just as my contemporaries don't understand me. Because men learn only what would be of use to their great-grandparents. The right way to live is something we can teach only the dead.

On the afternoon in which I write, the rain has finally let up. A gladness in the air feels almost too cool against the skin. The day is ending not in grey but in pale blue. A hazy blue is even reflecting off the stones of the street. It hurts to live, but the pain is remote. Feeling doesn't matter. One or another shop window lights up. In a window higher up, there are people looking down at the workers who are finishing up for the day. The beggar who brushes my shoulder would be shocked if he knew me.

The indefinite hour grows yet a little later in the now less pale and less blue blueness mirrored in the buildings.

Fall gently final hour of this day in which those who believe and are mistaken engage in their usual labours with the joy of unconsciousness, even in their pain. Fall gently, final wave of light, melancholy of this useless afternoon, fogless haze that seeps into my heart. Fall gently and lightly, shimmering blue paleness of this aquatic afternoon – gently, lightly, sadly over the cold and simple earth. Fall gently, invisible grey, embittered monotony, sleepless tedium.

192

During three straight days of heat without let-up, a storm lurked in the anxious stillness until finally drifting elsewhere, and then a gentle, almost cool warmth arrived to soothe the bright surface of things. So too, it sometimes happens in life that a soul weighed down by living suddenly feels relief, for no apparent reason.

I see us as climates over which storms threaten, before breaking elsewhere.

The empty immensity of things, the tremendous oblivion in the sky and on earth. . .

193

I've witnessed, incognito, the gradual collapse of my life, the slow foundering of all that I wanted to be. I can say, with a truth that needs no flowers to show it's dead, that there's nothing I've wanted – and nothing in which I've placed, even for a moment, the dream of only that moment – that hasn't disintegrated below my windows like a clod of dirt that resembled stone until it fell from a flowerpot on a high balcony. It would even seem that Fate has always tried to make me love or want things just so that it could show me, on the very next day, that I didn't have and could never have them.

But as an ironic spectator of myself, I've never lost interest in seeing what life brings. And since I now know beforehand that every vague hope will end in disillusion, I have the special delight of already enjoying the disillusion with the hope, like the bitter with the sweet that makes the sweet sweeter by way of contrast. I'm a sullen strategist who, having never won a battle, has learned to derive pleasure from mapping out the details of his inevitable retreat on the eve of each new engagement.

My destiny, which has pursued me like a malevolent creature, is to be able to desire only what I know I'll never get. If I see the nubile figure of a girl in the street and imagine for the slightest moment, however nonchalantly, what it would be like if she were mine, it's a dead certainty that ten steps past my dream she'll meet the man who's obviously her husband or lover. A romantic would make a tragedy out of this; a stranger to the situation would see it as a comedy; I, however, mix the two things, since I'm romantic in myself and a stranger to myself, and I turn the page to yet another irony.

Some say that without hope life is impossible, others that with hope it's empty. For me, since I've stopped hoping or not hoping, life is simply an external picture that includes me and that I look at, like a show without a plot, made only to please the eyes – an incoherent dance, a rustling of leaves in the wind, clouds in which the sunlight changes colour, ancient streets that wind every which way around the city.

I am, in large measure, the selfsame prose I write. I unroll myself in sentences and paragraphs, I punctuate myself. In my arranging and rearranging of images I'm like a child using newspaper to dress up as a king, and in the way I create rhythm with a series of words I'm like a lunatic adorning my hair with dried flowers that are still alive in my dreams. And above all I'm calm, like a rag doll that has become conscious of itself and occasionally shakes its head to make the tiny bell on top of its pointed cap (a component part of the same head) produce a sound, the jingling life of a dead man, a feeble notice to Fate.

But how often, in the middle of this peaceful dissatisfaction, my conscious emotion is slowly filled with a feeling of emptiness and tedium for thinking this way! How often I feel, as if hearing a voice behind intermittent sounds, that I myself am the underlying bitterness of this life so alien to human life – a life in which nothing happens except in its self-awareness! How often, waking up for a moment from this exile that's me, I get a glimpse of how much better it would be to be a complete nobody, the happy man who at least has real bitterness, the contented man who feels fatigue instead of tedium, who suffers instead of imagining he suffers, who kills himself, yes, instead of watching himself die!

I've made myself into the character of a book, a life one reads. Whatever I feel is felt (against my will) so that I can write that I felt it. Whatever I think is promptly put into words, mixed with images that undo it, cast into rhythms that are something else altogether. From so much self-revising, I've destroyed myself. From so much self-thinking, I'm now my thoughts and not I. I plumbed myself and dropped the plumb; I spend my life wondering if I'm deep or not, with no remaining plumb except my gaze that shows me – blackly vivid in the mirror at the bottom of the well – my own face that observes me observing it.

I'm like a playing card belonging to an old and unrecognizable suit – the sole survivor of a lost deck. I have no meaning, I don't know my worth, there's nothing I can compare myself with to discover what I am, and to make such a discovery would be of no use to anyone. And so, describing myself in image after image – not without truth, but with lies mixed in – I end up more in the images than in me, stating myself until I no longer exist, writing with my soul for ink, useful for nothing except writing. But the reaction ceases, and again I resign myself. I go back to whom I am, even if it's nothing. And a hint of tears that weren't cried makes my stiff eyes burn; a hint of anguish that wasn't felt gets caught in my dry throat. But I don't even know what I would have cried over, if I'd cried, nor why it is that I didn't cry over it. The fiction follows me, like my shadow. And what I want is to sleep.

194

A terrible weariness fills the soul of my heart. I feel sad because of whom I never was, and I don't know with what kind of nostalgia I miss him. I fell, with every sunset, against my hopes and certainties.

195

There are people who truly suffer because they weren't able, in real life, to live with Mr Pickwick or to shake Mr Wardle's hand. I'm one of those people. I've wept genuine tears over that novel, for not having lived in that time and with those people, real people.

The disasters of novels are always beautiful, because the blood in them isn't real blood and those who die in them don't rot, nor is rottenness rotten in novels.

When Mr Pickwick is ridiculous he's not ridiculous, for it all happens in a novel. Perhaps the novel is a more perfect life and reality, which God creates through us. Perhaps we live only to create it. It seems that civilizations exist only to produce art and literature; words are what speak for them and remain. How do we know that these extra-human figures aren't truly real? It tortures my mind to think this might be the case. . .

196

The feelings that hurt most, the emotions that sting most, are those that are absurd: the longing for impossible things, precisely because they are impossible; nostalgia for what never was; the desire for what could have been; regret over not being someone else; dissatisfaction with the world's existence. All these half-tones of the soul's consciousness create in us a painful landscape, an eternal sunset of what we are. The sensation we come to have of ourselves is of a deserted field at dusk, sad with reeds next to a river without boats, its glistening waters blackening between wide banks.

I don't know if these feelings are a slow madness born of disconsolation or if they're reminiscences of some other world in which we've lived – jumbled, criss-crossing remembrances, like things seen in dreams, absurd in the form they come to us but not in their origin, if we knew what it was. I don't know if we weren't in fact other beings, whose greater completeness we can sense today, incompletely, forming at best a sketchy notion of their lost solidity in the two dimensions of our present lives, mere shadows of what they were.

I know these thoughts of the emotion ache bitterly in the soul. Our inability to conceive of anything they could correspond to, the impossibility of finding a substitute for what they embrace in our imagination – all of this weighs like a harsh sentence handed down no one knows where, or by whom, or why.

But what remains from feeling all this is an inevitable disaffection with life and all its gestures, a foretasted weariness of all desires in all their manifestations, a generic distaste for all feelings. In these times of acute grief, it is impossible – even in dreams – to be a lover, to be a hero, to be happy. All of this is empty, even in our idea of what it is. It's all spoken in another language that we can't grasp – mere nonsense syllables to our understanding. Life is hollow, the soul hollow, the world hollow. All gods die a death greater than death. All is emptier than the void. All is a chaos of things that are nothing.

If, on thinking this, I look up to see if reality can quench my thirst, I see inexpressive façades, inexpressive faces, inexpressive gestures. Stones, bodies, ideas – all dead. All movements are one great standstill. Nothing means anything to me. Nothing is known to me, not because it's unfamiliar but because I don't know what it is. The world has slipped away. And in the bottom of my soul – as the only reality of this moment – there's an intense and invisible grief, a sadness like the sound of someone crying in a dark room.

197

I sorely grieve over time's passage. It's always with exaggerated emotion that I leave something behind, whatever it may be. The miserable rented room where I lived for a few months, the dinner table at the provincial hotel where I stayed for six days, even the sad waiting room at the station where I spent two hours waiting for a train – yes, their loss grieves me. But the special things of life – when I leave them behind and realize with all of my nerves' sensibility that I'll never see or have them again, at least not in that exact same moment – grieve me metaphysically. A chasm opens up in my soul and a cold breeze of the hour of God blows across my pallid face.

Time! The past! Something – a voice, a song, a chance fragrance – lifts the curtain on my soul's memories. . . That which I was and will never again be! That which I had and will never again have! The dead! The dead who loved me in my childhood. Whenever I remember them, my whole soul shivers and I feel exiled from all hearts, alone in the night of myself, weeping like a beggar before the closed silence of all doors.

198

Holiday Notes

The small cove with its small beach, cut off from the world by two miniature promontories, was my retreat from myself during those three days of holiday. The beach was reached by a crudely built stairway that began with wooden steps at the top and continued, halfway down, with steps cut directly into the rock, with a rusty iron handrail for support. And each time I went down that old stairway, and especially on the part made of stone, I stepped out of my own existence and found myself.

Occultists say (or at least some of them do) that the soul has supreme moments when it recalls, with the emotions or with some part of memory, a moment or an aspect or a shadow from a previous incarnation. And since the soul returns to a time that is closer than the present to the beginning and origin of things, it experiences a sensation of childhood and of liberation.

In descending that now little-used stairway and slowly stepping out on to the forever deserted beach, it was as if I were using some magical technique to find myself nearer the monad that I perhaps am. Certain aspects and characteristics of my daily existence – represented in my normal self by desires, aversions, worries – vanished from me like fugitives from the law, fading into the shadows beyond recognition, and I attained a state of inward distance in which it was hard to remember yesterday or to believe that the self who lives in me day after day really belongs to me. My usual emotions, my regularly irregular habits, my conversations with others, my adaptations to the world's social order – all of this seemed like things I'd read somewhere, like inert pages of a published biography, or details from some novel, in one of the middle chapters we read while thinking about something else, and the story-line slackens until it finally slithers away on the ground.

There on the beach, with no sound but that of the ocean waves and of the wind passing high overhead, like a large invisible aeroplane, I experienced dreams of a new sort – soft and shapeless things, marvels that made a deep impression, without images or emotions, clear like the sky and the water, and reverberating like the white whorls of ocean rising up from the depths of a vast truth: a tremulously slanting blue in the distance that acquired glistening, muddy-green hues as it approached, breaking with a great hissing its thousand crashing arms to scatter them over darkish sand where they left dry foam, and then gathering into itself all undertows, all return journeys to that original freedom, all nostalgias for God, all memories (like this one, shapeless and painless) of a prior state, blissful because it was so good or because it was different, a body made of nostalgia with a soul of foam, repose, death, the everything or the nothingness which – like a huge ocean – surrounds the island of castaways that is life.

And I slept without sleeping, already straying from what I'd seen through my feelings, a twilight of myself, a ripple of water among trees, the peace of wide rivers, the coolness of sad evenings, the slow panting in the white breast of the childhood sleep of contemplation.

199

The sweetness of having neither family nor companions, that pleasant taste as of exile, in which the pride of the expatriate subdues with a strange sensuality our vague anxiety about being far from home – all of this I enjoy in my own way, indifferently. Because one of the tenets of my mental attitude is that our attention to what we feel shouldn't be unduly cultivated, and even dreams should be regarded with condescension, with an aristocratic awareness that they couldn't exist without us. To give too much importance to a dream would be to give too much importance to something which, after all, broke away from us and set itself up as reality, at least as far as it could, thereby losing its right to special treatment from us.

200

Commonness is a hearthstone. Banality is a mother's lap. After a long incursion into lofty poetry, up to the heights of sublime yearning, to the cliffs of the transcendent and the occult, it tastes better than good, it feels like all that is warm in life, to return to the inn with its happily laughing fools and to drink with them as one more fool, as God made us, content with the universe we were given and leaving the rest to those who climb mountains to do nothing at the top.

I'm not impressed should someone tell me that a certain man I consider crazy or stupid surpasses a common man in many achievements and particulars of life. Epileptics have amazing strength when they go into seizure; paranoiacs have an ability to reason that few normal men can match; religious maniacs bring multitudes of believers together as few (if any) demagogues can, and with a force of conviction that the latter can't inspire in their followers. And all that this proves is that craziness is craziness. I prefer a defeat that knows the beauty of flowers to a victory in the desert, full of blindness in the soul, alone with its isolated nothingness.

How often even my futile dreaming makes me loathe my inner life and feel physically nauseated by mysticisms and contemplations. How quickly I then race from my apartment where I dream to the office, and when I see the face of Moreira it's as if I had finally docked at a port. When all is said and done, I prefer Moreira to the astral world; I prefer reality to truth; I prefer life, yes, to the very God who created it. Since this is the life he gave me, this is the life I'll live. I dream because I dream, but I don't suffer the indignity of considering my dreams anything more than my personal theatre, even as I don't consider wine – though I enjoy drinking it – to be a source of nourishment or a vital necessity.

201

Since early morning and against the solar custom of this bright city, the fog had wrapped a weightless mantle (which the sun slowly gilded) around the rows of houses, the cancelled open spaces, and the shifting heights of land and of buildings. But as the hours advanced towards midday, the gentle mist began to unravel until, with breaths like flapping shadows of veils, it expired altogether. By ten o'clock, the tenuous blueing of the sky was the only evidence that there had been fog.

The city's features were reborn once the blurry mask slipped away. As if a window had been opened, the already dawned day dawned. There was a slight change in all the sounds, which had also suddenly returned. A blue tint infiltrated even the stones of the streets and the impersonal auras of pedestrians. The sun was warm, but still humidly so, filtered by the vanished fog.

The awakening of a city, with or without fog, moves me far more than the breaking of dawn in the country. It's much more of a rebirth, there's much more to look forward to, when the sun – instead of just gilding the grasses, the shrubs' silhouettes and the trees' countless green hands with its murky, then moist, and finally luminously gold light – multiplies its possible effects on windows (in myriad reflections), walls (painting them different colours) and rooftops (shading each one uniquely) to make a glorious morning absolutely distinct from so many other distinctive realities. A dawning in the country does me good; a dawning in the city good and bad, and so it does me more than just good. Yes, because the greater hope it stirs in me has, like all hopes, that slightly bitter, nostalgic taste of not being reality. The country morning exists; the city morning promises. The former makes one live; the latter makes one think. And I'm doomed always to feel, like the world's great damned men, that it's better to think than to live.

202

After the heat began to wane at summer's end, it sometimes happened in late afternoon that certain softer hues in the broad sky and certain strokes of cold breezes already signalled the coming of autumn. There was still no discolouring or falling of leaves, nor yet that vague anxiety we naturally feel when we see death all around us, since we know ours will also come. But there was a sort of flagging of all effort, a vague slumber fallen over the last signs of action. Ah, with so much sad indifference in these afternoons, the autumn begins in us before it begins in things.

Each new autumn is closer to the last autumn we'll have, and the same is true of spring or summer; but autumn, by its nature, reminds us that all things will end, which is something we're apt to forget when we look around us in spring or summer.

It's still not autumn, there's still no yellow of fallen leaves in the air, still none of that damp sadness that marks the weather when it's on its way to becoming winter. But there is a hint of expected sadness – a sorrow dressed for the journey – in our hazy awareness of colours being smattered, of the wind's different sound, of that ancient stillness which spreads in the falling night across the ineluctable presence of the universe.

Yes, we will all pass, we will pass everything. Nothing will remain of the man who wore feelings and gloves, who talked about death and local politics. Just as one and the same light illumines the faces of saints and the gaiters of pedestrians, so too the same lack of light will cause darkness to engulf the nothing that remains of some having been saints and others having used gaiters. In the vast whirlwind where the whole world listlessly turns like so many dry leaves, kingdoms count no more than the dresses of seamstresses, and the pigtails of blonde girls go round in the same mortal whirl as the sceptres that stood for empires. All is nothing, and in the entrance hall to the Invisible, whose open door reveals merely a closed door beyond, all things dance, servants of the wind which churns them without hands – all things, big and small, which for us and in us formed the perceptible system of the universe. All is shadow mixed with dust, and there's no voice but in the sounds made by what the wind lifts up or sweeps forward, nor silence except from what the wind abandons. Some of us, light leaves, and therefore less earthbound, ascend high in the hall's whirl and fall farther away from the circle of the heavy. Others, almost invisible but still equally dust, different only if seen close up, form their own layer in the whirlwind. Still others, tree trunks in miniature, are dragged around and come to a halt here and there. One day, when everything is finally and fully revealed, that other door will open and all that we were – rubbish of stars and souls – will be swept outside the house, so that what exists can start over.

My heart hurts me like a foreign body. My brain sleeps all that I feel. Yes, it's the beginning of autumn which brings to the air and to my soul that unsmiling light whose lifeless yellow tinges the irregular, rounded edges of the sunset's several clouds. Yes, it's the beginning of autumn and the clear awareness, in the limpid hour, of the anonymous inadequacy of everything. Autumn, yes, autumn, the one that's here or that's yet to come, and the foretasted weariness of all acts, the foretasted disillusion of all dreams. What can I hope for and where would it come from? Already, in what I think of myself, I'm there among the leaves and dust of the entrance hall, in the meaningless orbit of nothing at all, making sounds of life on the clean flagstones gilded by the last rays of a sun setting I don't know where.

All that I've thought, all that I've dreamed, all that I have or haven't done – all will go in autumn, like used matches strewn over the floor and pointing various ways, or papers crumpled into fake balls, or the great empires, all religions, the philosophies that the drowsy children of the abyss invented for sport. All that constituted my soul, from my lofty ambitions to my humble rented room, from the gods I had to the boss – Senhor Vasques – that I also had, all will go in autumn, all in autumn, in the tender indifference of autumn. All in autumn, yes, all in autumn.

203

We don't even know if what ends with daylight terminates in us as useless grief, or if we are just an illusion among shadows, and reality just this vast silence without wild ducks that falls over the lakes where straight and stiff reeds swoon. We know nothing. Gone is the memory of the stories we heard as children, now so much seaweed; still to come is the tenderness of future skies, a breeze in which imprecision slowly opens into stars. The votive lamp flickers uncertainly in the abandoned temple, the ponds of deserted villas stagnate in the sun, the name once carved into the tree now means nothing, and the privileges of the unknown have been blown over the roads like torn-up paper, stopping only when some object blocked their way. Others will lean out the same window as the rest; those who have forgotten the evil shadow will keep sleeping, longing for the sun they never had; and I, venturing without acting, will end without regret amid soggy reeds, covered with mud from the nearby river and from my sluggish weariness, under vast autumn evenings in some impossible distance. And through it all, behind my daydream, I'll feel my soul like a whistle of stark anxiety, a pure and shrill howl, useless in the world's darkness.

204

Clouds. . . Today I'm conscious of the sky, but there are days when I just feel it and don't look at it, when I just live in the city and not in the world of nature that includes it. Clouds. . . Today they are the main reality, worrying me as if an overcast sky were one of the imminent dangers of my destiny. Clouds. . . They pass from the sea to the Castle, from west to east, in a scattered and naked tumult: white when they raggedly proceed at the forefront of who knows what; half-black when they linger, waiting for the purring wind to blow them away; and black with a dirty whiteness when – as if wishing to stay – they darken with their arrival more than with their shadow the illusory space opened up by the streets between the impassable rows of buildings.

Clouds... I exist without knowing it and will die without wanting to. I'm the gap between what I am and am not, between what I dream and what life has made of me, the fleshly and abstract average of things that are nothing, I being likewise nothing. Clouds... Such disquiet when I feel, such discomfort when I think, such futility when I desire! Clouds... They're still passing, some of them so huge it seems they'll fill the whole sky (though the buildings prevent us from seeing if they're really as large as they appear), while others are of indefinite size, being perhaps two together or one that's going to split in two, meaningless in the heights of the exhausted sky, and still others are small, as if they were playthings of powerful beings, odd-shaped balls of some absurd game and now placed to one side of the sky, in cold isolation.

Clouds... I question myself and don't know me. Nothing I've done has been useful, and nothing I do will be any different. I've wasted part of my life in confusedly interpreting nothing at all, and the rest of it in writing these verses in prose for my incommunicable sensations, which is how I make the unknown universe mine. I'm objectively and subjectively sick of myself. I'm sick of everything, and of the everythingness of everything. Clouds... They're everything: disintegrated fragments of atmosphere, the only real things today between the worthless earth and the non-existent sky, indescribable tatters of the tedium I ascribe to them, mist condensed into colourless threats, dirty wads of cotton from a hospital without walls. Clouds... They're like me, a ravaged passage between sky and earth, at the mercy of an invisible impulse, thundering or not thundering, whitely giving joy or blackly spreading gloom, stray fictions in the gap, far from the earth's noise but without the sky's peace. Clouds... They continue to pass, passing always, they will always continue, in a discontinuous rolling of dull-coloured skeins, in a scattered prolongation of false, broken sky.

205

The day's fluid departure ends in exhausted purples. No one would be able to say who I am, nor know who I've been. I came down from the unknown mountain to the unknown valley, and in the languid evening my steps were tracks left in the woods' clearings. Everyone I loved had forgotten me in the shade. No one knew when the last boat was. The post office had no information about the letter that nobody would ever write.

But it was all false. They told none of the stories that nobody told them, and no one knows anything for sure about the one who departed long ago, placing his hope in the false voyage, son of the fog and indecision to come. I have a name among those who tarry, and that name is shadow, like everything.

206

Forest

Ah, but not even the alcove was genuine – it was the old alcove of my lost childhood! It withdrew like a fog, passing materially through the white walls of my real room, which emerged from the shadows distinct and smaller, like life and the day, like the creaking of the wagon and the faint sound of the whip that puts muscles for standing up into the prone body of the tired animal.

207

How many things that we consider right or true are merely the vestiges of our dreams, the sleepwalking figures of our incomprehension! Does anyone know what's right or true? How many things we consider beautiful are merely the fashion of the day, the fiction of their time and place? How many things we consider ours are utterly foreign to our blood, we being merely their perfect mirrors or transparent wrappers!

The more I meditate on our capacity for self-deception, the more my certainties crumble, slipping through my fingers as fine sand. And when this meditation becomes a feeling that clouds my mind, then the whole world appears to me as a mist made of shadows, a twilight of edges and corners, a fiction of the interlude,* a dawn that never becomes morning. Everything transforms into a dead absolute of itself, into a stagnation of details. And even my senses, to where I transfer my meditation in order to forget it, are a kind of slumber, something remote and derivative, an in-betweenness, variation, by-products of shadows and confusion.

In times like these – when I could readily understand ascetics and recluses, were I able to understand how anyone can make an effort on behalf of absolute ends or subscribe to a creed that might produce an effort – I would create, if I could, a full-fledged aesthetics of despair, an inner rhythm like a crib's rocking, filtered by the night's caresses in other, far-flung homelands.

Today, at different times, I ran into two friends who'd had a fight. Each one told me his version of why they'd fought. Each one told me the truth. Each one gave me his reasons. They were both right. They were both absolutely right. It's not that one of them saw it one way and the other another way, or that one saw one side of what happened and the other a different side. No: each one saw things exactly as they'd happened, each one saw them according to the same criterion, but each one saw something different, and so each one was right.

I was baffled by this dual existence of truth.

208

Just as, whether we know it or not, we all have a metaphysics, so too, whether we like it or not, we all have a morality. I have a very simple morality: not to do good or evil to anyone. Not to do evil, because it seems only fair that others enjoy the same right I demand for myself –

not to be disturbed – and also because I think that the world doesn't need more than the natural evils it already has. All of us in this world are living on board a ship that is sailing from one unknown port to another, and we should treat each other with a traveller's cordiality. Not to do good, because I don't know what good is, nor even if I do it when I think I do. How do I know what evils I generate if I give a beggar money? How do I know what evils I produce if I teach or instruct? Not knowing, I refrain. And besides, I think that to help or clarify is, in a certain way, to commit the evil of interfering in the lives of others. Kindness depends on a whim of our mood, and we have no right to make others the victims of our whims, however humane or kind-hearted they may be. Good deeds are impositions; that's why I categorically abhor them.

If, for moral reasons, I don't do good to others, neither do I expect others to do good to me. When I get sick, what I hate most is if someone should feel obliged to take care of me, something I'd loathe doing for another. I've never visited a sick friend. And whenever I've been sick and had visitors, I've always felt their presence as a bother, an insult, an unwarranted violation of my wilful privacy. I don't like people to give me things, because it seems like they're obligating me to give something in return – to them or to others, it's all the same.

I'm highly sociable in a highly negative way. I'm inoffensiveness incarnate. But I'm no more than this, I don't want to be more than this, I can't be more than this. For everything that exists I feel a visual affection, an intellectual fondness – nothing in the heart. I have faith in nothing, hope in nothing, charity for nothing. I'm nauseated and outraged by the sincere souls of all sincerities and by the mystics of all mysticisms, or rather, by the sincerities of all sincere souls and the mysticisms of all mystics. This nausea is almost physical when the mysticisms are active – when they try to convince other people, meddle with their wills, discover the truth, or reform the world.

I consider myself fortunate for no longer having family, as it relieves me of the obligation to love someone, which I would surely find burdensome. Any nostalgia I feel is literary. I remember my childhood with tears, but they're rhythmic tears, in which prose is already being formed. I remember it as something external, and it comes back to me through external things; I remember only external things. It's not the stillness of evenings in the country that endears me to the childhood I spent there, it's the way the table was set for tea, it's the way the furniture was arranged in the room, it's the faces and physical gestures of the people. I feel nostalgia for scenes. Thus someone else's childhood can move me as much as my own; both are purely visual phenomena from a past I'm unable to fathom, and my perception of them is literary. They move me, yes, but because I see them, not because I remember them.

I've never loved anyone. The most that I've loved are my sensations – states of conscious seeing, impressions gathered by intently hearing, and aromas through which the modesty of the outer world speaks to me of things from the past (so easily remembered by their smells), giving me a reality and an emotion that go beyond the simple fact of bread being baked inside the bakery, as on that remote afternoon when I was coming back from the funeral of my uncle who so loved me, and I felt a kind of sweet relief about I'm not sure what.

This is my morality, or metaphysics, or me: passer-by of everything, even of my own soul, I belong to nothing, I desire nothing, I am nothing – just an abstract centre of impersonal sensations, a fallen sentient mirror reflecting the world's diversity. I don't know if I'm happy this way. Nor do I care.

209

To join in or collaborate or act with others is a metaphysically morbid impulse. The soul conferred on the individual shouldn't be lent out to its relations with others. The divine fact of existing shouldn't be surrendered to the satanic fact of coexisting.

When I act with others, there's at least one thing I lose – acting alone.

When I participate, although it seems that I'm expanding, I'm limiting myself. To associate is to die. Only my consciousness of myself is real for me; other people are hazy phenomena in this consciousness, and it would be morbid to attribute very much reality to them.

Children, who want at all costs to have their way, are closest to God, for they want to exist.

As adults our life is reduced to giving alms to others and receiving them in return. We squander our personalities in orgies of coexistence.

Every spoken word double-crosses us. The only tolerable form of communication is the written word, since it isn't a stone in a bridge between souls but a ray of light between stars.

To explain is to disbelieve. Every philosophy is a diplomacy dressed up as eternity . . . . . Like diplomacy, it has no real substance, existing not in its own right but completely and utterly on behalf of some objective.

The only noble destiny for a writer who publishes is to be denied a celebrity he deserves. But the truly noble destiny belongs to the writer who doesn't publish. Not who doesn't write, for then he wouldn't be a writer. I mean the writer in whose nature it is to write, but whose spiritual temperament prevents him from showing what he writes.

To write is to objectify dreams, to create an outer world as a material reward [?] of our nature as creators. To publish is to give this outer world to others; but what for, if the outer world common to us and to them is the 'real' outer world, the one made of visible and tangible matter? What do others have to do with the universe that's in me?

210

Aesthetics of Discouragement

To publish – the socialization of one's self. A vile necessity! But still not a real *act*, since it's the publisher who makes money, the printer who produces. It at least has the merit of being incoherent.

When a man reaches the age of lucidity, one of his main concerns is to actively and thoughtfully shape himself into the image and likeness of his ideal. Since inertia is the ideal that best embodies the logic of our soul's aristocratic attitude *vis-à-vis* the □ bustle and clamour of the modern world, our Ideal should be the Inert, the Inactive. Futile? Perhaps. But this will only trouble those who feel attracted to futility.

211

Enthusiasm is a vulgarity.

To give expression to enthusiasm is, above all else, to violate the rights of our insincerity.

We never know when we're sincere. Perhaps we never are. And even if we're sincere about something today, tomorrow we may be sincere about its complete opposite.

I myself have never had convictions. I've always had impressions. I could never hate a land in which I'd seen a scandalous sunset.

We externalize impressions not so much because we have them but to convince ourselves that we do.

212

To have opinions is to sell out to yourself. To have no opinion is to exist. To have every opinion is to be a poet.

213

Everything slips away from me. My whole life, my memories, my imagination and all it contains, my personality: it all slips away. I constantly feel that I was someone different, that a different I felt, that a different I thought. I'm watching a play with a different, unfamiliar setting, and what I'm watching is me.

In the commonplace clutter of my literary drawers I sometimes find things I wrote ten or fifteen years ago, or longer, and many of them seem to be written by a stranger; I can't recognize the voice as my own. But who wrote them, if not me? I felt those things, but in what seems to be another life, one from which I've now awoken, as if from someone else's sleep.

I often come across pages I wrote in my youth, when I was seventeen or twenty, and some of them reveal an expressive power I can't remember having back then. There are certain phrases and sentences written in the wake of my adolescence that seem like the product of the person I am now, with all that I've learned in the intervening years. I see I'm the same as what I was. And since in general I feel that I've greatly progressed from what I was, I wonder where the progress is, if back then I was the same as now.

There's a mystery here that discredits and disturbs me.

Just the other day I was bowled over by a short piece I wrote ages ago. I'm quite certain that the special care I take with language goes back only a few years, but in one of my drawers I found this much older piece of writing in which that same care was clearly evident. I must not have known myself at all back then. How did I develop into what I already was? How have I come to know the I that I never knew back then? And everything becomes a confusing labyrinth where I stray, in myself, away from myself.

I let my mind wander, and I'm sure that what I'm writing I've already written. I remember. And I ask the one in me who presumes to exist if in the Platonism of sensations there might not be another, less vertical anamnesis – another pre-existing life that we vaguely remember but that belongs only to this life. . .

My God, my God, who am I watching? How many am I? Who is I? What is this gap between me and myself?

214

Again I found pages of mine, this time in French, written some fifteen years ago. I've never been in France and was never in close contact with French people, so it's not as if I had a familiarity with the language that waned over the years. Today I read as much French as I ever did. I'm older and more practised in thought; I should have progressed. Yet these pages from my distant past denote a confidence in the use of French that I no longer possess; they have a fluid style that today I couldn't possibly achieve in that language; there are entire passages, complete sentences, grammatical forms and idioms that demonstrate a fluency I've lost without remembering that I ever had it. How can this be explained? Who did I replace inside myself?

It's easy enough to form a theory of the fluidity of things and souls, to understand ourselves as an inner flow of life, to imagine that we're a large quantity, that we traverse ourselves, that we have been many... But in this case there's something besides the flow of personality between its own banks: there's an absolute other, an extraneous self that was me. That with age I should lose my imagination, my emotion, a certain kind of intelligence, a way of feeling – all of this, while causing regret, wouldn't cause me any great wonder. But what am I confronting when I read myself as if reading a stranger? On what shore am I standing if I see myself in the depths?

At other times I find pages that I not only don't remember having written, which in itself doesn't astonish me, but that I don't even remember having been capable of writing, which terrifies me. Certain phrases belong to another mentality. It's as if I'd found an old picture that I know is of me, with a different height and with features I don't recognize, but undoubtedly me, terrifyingly I.

215

I have the most conflicting opinions, the most divergent beliefs. For it's never I who thinks, speaks or acts. It's always one of my dreams, which I momentarily embody, that thinks, speaks and acts for me. I open my mouth, but it's I-another who speaks. The only thing I feel to be really *mine* is a huge incapacity, a vast emptiness, an incompetence for everything that is life. I don't know the gestures for any real act .....

I never learned how to exist.

I obtain everything I want, as long as it's inside me.

I'd like the reading of this book to leave you with the impression that you've traversed a sensual nightmare.

What used to be moral is aesthetic for us. What was social is now individual.

Why should I look at twilights if I have within me thousands of diverse twilights – including some that aren't twilights – and if, besides seeing them inside me, I myself *am them*, on the inside and the outside?

216

The sunset spreads over the scattered clouds that dot the entire sky. Soft hues of every colour fill the lofty, spatial diversities, absently floating amid the sorrows on high. On the crests of the half-coloured, half-shaded rooftops, the last slow rays of the departing sun take on colours that are not their own nor of the things they light up. An immense calm hangs over the noisy city, which is also growing calmer. Everything breathes beyond colour and sound, in a deep and hushed sigh.

On the painted buildings that the sun doesn't see, the colours are beginning to grey. There's a coldness in these colours' diversity. A mild anxiety dozes in the pseudo-valleys formed by the streets. It dozes and grows calm. And little by little, in the lowest of the high clouds, the hues begin to be shadowy. Only in that tiny cloud – a white eagle hovering above everything – does the far-off sun still cast its smiling gold.

Everything I sought in life I abandoned for the sake of the search. I'm like one who absent-mindedly looks for he doesn't know what, having forgotten it in his dreaming as the search got under way. The thing being searched for becomes less real than the real motions of the hands that search – rummaging, picking up, putting down – and that visibly exist, long and white, with exactly five fingers on each.

All that I've had is like this high and diversely identical sky, tatters of nothing tinged by a distant light, fragments of pseudo-life gilded by death from afar with its sad smile of whole truth. All I've had has amounted to my not knowing how to search, like a feudal lord of swamps at twilight, solitary prince of a city of empty tombs.

All that I am or was, or that I think I am or was, suddenly loses – in these thoughts and in that high cloud's suddenly spent light – the secret, the truth, perhaps fortune, that was in some obscure thing that has life for a bed. All of this, like a sun that's missing, is all I have left. Over the diversely high rooftops the light lets its hands slip away until, in the unity of those same rooftops, the inner shadow of everything emerges.

Like a hazy flickering drop, in the distance the first small star glows.

217

All stirrings of our sensibility, even the most pleasant ones, are bound to disturb the inscrutable inner life of that same sensibility. Tiny concerns as well as large worries distract us from ourselves, hindering the peace of mind we all aspire to, whether we know it or not.

We almost always live outside ourselves, and life itself is a continual dispersion. But it's towards ourselves that we tend, as towards a centre around which, like planets, we trace absurd and distant ellipses.

218

I'm older than Time and Space, because I'm conscious. Things derive from me; the whole of Nature is the offspring of my sensations.

I seek and don't find. I want and can't have.

Without me the sun rises and expires; without me the rain falls and the wind howls. It's not because of me that there are seasons, the twelve months, time's passage.

Lord of the world in me which, like earthly lands, I can't take with me . . . . .

219

That locus of sensations known as my soul sometimes walks with me, consciously, through the city's nocturnal streets, in the wearisome hours when I feel like a dream among dreams of a different sort, by the □ gaslight, in the midst of the transitory sound of traffic.

As my body penetrates the lanes and side streets, my soul loses itself in intricate labyrinths of sensation. All that can disturbingly convey the notion of unreality and feigned existence, all that can demonstrate – not to abstract reason but □ and concretely – how the place occupied by the universe is hollower than hollow: all this objectively unfolds before my detached spirit. I don't know why, but I'm troubled by this objective network of wide and narrow streets, this succession of street lamps, trees, lighted and dark windows, opened and closed gates – heterogeneously nocturnal shapes which my near-sightedness makes even hazier, until they become subjectively monstrous, unintelligible and unreal.

Verbal snatches of envy, lust and triviality collide with my sense of hearing. Whispered murmurs □ ripple towards my consciousness.

Little by little I lose my clear awareness of the fact that I concurrently exist with all this, that I really move – seeing little but hearing – among shadows that represent beings and places where there actually are beings. It becomes gradually, darkly, indistinctly unintelligible to me how all of this can exist in the face of eternal time and infinite space.

Through a passive association of ideas, I start thinking about the men whose consciousness of that space and time was so analytically and intuitively acute that it lost touch with the world. It seems ludicrous that on nights no doubt like this one, in cities surely not very different from the one in which I contemplate, there were men such as Plato, Scotus Erigena,* Kant and Hegel who virtually forgot about all this, who became different from these □ people. And they were from the same human race . . . . .

With what horrible clarity even I, as I walk here and think these thoughts, feel distant, alien, confused and . . . . .

I end my solitary peregrination. A vast silence, impassive to slight sounds, assaults and overwhelms me. In both body and spirit I feel sorely weary of things, all things, of simply being here, of □ finding myself in this present state. I almost catch myself wanting to scream because of a feeling that I'm sinking in an ocean of □ whose immensity has nothing to do with the infinity of space or the eternity of time, nor with anything that can be measured and named. In these moments of supremely silent terror, I don't know what I materially am, what I normally do, what I usually want, feel and think. I feel cut off from myself, outside of my reach. The moral impulse to struggle, the intellectual effort to systematize and understand, the restless artistic yearning to produce something that I no longer fathom but that I remember having fathomed and that I call beauty – all of this vanishes from my sense of reality, all of this strikes me as not even worthy of being considered useless, empty and remote. I feel like a mere void, the illusion of a soul, the locus of a being, a conscious darkness where a strange insect □ vainly seeks at least the warm memory of a light.

220

Dolorous Interlude

What good is dreaming?

What did I make of myself? Nothing.

To be spiritualized in Night . . . . .

Inner Statue without contours, Outer Dream without a dream-essence.

221

I've always been an ironic dreamer, unfaithful to my inner promises. Like a complete outsider, a casual observer of whom I thought I was, I've always enjoyed watching my daydreams go down in defeat. I was never convinced of what I believed in. I filled my hands with sand, called it gold, and opened them up to let it slide through. Words were my only truth. When the right words were said, all was done; the rest was the sand that had always been.

If it weren't for my continuous dreaming, my perpetual state of alienation, I could very well call myself a realist – someone, that is, for whom the outer world is an independent nation. But I prefer not to give myself a name, to be somewhat mysterious about what I am and to be impishly unpredictable even to myself.

I feel a certain duty to dream continuously since, not being more nor wanting to be more than a spectator of myself, I have to put on the best show I can. And so I fashion myself out of gold and silks, in imaginary rooms, on a false stage, with ancient scenery: a dream created to invisible music and the play of soft lights.

I cherish, like the memory of a special kiss, my childhood remembrance of a theatre with a bluish, moonlit setting that depicted the terrace of an impossible palace, surrounded by a huge park, likewise painted. I spent my soul living all of that as though it were real. The music that softly played on this occasion of my mental experience of life gave the stage setting a feverish reality.

The setting was definitely bluish and moonlight, but I don't remember who appeared on stage. The play I place today in that remembered scenery comes from the verses of Verlaine and Pessanha,* but this isn't the play (which I've forgotten) that was performed on the actual stage and had nothing to do with that reality of blue music. It's my own, fluid play, a grandiose moonlit masquerade, a silver and nocturnal blue interlude.

Then came life. That night they took me to The Gold Lion* for dinner. I can still taste the steaks on the palate of my nostalgia – steaks (I know because I imagine*) such as nowadays no one makes or I, at any rate, don't eat. And it all gets mixed up – the childhood I live from afar, the tasty food at the restaurant, the moonlit setting, Verlaine future and I present – in a blurry diagonal, in a false gap between what I was and what I am.

222

As when a storm is brewing and the noises from the street talk in a loud and detached voice. . .

The street winced in the stark white light, and the dull darkness trembled all around the world with a boom of echoing crashes. The harsh sadness of the heavy rain accentuated the air's ugly black hue. Cold and warm and hot at the same time, the air was everywhere equivocal. Then a wedge of metallic light entered the large office, ripping into the peace of each human body, and a huge rock of sound struck with a chill shock on all sides, shattering into a hard silence. The sound of rain diminishes, becoming a soft voice. The noise from the street diminishes out of fear. A new light spreads its swift yellow over the silent darkness, but breathing was again possible before the fist of rumbling sound abruptly echoed from afar; like an angry farewell, the storm was beginning to draw away.

. . . with a drawling, moribund murmur, with no light in the increasing light, the rumble of the storm subsided in the distant expanses – it circled over Almada*. . .

A dreadful light suddenly cracked and splintered. It froze inside every brain and chamber. Everything froze. Hearts stopped for a moment. They're all very sensitive people. The silence terrifies, as if death had struck. The sound of increasing rain, as if everything were weeping, is a relief. The air is like lead.

223

A sword of faint lightning darkly whirled in the large room. The rumble that followed, breaking in on a widespread gulp, trailed off into the distance. The sound of rain wept loudly, like mourners in between their chit-chatting. Here inside, each tiny sound stood out clearly, nervously.

224

. . . that episode of the imagination which we call reality.

It's been raining for two straight days, and the rain that falls from the cold grey sky has a colour that afflicts my soul. For two straight days. . . I'm sad from feeling, and I reflect it at the window, to the sound of the dripping water and pouring rain. My heart is overwhelmed, and my memories have turned into anxieties.

Though I don't feel tired and have no reason to feel tired, I'd love to go to sleep right now. Back when I was a child and happy, the voice of a colourful green parrot lived in a house off the courtyard next door. On rainy days his talking never became mournful, and he would cry out – sure of his shelter – a constant sentiment that hovered in the sadness like a phonograph before its time.

Did I think about this parrot because I'm sad and my distant childhood brings it to mind? No, I actually thought about it because a parrot is right now frantically squawking in the courtyard opposite where I live today.

Everything is topsy-turvy. When it seems like I'm remembering, I'm thinking of something else; if I look, I don't recognize, and when distracted, I see clearly.

I turn my back to the grey window with its panes that are cold to the touch, and by some magic of the penumbra I suddenly see the interior of our old house, next to which there was a courtyard with a squawking parrot; and my eyes fall asleep from the irrevocable fact of having, in effect, lived.

225

Yes, it's the sunset. Slowly and distractedly I reach the end of the Rua da Alfândega and see, beyond the Terreiro do Paço,* a clear view of the sunless western sky. It's a blue sky tinged green and tending towards light grey, and on the left, over the hills of the opposite bank, there's a cowering mass of brownish to lifeless pink fog. An immense peace that I don't have is coldly present in the abstract fall air. Not having it, I experience the feeble pleasure of imagining it exists. But in reality there is no peace nor lack of peace, just sky, a sky with every fading colour: light blue, blue-green, pale grey between green and blue, fuzzy hues of distant clouds that aren't clouds, yellowishly darkened by an expiring red. And all of this is a vision that vanishes as soon as it occurs, a winged interlude between nothing and nothing that takes place on high, in shades of sky and grief, diffuse and indefinite.

I feel and forget. A nostalgia – the same one that everyone feels for everything – invades me as if it were an opium in the cold air. I have an inner, pseudo-ecstasy that comes from seeing.

Towards the ocean, where the sun's ceasing becomes increasingly final, the light dies out in a livid white which is blued by greenish cold. In the air there's a torpor of what is never achieved. The panorama of the sky loudly hushes.

In this moment when I'm bursting with feeling, I wish I had the gift of ruthless self-expression, the arbitrary whim of a style as my destiny. But no: this remote, lofty sky that's disintegrating is everything right now, and the emotion I feel, which is many confused emotions bunched together, is merely this useless sky's reflection in a lake in me – a lake secluded among steep rugged rocks, perfectly still, a kind of dead man's gaze in which the heights distractedly observe themselves.

So many times, so many, like now, it has oppressed me to feel myself feel – to feel anguish just because it's a feeling, restlessness because I'm here, nostalgia for something I've never known, the sunset of all emotions, myself yellowing, subdued to grey sadness in my external self-awareness.

Ah, who will save me from existing? It's neither death nor life that I want: it's that other thing shining in the depths of longing, like a possible diamond in a pit one can't descend. It's all the weight and sorrow of this real and impossible universe, of this sky like the flag of an unknown army, of these colours that are paling in the fictitious air, where the imaginary crescent of the moon, cut out of distance and insensibility, now emerges in a still, electric whiteness.

It all amounts to the absence of a true God, an absence that is the empty cadaver of the lofty heavens and the closed soul. Infinite prison – since you're infinite, there's no escaping you!

226

Ah, what transcendental □ sensuousness when at night, walking along the city streets and staring from within my soul at the building façades, all the structural differences, the architectural details, the lit windows, the potted plants that make each balcony unique – yes, looking at all this, what instinctive joy I felt when to the lips of my consciousness came this shout of redemption. But none of this is real!

227

I prefer prose to poetry as an art form for two reasons, the first of which is purely personal: I have no choice, because I'm incapable of writing in verse. The second reason applies to everyone, however, and I don't think it's just a shadow or disguised form of the first. It's worth looking at in some detail, for it touches on the essence of all art's value.

I consider poetry to be an intermediate stage between music and prose. Like music, poetry is bound by rhythmic laws, and even when these are not the strict laws of metre, they still exist as checks, constraints, automatic mechanisms of repression and censure. In prose we speak freely. We can incorporate musical rhythms, and still think. We can incorporate poetic rhythms, and yet remain outside them. An occasional poetic rhythm won't disturb prose, but an occasional prose rhythm makes poetry fall down.

Prose encompasses all art, in part because words contain the whole world, and in part because the untrammelled word contains every possibility for saying and thinking. In prose, through transposition, we're able to render everything: colour and form, which painting can render only directly, in themselves, with no inner dimension; rhythm, which music likewise renders only directly, in itself, without a formal body, let alone that second body which is the idea; structure, which the architect must make out of given, hard, external things, and which we build with rhythms, hesitations, successions and fluidities; reality, which the sculptor has to leave in the world, with no aura of transubstantiation; and poetry, finally, to which the poet, like the initiate of a secret society, is the servant (albeit voluntary) of a discipline and a ritual.

I'm convinced that in a perfect, civilized world there would be no other art but prose. We would let sunsets be sunsets, using art merely to understand them verbally, by conveying them in an intelligible music of colour. We wouldn't sculpt bodies but let them keep for themselves their supple contours and soft warmth that we see and touch. We would build houses only to live in them, which is after all what they're for. Poetry would be for children, to prepare them for prose, since poetry is obviously something infantile, mnemonic, elementary and auxiliary.

Even what we might call the minor arts have their echoes in prose. There is prose that dances, sings and recites to itself. There are verbal rhythms with a sinuous choreography, in which the idea being expressed strips off its clothing with veritable and exemplary sensuality. And there are also, in prose, gestural subtleties carried out by a great actor, the Word, which rhythmically transforms into its bodily substance the impalpable mystery of the universe.

228

Everything is interconnected. My readings of classical authors, who never speak of sunsets, have made many sunsets intelligible to me, in all their colours. There is a relationship between syntactical competence, by which we distinguish the values of beings, sounds and shapes, and the capacity to perceive when the blue of the sky is actually green, and how much yellow is in the blue green of the sky.

It comes down to the same thing – the capacity to distinguish and to discriminate. There is no enduring emotion without syntax. Immortality depends on the grammarians.

229

To read is to dream, guided by someone else's hand. To read carelessly and distractedly is to let go of that hand. To be only superficially learned is the best way to read well and be profound.

How shoddy and contemptible life is! Note that, for it to be shoddy and contemptible, all it takes is you not wanting it, it being given to you anyway, and nothing about it depending on your will or even on your illusion of your will.

To die is to become completely other. That's why suicide is a cowardice: it's to surrender ourselves completely to life.

230

Art is a substitute for acting or living. If life is the wilful expression of emotion, art is the intellectual expression of that same emotion. Whatever we don't have, don't attempt or don't achieve can be possessed through dreams, and these are what we use to make art. At other times our emotion is so strong that, although reduced to action, this action doesn't completely satisfy it; the leftover emotion, unexpressed in life, is used to produce the work of art. There are thus two types of artist: the one who expresses what he doesn't have, and the one who expresses the surplus of what he did have.

231

One of the soul's great tragedies is to execute a work and then realize, once it's finished, that it's not any good. The tragedy is especially great when one realizes that the work is the best he could have done. But to write a work, knowing beforehand that it's bound to be flawed and imperfect; to see while writing it that it's flawed and imperfect – this is the height of spiritual torture and humiliation. Not only am I dissatisfied with the poems I write now; I also know that I'll be dissatisfied with the poems I write in the future. I know it philosophically and in my flesh, through a hazy, gladiolated* foreglimpse.

So why do I keep writing? Because I still haven't learned to practise completely the renunciation that I preach. I haven't been able to give up my inclination to poetry and prose. I have to write, as if I were carrying out a punishment. And the greatest punishment is to know that whatever I write will be futile, flawed and uncertain.

I wrote my first poems when I was still a child. Though dreadful, they seemed perfect to me. I'll never again be able to have the illusory pleasure of producing perfect work. What I write today is much better. It's even better than what some of the best writers write. But it's infinitely inferior to what I for some reason feel I could – or perhaps should – write. I weep over those first dreadful poems as over a dead child, a dead son, a last hope that has vanished.

232

The more we live, the more convinced we become of two truths that contradict each other. The first is that next to the reality of life all the fictions of literature and art pale. It's true that they give us a nobler pleasure than what we get from life, but they're like dreams which, though offering us feelings not felt in life and joining together forms that never meet in life, are none the less dreams that dissipate when we wake up, leaving no memories or nostalgia with which we could later live a second life.

The other truth is that, since every noble soul desires to live life in its entirety – experiencing all things, all places and all feelings – and since this is objectively impossible, the only way for a noble soul to live life is subjectively; only by denying life can it be lived in its totality.

These two truths are mutually exclusive. The wise man won't try to reconcile them, nor will he dismiss one or the other. But he will have to follow one or the other, yearning at times for the one he didn't choose; or he'll dismiss them both, rising above himself in a personal nirvana.

Happy the man who doesn't ask for more than what life spontaneously gives him, being guided by the instinct of cats, which seek sunlight when there's sun, and when there's no sun then heat, wherever they find it. Happy the man who renounces his personality in favour of the imagination and who delights in contemplating other people's lives, experiencing not all impressions but the outward spectacle of all impressions. And happy, finally, the man who renounces everything, who has nothing that can be taken from him, nothing that can be diminished.

The rustic, the reader of novels, the pure ascetic – these three are happy in life, for these three types of men all renounce their personalities: one because he lives by instinct, which is impersonal, another because he lives by the imagination, which is forgetting, and the third because he doesn't live but merely (since he still hasn't died) sleeps.

Nothing satisfies me, nothing consoles me; everything that has been and that hasn't been jades me. I don't want to have my soul and don't want to renounce it. I want what I don't want and renounce what I don't have. I can't be nothing nor be everything: I'm the bridge between what I don't have and what I don't want.

233

. . . the solemn sadness that dwells in all great things – in high mountains and in great men, in profound nights and in eternal poems.

234

We can die if all we've done is love.

235

Only once was I truly loved. I've always been treated in a friendly manner, and even people I hardly know have rarely been rude or brusque or cold to me. In certain people that friendly manner, with my encouragement, might have been converted into love or affection, but I've never had the patience or mental concentration to even want to make the effort.

At first I thought (so little do we know ourselves!) that shyness was to blame for my soul's apparent apathy in this matter. But I came to realize that it actually had to do with the tedium I felt *vis-à-vis* emotions – not to be confused with the tedium of life. I didn't have the patience to commit myself to an ongoing feeling, especially when it would require an ongoing effort. 'What for?' thought the part of me that doesn't think. I have enough intellectual subtlety and psychological insight to know 'how'; the 'how of the how' is what has always escaped me. My weakness of will has always begun as a weakness of will to have any will. This was the case in my emotions as well as in my intellect, and in my very will, and in all my dealings with life.

But on that occasion when circumstances mischievously led me to suppose that I loved and to verify that the other person truly loved me, my first reaction was of bewildered confusion, as if I'd won a grand prize in an unconvertible currency. And then, because no human can avoid being human, I felt a certain vanity; this emotion, however, which would seem to be the most natural one, quickly vanished. It was followed by an uncomfortable feeling that's hard to define but that was composed of tedium, of humiliation, and of weariness.

Of tedium, as if Fate had obliged me to occupy my free evenings with some strange and unfamiliar labour. Of tedium, as if a new duty – that of a hideous reciprocity – had been ironically foisted on me as a privilege for which I was expected to thank Fate profusely. Of tedium, as if the irregular monotony of life weren't enough, so that on top of that I needed the obligatory monotony of a definite feeling.

And of humiliation – yes, humiliation. It took me a while to understand the presence of this feeling that seemed not at all justified by its cause. I should have loved being loved. It should have piqued my vanity that someone had heaped attention on me as a lovable human being. But apart from my brief feeling of actual vanity (and even that may have consisted of surprise more than of vanity itself), what I experienced was humiliation. I felt that I'd been given someone else's prize – a prize that was worth something only to the person who rightfully deserved it.

But most of all I felt weariness – a weariness beyond all tedium. I finally understood a phrase of Chateaubriand whose meaning, because of my lack of personal experience, had always eluded me. Chateaubriand writes of René, his personification, 'it wearied him to be loved' – *on le fatigait en l'aimant*. I realized with astonishment that this experience was identical to my own, and so I couldn't deny its validity.

The weariness of being loved, of being truly loved! The weariness of being the object of other people's burdensome emotions! Of seeing yourself – when what you wanted was to remain forever free – transformed into a delivery boy whose duty is to reciprocate, to have the decency not to flee, lest anyone think that you're cavalier towards emotions and would reject the loftiest sentiment that a human soul can offer. The weariness of your existence becoming absolutely dependent on a relationship with someone else's feeling! The weariness of having to feel something, of having to love at least a little in return, even if it's not a true reciprocity!

As it came, so it went, and today nothing of that shadowy episode remains in my intellect or in my emotions. It brought me no experience that I couldn't have deduced from the laws of human life, which I instinctively know because I'm human. It gave me no pleasure to look back on with regret, nor sorrow to remember with equal regret. It all seems like something I read somewhere, like an incident that happened to someone else, a novel I read halfway through and whose second half was missing, but I didn't care that it was missing, because the first half of the story was all there, and although it made no sense, I realized that no sense could ever be made of it, regardless of what happened in the part that was missing.

All that remains is my feeling of gratitude towards the one who loved me. But it's an abstract, bewildered gratitude, more intellectual than emotional. I'm sorry that I caused someone to feel sorrow; I'm sorry about that, and only about that.

It's unlikely that life will bring me another encounter with natural emotions. I almost wish it would, to see how I'd react the second time, after having thoroughly analysed the first experience. I might feel less emotion, or I might feel more. If Fate should bring it, then well and good. I'm curious about my emotions. Whereas I don't have the least curiosity about facts, whatever they are or will yet be.

236

To submit to nothing, whether to a man or a love or an idea, and to have the aloof independence of not believing in the truth or even (if it existed) in the usefulness of knowing it – this seems to me the right attitude for the intellectual inner life of those who can't live without thinking. To belong is synonymous with banality. Creeds, ideals, a woman, a profession – all are prisons and shackles. To be is to be free. Even ambition, if we take pride in it, is a hindrance; we wouldn't be proud of it if we realized it's a string by which we're pulled. No: no ties even to ourselves! Free from ourselves as well as from others, contemplatives without ecstasy, thinkers without conclusions and liberated from God, we will live the few moments of bliss allowed us in the prison yard by the distraction of our executioners. Tomorrow we will face the guillotine. Or if not tomorrow, then the day after. Let us stroll about in the sun before the end comes, deliberately forgetting all projects and pursuits. Without wrinkles our foreheads will glow in the sun, and the breeze will be cool for those who quit hoping.

I throw my pen against the slanted desk top and watch it roll down without bothering to catch it. I felt all of this without warning. And my happiness consists in this gesture of rage that I don't feel.

237

Notes for a Rule of Life

To need to dominate others is to need others. The commander is dependent.

Enlarge your personality without including anything from the outside – asking nothing from others and imposing nothing on others, but *being* others when you need them.

Reduce your necessities to a minimum, so as not to depend on anyone for anything.

It's true that such a life is impossible in the absolute. But it's not impossible relatively.

Let's consider a man who owns and runs an office. He should be able to do without his employees; he should be able to type, to balance the books, to sweep the office. He should depend on others because it saves him time, not because he's incompetent. Let him tell the office boy to put a letter in the post because he doesn't want to lose time going to the post office, not because he doesn't know where the post office is. Let him tell a clerk to take care of a certain matter because he doesn't want to waste time on it, not because he doesn't know how to take care of it.

238

There is no sure prize for virtue, and no sure punishment for sin. Nor would it be right for such prizes and punishments to exist. Virtue and sin are inevitable manifestations in organisms which, condemned to one thing or the other, serve their sentences of being good or of being bad. That's why all religions place rewards and punishments – deserved by people who were nothing and could do nothing, and therefore can deserve nothing – in other worlds, which no science can verify and no faith describe.

So let us renounce all sincere beliefs, along with all concern to influence others.

Life, said Tarde,* is the search for the impossible by way of the useless. Let us always search for the impossible, since that is our destiny, and let us search for it by way of the useless, since no path goes by any other way, but let us rise to the consciousness that nothing we search for can be found, and that nothing along the way deserves a fond kiss or memory.

We weary of everything, said the scholiast, except understanding. Let us understand, let us keep understanding, and let us make ghostly flowers out of this understanding, shrewdly entwining them into wreaths and garlands which are also doomed to wilt.

239

'We weary of everything, except understanding.' The meaning of the phrase is sometimes hard to grasp.

We weary of thinking to arrive at a conclusion, because the more we think and analyse and discern, the less we arrive at a conclusion.

And so we fall into that passive state in which we want to understand only the explanation of whatever is being proposed. It's an aesthetic attitude, since we don't care in the least whether what's proposed is or isn't true, and all we see in what we understand are the details of the explanation, the type of rational beauty it has for us.

We weary of thinking, of having our own opinions, of trying to think in order to act. But we don't weary of temporarily having other people's opinions, just to feel their intrusion and not follow their lead.

240

Rainy Landscape

Hour after hour, all night long, the patter of the rain rained down. All night long, as I tossed and turned, its cold monotony beat against the windows. A gust of wind sometimes whipped overhead, and the rain would wave with sound, passing its quick hands over the panes; at other times there was just a muffled sound that made everything sleep in the dead exterior. My soul, as always, whether among bedclothes or among people, was painfully conscious of the world. The day, like happiness, kept procrastinating – indefinitely, it seemed.

If happiness and the new day would never come! If at least we could never have the disillusion of getting what we wait and hope for!

The chance sound of a late-night car, jostling roughly over the cobblestones, became steadily louder, clacked rudely beneath my window, and faded away at the far end of the street, at the far end of my fitful sleep that never became true slumber. Now and then a neighbour's door would slam. At times there was a splashing of footsteps, a swishing sound of wet clothes. Once or twice, when the steps were numerous, they made a louder sound. Then they died out, the silence returned, and the rain relentlessly continued.

If I opened my eyes from my pretended slumber I could see, on the darkly visible walls of my room, floating snatches of dreams to be dreamed, dim lights, black lines, hazy shapes climbing up and down. The various pieces of furniture, larger than in the daytime, indistinctly blotted the dark's absurdity. The door was distinguishable as something no whiter or blacker than night, just different. The window I could only hear, not see.

Again, fluid and uncertain, the rain pattered. Time dragged to its accompaniment. My soul's solitude grew and spread, invading what I felt, what I wanted, and what I was going to dream. The room's hazy objects, which shared my insomnia in the shadows, moved with their sadness into my desolation.

241

Triangular Dream

The light had become an extremely sluggish yellow, a yellow that was filthy white. The distance between things had increased, and sounds were spaced differently, disconnectedly, and farther apart. As soon as they were heard, they suddenly ceased, as if cut short. The heat, which seemed to have intensified, was cold, though it was still heat. Through the crack between the window's two shutters, the only visible tree displayed an exaggeratedly expectant attitude. It had a different kind of green, which infused it with silence. The atmosphere, like a flower, had closed its petals. And in the composition of space itself, a different interrelationship of something like planes had changed and fragmented the way that sounds, lights and colours use space.

242

Even apart from our ordinary dreams – those abominations from the soul's sewers that no one would dare confess and that oppress our nights like foul phantoms, grimy bubbles and slime of our repressed sensibility – what ridiculous, frightening and unspeakable things the soul, with a little effort, can recognize in its corners!

The human soul is a madhouse of the grotesque. If a soul were able to reveal itself truthfully, if its shame and modesty didn't run deeper than all its known and named ignominies, then it would be – as is said of truth – a well, but a sinister well full of murky echoes and inhabited by abhorrent creatures, slimy non-beings, lifeless slugs, the snot of subjectivity.

243

All it would take to make a catalogue of monsters is to photograph in words the things the night brings to drowsy souls unable to sleep. These things have all the incoherence of dreams without the alibi of sleeping. They hover like bats over the soul's passivity, or like vampires that suck the blood of submission.

They're larvae from the debris on the hillside, shadows that fill the valley, remnants left by destiny. Sometimes they're worms, loathsome to the very soul that cradles and breeds them; sometimes they're ghosts that sinisterly skulk around nothing at all; sometimes they pop out as snakes from the absurd hollows of spent emotions.

Ballast of falseness, they're useful for nothing but to render us useless. They are doubts from the abyss that drag their cold and slithery bodies across the soul. They hang on as smoke, they leave tracks, and they never amounted to more than the sterile substance of our awareness of them. One or another is like an inner firework, sparking between dreams, and the rest is what our unconscious consciousness saw of them.

A dangling, untied ribbon, the soul doesn't exist in and of itself. The great landscapes belong to tomorrow, and we have already lived. The conversation was cut short and fizzled. Who would have thought life would turn out like this?

I'm lost if I find myself; I doubt what I discover; I don't have what I've obtained. I sleep as if I were taking a walk, but I'm awake. I wake up as if I'd been sleeping, and I don't belong to me. Life, in its essence, is one big insomnia, and all that we think or do occurs in a lucid stupor.

I'd be happy if I could sleep. This is what I think now, because I'm not sleeping. The night is an enormous weight beyond the silent blanket of dreams under which I smother myself. I have indigestion of the soul.

After this is over, morning will come as always, but it will be too late, as always. Everything sleeps and is happy except me. I rest a little, without even trying to sleep. And huge heads of non-existent monsters rise in confusion from the depths of who I am. They're Oriental dragons from the abyss, with their red tongues hanging outside of logic and their eyes deadly staring at my lifeless life that doesn't stare back.

The lid, for God's sake, the lid! Close the lid on unconsciousness and life! Fortunately, through the open shutters of the cold window, a bleak thread of pale light begins to chase darkness from the horizon. Morning, fortunately, is what's going to break. The disquiet that so wearies me has almost quieted down. A cock crows absurdly in the middle of the city. The wan day begins in my vague slumber. Eventually I'll sleep. The noise of wheels tells me there's a cart. My eyelids sleep, but not I. Everything, finally, is Destiny.

244

To be a retired major seems to me ideal. Too bad it's not possible to have eternally been nothing but a retired major.

My longing to be whole put me into this state of useless regret.

The tragic futility of life.

My curiosity – sister to the skylarks.

The treacherous anxiety of sunsets; the dawn's timid shroud.

Let's sit down here. From here we can see more of the sky. The vast expanse of these starry heights is soothing. Life hurts less as we look at them; a whiff of air from an invisible fan refreshes our life-wearied face.

245

The human soul is so inevitably the victim of pain that is suffers the pain of the painful surprise even with things it should have expected. A man who has always spoken of fickleness and unfaithfulness as perfectly normal behaviour in women will feel all the devastation of the sad surprise when he discovers that his sweetheart has been cheating on him, exactly as if he'd always held up female fidelity and constancy as a dogma or a rightful expectation. Another man, convinced that everything is hollow and empty, will feel like he's been struck by lightning when he learns that what he writes is considered worthless, or that his efforts to educate people are in vain, or that it's impossible to communicate his emotion.

We need not suppose that those who have experienced these and similar disasters were insincere in what they said or wrote, even if the disasters they suffered were foreseeable in their words. The sincerity of intellectual affirmation has nothing to do with the naturalness of spontaneous emotion. Strangely or not, it seems the soul may be given such surprises merely so that it won't lack pain, so that it will still know disgrace, so that it will have its fair share of grief in life. We are all equal in our capacity for error and suffering. Only those who don't feel don't experience pain; and the highest, most notable and most prudent men are those who experience and suffer precisely what they foresaw and what they disdained. This is what is known as Life.

246

To see all the things that happen to us as accidents or incidents from a novel, which we read not with our eyes but with life. Only with this attitude can we overcome the mischief of each day and the fickleness of events.

247

The active life has always struck me as the least comfortable of suicides. To act, in my view, is a cruel and harsh sentence passed on the unjustly condemned dream. To exert influence on the outside world, to change things, to overcome obstacles, to influence people – all of this seems more nebulous to me than the substance of my daydreams. Ever since

I was a child, the intrinsic futility of all forms of action has been a cherished touchstone for my detachment from everything, including me.

To act is to react against oneself. To exert influence is to leave home.

I've always pondered how absurd it is that, even when the substance of reality is just a series of sensations, there can be things so complexly simple as businesses, industries, and social and family relationships, so devastatingly unintelligible in light of the soul's inner attitude towards the idea of truth.

248

My abstention from collaborating in the existence of the outside world results in, among other things, a curious psychic phenomenon.

Abstaining entirely from action and taking no interest in Things, I'm able to see the outside world with perfect objectivity. Since nothing interests me or makes me think it should be changed, I don't change it.

And thus I'm able . . . . .

249

Beginning in the mid-eighteenth century, a terrible disease progressively swept over civilization. Seventeen centuries of consistently frustrated Christian aspirations and five centuries of forever postponed pagan aspirations (Catholicism having failed as Christianity, the Renaissance having failed as paganism, and the Reformation having failed as a universal phenomenon), the shipwreck of all that had been dreamed, the paltriness of all that had been achieved, the sadness of living a life too miserable to be shared by others, and other people's lives too miserable for us to want to share – all of this fell over souls and poisoned them. Minds were filled with a horror of all action, which could be contemptible only in a contemptible society. The soul's higher activities languished; only its baser, more organic functions flourished. The former having stagnated, the latter began to govern the world.

Thus was born a literature and art made of the lower elements of thought – Romanticism. And with it, a social life made of the lower elements of action – modern democracy.

Souls born to rule had no recourse but to abstain. Souls born to create, in a society where creative forces were flagging, had no world to mould to their will besides the social world of their dreams, the introspective sterility of their own soul.

We apply the name 'Romantics' both to the great men who failed and to the little men who showed themselves for what they were. But the only similarity between the two is in their overt sentimentality, which in the former denotes an inability to make active use of the intelligence, while in the latter it denotes the lack of intelligence itself. A Chateaubriand and a Hugo, a Vigny and a Michelet, are products of the same age. But Chateaubriand is a great soul that was diminished, Hugo a little soul that was inflated by the winds of the day. Vigny is a genius that had to flee, Michelet a woman that was forced to be a man of genius. In the father of them all, Jean Jacques Rousseau, the two tendencies coincide. He possessed, in equal measure, the intelligence of a creator and the sensibility of a slave. His social sensibility infected his theories, which his intelligence merely set forth with clarity. His intelligence served only to bemoan the tragedy of coexisting with such a sensibility.

Rousseau is the modern man, but more complete than any modern man. From the weaknesses that made him fail, he extracted – alas for him and for us! – the forces that made him triumph. The part of him that went forward conquered, but when he entered the city, the word 'Defeat' could be read at the bottom of his victory banners. And in the part of him that stayed behind, incapable of fighting to conquer, there were crowns and sceptres, a ruler's majesty and a conqueror's glory – his legitimate inner destiny.

II

We were born into a world that has suffered from a century and a half of renunciation and violence – the renunciation of superior men and the violence of inferior men, which is their victory.

No superior trait can assert itself in the modern age, whether in action or in thought, in the political sphere or in the theoretical sphere.

The downfall of aristocratic influence has created an atmosphere of brutality and indifference towards the arts, such that a refined sensibility has nowhere to take refuge. Contact with life is ever more painful for the soul, and all efforts are ever more arduous, because the outer conditions for making an effort are forever more odious.

The downfall of classical ideals made all men potential artists, and therefore bad artists. When art depended on solid construction and the careful observance of rules, few could attempt to be artists, and a fair number of these were quite good. But when art, instead of being understood as creation, became merely an expression of feelings, then anyone could be an artist, because everyone has feelings.

250

Even if I wanted to create . . . . .

The only true art is that of *construction*. But the present-day milieu makes it impossible for constructive qualities to appear in the human spirit.

That's why science developed. Machines are the only things today in which there's construction; mathematical proofs are the only arguments with a chain of logic.

Creativity needs a prop, the crutch of reality.

Art is a science. . .

It suffers rhythmically.

I can't read, for my hypercritical sensibility notices only flaws, imperfections, things that could be improved. I can't dream, for my dreams are so vivid that I compare them with reality and quickly realize they're unreal, hence without value. I can't enjoy innocently gazing at people and things, for my longing to dig deeper is inexorable, and since my interest can't exist without this longing, it must either die at its hands or wither [on its own]. I can't be satisfied by metaphysical speculation, for I know all too well (from my own experience) that all systems are defensible and intellectually possible, and to enjoy the intellectual art of constructing systems, I would have to be able to forget that the goal of metaphysical speculation is the search for truth.

A happy past in whose remembrance I would also be happy, with nothing in the present that would cheer or even interest me, with no dream or possibility of a future that could be any different from this present or have a past other than this past! – here lies my life, a conscious ghost of a paradise I never knew, a stillborn corpse of my unrealized hopes.

Happy those who suffer as unified selves – whom anxiety alters but doesn't divide, who believe at least in unbelief, and who can sit in the sun without mental reservations!

251

Fragments of an Autobiography

First I was engrossed in metaphysical speculations, then in scientific ideas. Finally I was attracted to sociological [concepts]. But in none of these stages of my search for truth did I find relief or reassurance. I didn't read much in these various fields, but what I did read was enough to make me weary of so many contradictory theories, all equally based on elaborate rationales, all equally probable and in accord with a selection of the facts that always gave the impression of being all the facts. If I raised my tired eyes from the books, or if I distractedly shifted focus from my thoughts to the outside world, I saw only one thing, which plucked one by one all the petals of the notion of effort, convincing me that all reading and thinking are useless. What I saw was the infinite complexity of things, the vast sum □, the utter attainability of even those few facts that would be necessary for the formation of a science.

◆

I gradually discovered the frustration of discovering nothing. I could find no reason or logic for anything except a scepticism that didn't even seek a self-justifying logic. It never occurred to me to cure myself of this. And indeed, why be cured of it? What would it mean to be 'healthy'? How could I be sure that this attitude meant I was sick? And if I was sick, who's to say that sickness wasn't preferable or more logical or more □ than health? If health was preferable, then wasn't I sick due to some natural cause? And if it was natural, why go against Nature, which for some purpose or other – if it has any purpose – must have wanted me to be sick?

I never found convincing arguments for anything other than inertia, and over time I became ever more keenly, sullenly aware of my inertia as an abdicator. Seeking out modes of inertia, pleading to evade all personal struggle and social responsibility – this is the □ substance from which I carved the imaginary statue of my existence.

I got tired of reading, and I stopped arbitrarily pursuing now this, now that aesthetic mode of life. Of the little I did read, I learned to extract only the elements useful for dreaming. Of the little I saw and heard, I strove to take away only what could be prolonged in me as a distant and distorted reflection. I endeavoured to make all my thoughts and all the daily chapters of my experience provide me with nothing but sensations. I gave my life an aesthetic orientation, and I made that aesthetic utterly personal, exclusively my own.

The next step in the development of my inner hedonism was to shun all sensibility to things social. I shielded myself against feeling ridiculous. I learned to be insensitive to the appeals of instinct and to the entreaties of . . . . .

I reduced my contact with others to a minimum. I did my best to lose all attachment to life . . . . . In time I even shed my desire for glory, like a sleepy man who takes off his clothes to go to bed.

◆

After studying metaphysics and □ sciences, I went on to mental occupations that were more threatening to my nervous equilibrium. I spent frightful nights hunched over tomes by mystics and cabbalists which I never had the patience to read except intermittently, trembling and . . . . . The rites and mysteries of the Rosicrucians, the □ symbolism of the Cabbala and the Templars . . . . . – all of this oppressed me for a long time. My feverish days were filled with pernicious speculations based on the demonic logic of metaphysics – magic, □ alchemy – and I derived a false vital stimulus from the painful and quasi-psychic sensation of being always on the verge of discovering a supreme mystery. I lost myself in the delirious subsystems of metaphysics, systems full of disturbing analogies and pitfalls for lucid thought, vast enigmatic landscapes where glimmers of the supernatural arouse mysteries on the fringes.

Sensations aged me. Too much thinking wore me out. My life became a metaphysical fever, always searching for the occult meanings of things, playing with the fire of mysterious analogies, denigrating [?] itself by putting off full lucidity and normal synthesis.

I fell into a complex state of mental indiscipline and general indifference. Where did I take refuge? My impression is that I didn't take refuge anywhere. I abandoned myself to I don't know what.

I limited and focused my desires to hone and refine them. To reach the infinite – and I believe it can be reached – we need to have a sure port, just one, from which to set out for the Indefinite.

Today I'm an ascetic in my religion of myself. A cup of coffee, a cigarette and my dreams can substitute quite well for the universe and its stars, for work, love, and even beauty and glory. I need virtually no stimulants. I have opium enough in my soul.

What dreams do I have? I don't know. I forced myself to reach a point where I'm no longer sure what I think, dream, or envision. I seem to dream ever more remotely, about vague and imprecise things that can't be visualized.

I have no theories about life. I don't know or wonder whether it's good or bad. In my eyes it's harsh and sad, with delightful dreams interspersed here and there. Why should I care what it is for others?

Other people's lives are of use to me only in my dreams, where I live the life that seems to suit each one.

252

Thinking is still a form of acting. Only in sheer reverie, where nothing active intervenes and even our self-awareness gets stuck in the mud – only there, in this warm and damp state of non-being, can total renunciation of action be achieved.

To stop trying to understand, to stop analysing. . . To see ourselves as we see nature, to view our impressions as we view a field – that is true wisdom.

253

. . . the sacred instinct of having no theories. . .

254

More than once, while roaming the streets in the late afternoon, I've been suddenly and violently struck by the bizarre presence of organization in things. It's not so much natural things that arouse this powerful awareness in my soul; it's the layout of the streets, the signs, the people dressed up and talking, their jobs, the newspapers, the logic of it all. Or rather, it's the fact that ordered streets, signs, jobs, people and society exist, all of them fitting together and going forward and opening up paths.

When I take a good look at man, I see that he's as unconscious as a dog or cat, that he speaks and organizes himself into society through a different kind of unconsciousness, patently inferior to the unconsciousness that guides ants and bees in their social life. And as if a light had turned on, the intelligence that creates and informs the world becomes as clear to me as the existence of organisms, as clear as the existence of logical and invariable physical laws.

On these occasions, I always recall the words of I can't remember which scholastic: *Deus est anima brutorum*, God is the soul of the beasts. This marvellous phrase was the author's way of explaining the certainty with which instinct guides inferior animals, which display no intelligence, or only a primitive outline of one. But we are all inferior animals, and speaking and thinking are merely new instincts, less dependable than others precisely because they're new. So that the beautifully accurate phrase of the scholastic has a wider application, and I say, 'God is the soul of everything.'

I've never understood how anyone who has stopped to consider the tremendous fact of this universal watch mechanism can deny the watchmaker, in whom not even Voltaire disbelieved. I understand why, in light of certain events that have apparently deviated from a plan (and only by knowing the plan could one know if they have deviated from it), someone might attribute an element of imperfection to this supreme intelligence. I understand this, although I don't accept it. And I understand why, in view of the evil that's in the world, one might not acknowledge that the creating intelligence is infinitely good. I understand this, although again I don't accept it. But to deny the existence of this intelligence, namely God, strikes me as one of those idiocies that sometimes afflict, in one area of their intelligence, men who in all other areas may be superior – those, for example, who systematically make mistakes in adding and subtracting, or who (considering now the intelligence that rules aesthetic sensibility) cannot feel music, or painting, or poetry.

I've said that I don't accept the notion of the watchmaker who is imperfect or who isn't benevolent. I reject the notion of the imperfect watchmaker, because those aspects of the world's government and organization that seem flawed or nonsensical might prove otherwise, if we only knew the plan. While clearly seeing a plan in everything, we also see certain things that apparently make no sense, but if there's a reason behind everything, then won't these things be guided by that same reason? Seeing the reason but not the actual plan, how can we say that certain things are outside the plan, when we don't know what it is? Just as a poet of subtle rhythms can insert an arrhythmic verse for rhythmic purposes, i.e. for the very purpose he seems to be going against (and a critic who's more linear than rhythmic will say that the verse is mistaken), so the Creator can insert things that our narrow logic considers arrhythmic into the majestic flow of his metaphysical rhythm.

I admit that the notion of an unbenevolent watchmaker is harder to refute, but only on the surface. One could say that since we don't really know what evil is, we cannot rightfully affirm that something is bad or good, but it's true that a pain, even if it's for our ultimate good, is obviously bad in itself, and this is enough to prove that evil exists in the world. A toothache is enough to make one disbelieve in the goodness of the Creator. The basic error in this argument seems to lie in our complete ignorance of God's plan, and our equal ignorance of what kind of an intelligent person the Intellectual Infinite might be. The existence of evil is one thing; the reason for its existence is another. The distinction may be subtle to the point of seeming sophistic, but it is nevertheless valid. The existence of evil cannot be denied, but one can deny that the existence of evil is evil. I admit that the problem persists, but only because our imperfection persists.

255

If there's one thing life grants us for which we should thank the Gods, besides thanking them for life itself, it's the gift of not knowing: of not knowing ourselves and of not knowing each other. The human soul is a murky and slimy abyss, a well on the earth's surface that's never used. No one would love himself if he really knew himself, and without the vanity which is born of this ignorance and is the blood of the spiritual life, our souls would die of anemia. No one knows anyone else, and it's just as well, for if he did, he would discover – in his very own mother, wife or son – his inveterate, metaphysical enemy.

We get along because we're strangers at heart. What would become of so many happy couples if they could see into one another's soul, if they could truly understand one another, as romantics say, without knowing the danger (albeit ultimately inconsequential) of what they're saying? All marriages are flawed, because each partner holds inside, in a secret corner where the soul belongs to the Devil, the wispy image of the desired man who is nothing like the husband, the hazy figure of the sublime woman whom the wife doesn't live up to. The happiest people are unaware of their frustrated inclinations; the less happy are aware but choose to ignore them, and only an occasional jerky movement or brusque remark evokes, on the casual surface of gestures and words, the hidden Demon, the ancient Eve, the Knight and the Sylph.

The life we live is a flexible, fluid misunderstanding, a happy mean between the greatness that doesn't exist and the happiness that can't exist. We are content thanks to our capacity, even as we think and feel, for not believing in the soul's existence. In the masked ball which is our life, we're satisfied by the agreeable sensation of the costumes, which are all that really count for a ball. We're servants of the lights and colours, moving in the dance as if in the truth, and we're not even aware – unless, remaining alone, we don't dance – of the so cold and lofty night outside, of the mortal body under the tatters that will outlive it, of all that we privately imagine is essentially us but that is actually just an inner parody of that supposedly true self.

All that we do, say, think or feel wears the same mask and the same costume. No matter how much we take off what we wear, we'll never reach nakedness, which is a phenomenon of the soul and not of removing clothes. And so, dressed in a body and soul, with our multiple costumes stuck to us like feathers on a bird, we live happily or unhappily – or without knowing how we live – this brief time given us by the gods that we might amuse them, like children who play at serious games.

One or another man, liberated or cursed, suddenly sees – but even this man sees rarely – that all we are is what we aren't, that we fool ourselves about what's true and are wrong about what we conclude is right. And this man, who in a flash sees the universe naked, creates a philosophy or dreams up a religion; and the philosophy spreads and the religion propagates, and those who believe in the philosophy begin to wear it as a suit they don't see, and those who believe in the religion put it on as a mask they soon forget.

Knowing neither ourselves nor each other, and therefore cheerfully getting along, we keep twirling round in the dance and chatting during the intervals – human, futile, and in earnest – to the sound of the great orchestra of the stars, under the aloof and disdainful gaze of the show's organizers.

Only they know we're the prey of the illusion they created for us. But what's the reason for this illusion, and why is there this or any illusion, and why did they, likewise deluded, give us the illusion they gave us? This, undoubtedly, not even they know.

256

I've always felt an almost physical loathing for secret things – intrigues, diplomacy, secret societies, occult sciences. What especially irks me are these last two things – the pretension certain men have that, through their understandings with Gods or Masters or Demiurges, they and they alone know the great secrets on which the world is founded.

I can't believe their claims, though I can believe someone else might. But is there any reason why all these people might not be crazy or deluded? The fact there are a lot of them proves nothing, for there are collective hallucinations.

What really shocks me is how these wizards and masters of the invisible, when they write to communicate or intimate their mysteries, all write abominably. It offends my intelligence that a man can master the Devil without being able to master the Portuguese language. Why should dealing with demons be easier than dealing with grammar? If through long exercises of concentration and willpower one can have so-called astral visions, why can't the same person – applying considerably less concentration and willpower – have a vision of syntax? What is there in the teachings and rituals of the Magic Arts that prevents their adherents from writing – I won't say with clarity, since obscurity may be part of the occult law – but at least with elegance and fluency, which can exist in the sphere of the abstruse? Why should all the soul's energy be spent studying the language of the Gods, without a pittance left over to study the colour and rhythm of the language of men?

I don't trust masters who can't be down-to-earth. For me they're like those eccentric poets who can't write like everybody else. I accept that they're eccentric, but I'd like them to show me that it's because they're superior to the norm rather than incapable of it.

There are supposedly great mathematicians who make errors in simple addition, but what I'm talking about here is ignorance, not error. I accept that a great mathematician can add two and two and get five: it can happen to anyone in a moment of distraction. What I don't accept is that he not know what addition is or how it's done. And this is the case of the overwhelming majority of occult masters.

257

Thought can be lofty without being elegant, but to the extent it lacks elegance it will have less effect on others. Force without finesse is mere mass.

258

To have touched the feet of Christ is no excuse for mistakes in punctuation.

If a man writes well only when he's drunk, then I'll tell him: Get drunk. And if he says that it's bad for his liver, I'll answer: What's your liver? A dead thing that lives while you live, whereas the poems you write live without while.

259

I enjoy speaking. Or rather, I enjoy wording. Words for me are tangible bodies, visible sirens, incarnate sensualities. Perhaps because real sensuality doesn't interest me in the least, not even intellectually or in my dreams, desire in me metamorphosed into my aptitude for creating verbal rhythms and for noting them in the speech of others. I tremble when someone speaks well. Certain pages from Fialho* and from Chateaubriand make my whole being tingle in all of its pores, make me rave in a still shiver with impossible pleasure. Even certain pages of Vieira,* in the cold perfection of their syntactical engineering, make me quiver like a branch in the wind, with the passive delirium of something shaken.

Like all who are impassioned, I take blissful delight in losing myself, in fully experiencing the thrill of surrender. And so I often write with no desire to think, in an externalized reverie, letting the words cuddle me like a baby in their arms. They form sentences with no meaning, flowing softly like water I can feel, a forgetful stream whose ripples mingle and undefine, becoming other, still other ripples, and still again other. Thus ideas and images, throbbing with expressiveness, pass through me in resounding processions of pale silks on which imagination shimmers like moonlight, dappled and indefinite.

I weep over nothing that life brings or takes away, but there are pages of prose that have made me cry. I remember, as clearly as what's before my eyes, the night when as a child I read for the first time, in an anthology, Vieira's famous passage on King Solomon: 'Solomon built a palace. . .' And I read all the way to the end, trembling and confused. Then I broke into joyful tears – tears such as no real joy could make me cry, nor any of life's sorrows ever make me shed. That hieratic movement of our clear majestic language, that expression of ideas in inevitable words, like water that flows because there's a slope, that vocalic marvel in which the sounds are ideal colours – all of this instinctively seized me like an overwhelming political emotion. And I cried. Remembering it today, I still cry. Not out of nostalgia for my childhood, which I don't miss, but because of nostalgia for the emotion of that moment, because of a heartfelt regret that I can no longer read for the first time that great symphonic certitude.

I have no social or political sentiments, and yet there is a way in which I'm highly nationalistic. My nation is the Portuguese language. It wouldn't trouble me at all if Portugal were invaded or occupied, as long as I was left in peace. But I hate with genuine hatred, with the only hatred I feel, not those who write bad Portuguese, not those whose syntax is faulty, not those who used phonetic rather than etymological spelling,* but the badly written page itself, as if it were a person, incorrect syntax, as someone who ought to be flogged, the substitution of *i* for *y*, as the spit that directly disgusts me, independent of who spat it.

Yes, because spelling is also a person. The word is complete when seen and heard. And the pageantry of Graeco-Roman transliteration dresses it for me in its authentic royal robe, making it a lady and queen.

260

Art consists in making others feel what we feel, in freeing them from themselves by offering them our own personality. The true substance of whatever I feel is absolutely incommunicable, and the more profoundly I feel it, the more incommunicable it is. In order to convey to someone else what I feel, I must translate my feelings into his language – saying things, that is, as if they were what I feel, so that he, reading them, will feel exactly what I felt. And since this someone is presumed by art to be not this or that person but everyone (i.e., that person common to all persons), what I must finally do is convert my feelings into a typical human feeling, even if it means perverting the true nature of what I felt.

Abstract things are hard to understand, because they don't easily command the reader's attention, so I'll use a simple example to make my abstractions concrete. Let's suppose that, for some reason or other (which might be that I'm tired of keeping the books or bored because I have nothing to do), I'm overwhelmed by a vague sadness about life, an inner anxiety that makes me nervous and uneasy. If I try to translate this emotion with close-fitting words, then the closer the fit, the more they'll represent my own personal feeling, and so the less they'll communicate it to others. And if there is no communicating it to others, it would be wiser and simpler to feel it without writing it.

But let's suppose that I want to communicate it to others – to make it into art, that is, since art is the communication to others of the identity we feel with them, without which there would be no communication and no need for it. I search for the ordinary human emotion that will have the colouring, spirit and shape of the emotion I'm feeling right now for the inhuman, personal reason of being a weary bookkeeper or a bored Lisboan. And I conclude that the ordinary emotion which in ordinary souls has the same characteristics as my emotion is nostalgia for one's lost childhood.

Now I have the key to the door of my theme. I write and weep about my lost childhood, going into poignant detail about the people and furniture of our old house in the country. I recall the joy of having no rights or responsibilities, of being free because I still didn't know how to think or feel – and this recollection, if it's well written and visually effective, will arouse in my reader exactly the same emotion I was feeling, which had nothing to do with childhood.

I've lied? No, I've understood. That lying, except for the childish and spontaneous kind that comes from wanting to be dreaming, is merely the recognition of other people's real existence and of the need to conform that existence to our own, which cannot be conformed to theirs. Lying is simply the soul's ideal language. Just as we make use of words, which are sounds articulated in an absurd way, to translate into real language the most private and subtle shifts of our thoughts and emotions (which words on their own would never be able to translate), so we make use of lies and fiction to promote understanding among ourselves, something that the truth – personal and incommunicable – could never accomplish.

Art lies because it is social. And there are two great forms of art: one that speaks to our deepest soul, the other to our attentive soul. The first is poetry, the second is the novel. The first begins to lie in its very structure; the second in its very intention. One purports to give us the truth through lines that keep strict metres, thus lying against the nature of speech; the other purports to give us the truth by means of a reality that we all know never existed.

To feign is to love. Whenever I see a pretty smile or a meaningful gaze, no matter whom the smile or gaze belongs to, I always plumb to the soul of the smiling or gazing face to discover what politician wants to buy our vote or what prostitute wants us to buy her. But the politician that buys us loved at least the act of buying us, even as the prostitute loved being bought by us. Like it or not, we cannot escape universal brotherhood. We all love each other, and the lie is the kiss we exchange.

261

In me all affections take place on the surface, but sincerely. I've always been an actor, and in earnest. Whenever I've loved, I've pretended to love, pretending it even to myself.

262

Today I was struck by an absurd but valid sensation. I realized, in an inner flash, that I'm no one. Absolutely no one. In that flash, what I'd supposed was a city proved to be a barren plain, and the sinister light that showed me myself revealed no sky above. Before the world existed, I was deprived of the power to be. If I was reincarnated, it was without myself, without my I.

I'm the suburbs of a non-existent town, the long-winded commentary on a book never written. I'm no one, no one at all. I don't know how to feel, how to think, how to want. I'm the character of an unwritten novel, wafting in the air, dispersed without ever having been, among the dreams of someone who didn't know how to complete me.

I always think, I always feel, but there's no logic in my thought, no emotions in my emotion. I'm falling from the trapdoor on high through all of infinite space in an aimless, infinitudinous,* empty descent. My soul is a black whirlpool, a vast vertigo circling a void, the racing of an infinite ocean around a hole in nothing. And in these waters which are more a churning than actual waters float the images of all I've seen and heard in the world – houses, faces, books, boxes, snatches of music and syllables of voices all moving in a sinister and bottomless swirl.

And amid all this confusion I, what's truly I, am the centre that exists only in the geometry of the abyss: I'm the nothing around which everything spins, existing only so that it can spin, being a centre only because every circle has one. I, what's truly I, am a well without walls but with the walls' viscosity, the centre of everything with nothing around it.

It's not demons (who at least have a human face) but hell itself that seems to be laughing inside me, it's the croaking madness of the dead universe, the spinning cadaver of physical space, the end of all worlds blowing blackly in the wind, formless and timeless, without a God who created it, without even its own self, impossibly whirling in the absolute darkness as the one and only reality, everything.

If only I knew how to think! If only I knew how to feel!

My mother died too soon for me to ever know her. . .

263

As prone as I am to tedium, it's odd that until now I've never seriously thought about just what it is. Today my soul is in that state of limbo where neither life nor anything else really appeals, and I've decided, since I've never done it before, to analyse tedium through my impressionistic thoughts, even though whatever analysis I dream up will naturally be somewhat factitious.

I don't know if tedium is merely the waking equivalent of a vagrant's drowsy stupor, or if it is something more noble. In my own experience, tedium occurs frequently but unpredictably, without following a set pattern. I can go an entire listless Sunday without tedium, or I can suddenly experience it, like a cloud overhead, in the middle of concentrated labour. As far as I can tell, it isn't related to my state of health (or lack thereof), nor does it result from causes residing in my visible, tangible self.

To say that it's a metaphysical anxiety in disguise, that it's an acute disillusion incognito, that it's a voiceless poetry of the bored soul sitting at the window which looks out on to life – to say this or something similar can colour tedium, like a child who colours over the outlines of a figure and effaces them, but it's no more to me than a din of words echoing in the cellar of the mind.

Tedium... To think without thinking, but with the weariness of thinking; to feel without feeling, but with the anxiety of feeling; to shun without shunning, but with the disgust that makes one shun – all of this is in tedium but is not tedium itself, being at best a paraphrase or translation of it. In terms of our immediate sensation, it's as if the drawbridge had been raised over the moat of the soul's castle, such that we can only gaze at the lands around the castle, without ever being able to set foot on them. There's something in us that isolates us from ourselves, and the separating element is as stagnant as we are, a ditch of filthy water around our self-alienation.

Tedium... To suffer without suffering, to want without desire, to think without reason... It's like being possessed by a negative demon, like being bewitched by nothing at all. Wizards and witches, by making images of us and subjecting them to torments, can supposedly cause those torments to be reflected in us through an astral transference. Transposing this image, I would say that my tedium is like the fiendish reflection of an elfin demon's sorceries, applied not to my image but to its shadow. It's on my internal shadow, on the outside of my inner soul, that papers are pasted or needles are poked. I'm like the man that sold his shadow,* or, rather, like the shadow that was sold.

Tedium... I work hard. I fulfil what the moralists of action would say is my social duty. I fulfil that duty, or fate, without too much effort and without gross incompetence. But sometimes right in the middle of my work, or in the middle of the rest which, according to the same moralists, I deserve and ought to enjoy, my soul overflows with a bitter inertia, and I'm tired, not of working or of resting, but of me.

Why of me, if I wasn't thinking about myself? Of what other thing, if I wasn't thinking about anything? The mystery of the universe that descends on my bookkeeping or on my repose? The universal sorrow of living which is suddenly particularized in my soul-turned-medium? Why so ennoble someone whose identity isn't even certain? It's a sensation of emptiness, a hunger without appetite, as noble as the sensations that come to our physical brain and stomach when we smoke too much or suffer from indigestion.

Tedium... Perhaps, deep down, it is the soul's dissatisfaction because we didn't give it a belief, the disappointment of the sad child (who we are on the inside) because we didn't buy it the divine toy. Perhaps it is the insecurity of one who needs a guiding hand and who doesn't feel, on the black path of profound sensation, anything more than the soundless night of not being able to think, the empty road of not being able to feel...

Tedium... Those who have Gods don't have tedium. Tedium is the lack of a mythology. For people without beliefs, even doubt is impossible, even their scepticism will lack the strength to question. Yes, tedium is the loss of the soul's capacity for self-delusion; it is the mind's lack of the non-existent ladder by which it might firmly ascend to truth.

264

I know, by analogy, what it means to overeat. I know it through my sensations, not my stomach. There are days when they've eaten too much, and my body gets heavy, my gestures are clumsy, and I don't feel like moving a muscle.

On these occasions, like a thorn in the side, a vestige of my vanished imagination nearly always emerges from out of my undisturbed torpor. And I make plans founded on ignorance, I raise edifices based on hypotheses, and I'm dazzled by what's bound to never happen.

At these strange times, my moral as well as material life are mere appendages to who I am. I forget not only about the notion of duty but also about the idea of being, and I feel physically tired of the whole universe. I sleep what I know and what I dream with an equal intensity that makes my eyes sore. Yes, at these times I know more about myself than I've ever known, and I'm every snooze of every beggar lying under the trees on the estate of Nobody.

265

The idea of travelling seduces me vicariously, as if it were the perfect idea for seducing someone I'm not. All the world's vast panorama traverses my alert imagination like a colourful tedium; I trace a desire as one who's tired of making gestures, and the anticipated weariness of potential landscapes scourges the flower of my drooping heart like a harsh wind.

And as with journeys, so with books, and as with books, so with everything. . . I dream of an erudite life in the quiet company of the ancients and the moderns, a life in which I would renew my emotions via the emotions of others, and fill myself with contradictory thoughts based on the contradiction between the meditators and those who almost thought (and who are the majority of writers). But the very idea of reading vanishes as soon as I pick up a book from the table, the physical act of reading abolishing all desire to read. In the same way, the idea of travelling withers if I happen to go near a platform or port of departure. And I return to the two worthless things that I (likewise worthless) am certain of: my daily life as an inconspicuous passer-by, and the waking insomnia of my dreams.

And as with books, so with everything. . . As soon as something occurs to me that might interrupt the silent procession of my days, I lift my eyes with heavy protest towards the sylph who belongs to me and who, poor thing, might have been a siren had she only learned to sing.

266

When I first came to Lisbon I used to hear, from the apartment above ours, the sound of scales played on a piano, the monotonous practising of a girl I never actually saw. Today I realize that in the cellar of my soul, by some mysterious process of infiltration, those scales persist, audible if the door below is opened, played over and over by the girl who is now someone else, a grown woman, or dead and enclosed in a white place where verdant cypresses blackly wave.

I'm no longer the child I was back then, but the sound of the playing is the same in my memory as it was in reality, so that whenever it gets up from where it pretends to be sleeping, it has the same slow finger work, the same rhythmic monotony. When I feel or think about it, I'm overwhelmed by a vague and anxious sadness that's my own.

I don't mourn the loss of my childhood; I mourn because everything, including (my) childhood, is lost. It's not the concrete passing of my own days but the abstract flight of time that torments my physical brain with the relentless repetition of the piano scales from upstairs, terribly anonymous and far away. It's the huge mystery of nothing lasting which incessantly hammers things that aren't really music, just nostalgia, in the absurd depths of my memory.

I summon up, insensibly, the vision of the sitting room that I never saw, where the pupil I never met is still playing today, finger by careful finger, the forever identical scales of what's already dead. I see, I see more and more, I reconstruct by seeing. And the entire household of the upstairs apartment, for which today I feel a nostalgia I didn't feel yesterday, is fictitiously constructed by my uncertain contemplation.

I suspect, however, that all of this is vicarious, that the nostalgia I feel isn't truly mine or truly abstract but is the emotion intercepted from an unidentified third party, for whom these emotions, which in me are literary, are – as Vieira* would say – literal. Conjectured feelings are what grieve and torment me, and the nostalgia that makes my eyes well with tears is conceived and felt through imagination and projection.

And with a relentlessness that comes from the world's depths, with a persistence that strikes the keys metaphysically, the scales of a piano student keep playing over and over, up and down the physical backbone of my memory. It's the old streets with other people, the same streets that today are different; it's dead people speaking to me through the transparency of their absence; it's remorse for what I did or didn't do; it's the rippling of streams in the night, noises from below in the quiet building.

I feel like screaming inside my head. I want to stop, to break, to smash this impossible phonograph record that keeps playing inside me, where it doesn't belong, an intangible torturer. I want my soul, a vehicle taken over by others, to let me off and go on without me. I'm going crazy from having to hear. And in the end it is I – in my odiously impressionable brain, in my thin skin, in my hypersensitive nerves – who am the keys played in scales, O horrible and personal piano of our memory.

And always, always, as if in a part of my brain that had become autonomous, the scales play, play, play, below me and above me, in the first building I lived in when I came to Lisbon.

267

It's the last death of Captain Nemo. Soon I too will die.

All of my childhood was deprived, in that moment, of any possibility of enduring.

268

Smell is a strange way of seeing. It evokes sentimental scenes, sketched all of a sudden by the subconscious. I've often experienced this. I'm walking down a street. I see nothing, or rather, I look all around and see the way everyone sees. I know I'm walking down a street and don't know that it exists with two sides comprised of variously shaped buildings made by human hands. I'm walking down a street. The smell of bread from a bakery nauseates me with its sweetness, and my childhood rises up from a distant neighbourhood, and another bakery emerges from that fairyland which is everything we ever had that has died. I'm walking down a street. Suddenly I smell the fruit on the slanted rack of the small grocery, and my short life in the country – I can't say from when or where – has trees in the background and peace in what can only be my childhood heart. I'm walking down a street. I'm unexpectedly thrown off balance by the smell of crates from the crate-maker's: my dear Cesário!* You appear before me and at last I'm happy, for I've returned by way of memory to the only truth, which is literature.

269

One of my life's greatest tragedies is to have already read *The Pickwick Papers*. (I can't go back and read them for the first time.)

270

Art frees us, illusorily, from the squalor of being. While feeling the wrongs and sufferings endured by Hamlet, prince of Denmark, we don't feel our own, which are vile because they're ours and vile because they're vile.

Love, sleep, drugs and intoxicants are elementary forms of art, or rather, of producing the same effect as art. But love, sleep and drugs all have their disillusion. Love wearies or disappoints. We wake up from sleep, and while sleeping we haven't lived. And we pay for drugs with the ruin of the very body they served to stimulate. But in art there is no disillusion, since illusion is accepted from the start. There's no waking up from art, because we dream but don't sleep in it. Nor do we pay a tax or penalty for having enjoyed art.

Since the pleasure we get from art is in a sense not our own, we don't have to pay for it or regret it later.

By art I mean everything that delights us without being ours – the trail left by what has passed, a smile given to someone else, a sunset, a poem, the objective universe.

To possess is to lose. To feel without possessing is to preserve and keep, for it is to extract from things their essence.

271

It's not love but love's outskirts that are worth knowing...

The repression of love sheds much more light on its nature than does the actual experience of it. Virginity can be a key to profound understanding. Action has its rewards but brings confusion. To possess is to be possessed, and therefore to lose oneself. Only the idea can fathom reality without getting ruined.

272

Christ is a form of emotion.

In the Pantheon there's room for all the gods that mutually exclude each other; all have their throne and their sovereignty. Each one can be everything, for here there are no limits, not even logical ones, and the mingling of various immortals allows us to enjoy the coexistence of diverse infinities and assorted eternities.

273

Nothing is ever sure in history. There are periods of order when everything is contemptible and periods of disorder in which all is lofty. Decadent eras abound in mental vitality, mighty eras in intellectual weakness. Everything mixes and criss-crosses, and truth exists only in so far as it is presumed.

So many noble ideas fallen into the dung heap, so many heartfelt desires lost in the torrent!

Gods and men – they're all the same to me in the rampant confusion of unpredictable fate. They march through my dreams in this anonymous fourth-floor room, and they're no more to me than they were to those who believed in them. Idols of leery, wide-eyed Africans, animal deities of hinterland savages, the Egyptians' personified symbols, luminous Greek divinities, stiff Roman gods, Mithras lord of the Sun and of emotion, Jesus lord of consequences and charity, various versions of the same Christ, new holy gods of new towns – all of them make up the funeral march (be it a pilgrimage or burial) of error and illusion. They all march, and behind them march the dreams that are just empty shadows cast on the ground but that the worst dreamers suppose are firmly planted there: pathetic concepts without body or soul – Liberty, Humanity, Happiness, a Better Future, Social Science – moving forward in the solitude of darkness like leaves dragged along by the train of a royal robe stolen by beggars.

274

Revolutionaries make a crass and grievous error when they distinguish between the bourgeoisie and the masses, the nobility and the common people, the ruling and the ruled. The only distinction is between those who adapt and those who don't; the rest is literature, and bad literature. The beggar, if he adapts, can become king tomorrow, though in doing so he'll forfeit the virtue of being a beggar. He'll have crossed the border, losing his nationality.

These thoughts console me in this cramped office, whose grimy windows overlook a joyless street. These thoughts console me, and for company I have my fellow creators of the world's consciousness – the reckless playwright William Shakespeare, John Milton the schoolteacher, Dante Alighieri the tramp, ... and even, if the reference be permitted, Jesus Christ, who was nothing in the world, his very existence being doubted by history. Quite a different class of men is formed by the likes of the state councillor Johann Wolfgang von Goethe,

the senator Victor Hugo, the chief of state Lenin, the chief of state Mussolini . . . . .

Those of us in the shade, among the delivery boys and the barbers, constitute humanity . . . . .

On the one hand there are the kings with their prestige, the emperors with their glory, the geniuses with their aura, the saints with their haloes, the leaders with their supremacy, the prostitutes, the prophets and the rich. . . On the other hand there's us – the delivery boy on the corner, the reckless playwright William Shakespeare, the barber with his jokes, John Milton the schoolteacher, the shop assistant, Dante Alighieri the tramp, those whom death forgets or consecrates and whom life forgot without ever consecrating.

275

Government of the world begins in us. It's not the sincere who govern the world, but neither is it the insincere; it's those who create in themselves a real sincerity by artificial and automatic means. This sincerity is what makes them strong, and it outshines the less false sincerity of others. To be adept at deluding oneself is the first prerequisite for a statesman. Only poets and philosophers see the world as it really is, for only to them is it given to live without illusions. To see clearly is to not act.

276

An opinion is a vulgarity, even when it's not sincere.

Every instance of sincerity is an intolerance. There are no sincere liberal minds. There are, for that matter, no liberal minds.

277

There everything is feeble, anonymous and gratuitous. There I saw great demonstrations of compassion, which seemed to reveal the depths of tragically sad souls, but I discovered that the demonstrations lasted no longer than the moment in which they were words, and that they originated – how often I observed this with the discernment of the silent – in something analogous to pity, lost as swiftly as the novelty of the observation, or else in the wine of the compassionate soul's dinner. There was always a direct relationship between the humanitarian sentiments expressed and the amount of brandy consumed, and many a grand gesture suffered from one glass too many or from a pleonastic thirst.

All of these individuals had sold their souls to a devil from hell's riff-raff, a devil that craved sordidness and idleness. They lived drunken lives of vanity and sloth, and limply died in the cushions of words, in a morass of scorpions whose venom is mere drool.

The most extraordinary thing about all of these people was their complete and unanimous lack of importance, in every sense of the word. Some wrote for the major newspapers and succeeded in not existing. Others figured prominently in the professional register and succeeded in doing nothing in life. Others were even poets of renown, but one and the same ashen dust paled their foolish faces, and they were all a graveyard of embalmed stiffs, positioned with their hands on their hips, in postures of the living.

From the short time that I stagnated in that exile of mental cleverness, I've retained the memory of a few good and genuinely amusing moments, of many dull and unhappy moments, of several profiles standing out from the nothingness, of some gestures directed at whatever waitress happened to be on duty – in short, a physically nauseating tedium and the remembrance of a funny joke or two.

Interspersed among them like blank spaces there were a few older men, who with their outmoded witticisms would backbite like the others, and about the same people.

I've never felt so much sympathy for the minor figures of public glory as when I saw them vilified by these minor men who grudge them their petty glory. I understood then why the pariahs of Greatness are able to triumph: because they triumph in relation to these men and not in relation to humanity.

Poor devils with their insatiable hunger – either hungry for lunch, hungry for fame, or hungry for life's desserts. Anyone who hears them for the first time will imagine he's listening to Napoleon's tutors and Shakespeare's teachers.

Some triumph in love, some triumph in politics, and some triumph in art. The first group has the advantage of storytelling, since one can be highly successful in love without there being public knowledge of what happened. Of course, on hearing one of these men recount his sexual marathons, we begin to have our doubts after about the seventh conquest. Those who are the lovers of aristocratic or well-known ladies (and it seems to be the case for nearly all of them) ravage so many countesses that a tally of their conquests would shatter the gravity and composure of even the great-grandmothers of young women with titles.

Some specialize in physical conflict, killing the boxing champions of Europe in nocturnal revelries on the street corners of Chiado.* Others have influence over all the ministers of all the ministries, and these are the ones whose claims are at least plausible.

Some are terrible sadists, others are inveterate pederasts, and still others confess in a loud, sad voice that they're brutal with women, having brought them along life's paths by the whip. They always let someone else pay for their coffee.

Some are poets, some are . . . . .

I know no better antidote for that torrent of shadows than direct acquaintance with common human life – in its commercial reality, for instance, as exhibited on the Rua dos Douradores. With what relief I used to return from that madhouse of puppets to the real presence of Moreira, my supervisor, a genuine and competent bookkeeper, badly dressed and out of shape, but at any rate a man, something none of these others have succeeded in being.

278

Most men spontaneously live a fictitious and alien life. 'Most people are other people,'* said Oscar Wilde, and he was right. Some spend their lives in pursuit of something they don't want; others pursue something they want that's useless to them; still others lose themselves . . . . .

But most men are happy and enjoy life for no reason. Man usually doesn't weep much, and when he complains, that's his literature. Pessimism isn't viable as a democratic formula. Those who lament the world's woes are isolated – they lament only their own. A Leopardi or an Antero de Quental* doesn't have a sweetheart? Then the universe is a torment. A Vigny feels he's inadequately loved? The world is a prison. A Chateaubriand dreams the impossible? Human life is tedious. A Job is covered with boils? Earth is covered with boils. People step on some sad fellow's corns? Alas for his feet, the suns and the stars!

Indifferent to all this, humanity keeps on eating and loving, weeping over only what it must weep, and for as short a time as possible – over the death of a son, for instance, who is soon forgotten except on his birthday, or over the loss of money, which only causes weeping until more money comes along or one gets used to the loss.

The will to live recovers and carries on. The dead are buried. Our losses are forgotten.

279

He left today for his home town, apparently for good. I mean the so-called office boy, the same man I'd come to regard as part of this human corporation, and therefore as part of me and my world. He left today. In the corridor, casually running into each other for the expected surprise of our farewell, he timidly returned my embrace, and I had enough self-control not to cry, as in my heart – independent of me – my ardent eyes wanted.

Whatever has been ours, because it was ours, even if only as a casual presence in our daily routine or in what we see, becomes part of us. The man who left today for a Galician town I've never heard of was not, for me, the office boy; he was a vital part, because visible and human, of the substance of my life. Today I was diminished. I'm not quite the same. The office boy left today.

Everything that happens where we live happens in us. Everything that ceases in what we see ceases in us. Everything that has been, if we saw it when it was, was taken from us when it went away. The office boy left today.

Wearier, older, and less willing, I sit down at the high desk and continue working from where I left off yesterday. But today's vague tragedy, stirring thoughts I have to dominate by force, interrupts the automatic process of good bookkeeping. The only way I'm able to work is through an active inertia, as my own slave. The office boy left today.

Yes, tomorrow or another day, or whenever the bell will soundlessly toll my death or departure, I'll also be one who's no longer here, an old copier stowed away in the cabinet under the stairs. Yes, tomorrow or when Fate decides, the one in me who pretended to be I will come to an end. Will I go to my home town? I don't know where I'll go. Today the tragedy is visible because of an absence, considerable because it doesn't deserve consideration. My God, my God, the office boy left today.

280

O night in which the stars feign light, O night that alone is the size of the Universe, make me, body and soul, part of your body, so that – being mere darkness – I'll lose myself and become night as well, without any dreams as stars within me, nor a hoped-for sun shining with the future.

281

First it's a sound that makes another sound, in the nocturnal hollow of things. Then it's a low howl, accompanied by the creaking of the street's swaying signboards. And then the voice of space becomes a shout, a roar, and everything shudders, nothing sways, and there's silence in the dread of all this, like a speechless dread that sees another dread when the first one has passed.

Then there's nothing but wind, just wind, and I sleepily notice how the doors shake in their frames and how the glass in the windows loudly resists.

I don't sleep. I interexist.* A few vestiges of consciousness persist. I feel the weight of slumber but not of unconsciousness. I don't exist. The wind. . . I wake up and go back to sleep without yet having slept. There's a landscape of loud and indistinct sound beyond which I'm a stranger to myself. I cautiously delight in the possibility of sleeping. I really do sleep, but don't know if I'm sleeping. In what seems to me like a slumber there is always a sound of the end of all things, the wind in the darkness, and, if I listen closely, the sound of my own lungs and heart.

282

After the last stars whitened into nothing in the morning sky and the breeze turned less cold in the oranged yellow of the light falling over several low-lying clouds, I finally succeeded in dragging my body – exhausted from nothing – out of the bed where I had sleeplessly pondered the universe.

I walked to the window with eyes that were burning from having stayed open all night. The light reflected off the crowded rooftops in various shades of pale yellow. I contemplated everything with the grand stupidity that comes from not sleeping. The yellow was wispy and insignificant against the hulking figures of the tall buildings. Far off in the west (the direction I was facing), the horizon was already a greenish white.

I know that today will oppress me as when I can't grasp a thing. I know that everything I do today will be marked not by weariness from the sleep I didn't have, but by the insomnia I did have. I know that my existence will feel even more like sleep-walking than usual, not just because I haven't slept but because I couldn't sleep.

There are days that are philosophies, that suggest interpretations of life, that are marginal notes – full of critical observations – in the book of our universal destiny. This seems to be one of those days. I have the ludicrous impression that it is my heavy eyes and my empty brain that trace, like an absurd pencil, the letters of my profound and useless commentary.

283

Freedom is the possibility of isolation. You are free if you can withdraw from people, not having to seek them out for the sake of money, company, love, glory or curiosity, none of which can thrive in silence and solitude. If you can't live alone, you were born a slave. You may have all the splendours of the mind and the soul, in which case you're a noble slave, or an intelligent servant, but you're not free. And you can't hold this up as your own tragedy, for your birth is a tragedy of Fate alone. Hapless you are, however, if life itself so oppresses you that you're forced to become a slave. Hapless you are if, having been born free, with the capacity to be isolated and self-sufficient, poverty should force you to live with others. This tragedy, yes, is your own, and it follows you.

To be born free is the greatest splendour of man, making the humble hermit superior to kings and even to the gods, who are self-sufficient by their power but not by their contempt of it.

Death is a liberation because to die is to need no one. In death the wretched slave is forcibly set free from his pleasures, from his sufferings, from his coveted and ongoing life. The king is freed of the domains he didn't want to give up. Women who spread love are freed of the triumphs they cherish. Men who conquered are freed of the victories for which their lives were predestined.

Death ennobles, dressing our poor ridiculous bodies in finery they have never known. In death a man is free, even if he didn't want freedom. In death he's no longer a slave, even if he wept on giving up his slavery. Like a king whose greatest glory is his kingly title, and who as a man may be laughable but as a king is superior, so the dead man may be horribly deformed but is still superior, because death has freed him.

Tired, I close the shutters of my windows, I exclude the world, and I have a few moments of freedom. Tomorrow I'll go back to being a slave, but right now – alone, needing no one, and worried only that some voice or presence might disturb me – I have my little freedom, my moment of excelsis.

Leaning back in my chair, I forget the life that oppresses me. Nothing pains me besides having felt pain.

284

Let's not even touch life with the tips of our fingers.

Let's not even love in our minds.

May we never know the feel of a woman's kiss, not even in our dreams.

Artisans of morbidity, let us excel in teaching others how to cast off all illusions. Spectators of life, let us peer over all walls, with the pre-weariness of knowing that we'll see nothing new or beautiful.

Weavers of despair, let us weave only shrouds – white shrouds for the dreams we never dreamed, black shrouds for the days that we died, grey shrouds for the gestures we merely dreamed, and royal purple shrouds for our useless sensations.

On the hills and in the valleys and along swampy □ shores, hunters hunt wolves, deer, and wild ducks. Let us hate them, not because they kill but because they enjoy themselves (and we don't).

May our facial expression consist of a wan smile, like that of someone who's about to cry, a far-away gaze, like that of someone who doesn't want to see, and a disdain in all its features, as when someone despises life and lives only to despise it.

And may our disdain be for those who work and struggle, and our hatred for those who hope and trust.

285

I'm almost convinced that I'm never awake. I'm not sure if I'm not in fact dreaming when I live, and living when I dream, or if dreaming and living are for me intersected, intermingled things that together form my conscious self.

Sometimes, when I'm actively engaged in life and have as clear a notion of myself as the next man, my mind is beset by a strange feeling of doubt: I begin to wonder if I exist, if I might not be someone else's dream. I can imagine, with an almost carnal vividness, that I might be the character of a novel, moving within the reality constructed by a complex narrative, in the long waves of its style.

I've often noticed that certain fictional characters assume a prominence never attained by the friends and acquaintances who talk and listen to us in visible, real life. And this makes me fantasize about whether everything in the sum total of the world might not be an interconnected series of dreams and novels, like little boxes inside larger boxes that are inside yet larger ones, everything being a story made up of stories, like *A Thousand and One Nights*, unreally taking place in the never-ending night.

If I think, everything seems absurd to me; if I feel, everything seems strange; if I want, it's something in me that does the wanting. Whenever there's action in me, I'm sure I wasn't responsible for it. If I dream, it seems I'm being written. If I feel, it seems I'm being painted. If I want, it seems that I've been placed in a vehicle, like freight to be delivered, and that I continue with a movement I imagine is my own towards a destination I don't want until I get there.

How confusing it all is! How much better it is to see rather than think, to read rather than write! What I see may deceive me, but I don't consider it mine. What I read may distress me, but I don't have to feel bad for having written it. How painful everything is when we think of it as conscious thinkers, as contemplative beings whose consciousness has reached that second stage by which we know that we know! Although the day is gorgeous, I can't help but think this way. To think or to feel? Or what third thing among the stage-sets in the back? Tedium of twilight and disarray, shut fans, weariness from having had to live...

286

We walked, still young, beneath the tall trees and the forest's soft rustling. The moonlight made ponds out of the clearings that sprang into view along our aimless path, and their branch-tangled shores were more night than the night itself. The breeze of woodlands sighed among the trees. We talked about impossible things, and our voices were part of the night, the moon and the forest. We heard them as if they belonged to others.

The obscure forest wasn't entirely pathless. Our steps wended along trails that we instinctively knew, among dappling shadows and streaks of cold, hard moonlight. We talked about impossible things, and the whole of that real-life landscape was just as impossible.

287

We worship perfection because we can't have it; if we had it, we would reject it. Perfection is inhuman, because humanity is imperfect.

We harbour a secret hatred of paradise. Our yearnings are like those of the poor wretch who hopes for the countryside in heaven. It's not abstract ecstasies or marvels of the absolute that can enchant a feeling soul; it's homesteads and hillsides, green islands in blue seas, wooded paths and restful hours spent on ancestral farms, even if we've never had these things. If there's no land in heaven, then better there were no heaven. Better that everything be nothing and that the plotless novel come to an end.

To achieve perfection would require a coldness foreign to man, and he would lose the human heart that makes him love perfection.

In awe we worship the impulse to perfection of great artists. We love their approximation to perfection, but we love it because it is only an approximation.

288

How tragic not to believe in human perfectibility!

And how tragic to believe in it!

289

If I had written *King Lear*, I would be plagued by remorse for the rest of my life. For the sheer greatness of this work grossly magnifies its defects, its monstrous defects, the tiniest things that stand between certain scenes and their possible perfection. It's not the sun marred by spots; it's a broken Greek statue. All that has ever been done is ridden with errors, faulty perspectives, ignorance, signs of bad taste, shortcomings and oversights. To write a masterpiece large enough to be great and perfect enough to be sublime is a task no one has had the fortune or divine capacity to accomplish. Whatever can't be done in a single burst suffers from the unevenness of our spirit.

This thought causes my imagination to be overwhelmed by regret, by a painful certainty that I'll never be able to do anything good and useful for Beauty. The only method for achieving Perfection is to be God. Our greatest effort takes time; the time it takes passes through various stages of our soul, and each stage of the soul, being unlike any other, taints the character of the work with its own personality. All we can be certain of when we write is that we write badly; the only great and perfect works are the ones we never dream of realizing.

Listen still, with a sympathetic ear. Hear me out and then tell me if dreaming isn't better than life...

Hard work never pays off. Effort never leads anywhere. Only abstention is noble and lofty, for it alone recognizes that realization is always inferior, that the work we produce is always the grotesque shadow of the work we dreamed.

How I would love to be able to record, in words on paper that could be read out loud and listened to, the dialogues of the characters in my imagined dramas! The action in these dramas flows perfectly and the dialogues are flawless, but the action isn't spatially delineated in me such that I could materially project it, nor does the substance of these inner dialogues consist of actual words which I could listen to closely and transcribe on paper.

I love certain lyric poets precisely because they weren't epic or dramatic poets, because they had the intuitive wisdom never to want to express more than an intensely felt or dreamed moment. What can be written unconsciously is the exact measure of the perfection that is possible. No Shakespearian drama satisfies like a lyric poem of Heine. The poetry of Heine is perfect, whereas all drama – of Shakespeare or anyone else – is inevitably imperfect. Ah, to be able to construct a complete Whole, to compose something that would be like a human body, with perfect harmony among all its parts, and with a life, a life of unity and congruency, uniting the scattered traits of its various parts!*

You who listen but hardly hear me have no idea what a tragedy this is! To lose father and mother, to attain neither glory nor happiness, to have neither friend nor lover – all of that can be endured; what cannot be endured is to dream something beautiful that's impossible to achieve in word or deed.

The awareness that a work is perfect, the satisfaction of a work achieved... – soothing is the sleep under this shady tree in the calm of summer.

290

When I lean back and belong only remotely to life, then how fluently I dictate to my inertia the phrases I'll never write and how clearly I describe in my meditation the landscapes I could never describe! I fashion complete sentences with not a word out of place; detailed dramatic plots unroll in my mind; I sense the verbal and metrical cadence of great poems in each and every word, and a great enthusiasm follows me like an invisible slave in the shadows. But if I get up from the chair, where these nearly actualized sensations loll, and step over to the table to write them down, then the words flee, the dramas die, and the vital nexus underlying the rhythmic murmur vanishes, leaving only a distant nostalgia, a vestige of sunlight on faraway mountains, a wind that stirs leaves on the edge of a wilderness, a kinship that's never revealed, the orgy other people enjoy, the woman whom we expect to turn around and look but who never quite exists.

I've undertaken every project imaginable. The *Iliad* composed by me had a structural logic in its organic linking of epodes such as Homer could never have achieved. The meticulous perfection of my unwritten verses makes Virgil's precision look sloppy and Milton's power slack. My allegorical satires surpassed all of Swift's in the symbolic exactitude of their rigorously interconnected particulars. How many Horaces* I've been!

And whenever I've stood up from the chair where in fact these things were not totally dreamed, I've experienced the double tragedy of realizing that they're worthless and that they weren't pure dream, that something of them remains on the abstract threshold of my thinking and their being.

I was a genius in more than dreams and in less than life. That is my tragedy. I was the runner who led the race until he fell down, right before the finishing line.

291

If in art there were the office of improver, then I would have a function in life, at least in my life as an artist.

To begin with somebody else's creation, working only on improving it. . . Perhaps that is how the *Iliad* was written.

Anything but to have to struggle with original creation!

How I envy those who produce novels, those who begin them and write them and finish them! I can imagine novels chapter by chapter, sometimes with the actual phrases of dialogue and the narrative commentary in between, but I'm incapable of committing these dreams of writing to paper . . . . .

292

Every form of action, from war to logical reasoning, is false; and every abdication is also false. If only I could not act and not abdicate from acting! That would be the Dream-Crown of my glory, the Sceptre-of-Silence of my greatness.

I don't even suffer. My disdain for everything is so complete that I even disdain myself. The contempt I have for the sufferings of others I also have for my own. And so all my suffering is crushed under the foot of my disdain.

Ah, but this makes me suffer more. . . Because to value one's own suffering is to gild it with the sun of pride. Intense suffering can give the sufferer the illusion of being the Chosen One of Pain. Thus . . . . .

293

DOLOROUS INTERLUDE

Like someone whose eyes, when lifted up after staring at a book for a long time, wince at the mere sight of a naturally bright sun, so too, when I lift my eyes from looking at myself, it hurts and stings me to see the vivid clarity and independence-from-me of the world outside, of the existence of others, of the position and correlation of movements in space. I stumble on the real feelings of others. The antagonism of their psyches towards mine shoves me and trips up my steps. I slide and tumble above and between the sounds of their strange words in my ears, the hard and definite falling of their feet on the actual floor, their motions that really exist, their various and complex ways of being persons who are not mere variants of my own.

And once I've hurled myself into these souls, I suddenly feel helpless and empty, as if I'd died and yet I live, a sore and pale shade, which the first breeze will knock to the ground and the first physical contact dissolve into dust.

And then I wonder: Was it worth all the effort I put into isolating and raising myself up? Was it worth making my life into a long-drawn-out calvary for the sake of my Crucified Glory? And even if I know that it was worth it, in these moments I'm overwhelmed by the feeling that it wasn't and will never be worth it.

294

Money, children, lunatics . . . . .

Wealth should never be envied except platonically. Wealth is freedom.

295

Money is beautiful, because it frees us.

To want to die in Peking and not be able to is one of the things that weigh on me like a feeling of impending doom.

The buyers of useless things are wiser than is commonly supposed – they buy little dreams. They become children in the act of acquisition. When people with money succumb to the charms of those useless little objects, they possess them with the joy of a child gathering sea shells on the beach – the image that best expresses the child's happiness. He gathers shells on the beach! No two are ever alike for a child. He falls asleep with the two prettiest ones in his hand, and when they're lost or taken from him (A crime! They've made off with outward bits of his soul! They've stolen pieces of his dream!), he weeps like a God robbed of a just-created universe.

296

The love of absurdity and paradox is the animal happiness* of the sad. Just as the normal man talks nonsense and slaps others on the back out of zest and vitality, so those incapable of joy and enthusiasm do somersaults in their minds and perform, in their own cold way, the warm gestures of life.

297

Reductio ad absurdum is one of my favourite drinks.

298

Everything is absurd. One man spends his life earning and saving up money, although he has no children to leave it to nor any hope that some heaven might reserve him a transcendent portion. Another man strives to gain posthumous fame without believing in an afterlife that would give him knowledge of that fame. Yet another wears himself out in pursuit of things he doesn't really care for. Then there's one who . . . . .

One man reads so as to learn, uselessly. Another man enjoys himself so as to live, uselessly.

I'm riding on a tram and, as usual, am closely observing all the details of the people around me. For me these details are like things, voices, phrases. Taking the dress of the girl in front of me, I break it down into the fabric from which it's made and the work that went into making it (such that I see a dress and not just fabric), and the delicate embroidery that trims the collar decomposes under my scrutiny into the silk thread with which it was embroidered and the work it took to embroider it. And immediately, as in a textbook of basic economics, factories and jobs unfold before me: the factory where the cloth was made; the factory where the darker-coloured silk was spun to trim with curlicues its place around the neck; the factories' various divisions, the machines, the workers, the seamstresses. My inwardly turned eyes penetrate into the offices, where I see the managers trying to stay calm, and I watch everything being recorded in the account books. But that's not all: I see beyond all this to the private lives of those who live their social existence in these factories and offices. The whole world opens up before my eyes merely because in front of me – on the nape of a dark-skinned neck whose other side has I don't know what face – I see a regularly irregular dark-green embroidery on a light-green dress.

All humanity's social existence lies before my eyes.

And beyond this I sense the loves, the secrets and the souls of all who laboured so that the woman in front of me in the tram could wear, around her mortal neck, the sinuous banality of a dark-green silk trim on a less-dark-green cloth.

I get dizzy. The seats in the tram, made of tough, close-woven straw, take me to distant places and proliferate in the form of industries, workers, their houses, lives, realities, everything.

I get off the tram dazed and exhausted. I've just lived all of life.

299

Every time I go somewhere, it's a vast journey. A train trip to Cascais* tires me out as if in this short time I'd travelled through the urban and rural landscapes of four or five countries.

I imagine myself living in each house I pass, each chalet, each isolated cottage whitewashed with lime and silence – happy at first, then bored, then fed up. It all happens in a moment, and as soon as I've abandoned one of these homes, I'm filled with nostalgia for the time I lived there. And so every trip I make is a painful and happy harvest of great joys, great boredoms, and countless false nostalgias.

And as I pass by those houses, villas and chalets, I also live the daily lives of all their inhabitants, living them all at the same time. I'm the father, mother, sons, cousins, the maid and the maid's cousin, all together and all at once, thanks to my special talent for simultaneously feeling various and sundry sensations, for simultaneously living the lives of various people – both on the outside, seeing them, and on the inside, feeling them.

I've created various personalities within. I constantly create personalities. Each of my dreams, as soon as I start dreaming it, is immediately incarnated in another person, who is then the one dreaming it, and not I.

To create, I've destroyed myself. I've so externalized myself on the inside that I don't exist there except externally. I'm the empty stage where various actors act out various plays.

300

Triangular Dream

In my dream on the deck I shuddered: a chilling presentiment ran through my Far-away Prince's soul.

A noisy, threatening silence invaded the room's visible atmosphere like a livid breeze.

It all comes down to a harsh, troubling brilliance in the moonlight over the ocean that no longer tosses but still waves. Though I still couldn't hear them, it became clear that there were cypresses next to the Prince's palace.

The sword of the first lightning bolt vaguely whirled in the beyond. The moonlight over the high sea is the colour of lightning, and what it all means is that the palace of the prince I never was is now ruins in a distant past.

As the ship draws near with a sullen sound, the room lividly darkens, and he didn't die, nor is he captive, but I don't know what has become of him, the prince. What cold and unknown thing is his destiny now?

301

The only way you can have new sensations is by forging a new soul. It's useless to try to feel new things without feeling them in a new way, and you can't feel in a new way without changing your soul. For things are what we feel they are – how long have you known this without yet knowing it? – and the only way for there to be new things, for us to feel new things, is for there to be some novelty in how we feel them.

Change your soul. How? That's for you to figure out.

From the time we're born until we die, our soul slowly changes, like the body. Find a way to make it change faster, even as our body changes more rapidly when suffering or recovering from certain diseases.

We should never stoop down to delivering lectures, lest anyone think we have opinions or would condescend to speak with the public. Let the public read us, if they wish.

The lecturer, moreover, resembles an actor – an errand boy of Art, a figure despised by any good artist.

302

I've discovered that I'm always attentive to, and always thinking about, two things at the same time. I suppose everyone is a bit like that. Certain impressions are so vague that only later, because we remember them, do we even realize we had them. I believe these impressions form a part – perhaps the internal part – of the dual attention we all possess. In my case the two realities that hold my attention are equally vivid. This is what constitutes my originality. This, perhaps, is what constitutes my tragedy, and what makes it comic.

Hunched over the ledger, I attentively record the entries that tell the useless history of an obscure firm, while at the same time and with equal attention my thoughts follow the route of a non-existent ship past landscapes of an unreal Orient. For me the two things are equally visible and equally distinct: the ruled pages on which I carefully write the commercial epic of Vasques & Co., and the deck where I carefully observe – beyond the ruled pattern of the floorboards' tarred joints – the rows of lounge chairs and the stretched legs of passengers relaxing on the voyage. (If I were run over by a child's bicycle, the child's bicycle would become part of my history.) The smoking room blocks the view; that's why only their legs can be seen.

As I dip my pen in the inkwell, the door of the smoking room opens up – almost right next to where I feel I am – to reveal the face of the stranger. He turns his back to me and walks towards the others. His gait is slow and his hips don't tell much. He's English. I begin another entry. I try to figure out where I was going wrong. The Marques account should be debited rather than credited. (I see him as a chubby and affable jokester, and suddenly the ship disappears.)

303

The world belongs to those who don't feel. The essential condition for being a practical man is the absence of sensibility. The chief requisite for the practical expression of life is will, since this leads to action. Two things can thwart action – sensibility and analytic thought, the latter of which is just thought with sensibility. All action is by nature the projection of our personality on to the external world, and since the external world is largely and firstly made up of human beings, it follows that this projection of personality is basically a matter of crossing other people's path, of hindering, hurting or overpowering them, depending on the form our action takes.

To act, then, requires a certain incapacity for imagining the personalities of others, their joys and sufferings. Sympathy leads to paralysis. The man of action regards the external world as composed exclusively of inert matter – either intrinsically inert, like a stone he walks on or kicks out of his path, or inert like a human being who couldn't resist him and thus might as well be a stone as a man since, like a stone, he was walked on or kicked out of the way.

The best example of the practical man is the military strategist, in whom extreme concentration of action is joined to its extreme importance. All life is war, and the battle is life's synthesis. The strategist is a man who plays with lives like the chess player with chess pieces. What would become of the strategist if he thought about how each of his moves brings night to a thousand homes and grief to three thousand hearts? What would become of the world if we were human? If man really felt, there would be no civilization. Art gives shelter to the sensibility that action was obliged to forget. Art is Cinderella, who stayed at home because that's how it had to be.

Every man of action is basically cheerful and optimistic, because those who don't feel are happy. You can spot a man of action by the fact he's never out of sorts. A man who works in spite of being out of sorts is an auxiliary to action. He can be a bookkeeper, as it were, in the vast general scheme of life, as I happen to be in my own particular life, but he cannot be a ruler over things or men. Rulership requires insensibility. Whoever governs is happy, since to be sad one has to feel.

Today my boss, Senhor Vasques, closed a deal that brought a sick man and his family to ruin. As he negotiated the deal he completely forgot that this man existed, except as the opposing commercial party. After the deal was closed, he was touched by sensibility. Only afterwards, of course, since otherwise the deal would never have been made. 'I feel sorry for the fellow,' he told me. 'He's going to wind up being destitute.' Then, lighting up a cigar, he added: 'Well, if he needs anything from me' – meaning some kind of charity – 'I won't forget that I have him to thank for a good business deal and a few thousand escudos.'

Senhor Vasques isn't a crook; he's a man of action. The loser in this game can indeed count on my boss's charity in the future, for he's a generous man.

Senhor Vasques is like all men of action, be they business leaders, industrialists, politicians, military commanders, social and religious idealists, great poets, great artists, beautiful women, or children who do what they please. The one who ordains is the one who doesn't feel. The one who succeeds is the one who thinks only of what is needed for success. The remaining general lot of humanity – amorphous, sensitive, imaginative and fragile – is no more than the backdrop against which these stage actors perform until the puppet show ends, no more than the flat and lifeless chess board over which the pieces move until they're put away by the Great Player, who, fooling himself with a double personality, plays against his own person* and is always entertained.

304

Faith is the instinct of action.

305

My vital habit of disbelieving everything (especially instinctive things) and my natural inclination to insincerity neutralize all obstacles to the constant application of my method.

What I basically do is convert other people into my dreams. I take up their opinions, which I develop through my reason and intuition in order to make them my own (having no opinions, I can adopt theirs as well as any others) and to conform them to my taste, turning their personalities into things that have an affinity with my dreams.

I've so favoured dreaming over real life that I'm able, in my verbal encounters (the only kind I have), to keep on dreaming and to keep following, through the opinions and feelings of others, the fluid course of my own amorphous personality.

Other people are channels or conduits in which the ocean's water flows according to their fancy, and the shimmering of that water in the sunlight defines their curved path much better than their empty dryness could do.

Although it sometimes seems to my hasty analysis that I'm the parasite of others, what really occurs is that I force them to be parasites of my subsequent emotion. My life inhabits the shells of their personalities. I reproduce their footsteps in my spirit's clay, absorbing them so thoroughly into my consciousness that I, in the end, have taken their steps and walked in their paths even more than they.

Due to my habit of dividing myself, following two distinct mental operations at the same time, it's generally the case that as I lucidly and intensely adapt myself to what others are feeling, I simultaneously undertake a rigorously objective analysis of their unknown self, what they think and are. And thus in my dreaming, without ever interrupting my reverie, I not only live the distilled essence of their sometimes dead emotions, I also discover and classify the intricate links between their various intellectual and spiritual energies, which were often lying dormant in their soul.

Nor, while all this is going on, do their physiognomies and dress and gestures escape my notice. I live their dreams, their instinctive nature, and their body and its postures all at the same time. In a sweeping, unified dispersion, I ubiquitize* myself in them, and at each moment of our conversation I create, and am, a multitude of selves – conscious and unconscious, analysed and analytical – joined together as in a spread fan.

306

I belong to a generation that inherited disbelief in the Christian faith and created in itself a disbelief in all other faiths. Our fathers still had the believing impulse, which they transferred from Christianity to other forms of illusion. Some were champions of social equality, others were wholly enamoured of beauty, still others had faith in science and its achievements, and there were some who became even more Christian, resorting to various Easts and Wests in search of new religious forms to entertain their otherwise hollow consciousness of merely living.

We lost all of this. We were born with none of these consolations. Each civilization follows the particular path of a religion that represents it; turning to other religions, it loses the one it had, and ultimately loses them all.

We lost the one, and all the others with it.

And so we were left, each man to himself, in the desolation of feeling ourselves live. A ship may seem to be an object whose purpose is to sail, but no, its purpose is to reach a port. We found ourselves sailing without any idea of what port we were supposed to reach. Thus we reproduced a painful version of the argonauts' adventurous precept:* living doesn't matter, only sailing does.

Without illusions, we live by dreaming, which is the illusion of those who can't have illusions. Living off our inner selves has diminished us, for the complete man is the one who doesn't know himself. Without faith, we have no hope, and without hope we have no real life. Having no idea of the future, we likewise have no idea of today, because today, for the man of action, is nothing but a prologue to the future. The energy to fight was stillborn in us, for we were born without the fighting spirit.

Some of us stagnated in the idiotic conquest of the ordinary, contemptibly seeking our daily bread without ever sweating for it, without making a conscious effort, without the nobility of achievement.

Others of us, more high-minded, spurned state and society, wanting and desiring nothing, and trying to take to the calvary of oblivion the cross of simply existing – an impossible endeavour for whoever doesn't have, like the bearer of the Cross, the consciousness of a divine origin.

Still others, busy on the outside of the soul, devoted themselves to the cult of noise and confusion, thinking they were living whenever they heard themselves, and supposing they loved whenever they brushed love's outward forms. Living was painful because we knew we were alive; dying didn't scare us, for we had lost the normal notion of what death is.

But those who formed the Terminal Race, the spiritual limit of the Deadly Hour, didn't even have courage enough for true denial and asylum. What we lived was in denial, discontent and disconsolation, but we lived it within, without moving, forever closed (at least in the way we lived) inside the four painted walls of our room and the four stone walls of our inability to act.

307

Aesthetics of Discouragement

Since we can't extract beauty from life, let's at least try to extract beauty from not being able to extract beauty from life. Let's make our failure into a victory, into something positive and lofty, endowed with columns, majesty and our mind's consent.

If life has given us no more than a prison cell, let's at least decorate it as best we can – with the shadows of our dreams, their colourful patterns engraving our oblivion on the static surface of the walls.

Like every dreamer, I've always felt that my calling was to create. Since I've never been able to make an effort or carry out an intention, creation for me has always meant dreaming, wanting or desiring, and action has meant dreaming of the acts I wish I could perform.

308

I called my incapacity for living genius, and I dressed up my cowardice by calling it refinement. I placed myself – God gilded with false gold – on an altar of cardboard painted to look like marble.

But I didn't succeed in fooling myself, nor [. . .] my self-delusion.

309

The pleasure of praising ourselves. . .

Rainy Landscape

It smells to me of coldness, of regret, of the hopelessness of every road and of every ideal ever dreamed up.

Women today take so much care with how they look and move that they give the excruciating impression of being ephemeral and irreplaceable.

Their □ and embellishments so paint and colour them that they become more decorative than carnally alive. Friezes, pictures, paintings – that's all they amount to, visually speaking.

The mere gesture of wrapping a shawl around their shoulders is done with a greater awareness of its visual effect than ever before. The shawl used to be part of a woman's basic attire; now it's an optional feature, depending solely on notions of aesthetic taste.

In these colourful times when almost nothing escapes being turned into art, everything plucks petals from the conscious sphere and merges □ into flights of fancy.

These female figures are all like fugitives from pictures that were never painted. Some of them are too full of details. . . Certain profiles stand out too sharply, as if they were trying to look unreal, so detached are their pure lines from the background.

310

My soul is a secret orchestra, but I don't know what instruments – strings, harps, cymbals, drums – strum and bang inside me. I only know myself as the symphony.

Every effort is a crime, because every gesture is a dead dream.

Your hands are captive doves. Your lips are silent doves (that come to coo before my eyes).

All of your gestures are birds. You're a swallow when you stoop, a condor when you look at me, and an eagle in your disdainful lady's ecstasies. I look at you and see a pond full of flapping wings . . . . .

You are nothing but wings . . . . .

Rain, rain, rain. . .

Groaning, unrelenting rain . . . . .

My body makes even my soul shiver, not with a coldness that's in the air, but with a coldness that comes from watching the rain.

Every pleasure is a vice, because to seek pleasure is what everyone does in life, and the only black vice is to do what everyone else does.

311

Sometimes, without expecting it and with no reason to expect it, the oppressiveness of common life makes me gag, and I feel physically nauseated by the voice and gestures of my so-called fellow man. It's an instant physical nausea, automatically felt in my stomach and head, an impressive but stupid consequence of my alert sensibility. Everyone who talks to me, each face whose eyes gaze at me, hits me like an insult or a piece of filth. I brim with disgust at the whole lot. I get dizzy from feeling myself feel them.

And in these moments of abdominal distress, there's nearly always a man, a woman or even a child that stands before me as a live representative of the banality that torments me. Not a representative according to my subjective, pondered emotion but by an objective truth, outwardly corresponding to what I inwardly feel and appearing to me by analogical magic as the perfect example for the rule I conceive.

312

There are days when everyone I meet, and especially the people I'm forced to have daily contact with, appear as symbols, and individually or together they form a prophetic or occult writing that obscurely describes my life. The office becomes a page with people for its words; the street is a book; the words I exchange with familiar or unfamiliar faces are phrases for which I have no dictionary, though I have an idea of what they mean. They speak, they tell, but it's not of themselves that they speak or tell; they're words, as I've said, that don't disclose their meaning, but they allow glimpses. In my twilight vision I only vaguely distinguish what these sudden glass panes on the surfaces of things let show from the interior that they veil and reveal. I understand without knowledge, like a blind man when someone tells him about colours.

Walking along the street, I often hear snatches of private conversations, and they're almost all about another woman, another man, a friend's boyfriend or someone else's girlfriend . . . . .

Just to hear these shadows of human speech (which is all that occupies most conscious lives) fills me with a sickening tedium, an anguished feeling of being exiled among spiders, and a sudden awareness of my humiliation among real people, condemned to being looked upon by the landlord and the whole neighbourhood as a tenant just like everyone else on the block. And it's with loathing that I peer through the bars of the storeroom's back windows, seeing everybody's rubbish heaped up in the rain in the grimy courtyard which is my life.

313

I loathe the happiness of all these people who don't know they're unhappy. Their human life is full of what, in a true sensibility, would produce a surfeit of anxieties. But since their true life is vegetative, their sufferings come and go without touching their soul, and they live a life that can be compared only to that of a man with a toothache who won a fortune – the genuine good fortune of living unawares, the greatest gift granted by the gods, for it is the gift of being like them, superior just as they are (albeit in a different fashion) to happiness and pain.

That's why, in spite of everything, I love them all. My dear vegetables!

314

I'd like to develop a code of inertia for superior souls in modern societies.

Society would govern itself spontaneously if it didn't contain sensitive and intelligent people. You can be sure that they're the only thing that hinders it. Primitive societies were happy because they didn't have such people.

Unfortunately, superior souls would die if expelled from society, because they don't know how to work. And without any stupid blanks between them, perhaps they would die of boredom. But my concern here is with overall human happiness.

Each superior soul who appeared in society would be exiled to the Island of the superiors.* The superiors would be fed, like animals in cages, by normal society.

Believe me: if there were no intelligent people to point out humanity's various woes, humanity wouldn't even notice them. And sensitive people who suffer cause the rest to suffer by association.

For the time being, since we live in society, our one duty as superiors is to reduce to a minimum our participation in the life of the tribe. We shouldn't read newspapers, for example, or should read them only to find out what anecdotal and unimportant things are happening. You can't imagine the delight I get from the provincial news round-up. The very names make doors to the indefinite open up in me.

The highest honour for a superior man is to not know the name of his country's chief of state, or whether he lives under a monarchy or a republic.

He should be careful to position his soul in such a way that passing things and events can't disturb him. Otherwise he'll have to take an interest in others, in order to look out for himself.

315

There's an aesthetics to wasting time. For those who cultivate sensations there's an unwritten handbook on inertia, with recipes for all the forms of lucidity. To develop the right strategy for fighting against the notion of social mores, against the impulses of our instincts and against the solicitations of sentiment requires a study that not every aesthete is prepared to undertake. A rigorous aetiology of our scruples should be followed by an ironic diagnosis of our concessions to normality. We must also learn how to ward off life's intrusions; a □ caution is necessary to make us impervious to outside opinions, and a velvety indifference to insulate our soul against the invisible blows of coexisting with others.

316

A life of aesthetic quietism, to prevent the insults and humiliations of life and the living from getting any closer than a loathsome periphery of our sensibility, outside the walls of our conscious soul.

All of us, in some part or other, are loathsome. We all harbour a crime we've committed, or a crime our soul is begging us to commit.

317

One of my constant preoccupations is to understand how other people can exist, how there can be souls that aren't mine, consciousnesses that have nothing to do with my own, which – because it's a consciousness – seems to me like the only one. I accept that the man standing before me, who speaks with words like mine and gesticulates as I do or could do, is in some sense my fellow creature. But so are the figures from illustrations that fill my imagination, the characters I meet in novels, and the dramatic personae that move on stage through the actors who represent them.

No one, I suppose, genuinely admits the real existence of another person. We may concede that the person is alive and that he thinks and feels as we do, but there will always be an unnamed element of difference, a materialized inequality. There are figures from the past and living images from books that are more real to us than the incarnate indifferences that talk to us over shop counters, or happen to glance at us in the trams, or brush against us in the dead happenstance of the streets. Most people are no more for us than scenery, generally the invisible scenery of a street we know by heart.

I feel more kinship and intimacy with certain characters described in books and certain images I've seen in prints than I feel with many so-called real people, who are of that metaphysical insignificance known as flesh and blood. And 'flesh and blood' in fact describes them rather well: they're like chunks of meat displayed in the window of a butcher's, dead things bleeding as if they were alive, shanks and cutlets of Destiny.

I'm not ashamed of feeling this way, as I've discovered that's how everyone feels. What seems to lie behind people's mutual contempt and indifference, such that they can kill each other like assassins who don't really feel they're killing, or like soldiers who don't think about what they're doing, is that no one pays heed to the apparently abstruse fact that other people are also living souls.

On certain days, in certain moments, brought to me by I don't know what breeze and opened to me by the opening of I don't know what door, I suddenly feel that the corner grocer is a thinking entity, that his assistant, who at this moment is bent over a sack of potatoes next to the entrance, is truly a soul capable of suffering.

When I was told yesterday that the employee of the tobacco shop had committed suicide, it seemed like a lie. Poor man, he also existed! We had forgotten this, all of us, all who knew him in the same way as all those who never met him. Tomorrow we'll forget him even better. But he evidently had a soul, for he killed himself. Passion? Anxiety? No doubt. . . But for me, as for all humanity, there's only the memory of a dumb smile and a shabby sports coat that hung unevenly from the shoulders. That's all that remains to me of this man who felt so much that he killed himself for feeling, since what else does one kill himself for? Once, as I was buying cigarettes from him, it occurred to me that he would go bald early. As it turns out, he didn't have time enough to go bald. That's one of the memories I have of him. What other one can I have, if even this one is not of him but of one of my thoughts?

I suddenly see his corpse, the coffin where they placed him, the so alien grave where they must have lowered him, and it dawns on me that the cashier of the tobacco shop, with crooked coat and all, was in a certain way the whole of humanity.

It was only a flash. What's clear to me now, today, as the human being I am, is that he died. That's all.

No, others don't exist. . . It's for me that this heavy-winged sunset lingers, its colours hard and hazy. It's for me that the great river shimmers below the sunset, even if I can't see it flow. It's for me that this square was built overlooking the river, whose waters are now rising. Was the cashier of the tobacco shop buried today in the common grave? Then the sun isn't setting for him today. But because I think this, and against my will, it has also stopped setting for me.

318

... ships passing in the night that neither signal nor recognize each other.

319

I realize now that I've failed, and it only surprises me that I didn't foresee that I was going to fail. What was there in me to suggest I might triumph? I had neither the conqueror's blind force nor the madman's sure vision. I was lucid and sad, like a cold day.

Clear things console me, and sunlit things console me. To see life passing by under a blue sky makes up for a lot. I forget myself indefinitely, forgetting more than I could ever remember. The sufficiency of things fills my weightless, translucent heart, and just to look is a sweet satisfaction. I've never been more than a bodiless gaze, whose only soul was a slight breeze that passed by and saw.

I have something of the spirit of a bohemian, of those who let life slip away, like something that slips through one's fingers because the gesture to seize it falls asleep at the mere idea. But I never had the outward compensation of the bohemian spirit – the carefree acceptance of come-and-go emotions. I was never more than an isolated bohemian, which is an absurdity; or a mystic bohemian, which is an impossibility.

I've lived certain moments of respite in the presence of Nature, moments sculpted out of tender isolation, that will always be like medals for me. In these moments I forgot all of my life's goals, all of the paths I wanted to follow. An immense spiritual tranquillity fell into the blue lap of my aspirations and allowed me to enjoy being nothing. But I've probably never enjoyed an incorruptible moment, free of any underlying spirit of failure and gloom. In all my moments of spiritual liberation there was a dormant sorrow, vaguely blooming in gardens beyond the walls of my consciousness, and the scent and the very colour of those sad flowers intuitively passed through the stone walls, whose far side (where the roses bloomed) never ceased being a hazy near side in the obscure mystery of who I am, in the drowsiness of my daily existence.

It was in an inner sea that the river of my life ended. All around my dreamed mansion the trees were yellow with autumn. This circular landscape is my soul's crown of thorns. The happiest moments of my life were dreams, and dreams of sorrow, and I saw myself in their ponds like a blind Narcissus who enjoyed the coolness as he bent over the water, aware of his reflection there through an inner, nocturnal vision that was confided to his abstract emotions and maternally adored in the recesses of his imagination.

Your necklaces of imitation pearls loved with me my finest hours. Carnations were our preferred flower, perhaps because they didn't suggest pomp. Your lips solemnly celebrated the irony of your own smile. Did you really understand your destiny? It was because you knew it without understanding it that the mystery written in the sadness of your eyes had cast a pall on your resigned lips. Our Homeland was too far away for roses. In the cascades of our gardens the water was pellucid with silences. In the tiny hollows of the rocks over which the water flowed, there were secrets from our childhood and dreams the same size as our toy soldiers of old, which we could station on the cascades' stones, in the static execution of a huge military operation, with nothing lacking in our dreams, and nothing lagging in our imagination.

I know I've failed. I enjoy the vague voluptuosity of failure like one who, in his exhaustion, appreciates the fever that laid him up.

I had a certain talent for friendship, but I never had any friends, either because they simply didn't turn up, or because the friendship I had imagined was an error of my dreams. I've always lived alone, and ever more alone as I've become more self-aware.

320

Towards the end of summer, when the dull sun's heat had lost its harshness, autumn began before it was autumn, with a mild and endlessly indefinite sadness, as if the sky didn't feel like smiling. Its blue was sometimes lighter, sometimes greener, from the lofty colour's own lack of substance. There was a kind of forgetfulness in the subdued purple tones of the clouds. It was no longer a torpor but a tedium that filled the lonely expanses where the clouds go by.

The real beginning of autumn was announced by a coldness in the air's non-coldness, by a subduing of the still unsubdued colours, by something of shadow and distance in the tint of the landscapes and the fuzzy countenance of things. Nothing was going to die yet, but everything – as in a still unformed smile – looked longingly back at life.

Finally the full autumn came. The air turned cold and windy; leaves rustled with a dry sound, even if they weren't dry; the ground took on the colour and impalpable shape of a shifting swamp. What had been a final smile faded as eyelids drooped and gestures flagged. And so everything that feels, or that we imagine feels, pressed its own farewell tight against its breast. A sound of whirling wind in a courtyard wafted through our consciousness of something else. Convalescence appealed as a way of at least truly feeling life.

But the first rains of winter, falling already in the now harsh autumn, washed away these halftones without respect. High winds howled against whatever was fixed, stirred up whatever was tied, swept along whatever was movable, and pronounced – between the rain's loud outbursts – absent words of anonymous protest, sad and almost angry sounds of glum despair.

And at last autumn coldly and greyly ceased. What came now was an autumn of winter, with the dust of everything becoming the mud of everything, but there was also a foretaste of the winter cold's good side: the harsh summer behind us, spring on its way, and autumn finally taking shape as winter. And in the lofty sky, whose dull tones no longer recalled heat or sadness, everything was propitious to night and indefinite meditations.

That's how it was for me before I thought about it. If I write it down today, it's because I remember it. The autumn I have is the one I lost.

321

Opportunity is like money, which, come to think of it, is nothing but an opportunity. For those who act, opportunity concerns the will, and the will doesn't interest me. For those like me who don't act, opportunity is the song of no sirens existing; it should be voluptuously spurned, stowed high away for no use at all.

'To have occasion to. . .' In this space the statue of renunciation will be raised.

O sprawling fields in the sun, the spectator for whom you alone exist is gazing at you from the shade.

O alcohol of grand words and long phrases that swell, like waves, with the breathing of their rhythms and then crash, smiling, with the irony of twisting snakes of foam and the sad magnificence of glimmering shadows. . .

322

Every gesture, however simple, violates an inner secret. Every gesture is a revolutionary act; an exile, perhaps, from the true □ of our intentions.

Action is a disease of thought, a cancer of the imagination. Action is self-exile. Every action is incomplete and flawed. The poem I dream has no flaws until I try to realize it. We find this recorded in the myth of Jesus. God, becoming man, cannot help but end in martyrdom. The supreme dreamer has the supreme martyr for a son.

The leaves' tattered shadows, the birds' tremulous song, the river's long arms shimmering coolly in the sun, the plants, the poppies, and the simplicity of sensations – even while feeling all this, I'm nostalgic for it, as if in feeling it I didn't feel it.

Time, like a wagon at the close of day, creakingly returns through the shadows of my thoughts. If I lift up my eyes from my thinking, they smart at the sight of the world.

To realize a dream, one must forget it, tearing away his attention from it. To realize is thus to not realize. Life is full of paradoxes, as roses are of thorns.

I'd like to write the encomium of a new incoherence that could serve as the negative charter for the new anarchy of souls. I've always felt that a digest of my dreams might be useful to humanity, which is why I've never tried to compile one. The idea that something I did might be helpful galled me and made me feel sapped.

I have country homes on the outskirts of life. I escape from the city of my actions to the trees and flowers of my reverie. Not a single echo from the life of my acts reaches my green retreat. I'm lulled by my memory as by an endless procession. From the goblets of my meditation I drink only the smile of the golden wine; I drink it only with my eyes, closing them, and Life passes by like a sail in the distance.

Sunny days smack of what I don't have. The blue sky and white clouds, the trees, the flute that's missing – eclogues left unfinished by the branches' rustling... All this is the silent harp, grazed by the lightness of my fingers.

The vegetable academy of silences... your name that sounded like poppies... the ponds... my going home... the crazy priest who went out of his mind during Mass... These memories are from my dreams... I keep my eyes open but see nothing... The things I do see aren't here... Waters*...

The lush green of the trees, through a jumble of entanglements, is part of my blood. Life throbs in my distant heart... I wasn't meant for reality, but life came and found me.

The agony of fate! I could die tomorrow! Even today something terrible could befall my soul! When I think of these things, I'm sometimes appalled at the supreme tyranny that obliges us to take steps without knowing where our uncertain paths will lead.

323

The rain kept sadly falling, but now with less force, as if seized by a cosmic weariness. There was no lightning, and only very occasionally would a distant, short roll of thunder harshly rumble, haltingly at times, as if it too were weary. Suddenly the rain let up even more. One of the employees opened the windows facing on to the Rua dos Douradores. A cool air, with dead remnants of warmth, drifted into the large office. The voice of Senhor Vasques talked loudly on the phone in his private office: 'You mean the line's still busy?' And then there was a dryly spoken aside – presumably an obscene remark to the receptionist on the other end.

324

To be able to have dreams, it's crucial that you know how to have no illusions.

In this way you'll reach the summit of dreamy abstention, where senses blend, feelings overflow, and ideas intermingle. There colours and souls taste like each other, hatreds taste like loves, and concrete things like abstract things, abstract things like concrete. The ties that joined everything but also separated everything – because they isolated each element – are broken. Everything melds and merges.

325

Fictions of the interlude,* colourfully covering the torpor and sloth of our underlying disbelief.

326

And I don't dream, I don't live; I dream real life. All ships are dreamed ships if we have the power to dream them. What kills the dreamer is to not live while he dreams; what hurts the man of action is to not dream while he lives. I fused the beauty of dreaming and the reality of life into a single, blissful colour. However much a dream may be ours, we can never possess it like the handkerchief in our pocket or, if you will, like our own flesh. However much one lives a life of full, boundless and triumphant action, he will never be free from the □ of contact with others, from stumbling over obstacles, even if small, and from feeling the passage of time.

To kill our dream life would be to kill ourselves, to mutilate our soul. Dreaming is the one thing we have that's really ours, invulnerably and inalterably ours.

Life and the Universe – be they reality or illusion – belong to everyone. Everyone can see what I see and have what I have, or can at least imagine himself seeing it and having it, and this is . . . . .

But no one besides me can see or have the things I dream. And if I see the outer world differently from how others see it, it's because I inadvertently incorporate, into what I see, the things from my dreams that have stuck to my eyes and ears.

327

On this clear bright day even the softness of the sounds is golden. There's gentleness everywhere. If I were told that a war had broken out, I would say there was no war. A day like today cannot admit anything that would disturb this gentleness that is everything.

328

Join your hands, and put them in mine, and listen, my love.

I want to tell you, with the soft and soothing voice of a confessor giving counsel, how much our yearning to attain falls short of what we do attain.

With my voice and your attention, I want us to pray together the litany of despair.

There is no artist's work that could not have been more perfect. When read line by line, the greatest of poems has few verses that couldn't be improved, few scenes that couldn't have been told more vividly, and the overall result is never so good that it couldn't have been vastly better.

Woe to the artist who notices this, who one day happens to think about it! Never again will he work with joy or sleep in peace. He'll be a young man without youth, and grow old dissatisfied.

And why should anyone express himself? What little he may say would be better left unsaid.

If I could really convince myself that renunciation is beautiful, how dolefully happy I would always be!

For you do not love the things I say with the same ears I use to hear myself say them. Even my ears, should I speak out loud, do not hear the words I speak in the same way as my inner ear hears the words I think. If even I, when I hear myself, get confused and am not always sure what I meant, then how much more other people are bound to misunderstand me!

What elaborate misconceptions form other people's understanding of us!

The joy of being understood by others cannot be had by those who want to be understood, for they are too complex to be understood; and simple people, who can be understood by others, never have the desire to be understood.

329

Have you ever considered, beloved Other, how invisible we all are to each other? Have you ever thought about how little we know each other? We look at each other without seeing. We listen to each other and hear only a voice inside ourself.

The words of others are mistakes of our hearing, shipwrecks of our understanding. How confidently we believe in *our* meanings of other people's words. We hear death in words they speak to express sensual bliss. We read sensuality and life in words they drop from their lips without the slightest intention of being profound.

The voice of brooks that you interpret, pure explicator... The voice of trees whose rustling means what we say it means... Ah, my unknown love, this is all just us and our fantasies, all ash, trickling down the bars of our cell!

330

Since perhaps not everything is false, may nothing cure us, my love, of the almost ecstatic pleasure of lying.

Ultimate subtlety! Supreme perversion! The absurd lie has all the charm of the perverse with the even greater, ultimate charm of being innocent. The deliberately innocent perversion – who can go beyond this supreme subtlety? The perversion that doesn't even aspire to give us pleasure and that lacks the fury to cause us pain, falling to the ground between pleasure and pain, useless and absurd like a shoddy toy with which an adult tries to amuse himself!

Don't you know, Exquisite One, the pleasure of buying things you don't need? Don't you know the delight of roads which, when we're distracted, we take by mistake? What human act has a colour as lovely as a spurious one ..... which lies to its own nature and contradicts its own intention?

How sublime to waste a life that could have been useful, never to execute a work of art that was certain to be beautiful, to abandon midway a sure road to victory!

Ah, my love, the glory of works which have been lost for ever, of treatises which today are mere titles, of libraries which burned down, of statues which were demolished!

How blessed with Absurdity are the artists who set fire to a beautiful work! Or the artists who could have made a beautiful work but deliberately made it ordinary! Or the great poets of Silence who, knowing they were capable of writing an absolutely perfect work, preferred to crown it with the decision never to write it. (For an imperfect work, it makes no difference.)

How much more beautiful the Mona Lisa would be if we couldn't see it! And if someone were to rob it just to burn it, what an artist he would be, even greater than the one who painted it!

Why is art beautiful? Because it's useless. Why is life ugly? Because it's all aims, objectives and intentions. All of its roads are for going from one point to another. If only we could have a road connecting a place no one ever leaves from to a place where no one goes! If only someone would devote his life to building a road from the middle of one field to the middle of another – a road that would be useful if extended at each end, but that would sublimely remain as only the middle stretch of a road!

The beauty of ruins? That they're no longer good for anything.

The sweetness of the past? Our memory of it, since to remember it is to make it present, and it isn't present nor ever can be – absurdity, my love, absurdity.

And I who am saying all this – why am I writing this book? Because I realize it's imperfect. Dreamed, it would be perfection; written, it becomes imperfect; that's why I'm writing it. And above all else, because I advocate uselessness, absurdity, □ – I write this book to lie to myself, to be unfaithful to my own theory.

And the supreme glory of all this, my love, is to think that perhaps none of it is true and that I don't even believe it's true.

And when lying begins to bring us pleasure, let's give it the lie by telling the truth. And when lying causes us anxiety, let's stop so that the suffering can't become even perversely pleasurable.

331

I'm suffering from a headache and the universe. Physical aches, more blatantly painful than moral ones, reflect in the spirit and set off tragedies not contained in them. They make the sufferer cross with everything, and everything naturally includes every star.

I do not share, have never shared, and can't imagine ever sharing that degenerate concept that regards us, as living souls, to be consequences of a material thing called the brain, which originates and resides in another material thing known as the cranium. I cannot be a materialist, which I believe is what one calls an adherent to this concept, for I cannot establish a clear relationship – I mean a visual relationship – between a tangible mass of grey or otherwise coloured matter and this thing known as the I that behind my gaze sees the skies and thinks about them, and imagines skies that don't exist. But even if I cannot fall into the pit of supposing that one thing is another just because they're in the same place, like a wall and my shadow on it, or that my soul's dependence on my brain is any greater than my dependence, when travelling, on the vehicle that carries me, I do believe there is a social relationship between what in us is pure spirit and what in us is the body's spirit, such that quarrels can occur between them. And what usually occurs is that the more ordinary of the two persons gets on the other's nerves.

My head aches today, and perhaps my stomach is the source of its aching. But the ache, once it is suggested by my stomach to my head, interrupts the meditation that goes on behind my thinking brain. Covering my eyes won't blind me, but it will keep me from seeing. And so now, because my head aches, I find nothing at all admirable or worthwhile in the show going on outside me which, in this absurd and monotonous moment, I don't even wish to see as the world. My head aches, which means I'm aware that matter has offended me, and, as happens when one is offended, I'm resentful and apt to be irritable with everyone, including whoever hasn't offended me but happens to be near by.

What I feel like doing is dying, at least temporarily, but this, as I've indicated, is only because my head aches. And it suddenly occurs to me how much more eloquently a great prose stylist would say this. Sentence by sentence he would elaborate on the anonymous grief of the world; the imagining eyes behind his paragraphs would scan the earth's various human dramas; and through the feverish throbbing of his temples an entire metaphysics of woe and misery would take shape on paper. But I don't have an eloquent style. My head aches because my head aches. The universe hurts me because my head hurts. But the universe that actually hurts me is not the true one, which exists because it doesn't know I exist, but that other universe which belongs only to me and which, should I pass my hands through my hair, makes me feel that each strand suffers for no other reason than to make me suffer.

332

I'm astonished by my capacity for anxiety. Though not generally inclined to metaphysical speculation, for some days now I've been filled with intense, even physical anxiety as I grope for answers to the metaphysical and religious problems. . . I quickly realized that for me the solution to the religious problem meant solving an emotional problem in rational terms.

333

No problem has a solution. None of us can untie the Gordian knot; either we give up or we cut it. We brusquely resolve intellectual problems with our feelings, either because we're tired of thinking, or because we're afraid to draw conclusions, or because of an inexplicable need to latch on to something, or because of a gregarious impulse to return to other people and to life.

Since we can never know all the factors that a problem entails, we can never solve it.

To arrive at the truth we would need more data, along with the intellectual resources for exhaustively interpreting the data.

334

It's been months since I last wrote. I've lived in a state of mental slumber, leading the life of someone else. I've felt, very often, a vicarious happiness. I haven't existed. I've been someone else. I've lived without thinking.

Today I suddenly returned to whom I am or dream I am. It was during a moment of great fatigue, after finishing a tedious assignment. I propped my elbows on the high slanted desk, rested my head against my hands, closed my eyes, and rediscovered myself.

In a far-away pseudo-slumber I remembered everything I had ever been, and as vividly as if it stood before my eyes I suddenly saw, before or after everything, the side of the old farm that opened on to the fields, and in the middle of the scene appeared the threshing-floor, empty.

I immediately felt how futile life is. As if prompted by a dull pain in my elbows, everything I was seeing, feeling, remembering and forgetting merged with the faint din from the street and the slight sounds of work as usual in the quiet office.

When I laid my hands on the desk and looked at what was there with a gaze that must have been heavy with dead worlds, the first thing I saw, with my physical eyes, was a blowfly (that soft buzzing that didn't belong to the office!) poised on top of the inkstand. I looked at it from the depths of the abyss, anonymous and attentive. It was coloured by green shades of black-blue, and its shiny repulsiveness wasn't ugly. A life!

Who knows for what supreme forces – gods or demons of Truth in whose shadow we roam – I may be nothing but a shiny fly that alights in front of them for a moment or two? A facile hypothesis? Trite observation? Philosophy with no real thought? Maybe. But I didn't think: I felt. It was carnally, directly, with profound and dark horror that I made this ludicrous comparison. I was a fly when I compared myself to one. I really felt like a fly when I imagined I felt like one. And I felt I had a flyish soul, slept flyishly and was flyishly withdrawn. And what's more horrifying is that I felt, at the same time, like myself. I automatically raised my eyes towards the ceiling, lest a lofty wooden ruler should swoop down to swat me, as I might swat that fly. When I lowered my eyes, the fly had fortunately disappeared without a sound, at least not any I could hear. The involuntary office was again without philosophy.

335

'To feel is a pain in the neck.' This offhand remark, spoken by a stranger I met in a restaurant, has been glowing ever since on the floor of my memory. The very earthiness of the language gives the sentence spice.

336

I wonder how many have contemplated, with the attention it merits, a deserted street with people in it. This sentence, by its phrasing, seems to want to say something else, and indeed it does. A deserted street is not a street no one walks on, but a street on which people walk as if it were deserted. This isn't hard to understand, provided one has seen it: a zebra can't be grasped by a man who doesn't know more than a donkey.

Our sensations change according to how we understand them and to what extent. There are ways of understanding that have special ways of being understood.

There are days when a tedium, a bitterness, an anxiety about life seems to rise to my head from the ground underneath me, and I would say it's intolerable if I didn't in fact tolerate it. It's a strangling of the life inside me, a longing to be another in all of my pores, a brief glimpse of the end.

337

What I most of all feel is weariness, and the disquiet that is its twin when the weariness has no reason to exist but to exist. I dread the gestures I have to make and am intellectually shy about the words I have to speak. Everything strikes me in advance as futile.

The unbearable tedium of all these faces, silly with intelligence or without it, nauseatingly grotesque in their happiness or unhappiness, hideous because they exist, an alien tide of living things that don't concern me...

338

I've always worried, in those occasional moments of detachment when we become conscious of ourselves as individuals who are seen as 'others' by other people, about the physical and even moral impression I must make on those who observe me and talk to me, whether on a daily basis or in a chance meeting.

We're all used to thinking of ourselves as primarily mental realities, and of other people as immediately physical realities. We vaguely see ourselves as physical people, in so far as we consider how we look to others. And we vaguely see others as mental realities, though only when we're in love or in conflict does it really dawn on us that they, like we, are predominantly soul.

And so sometimes I lose myself in futile speculations about the sort of person I am in the eyes of others: how my voice sounds, what kind of impression I leave in their involuntary memory, how my gestures, my words and my visible life are inscribed on the retinas of their interpretation. I've never succeeded in seeing myself from the outside. No mirror can show us ourself from outside, because no mirror can take us out of ourself. We would need a different soul, a different way of looking and thinking. If I were an actor projected on a screen, or if I recorded my voice on records, I'm certain that I still wouldn't know what I am on the outside, because like it or not, and no matter what I might record of myself, I'm always here inside, enclosed by high walls, on the private estate of my consciousness of me.

I don't know if others are like me, or if the science of life consists essentially in being so alienated from oneself that this alienation becomes second nature, such that one can participate in life as an exile from his own consciousness. Or perhaps other people, even more self-absorbed than I, are completely given over to the brutishness of being only themselves, living outwardly by the same miracle that enables bees to form societies more highly organized than any nation and allows ants to communicate with a language of tiny antennae whose results surpass our complex system of mutual understanding.

The geography of our consciousness of reality is an endless complexity of irregular coasts, low and high mountains, and myriad lakes. And if I ponder too much, I see it all as a kind of map, like that of the *Pays du Tendre** or of *Gulliver's Travels*, a fantasy of exactitude inscribed in an ironic or fanciful book for the amusement of superior beings, who know where countries are really countries.

Everything is complex for those who think, and no doubt thought itself takes delight in making things yet more complex. But those who think need to justify their abdication with a vast programme of understanding, which they set forth – like liars their explanations – with heaps of exaggerated detail that eventually reveal, once the earth is swept away, the lying root.

Everything is complex, or I'm the one who's complex. But at any rate it doesn't matter, because at any rate nothing matters. All of this, all these considerations that have strayed off the broad highway, vegetate in the gardens of excluded gods like climbing plants detached from their walls. And on this night as I conclude these inconclusive considerations, I smile at the vital irony which makes them appear in a human soul that was already, even before there were stars, an orphan of Fate's grand purposes.

339

The golden tint that still glows on waters abandoned by the setting sun is hovering on the surface of my weariness. I see myself as I see the lake I've imagined, and what I see in that lake is myself. I don't know how to explain this image, or this symbol, or this I that I envision. But I know I see, as if in reality I were seeing, a sun behind the hills that casts its doomed rays on to this lake that dark-goldenly shimmers.

One of the perils of thinking is to see while thinking. Those who think with their reason are distracted. Those who think with their emotion are sleeping. Those who think with their desire are dead. I, however, think with my imagination, and all reason, sorrow and impulse in me are reduced to something remote and irrelevant, like this lifeless lake among rocks where the last light of the sun unlastingly hovers.

Because I stopped, the waters trembled. Because I pondered, the sun withdrew. I close my slow and sleepy eyes, and there's nothing in me but a lake region where night begins to replace the day on the shimmering, dark-brown surface of waters in which seaweed floats.

Because I wrote, I said nothing. My impression is that what exists is always in another region, beyond the hills, and that there are great journeys to be made if we have soul enough to make them.

I've ceased, like the sun in my landscape. Nothing remains of what I said or saw except for an already fallen night, full of a lifeless glimmer of lakes on a lowland with no wild ducks, fluid and dead, humid and sinister.

340

No, I don't believe in the landscape. I don't say it because I believe in Amiel's* 'the landscape is a state of emotion', one of the better verbal moments of his unbearable interiorizing. I say it because I don't believe.

341

Day after day, in my ignoble and profound soul, I register the impressions that form the external substance of my self-awareness. I put them in vagabond words that desert me as soon as they're written, wandering on their own over slopes and meadows of images, along avenues of concepts, down footpaths of confusions. None of this is of any use to me, because nothing is of use to me. But writing makes me calmer, as when a sick man breathes easier without the sickness having passed.

Some people absent-mindedly scribble lines and absurd names on their desk blotter. These pages are the scribbles of my intellectual self-unawareness. I trace them in a stupor of feeling whatever I feel, like a cat in the sun, and I sometimes reread them with a vague, belated astonishment, as when I remember something I forgot ages ago.

When I write, I pay myself a solemn visit. I have special chambers, remembered by someone else in the interstices of my imagining, where I take delight in analysing what I don't feel, and I examine myself like a picture in a dark corner.

I lost my ancient castle before I was born. The tapestries of my ancestral palace were sold before I existed. My manor house from before I had life fell into ruins, and only in certain moments, when the moon shines in me over the river's reeds, do I shiver with nostalgia for the place where the toothless remains of the walls blackly stand out against the dark-blue sky made less dark by a milky yellow tinge.

I sphinxly discern myself. And from the lap of the queen I'm missing falls the forgotten ball of thread that's my soul – a little mishap of her useless embroidery. It rolls under the inlaid chest of drawers, where part of me follows it like a pair of eyes, until it vanishes in a nameless, mortuary horror.

342

I never sleep. I live and I dream; or rather, I dream in life and in my sleep, which is also life. There's no break in my consciousness: I'm aware of what's around me if I haven't fallen asleep yet or if I sleep fitfully, and I start dreaming as soon as I'm really asleep. And so I'm a perpetual unfolding of images, connected or disconnected but always pretending to be external, situated among people in the daylight, if I'm awake, or among phantoms in the non-light that illumines dreams, if I'm asleep. I honestly don't know how to distinguish one state from the other, and it may be that I'm actually sleeping when I'm awake and that I wake up when I fall asleep.

Life is a ball of yarn that someone got all tangled. It would make sense if it were rolled up tight, or if it were unrolled and completely stretched out. But such as it is, life is a problem without shape, a confusion of yarn leading nowhere.

I'm only half asleep, and as I think these things which I'll write down later (I'm already dreaming of the sentences I'll use), I'm seeing the landscapes of my vague dreams and hearing the patter of the rain outside, which makes my dreams even vaguer. They're riddles from the void, quivering with nothingness, and through them trickles the useless, external moaning of the constant rain, the one incessantly repeated detail of the auditory landscape. Hope? None. The wind-whipped shower of grief noisily pours down from the invisible sky. I keep on sleeping.

It was undoubtedly in the promenades of the park that the tragedy resulting in life occurred. There were two of them, both beautiful, and they wanted to be something else; their love was waiting for them in the tedium of the future, and their nostalgia for what was yet to come arrived as the daughter of the love they hadn't experienced. And so with no desires or hopes, by the light of the moon filtering through the nearby woods, they strolled hand in hand through the desert of the abandoned pathways. They were perfect children, because they weren't really children. Taking path after path, cutting silhouettes among the trees, they moved like cardboard figures across the stage setting of no one. And finally, ever closer and more separate, they vanished from sight in the vicinity of the pools, and the patter of the vague rain that's now letting up is the sound of the fountains they were heading to. I am the love they shared, which is why I'm able to hear them on this night when I can't sleep, and also why I'm able to live without joy.

343

A DAY (ZIGZAG)

If only I had been the Madame of a harem! What a pity this didn't happen to me!

What remains at the end of this day is what remained yesterday and will remain tomorrow: the boundless, insatiable longing to be always the same and other.

Come down from your unreality by the steps of my dreams and fatigues. Come down and replace the world.

344

IN PRAISE OF STERILE WOMEN

Should I one day take an earthly woman to wife, pray for me the following: that she at any rate be sterile. But also ask, should you pray for me, that I never come to have this hypothetical wife.

Only sterility is noble and worthy. Only to kill what never was is lofty, perverse* and absurd.

345

I don't dream of possessing you. Why should I? It would only debase my dream life. To possess a body is to be banal. And to dream of possessing a body is perhaps even worse, if that's possible: it's to dream of being banal – the supreme horror.

And since we wish to be sterile, let us also be chaste, for there is nothing more shameful and ignoble than to forswear what in Nature is fertile while holding on to the part we like in what we've forsworn. There are no halfway noble attitudes.

Let us be chaste like dead lips,* pure like dreamed bodies, and resigned to being this way, like mad nuns.

May our love be a prayer... Anoint me with seeing you, and I will make the moments I dream of you into a rosary, with my tediums for Our Fathers and my anxieties for Hail Marys.

Let us remain eternally like a male figure in one stained-glass window opposite a female figure in another stained-glass window... And between us humanity passing by, shadows whose footsteps coldly echo... Murmurs of prayers, secrets of ..... Sometimes the air fills up with □ incense. At other times a statuesque figure sprinkles holy water on this side and that side... And we will always be the same stained-glass windows, with the same colours when the sun strikes us, the same outlines when the night falls... The centuries will not touch our vitreous silence... In the world outside civilizations will come and go, revolutions will break out, feasts will whirl and rage, peaceful and orderly peoples will carry on... While we, my unreal love, will always have the same useless expression, the same false existence, and the same .....

Until one day, at the end of various centuries and empires, the Church will finally collapse and everything will cease...

But we, oblivious to it, will remain – I don't know how, or in what space, or for how long – eternal stained-glass windows, hours of naïve design and coloration executed by some artist who for ages has slept in a Gothic tomb on which two angels, their hands pressed together, freeze the idea of death in marble.

346

The things we dream have just one side. We can't walk around them to see what's on the other side. The problem with the things of life is that we can look at them from all sides. The things we dream have, like our souls,* only the side that we see.

347

A Letter Not to Post

I hereby excuse you from appearing in my idea of you.

Your life . . . . .

This is not my love; it's merely your life.

I love you the way I love the sunset or the moonlight: I want the moment to remain, but all I want to possess in it is the sensation of possessing it.

348

Nothing is more oppressive than the affection of others – not even the hatred of others, since hatred is at least more intermittent than affection; being an unpleasant emotion, it naturally tends to be less frequent in those who feel it. But hatred as well as love is oppressive; both seek us, pursue us, won't leave us alone.

My ideal would be to live everything through novels and to use real life for resting up – to read my emotions and to live my disdain of them. For someone with a keen and sensitive imagination, the adventures of a fictional protagonist are genuine emotion enough, and more, since they are experienced by us as well as the protagonist. No greater romantic adventure exists than to have loved Lady Macbeth with true and directly felt love. After a love like that, what can one do but take a rest, not loving anyone in the real world?

I don't know the meaning of this journey I was forced to make, between one and another night, in the company of the whole universe. I know I can read to amuse myself. Reading seems to me the easiest way to pass the time on this as on other journeys. I occasionally lift my eyes from the book where I'm truly feeling and glance, as a foreigner, at the scenery slipping by – fields, cities, men and women, fond attachments, yearnings – and all this is no more to me than an incident in my repose, an idle distraction to rest my eyes from the pages I've been reading so intently.

Only what we dream is what we truly are, because all the rest, having been realized, belongs to the world and to everyone. If I were to realize a dream, I'd be jealous, for it would have betrayed me by allowing itself to be realized. 'I've achieved everything I wanted,' says the feeble man, and it's a lie; the truth is that he prophetically dreamed all that life achieved through him. We achieve nothing. Life hurls us like a stone, and we sail through the air saying, 'Look at me move.'

Whatever be this interlude played out under the spotlight of the sun and the spangles of the stars, surely there's no harm in knowing it's an interlude. If what's beyond the theatre doors is life, then we will live, and if it's death, we will die, and the play has nothing to do with this.

That is why I never feel so close to truth, so initiated into its secrets, as on the rare occasions when I go to the theatre or the circus: then I know that I'm finally watching life's perfect representation. And the actors and actresses, the clowns and magicians, are important and futile things, like the sun and the moon, love and death, the plague, hunger and war among humanity. Everything is theatre. Is it truth I want? I'll go back to my novel. . .

349

The most abject of all needs is to confide, to confess. It's the soul's need to externalize.

Go ahead and confess, but confess what you don't feel. Go ahead and tell your secrets to get their weight off your soul, but let the secrets you tell be secrets you've never had.

Lie to yourself before you tell that truth. Expressing yourself is always a mistake. Be resolutely conscious: let expression, for you, be synonymous with lying.

350

I don't know what time is. I don't know what its real measure is, presuming it has one. I know that the clock's measure is false, as it divides time spatially, from the outside. I know that our emotions' way of measuring is just as false, dividing not time but our sensation of it. The way our dreams measure it is erroneous, for in dreams we only brush against time, now leisurely, now hurriedly, and what we live in them is fast or slow, depending on something in their flowing that I can't grasp.

Sometimes I think that everything is false, and that time is just a frame placed around things that are extraneous to it. In the remembrance I have of my past life, the times are arranged in absurd levels and planes, so that I'm younger in a certain episode from my serious-minded fifteenth year than in another from my childhood surrounded by toys.

My mind gets confounded if I think about these things. I sense there's a mistake in all this, but I don't know where it is. It's as if I were watching a magic show and knew I was being tricked, but couldn't work out the technique, or mechanism, behind the trick.

And then I'm visited by thoughts which are absurd but which I can't reject as completely absurd. I wonder if a man who slowly thinks in a fast-moving car is going fast or slow. I wonder if the identical speeds of a suicide who jumps into the sea and a man on a terrace who accidentally falls in are equal. I wonder if my actions of smoking a cigarette, writing this passage and obscurely thinking – all of which occupy the same interval of time – are truly synchronous.

We can imagine that one of two wheels on the same axle will always be in front of the other, if only by a fraction of a millimetre. A microscope would magnify this fractional distance until it became almost unbelievable – impossible, were it not real. And why shouldn't the microscope be right rather than our poor eyesight?

These considerations are useless? Indeed they are. They're tricks of reason? I don't deny it. But what is this thing that without any measure measures us, and without existing kills us? It's in these moments, when I don't even know if time exists, that it seems to me like a person, and I feel like going to sleep.

351

Games of Solitaire

On evenings lit by kerosene lamps in large and echoing country houses, the old aunts of those who had them passed the time by playing solitaire while the maid dozed off to the simmering sound of the tea kettle [. . .]. Someone in me who has taken my place feels nostalgia for this useless peace. The tea arrives and the old deck of cards is placed in a neat stack on a corner of the table. The shadow of the enormous china cabinet makes the dusky dining room still darker. The maid's face sweats with sleepiness as she slowly hurries to finish. I see all of this, inside myself, with an anguish and nostalgia that aren't related to anything. And I find myself considering the state of mind of someone playing solitaire.

352

It's not in open fields or in large gardens that I see spring arrive. It's in the several scrawny trees of a small city square. There the greenness stands out like a special gift and is joyful like a warm sorrow.

I love these lonely squares, tucked between streets with little traffic, and themselves with just as little. They are useless clearings, always there waiting, in between forgotten tumults. They're a bit of village in the city.

I come to a square, walk up one of the streets that runs into it, then back down the same street. Seen from the other direction, the square is different, but the same peace gilds with sudden nostalgia – the setting sun – the view I didn't see when I walked up the street.

Everything is useless, and I feel it as such. All that I've lived I've forgotten, as if I'd only vaguely heard it. All that I'll be reminds me of nothing, as if I'd lived and forgotten it.

A sunset of mild sorrow hovers all around me. Everything turns chilly, not because it's colder, but because I've entered a narrow street and the square is gone.

353

The not-cold, not-warm morning glided over the few houses dotting the slopes at the edge of town. A thin, wide-awake fog was disintegrating into shapeless shreds on the drowsy slopes. (It wasn't cold except for the fact life had to resume.) And all of this – all this moist coolness of a gentle morning – was analogous to a happiness he had never been able to feel.

The tram slowly descended towards the avenues. As it approached the denser concentration of houses, he was vaguely seized by a sense of loss. Human reality was beginning to be visible.

In these early morning hours, when the shadows have vanished but their light weight still lingers, the spirit that yields to the moment's suggestion hankers for arrival and the sun-bathed port of old. One would like not so much to have the moment stand still, as it does for solemn landscapes or for the moon when it so peacefully shines on the river, but to have had a different life, so that this moment could have a different flavour, more akin to one's self.

The uncertain fog thinned even more. The sun penetrated things more deeply. The sounds of life were growing everywhere louder.

At times like these, the right thing would be never to arrive at the human reality for which our lives are destined. To hover imponderably in the fog and the morning, not in spirit but in spiritualized body, in winged real-life – that is what would most satisfy our desire to seek a refuge, although there's no reason to seek one.

To feel everything in fine detail makes us indifferent, save towards what we can't obtain: sensations our soul is still too embryonic to grasp, human activities congruent with feeling things deeply, passions and emotions lost among more visible kinds of achievement.

The trees that lined the avenues were independent of all this.

The morning hour came to an end in the city, like the slope on the other side of the river when the boat touches the wharf. As long as it didn't dock, it bore the scenic view of the far shore on its hull; the scenery fell away at the sound of the hull scraping against the rocks. A man whose trousers were rolled up past his knees placed a clamp on the rope; his gesture was definitive, perfectly natural, and it metaphysically concluded with my soul no longer being able to enjoy a doubtful anxiety. The boys on the wharf looked at me as at a normal man, one who would never feel such undue emotion for the practical aspects of docking a boat.

354

Heat, like an invisible piece of clothing, makes one feel like taking it off.

355

I was already feeling uneasy. Without warning the silence had stopped breathing.

Suddenly, the light of all hells* cracked like steel. I crouched like an animal against the top of the desk, my hands lying flat like useless paws. A soulless light had swept through all nooks and souls, and the sound of a nearby mountain tumbled down from on high, rending the hard veil of the abyss* with a boom. My heart stopped.

My throat gulped. My consciousness saw only a blot of ink on a sheet of paper.

356

After the heat had lulled and the light beginning of rain increased until it could be heard, there was a tranquillity that the air didn't have when it was hot, a new peace in which the water blew its own breeze. So clear was the joy of this soft rain, with no darkness or threat of storm, that even those without raincoats or umbrellas (which was almost everyone) laughingly talked as they stepped quickly down the glistening street.

During an idle moment I walked over to the open office window – the heat had caused it to be opened, but the rain hadn't caused it to be shut – and looked with intense and indifferent concentration, as is my custom, at what I just finished accurately describing before I saw it. Yes, there went the joy of two banal souls, smiling as they talked in the fine rain, walking more briskly than hurriedly in the veiled yet luminous, limpid day.

But suddenly, popping into my view from behind a corner, there appeared an old, mean-looking, poor and unhumble man who impatiently made his way in the rain that was letting up. He surely had no special aim, but at least he had impatience. I looked at him with concentration, no longer the careless kind applied to things, but the kind that discerns symbols. He was the symbol of nobody, which is why he was in a hurry. He was the symbol of those who were never anything; that is why he suffered. He belonged not to those who smile as they feel the rain's joyful discomfort, but to the rain itself – a man so unconscious that he felt reality.

That's not what I wanted to say, however. Something stepped in between my observation of the passer-by (whom I had at any rate lost from view, because I'd stopped looking at him) and the thread of my reflections; some mystery from the unobserved, some urgency of the soul, stepped in and prevented me from continuing. And in the depths of my distraction I hear, without hearing, the voices of the packers at the far end of the office, where the warehouse begins, and without seeing I see the twine used for parcels, doubly knotted and doubly strung around the volumes wrapped in heavy brown paper, on the table next to the back window, among jokes and scissors.

To see is to have seen.

357

It's a rule of life that we can, and should, learn from everyone. There are solemn and serious things we can learn from quacks and crooks, there are philosophies taught us by fools, there are lessons in faithfulness and justice brought to us by chance and by those we chance to meet. Everything is in everything.

In certain particularly lucid moments of contemplation, like those of early afternoon when I observantly wander through the streets, each person brings me a novelty, each building teaches me something new, each placard has a message for me.

My silent stroll is a continual conversation, and all of us – men, buildings, stones, placards and sky – are a huge friendly crowd, elbowing each other with words in the great procession of Destiny.

358

Yesterday I saw and heard a great man. I don't mean a man reputed to be great, but a man who really is great. He is a man of worth, if there's worth in this world, and people see it, and he knows they see it. Thus he meets all the conditions necessary for me to call him a great man. And that's what I call him.

His physical appearance is that of a tired businessman. His face shows signs of fatigue, which could be from thinking too much, or simply from not leading a healthy life. His gestures are unremarkable. His gaze has a certain sparkle – the privilege of not being near-sighted. His voice is a bit garbled, as if the beginnings of a general paralysis had affected this particular expression of his soul. And his soul, thus expressed, goes on about party politics, about the devaluation of the escudo, and about what's wrong with his colleagues in greatness.

If I didn't know who he is, I wouldn't be able to tell by his appearance. I realize that great men need not conform to that heroic ideal of simple souls, whereby a great poet is always an Apollo in body and a Napoleon in expression, or at the very least a man of distinction with an expressive face. I realize that such notions are as absurd as they are human. But if we can't expect everything, or almost everything, we can still expect something. And passing from the figure we see to the soul that speaks, although we can't expect vivacity or verve, we should at least be able to count on intelligence and a hint of grandeur.

All this – these human disillusions – forces us to question what truth there is, if any, in our common notion of inspiration. It seems that this body of a businessman and this soul of a polite, educated fellow must, when all by themselves, be mysteriously endowed with some inner thing that's extraneous to them. It seems that they don't speak but that some voice speaks through them, uttering what would be falsehood if they said it.

These are casual and useless speculations. I sometimes regret indulging in them. They don't diminish the worth of the man, nor increase his body's expressiveness. But then, there isn't anything that changes anything, and what we say or do merely brushes the tops of the hills, in whose valleys everything sleeps.

359

No one understands anyone else. We are, as the poet* said, islands in the sea of life; between us flows the sea that defines and separates us. However much one soul strives to know another, he can know only what is told him by a word – a shapeless shadow on the ground of his understanding.

I love expressions, because I know nothing of what they express. I'm like the master of St Martha:* I'm satisfied with what I've been given. I see, and that's quite enough. Who can understand anything?

Perhaps it's this scepticism *vis-à-vis* our understanding that makes me look at a tree and a face, a poster and a smile, in exactly the same way. (Everything is natural, everything artificial, everything equal.) Everything I see is for me the merely visible, whether it be the lofty blue sky tinted with the whitish green of a pre-dawn morning, or the false frown on the face of someone suffering the death of a loved one before witnesses.

Sketches, illustrations, pages we look at and then turn. . . My heart isn't in them, and my gaze merely passes over them on the outside, like a fly over a sheet of paper.

Do I even know if I feel, if I think, if I exist? I know only that there's an objective scheme of colours, shapes and expressions of which I'm the useless shifting mirror for sale.

360

Compared with real, ordinary men who walk down the streets of life with a natural, fortuitous goal in mind, those who sit around in cafés cut a figure that can be described only by comparing them to certain elves from dreams – creatures that aren't exactly nightmarish or anguishing but whose remembrance, when we wake up, leaves a foul taste in our mouth that we don't quite understand, a feeling of deep disgust that's not for them, directly, but for something they embody.

I see the world's true geniuses and conquerors – both great and small – sailing in the night of things, oblivious to what their haughty prows are cutting through, in that gulfweed sea of packing straw and crumbled cork.

Everything is summed up in those cafés, just like in the inner court behind the office building, which through the grating of the warehouse window looks like a jail cell for confining rubbish.

361

The search for truth – be it the subjective truth of belief, the objective truth of reality, or the social truth of money or power – always confers, on the searcher who merits a prize, the ultimate knowledge of its non-existence. The grand prize of life goes only to those who bought tickets by chance.

The value of art is that it takes us away from here.

362

It's legitimate to break ordinary moral laws in obedience to a higher moral law. Hunger is no excuse for stealing a loaf of bread, but an artist can be excused for stealing ten thousand escudos to guarantee his sustenance and tranquillity for two years, provided his work seeks to advance human civilization; if it's merely an aesthetic work, then the argument doesn't hold.

363

We cannot love, son. Love is the most carnal of illusions. Listen: to love is to possess. And what does a lover possess? The body? To possess it we would have to incorporate it, to eat it, to make its substance our own. And this impossibility, were it possible, wouldn't last, because our own body passes on and transforms, because we don't even possess our body (just our sensation of it), and because once the beloved body were possessed it would become *ours* and stop being *other*, and so love, with the disappearance of the other, would likewise disappear.

Do we possess the soul? Listen carefully: no, we don't. Not even our own soul is ours. And how could a soul ever be possessed? Between one and another soul lies the impassable chasm of the fact that they're two souls.

What do we possess? What do we possess? What makes us love? Beauty? And do we possess it when we love? If we vehemently, totally possess a body, what do we really possess? Not the body, not the soul, and not even beauty. When we grasp an attractive body, it's not beauty but fatty and cellular flesh that we embrace; our kiss doesn't touch the mouth's beauty but the wet flesh of decaying, membranous lips; and even sexual intercourse, though admittedly a close and ardent contact, is not a *true* penetration, not even of one body into another. What do we possess? What do we really possess?

Our own sensations, at least? Isn't love at least a means of possessing ourselves through our sensations? Isn't it at least a way of dreaming vividly, and therefore more gloriously, the dream that we exist? And once the sensation has vanished, doesn't the memory at least stay with us always, so that we really possess. . .

Let's cast off even this delusion. We don't even possess our own sensations. Don't speak. Memory is no more than our sensation of the past. And every sensation is an illusion. . .

Listen to me, keep listening. Listen and don't look out the window at the river's far shore, so flat and smooth, nor at the twilight □, nor towards the train whistle cutting the empty distance . . . . . Listen to me carefully:

We do not possess our sensations, and through them we cannot possess ourselves.

(The tilted urn of twilight pours out on us an oil □ in which the hours, like rose petals, separately float.)

364

How can I possess with my body, when I don't even possess my body? How can I possess with my soul, when I don't possess my soul? How can I understand with my mind, when I don't understand my mind?

There is no body or truth we possess, nor even any illusion. We are phantoms made of lies, shadows of illusions, and our life is hollow on both the outside and the inside.

Does anyone know the borders of his soul, that he can say 'I am I'?

But I know that I'm the one who feels what I feel.

When someone else possesses this body, does he possess the same thing in it as I? No. He possesses another sensation.

Is there anything that we possess? If we don't know who we are, how can we know what we possess?

If, referring to what you eat, you were to say, 'I possess this', then I would understand you. Because you obviously incorporate what you eat into yourself, you transform it into your substance, you feel it enter into you and belong to you. But it's not with regard to what you eat that you speak of possession. What do you call possessing?

365

The madness known as affirmation, the sickness called belief, the infamy of being happy – all of this reeks of the world, it smacks of this sad thing that's the earth.

Be indifferent. Love the sunset and the dawn because it does no good, not even for you, to love them. Dress yourself in the gold of the dying afternoon, like a king deposed on a morning of roses in full bloom, with May in the white clouds and the smile of virgins in secluded villas. Let your yearning perish among myrtles, your tedium cease among tamarinds, and may the sound of water accompany all of this as if it were twilight on the banks of a river whose only meaning is to flow – eternal – towards distant seas. The rest is but the life that leaves us, the sparkle in our eyes that fades, the purple robes worn thin even before we don them, the moon that shines down on our exile, the stars that spread their silence over our hour of disillusionment.

Assiduous is the sterile and friendly grief that clasps us against its breast with love.

Decadence is my destiny.

My domain of old was in deep valleys. The water that trickled in my dreams was never tainted by blood. The trees' foliage that forgets life was always green in my forgetting. The moon was fluid like water between stones. Love never reached that valley, which is why life was happy there. Neither love, nor dreams, nor gods in temples – and we walked in the breeze and the indivisible hour without any nostalgia for drunken, useless beliefs.

366

Useless landscapes like those that wind around Chinese teacups, starting out from the handle and abruptly ending at the handle. The cups are always so small. . . Where would the landscape lead to, and with what ☐ of porcelain, if it could continue past the teacup handle?

Certain souls are capable of feeling heartfelt grief because the painted landscape on a Chinese fan isn't three-dimensional.

367

. . . and the chrysanthemums languish their sickly life in gardens made gloomy by their presence.

. . . the Japanese luxuriance of having only two apparent dimensions.

. . . the colourful existence of Japanese figures circling the teacups' dull translucence.

A table set for a discreet tea – a mere pretext for perfectly sterile conversations – has always struck me as a kind of living thing, an individuality with soul. It forms, like an organism, a synthetic whole, which is not the mere sum of its component parts.

368

And the dialogues in those fantastical gardens that indefinitely circle certain teacups? What sublime words the two figures seated on the other side of that teapot must be exchanging! And I without ears to hear them, a dead member of polychromatic humanity!

Exquisite psychology of truly static things, a psychology woven by eternity! And the expression of a painted figure, from the summit of its visible eternity, disdains our transitory fever, which never lingers at the windows of an attitude* nor pauses at the gates of a gesture.

Just imagine the folklore of the colourful people who inhabit paintings! The loves of embroidered figures – loves marked by a two-dimensional, geometric chastity – should be [probed] for the entertainment of venturesome psychologists.

We don't love, we only pretend to. True love, immortal and useless, belongs to those figures whose feelings never change, since by nature they are static. Ever since I've known the Japanese man who sits on the convex [surface] of my teapot, he has yet to make a move. He has never savoured the hand of the woman who is forever out of reach. Enervated colours, like those of an emptied, poured-out sun, eternally unrealize the slopes of that hill. And the whole scene observes a moment of sorrow – a sorrow more faithful than the one that right now fills, without filling, the hollowness of my weary hours.

369

In this metallic age of barbarians, only a relentless cultivation of our ability to dream, to analyse and to captivate can prevent our personality from degenerating into nothing or else into a personality like all the rest.

Whatever is real in our sensations is precisely what they have that isn't ours. The sensations common to us all are what constitute reality. Our sensations' individuality, therefore, lies in whatever they have that's erroneous. What joy it would give me to see a scarlet-coloured sun! How totally and exclusively mine it would be!

370

I never let my feelings know what I'm going to make them feel. I play with my sensations like a bored princess with her large, viciously agile cats.

I slam doors within me where certain sensations were about to pass in order to be realized. I quickly clear their path of mental objects that might cause them to make gestures.

Little nonsense phrases inserted into the conversations we pretend to be having, meaningless affirmations made from the ashes of other, equally meaningless affirmations. . .

– Your gaze reminds me of music played on a boat in the middle of a mysterious river with woods on the facing shore. . .

= Don't say that it's a chilly moonlit night. I abhor moonlit nights. . . There are people who actually play music on moonlit nights. . .

– That's also a possibility. . . An unfortunate one, of course. . . But your gaze evidently wants to be nostalgic about something. . . It lacks the feeling it expresses. . . In the falseness of your expression I can see many of the illusions that I've had. . .

= I can assure you that I sometimes feel what I say and even, despite being a woman, what I say through my gaze. . .

– Aren't you being harsh on yourself? Do we really feel what we think we're feeling? Does this conversation, for example, have any semblance of reality? Surely not. It would be unacceptable in a novel.

= And with good reason. . . Look, I'm not absolutely certain that I'm talking with you. . . In spite of being a woman, I made it my duty to be an illustration in the picture book of a mad artist. . . Some of my detail is overly precise. . . I realize it gives the impression of an overwrought, somewhat forced reality. . . To be an illustration seems to me the only ideal worthy of a contemporary woman. As a child I wanted to be the queen of one of the suits in a deck of old cards we had at home. . . This seemed to me like such a compassionately heraldic vocation. . . For a child, of course, such moral aspirations are common. . . Only later, when all our aspirations are immoral, do we really think about this. . .

– Since I never talk to children, I believe in their artistic instinct. . . You know, even now as I'm talking I'm trying to fathom the true meaning of the things you've been telling me. Do you forgive me?

= Not entirely. . . We should never plumb the feelings that other people pretend to have. They're always too intimate. . . Don't think it doesn't hurt me to share these intimate secrets, all of which are false but which represent true tatters of my pathetic soul. . . The most pitiful thing about us, believe me, is what we really aren't, and our worst tragedies take place in the idea we have of ourselves.

– That's so true. . . Why say it? You've hurt me. Why ruin the constant unreality of our conversation? This way it almost becomes a plausible interchange at a table set for tea, between a beautiful woman and a dreamer of sensations.

= You're right. . . Now it's my turn to ask forgiveness. . . But I was distracted and really didn't notice that I'd said something that makes sense. . . Let's change the subject. . . How late it always is!. . . Don't get upset again – the sentence I just said, after all, is complete nonsense. . .

– Don't apologize, and don't pay any attention to what we're talking about. . . Every good conversation should be a two-way monologue. . . We should ultimately be unable to tell whether we really talked with someone or simply imagined the conversation. . . The best and profoundest conversations, and the least morally instructive ones, are those that novelists have between two characters from one of their books. For example. . .

= For heaven's sake! Don't tell me you were going to cite an example! That's only done in grammars; perhaps you've forgotten that we don't even read them.

– Did you ever read a grammar?

= Never. I've always despised knowing the correct way to say something... All I ever liked in grammar books were the exceptions and pleonasms... To dodge the rules and say useless things sums up the essentially modern attitude. Did I say that correctly?...

– Absolutely... What's especially irritating in grammars (have you noticed how exquisitely impossible it is for us to be talking about this?) – the most irritating part of grammars is the chapter on verbs, since these are what give meaning to sentences... An honest sentence should always have any number of possible meanings... Verbs!... A friend of mine who committed suicide – every time I have a longish conversation I suicide a friend – was going to dedicate his life to destroying verbs...

= Why did he commit suicide?

– Wait, I still don't know... He wanted to discover and develop a method for surreptitiously not completing sentences. He used to say that he was searching for the microbe of meaning... He committed suicide – yes, of course – because one day he realized what a tremendous responsibility he'd assumed... The enormity of the problem made him go nuts... A revolver and...

= No, that's preposterous... Don't you see that it could never be a revolver? A man like that never shoots himself in the head... You understand very little about the friends you've never had... That's a serious defect, you know... My best girlfriend, a ravishing young man I invented...

– Do you get along?

= As best we can... But this girl, you can't imagine .....

The two figures sitting at the table set for tea surely didn't have this conversation. But they were so well groomed and dressed that it seemed a pity for them not to talk this way... That's why I wrote this conversation for them to have had... Their gestures, mannerisms, playful glances and smiles – those short interludes in the conversation when we stop feeling our own existence – clearly expressed what I faithfully pretend to be reporting... After they go their separate ways, each marrying someone else (since they think too much alike to marry each other), if one day they happen to look at these pages, I think they will recognize what they never said and will be grateful to me for so accurately interpreting not only what they really are but also what they never wished to be nor ever knew they were...

If they read me, may they believe that this was what they really said. In the words that they apparently heard from each other there were so many □ things missing, such as the fragrance in the air, the tea's aroma, the meaning of the corsage of □ which she wore on her chest... Although never stated, these things formed part of the conversation... All these things were there, and so my task isn't really to write literature but history. I reconstruct, completing what's missing, and this will serve as my excuse to them for having eavesdropped on what they didn't say and wouldn't have wanted to say.*

371

In Praise of Absurdity

I speak in earnest and with sadness. This is not a matter for joy, because the joys of dreaming are contradictory and gloomy, and must be enjoyed in a special, mysterious way.

Sometimes I inwardly, objectively observe delightful and absurd things which I can't even imagine seeing, for they're illogical to our eyesight – bridges that connect nothing to nothing, roads without beginning or end, upside-down landscapes ..... – the absurd, the illogical, the contradictory, everything that detaches and removes us from reality and its vast entourage of practical thoughts, human feelings, and all notions of useful and profitable action. Absurdity prevents the state of spirit in which dreaming is a sweet fury from ever becoming too tedious.

And I have a peculiar, mysterious way of envisioning these absurdities. In some way I can't explain, I'm able to see these things that are inconceivable for any kind of human vision.

372

In Praise of Absurdity

Let's absurdify life, from east to west.

373

Life is an experimental journey that we make involuntarily. It is a journey of the mind through matter, and since it is the mind that journeys, that is where we live. And so there are contemplative souls who have lived more intensely, more widely and more turbulently than those who live externally. The end result is what counts. What was felt is what was lived. A dream can tire us out as much as physical labour. We never live as hard as when we've thought a great deal.

The man in the corner of the dance-hall dances with all the dancers. He sees everything, and because he sees everything, he lives everything. Since everything is ultimately our own sensation, to have actual contact with a body counts for no more than seeing it or just remembering it. I dance, therefore, when I see someone dance. I second the English poet* who, lying in the grass and watching three mowers in the distance, said: 'A fourth man is mowing, and that fourth am I.'

All of this, told the way I feel it, has to do with the great weariness that came over me today, suddenly and for no apparent reason. I'm not only weary, but embittered; and the bitterness is also a mystery. I feel so anguished I'm on the verge of tears – not the kind that are wept but the kind that stay inside: tears caused by a sickness of the soul, not by a sensible pain.

How much I've lived without having lived! How much I've thought without having thought! I'm exhausted from worlds of static violence, from adventures I've experienced without moving a muscle. I'm surfeited with what I've never had and never will, jaded by gods that so far don't exist. I bear the wounds of all the battles I avoided. My muscles are sore from all the effort I have never even thought of making.

Dull, silent, futile... The lofty sky is of a flawed, dead summer. I look at it as if it weren't there. I sleep what I think, I'm lying down as I walk. I suffer without feeling anything. My enormous nostalgia is for nothing, is nothing, like the lofty sky that I don't see, and that I'm staring at impersonally.

374

In the day's limpid perfection, the sun-filled air nevertheless stagnates. It's not the present pressure of the future storm, not a malaise in our involuntary bodies, not a vague haziness in the truly blue sky. It's the torpor that the thought of not working makes us feel, a feather tickling our dozing face. It's sultry but it's summer. The countryside appeals even to those who don't like it.

If I were someone else, this would no doubt be a happy day for me, because I'd feel it without thinking about it. I would look forward to finishing my normal day's work – which to me is monotonously abnormal day after day – and then take the tram to Benfica* with some friends. We would eat dinner right as the sun was setting, in one of the garden restaurants. Our happiness in that moment would be part of the landscape, and recognized as such by all who saw us.

But since I am me, I merely take a little pleasure in the little that it is to imagine myself as that someone else. Yes, soon he-I, under a tree or bower, will eat twice what I can eat, drink twice what I dare drink, and laugh twice what I can conceive of laughing. Soon he, now I. Yes, for a moment I was someone else: in someone else I saw and lived this human and humble joy of existing as an animal in shirtsleeves. Great day that made me dream all this! The sky is sublimely blue, like my fleeting dream of being a hale and hearty sales representative on a sort of holiday when the day's work is over.

375

The countryside is always where we aren't. There, and there alone, do real trees and real shade exist.

Life is the hesitation between an exclamation and a question. Doubt is resolved by a period.

Miracles are God's laziness – or rather, the laziness we ascribe to God when we invent miracles.

The Gods are the incarnation of what we can never be.

The weariness of all hypotheses. . .

376

The slight inebriation of a mild fever, with its soft and penetrating discomfort that's cold in our aching bones and warm in our eyes, under our throbbing temples – I adore that discomfort like a slave his beloved oppressor. It puts me in that state of feeble, quivering passivity in which I glimpse visions, turn corners of ideas and get lost among sudden and unexpected feelings.

Thinking, feeling and wanting become a single confused thing. Beliefs, sensations, imagined things and real things get all mixed up, like the contents of various drawers overturned on to the floor.

377

There's a kind of sad happiness in the feeling of convalescence, especially if the sickness that preceded it affected the nerves.* There's an autumn in our emotions and thoughts, or rather, a beginning of spring that except for the absence of falling leaves seems, in the air and in the sky, like autumn.

Our fatigue is pleasant, and the pleasantness hurts just a little. We feel a bit removed from life, though still in it, as if on the balcony of life's house. We become pensive without actually thinking; we feel without any definable emotion. Our will grows calm, for we have no need of it.

That's when certain memories, certain hopes and certain vague desires slowly climb the slope of consciousness, like indistinct wayfarers seen from the top of a mountain. Memories of futile things: hopes whose non-fulfilment didn't particularly matter; desires that weren't violent in nature or in their manifestation, that weren't ever able to want really to be.

When the day is in keeping with these sensations – today, for example, which is rather cloudy even though it's summer, with a slight wind that feels almost chilly for not being warm –, then the particular mood in which we think, feel and live these impressions is accentuated. Not that the memories, hopes and desires we've had become any clearer. But we feel them more, and their indefinite sum total weighs a little, absurdly, on the heart.

In this moment I feel strangely far away. I'm on the balcony of life, yes, but not exactly of this life. I'm above life, looking down on it. It lies before me, descending in a varied landscape of dips and terraces towards the smoke from the white houses of the villages in the valley. If I close my eyes, I keep seeing, because I'm not really seeing. If I open them I see no more, because I wasn't really seeing in the first place. I'm nothing but a vague nostalgia, not for the past nor for the future but for the present – anonymous, unending and unintelligible.

378

The classifiers of things, by which I mean those scientists whose science is merely to classify, generally don't realize that what's classifiable is infinite and thus cannot be classified. But what really astounds me is that they don't realize there are things hidden in the cracks of knowledge – things of the soul and of consciousness – that can also be classified.

Perhaps because I think too much or dream too much, or perhaps for some other reason, I don't distinguish between the reality that exists and the world of dreams, which is the reality that doesn't exist. And so in my ruminations about the sky and the earth, I insert things that aren't lit up by the sun or trod on by feet – fluid wonders of my imagination.

I gild myself with sunsets I invent, but what I invent is alive in my invention. I rejoice in imaginary breezes, but the imaginary lives while it's being imagined. I have a soul, according to various hypotheses, and each of these hypotheses has its own soul, which it gives to me.

The only problem is that of reality, as insoluble as it is alive. What do I know about the difference between a tree and a dream? I can touch the tree; I know that I have the dream. What is all this really?

What is all this? It's that I, alone in the deserted office, can imaginatively live without abstaining from my intelligence. My thinking isn't interrupted by the vacant desks and the shipping division that's empty except for brown paper and balls of string. I'm not at my stool but leaning back in Moreira's comfortable armchair, enjoying a premature promotion. Perhaps it's the influence of my surroundings that has anointed me with distraction. These dog days make me tired; I sleep without sleeping, for lack of energy. And that's why I think this way.

379

Dolorous Interlude

I'm tired of the street, but no, I'm not tired of it – the street is all of life. There's the tavern opposite, which I can see if I look over my right shoulder, and there are the piled-up crates, which I can see by looking over my left shoulder; and in the middle, which I can only see if I turn around completely, there's the steady sound of the shoemaker's hammer, at the entrance to the offices of the Africa Company. I don't know what's on the upper floors. On the third floor there's a rooming house which is said to be immoral, but so it is with everything, life.

Tired of the street? Only thinking makes me tired. When I look at the street, or feel it, then I don't think: I do my work with great inner repose, ensconced in my corner, bookkeepingly nobody. I have no soul, nobody here does – it's all just work in this large office. Where millionaires live the good life, always in some foreign country or other, there is likewise work, and likewise no soul. And all that will remain is one or another poet. If only a phrase of mine could remain, just one thing I've written that would make people say 'Well done!', like the numbers I register, copying them in the book of my entire life.

I think that I shall always be an assistant bookkeeper in a fabric warehouse. I hope, with absolute sincerity, never to be promoted to head bookkeeper.

380

For a long time – I'm not sure if for days or for months – I haven't recorded any impressions; I don't think, therefore I don't exist. I've forgotten who I am. I'm unable to write because I'm unable to be. Through an oblique slumber, I've been someone else. To realize I don't remember myself means that I've woken up.

I fainted for a spell, cut off from my life. I return to myself without remembering what I've been, and the memory of what I used to be suffers from having been interrupted. I have a confused impression of a mysterious interlude; part of my memory is vainly struggling to find the other part. I can't pull myself together. If I've lived during this time, I forgot to be aware of it.

It's not that this first day that really feels like autumn – the first uncomfortably cool one to dress the dead summer with less light – gives me, through a kind of distracted clarity, a sensation of dead purpose and false desire. It's not that in this interlude of lost things there's a pale trace of useless memory. It's more painful than that. It's a tedium of trying to remember what can't be recalled, an anguish over what my consciousness has lost among reeds and seaweed, on the seashore of who knows what.

I know that the clear, still day has a veritable sky whose blue is less vivid than a deep blue. I know that the sun, slightly less golden than it was, bathes the walls and windows with its humid glimmers. I know that, although there is no wind, nor a breeze to recall and negate it, a wakeful coolness dozes in the hazy city. I know all this, without thinking or wanting to, and I'm sleepy only because I remember to be sleepy, nostalgic only because I'm disquieted.

I remotely and futilely convalesce from the sickness I never had. Wide awake, I prepare myself for what I don't dare. What sleepiness kept me from sleeping? What endearment refused to speak to me? How good to be someone else taking in a deep, cold breath of vigorous spring! How good – much better than life – to be able at least to imagine it, while in the distance, in the image I remember, the blue-green reeds bow along the riverside where there's not a hint of wind!

How often, remembering who I wasn't, I think of myself young and forget all the rest! The landscapes that existed but that I never saw were different then, and the landscapes that didn't exist but that I did see were new to me. Why do I care? I ended up in interstices, led on by chance, and now, as the sun itself seems to radiate coolness, the dark reeds by the river sleep coldly in the sunset that I see but do not have.

381

No one has yet defined tedium in a language comprehensible to those who have never experienced it. What some people call tedium is merely boredom; others use the term to mean a nagging discomfort; still others consider tedium to be weariness. But while tedium includes weariness, discomfort and boredom, it doesn't resemble them any more than water resembles the hydrogen and oxygen of which it is composed.

If some have a limited and incomplete notion of tedium, a few people give it a meaning that in a certain way transcends it – as when they use the word to signify intellectual and visceral dissatisfaction with the world's diversity and uncertainty. What makes us yawn, which we call boredom, what makes us fidget and is known as discomfort, and what makes us practically immobile, namely weariness – none of these things is tedium; but neither is tedium the profound sense of life's emptiness that causes frustrated ambition to surface, disappointed longings to rise up, and the seed to be planted in the soul of the future mystic or saint.

Tedium, yes, is boredom with the world, the nagging discomfort of living, the weariness of having lived; tedium is indeed the carnal sensation of the endless emptiness of things. But tedium, even more than all that, is a boredom with other worlds, whether real or imaginary; the discomfort of having to keep living, albeit as someone else, in some other way, in some other world; a weariness not only of yesterday and today but also of tomorrow and of eternity, if such exists, or of nothingness, if that's what eternity is. It's not only the emptiness of things and living beings that troubles the soul afflicted by tedium, it's also the emptiness of something besides things and beings – the emptiness of the very soul that feels this vacuum, that feels itself to be this vacuum, and that within this vacuum is nauseated and repelled by its own self.

Tedium is the physical sensation of chaos, a chaos that is everything. The bored, the uncomfortable and the weary feel like prisoners in a narrow cell. Those who abhor the narrowness of life itself feel shackled inside a large cell. But those who suffer tedium feel imprisoned in the worthless freedom of an infinite cell. The walls of the narrow cell may collapse and bury those who are bored, uncomfortable or tired. The shackles may fall and allow the man who abhors life's puniness to escape, or they may cause him pain as he struggles in vain to remove them and, through the feeling of that pain, revive him without his old abhorrence. But the walls of the infinite cell cannot crumble and bury us, because they don't exist; nor can we be revived by the pain of shackles no one has put on us.

This is what I feel before the placid beauty of this eternally dying afternoon. I look at the lofty, clear sky where I see fuzzy, pinkish shapes like the shadows of clouds, an impalpable soft down of a winged and far-away life. I look below me at the river, whose ever-so-slightly shimmering water is of a blue that seems to mirror a deeper sky. I raise my eyes back to the sky, where the coloured fuzziness that shredlessly unravels in the invisible air is now tinged by a frigid shade of dull white, as if something in the higher, more rarefied sphere of things had its own material tedium, an impossibility of being what it is, an imponderable body of anguish and desolation.

But what's in the lofty air besides the lofty air, which is nothing? What's in the sky besides a colour that's not its own? What's in these tatters that aren't even of clouds (and whose very existence I doubt) besides a few glimmers of materially arriving rays from an already resigned sun? What's in all this besides myself? Ah, but that, and that alone, is tedium. In all of this – the sky, the earth, the world – there is nothing at all but me!

382

I've reached the point where tedium is a person, the incarnate fiction of my own company.

383

The outer world exists like an actor on stage: it's there but is something else.

384

. . . and everything is an incurable sickness.

The indolence of feeling, the frustration of never knowing how to do anything, the inability to take action . . . . .

385

Fog or smoke? Was it rising from the ground or descending from the sky? Impossible to say: it seemed more like a disease of the air than an emanation or something descended. Sometimes it seemed more like an ailment of the eyes than a reality of nature.

Whatever it was, the entire landscape was cloaked by a hazy uneasiness made of forgetfulness and attenuation. It was as if the silence of the delinquent sun had taken shape in an imperfect body, or as if a general intuition that something was going to happen had caused the visible world to disguise itself.

It was hard to tell if the sky was filled with clouds or fog. It was all a torpid haze that was coloured here and there, a greyness with just a hint of yellow, except where it had dissolved into a false pink or had bluely stagnated, though this blue may have been the sky showing through rather than another blue overlaying it.

Nothing was definite, not even the indefinite. That's why it was only natural to call the fog smoke, since it didn't seem like fog, or to ask whether it was fog or smoke, it being impossible to determine. Even the air's temperature contributed to the doubt. It wasn't hot or cold or in between, but seemed to be composed of elements that had nothing to do with heat. Indeed, the fog that felt cool to the eyes seemed hot to the touch, as if sight and touch were two distinct modes of the same faculty of perception.

One couldn't even find, around the outlines of the trees or the corners of buildings, that blurring of contours and edges caused by true fog when it sets in, nor that slipping into view and out of view caused by real smoke. It was as if each thing projected its own vaguely diurnal shadow, in all directions, without a source of light to explain it as shadow, and without a specific place where it was projected to justify it as something visible.

Nor, in fact, was it visible: it was like something about to appear, equally throughout, as if it hesitated to be revealed.

And what feeling prevailed? The impossibility of having any feeling, the heart all broken to pieces in the mind, feelings all in a jumble, conscious existence in a stupor, and the heightening of some faculty akin to hearing – but in the soul – in order to apprehend a definitive, useless revelation that's always on the verge of appearing, like truth, and that always remains, like truth, the twin of what never appears.

Even the desire to sleep, remembered by the mind, has withered because mere yawning seems like too much of an effort. Even to stop seeing hurts the eyes. And in the soul's complete and colourless renunciation, only external, distant sounds constitute what's left of the impossible world.

Ah, another world, other things, another soul with which to feel them, another mind with which to know this soul! Anything, even tedium – anything but this general blurring of the soul and things, this bluish, forlorn indefiniteness of everything!

386

Together and apart we walked along the forest's sharply turning paths. Foreign to us, our steps were united, for they went in unison over the crackling softness of the yellow and half-green leaves that matted the ground's unevenness. But they also went separately, for we were two minds, with nothing in common except for the fact that what we weren't was treading in unison over the same resonant ground.

Autumn had already begun, and besides the leaves under our feet we could hear, in the wind's rough accompaniment, the constant falling of other leaves, or sounds of leaves, wherever we walked or had walked. There was no landscape but the forest, which veiled all others. But it was a good enough place for people like us, whose only life was to walk diversely and in unison over a moribund ground. I believe it was the close of day, the close of that day or any day, or perhaps all days, in an autumn that was all autumns, in the symbolic and true forest.

Not even we could say what homes, duties and loves we'd left behind. We were, in that moment, no more than wayfarers between what we had forgotten and what we didn't know, knights on foot defending an abandoned ideal. But that explained, along with the steady sound of trampled leaves and the forever rough sound of an unsteady wind, the reason for our departure, or for our return, since, not knowing what the path was, or why, we didn't know if we were coming or going. And always, all around us, the sound of leaves we couldn't see, falling we didn't know where, lulled the forest to sleep with sadness.

Although we paid no attention to each other, neither of us would have continued alone. We kept each other company with the drowsiness we both felt. The sound of our steps in unison helped each of us to think without the other, whereas our own solitary steps would have brought the other to mind. The forest was all false clearings, as if the forest itself were false, or were ending, but neither it nor the falseness was going to end. Our steps kept going in unison, and around the sound of the leaves we were trampling we heard a very soft sound of leaves falling in the forest that had become everything, in the forest that was the universe.

Who were we? Were we two, or two forms of one? We didn't know and we didn't ask. A hazy sun presumably existed, for it wasn't night in the forest. A vague aim presumably existed, for we were walking. Some world or other presumably existed, since a forest existed. But what it was or might be was foreign to us, two perpetual walkers treading in unison over dead leaves, anonymous and impossible listeners to falling leaves. Nothing else. A now harsh now gentle murmur of the inscrutable wind, a now loud now soft rustle of the unfallen leaves, a vestige, a doubt, a goal that had perished, an illusion that never was – the forest, the two walkers, and I, I, unsure of which one I was, or if I was both, or neither, and without seeing it to the end I watched the tragedy of nothing ever having existed but the autumn and the forest, the always rough and unsteady wind, and the always fallen or falling leaves. And always, as if surely there were a sun and day out there, one could see clearly – to nowhere – in the clamorous silence of the forest.

387

I suppose I'm what they call a decadent, one whose spirit is outwardly defined by those sad glimmers of artificial eccentricity that incarnate an anxious and artful soul in unusual words. Yes, I think that's what I am, and that I'm absurd. That's why, in the spirit of a classical writer, I try at least to place into an expressive mathematics the decorative sensations of my substituted soul. At a certain point in my written cogitation, I no longer know where the centre of my attention lies – whether in the scattered sensations I attempt to describe like enigmatic tapestries, or in the words which absorb me as I try to describe the act of describing and which, absorbing me, distract me and cause me to see other things. Beset by lucid and free associations of ideas, images and words, I say what I imagine I'm feeling as much as what I'm really feeling, and I'm unable to distinguish between the suggestions of my soul and the fruits born of images that fell from my soul to the ground, nor do I know whether the sound of a discordant word or the rhythm of an incidental phrase might not be diverting me from the already hazy point, from the already stowed sensation, thereby absolving me from thinking and saying, like long voyages designed to distract us. And all of this, which even as I'm telling it should stir in me a sense of futility, failure and anguish, gives me only wings of gold. As soon as I start talking about images, even if it's to say they should be used sparingly, images are born in me; as soon as I stand up from myself to repudiate something I don't feel, I start feeling that very thing, and even my repudiation becomes a feeling trimmed with embroidery; as soon as I want to abandon myself to the wind, having lost faith in my efforts, a placid phrase or a sober, concrete adjective suddenly, like sunlight, makes me clearly see the dormantly written page before me, and the letters drawn in my ink are an absurd map of magic signs. And I lay myself aside like my pen, and wrap myself in the flowing cape of obliviously leaning back, far away, intermediate and submissive, doomed like a castaway drowning within sight of marvellous islands, engulfed by the same purplish seas that he had so truly dreamed in distant beds.

388

Let's make the receptivity of our senses purely literary, and let's convert our emotions, when they stoop to becoming apparent, into visible matter that can be sculpted into statues with fluid, glowing words.

389

'Creator of indifferences' is the motto I want for my spirit today. I'd like my life's activity to consist, above all, in educating others to feel more and more for themselves, and less and less according to the dynamic law of collectiveness. To educate people in that spiritual antisepsis which precludes contamination by commonness and vulgarity is the loftiest destiny I can imagine for the pedagogue of inner discipline that I aspire to be. If all who read me would learn – slowly, of course, as the subject matter requires – to be completely insensitive to other people's opinions and even their glances, that would be enough of a garland to make up for my life's scholastic stagnation.

My inability to act has always been an ailment with a metaphysical aetiology. I've always felt that to perform a gesture implied a disturbance, a repercussion, in the outer universe; I've always had the impression that any movement I might make would unsettle the stars and rock the skies. And so the tiniest gesture assumed for me early on a metaphysical significance of astonishing proportions. I developed an attitude of transcendental honesty with respect to all action, and ever since this attitude took firm hold in my consciousness, it has prevented me from having intense relations with the tangible world.

390

To know how to be superstitious is still one of the arts which, developed to perfection, distinguishes the superior man.

391

Ever since I've been using my idle moments to observe and meditate, I've noticed that people don't agree or know the truth about anything that's of real importance in life or that would be useful for living it. The most exact science is mathematics, which lives in the cloister of its own laws and rules; when applied, yes, it elucidates other sciences, but it can elucidate only what they discover – it cannot help in the discovery. In the other sciences, the only sure and accepted facts are those that don't matter for life's supreme ends. Physics knows the expansion coefficient for iron, but it doesn't know the true mechanics of the world's composition. And the more we advance in what we'd like to know, the more we fall behind in what we do know. Metaphysics would seem to be the supreme guide, since it alone is concerned with ultimate truth and life's supreme ends, but it isn't even a scientific theory, just a pile of bricks that these or those hands form into awkward houses with no mortar holding them together.

I've also noticed that the only difference between humans and animals is the way they deceive themselves and remain ignorant about the life they live. Animals don't know what they do: they're born, they grow up, they live and they die without thought, reflection or a real future. And how many men live differently from animals? We all sleep, and the only difference is in what we dream, and in the degree and quality of our dreaming. Perhaps death will awaken us, but we can't even be sure of that unless it's by faith (for which believing is having), by hope (for which wanting is possessing), or by charity (for which giving is receiving).

It's raining on this cold and sad winter afternoon as if it had been raining, just as monotonously, since the first page of the world. It's raining, and as if the rain had made them hunch forward, my feelings lower their stupid gaze to the ground, where water flows and nourishes nothing, washes nothing, cheers up nothing. It's raining, and I suddenly feel the terrible weight of being an animal that doesn't know what it is, dreaming its thought and emotion, withdrawn into a spatial region of being as into a hovel, satisfied by a little heat as by an eternal truth.

392

'The people' are a regular chap.

The people are never humanitarian. What most characterizes this fellow called 'the people' is a narrow focus on his own interests, and a careful exclusion – as far as possible – of the interests of others.

When the people lose their tradition, it means that the social bond has been severed; and when the social bond is severed, then the bond between the people and the minority who aren't like them is also severed. And the severing of the social bond between the minority and the people spells the death of art and true science, the end of the main agencies on whose existence civilization depends.

To exist is to deny. What am I today, living today, but the denial of who and what I was yesterday? To exist is to contradict oneself. Nothing better symbolizes life than those news articles that contradict today what the newspaper said yesterday.

To want is to be unable to achieve. The man who wanted something he achieved didn't want it until it was already in his power to achieve. The man who wants will never achieve, because he loses himself in wanting. These principles seem fundamental to me.

393

. . . contemptible like the aims we live for, without our having chosen those aims.

Most if not all men live a contemptible life: contemptible in all its joys, and contemptible in almost all its sorrows, except those that have to do with death, since Mystery plays a part in these.*

Through the filter of my inattention, I hear fluid, scattered sounds which rise like intermittently flowing waves from outside, as if they came from another world: cries of vendors selling what's natural, such as vegetables, or what's social, such as lottery tickets; the round scraping of wheels from carts and wagons that hurriedly jerk forward;

cars whose veering makes more noise than their motors; the shaking of some sort of cloth out of some window; the whistle of a little boy; the laughter from an upper floor; the metallic groan of the tram one street over; the jumble of sounds issuing from the cross street; a mishmash of loud noises, soft noises and silences; halting rumbles of traffic; some footsteps; beginnings, middles and ends of people's utterances – and all of this exists for me, who am sleeping while thinking of it, like a stone poking out of a patch of grass where it doesn't belong.

Next, and coming through the wall of my rented room, it's domestic sounds that flow together in a stream: footsteps, dishes, the broom, a song (fado?*) that's cut short, last night's balcony rendezvous, irritation because something is missing from the dining table, someone asking for the cigarettes left on top of the cabinet – all of this is reality, the anaphrodisiac reality that has no part in my imagination.

Lightly fall the steps of the junior maid, whose slippers I picture having a red and black braid, and since that's how I picture them, their sound takes on something of a red and black braid; loudly fall the boots of the family's son, who's going out and yells goodbye, the slam of the door cutting the echo of the *later* that follows the *see you*; a dead calm, as if the world on this fourth floor had ended; dishes being taken to the kitchen to get washed; water running; 'Didn't I tell you that'. . . and silence whistling from the river.

But I dreamily and digestively drowse. I have time, between synaesthesias. And it's extraordinary to think that, if I were asked right now what I want for this short life, I could think of nothing better than these long, slow minutes, this absence of thought and emotion, of action and almost of sensation itself, this inner sunset of dissipated desire. And then it occurs to me, almost without thinking, that most if not all people live like this, with greater or lesser consciousness, moving forward or standing still, but with the very same indifference towards ultimate aims, the same renunciation of their personal goals, the same watered-down life.* Whenever I see a cat lying in the sun, I think of humanity. Whenever I see someone sleep, I remember that everything is slumber. Whenever someone tells me he dreamed, I wonder if he realizes that he has never done anything but dream. The sound from the street gets louder, as if a door had opened, and the doorbell rings.

It was nothing, for the door shut immediately. The footsteps die out at the end of the hallway. The washed plates raise their voice of water and porcelain. [. . .] A passing truck shakes the back of the apartment, and since all things end, I get up from my thinking.

394

And I reason at will, in the same way I dream, for reasoning is just another kind of dreaming.

O prince of better days, I was once your princess, and we loved each other with another kind of love, whose memory makes me grieve.

395

The so gentle and ethereal hour was an altar for prayer. The horoscope of our meeting was surely ruled by auspicious conjunctions – so subtle and silken was the vague substance of glimpsed dreams that had mingled with our awareness of feeling. Our bitter conviction that life wasn't worth living had come to an end, like one more summer. There was a rebirth of that spring which we could now, albeit fallaciously, imagine had been ours. With humiliating similarity to humans, the pools among the trees also lamented, along with the roses in the unshaded flower beds and the indefinite melody of living – all irresponsibly.

It's useless to discern or foresee. The whole of the future is a mist that surrounds us, and when we glimpse tomorrow, it tastes like today. My destinies are the clowns that the caravan left behind, with no better moonlight than that of the open road, nor any quivering in the leaves except what the breeze causes, and the uncertainty of the moment, and our belief that they are quivering. Distant purples, fleeting shadows, the dream incomplete and no hope of death's completing it, the rays of a dying sun, the light in the house on the hill, the anguished night, the perfume of death here among these books, all alone, with life outside, the trees smelling greenly in the vast night that is starrier on the other side of the hill. . . And so your sorrows had their solemn and benevolent union; your few words royally consecrated the voyage, no ships ever returned, not even the real ones, and the smoke of living stripped everything of its contours, leaving only the shadows and skeletons, the bitter waters of eerie ponds among boxwoods seen through gates that from a distance recall Watteau, anguish, and never again. Millenniums just for you to come, but the road has no curves and so you can never arrive. Goblets reserved for the inevitable hemlocks – not yours, but the life of us all, and even the street lamps, the nooks and crannies, the faint wings we only hear, while in the restless, suffocating night our thought slowly rises and paces across its anxiety. . . Yellow, green-black, love-blue: all dead, my divine nursemaid, all dead, and all ships are the ship that never set sail! Pray for me, and perhaps God will exist because it's for me that you pray. The fountain softly pattering in the distance, life uncertain, the smoke fading to nothing in the village where night is falling, my memory so hazy, the river so far away. . . Grant that I may sleep, grant that I may forget myself, lady of Obscure Designs, Mother of Endearments and of Blessings incompatible with their own existence. . .

396

After the last rains left the sky for earth, making the sky clear and the earth a damp mirror, the brilliant clarity of life that returned with the blue on high and that rejoiced in the freshness of the water here below left its own sky in our souls, a freshness in our hearts.

Whether we like it or not we're servants of the hour and its colours and shapes, we're subjects of the sky and earth. Even those who delve only in themselves, disdaining what surrounds them, delve by different paths when it rains and when it's clear. Obscure transmutations, perhaps felt only in the depths of abstract feelings, occur because it rains or stops raining. They're felt without our feeling them because the weather we didn't feel made itself felt.

Each of us is several, is many, is a profusion of selves. So that the self who disdains his surroundings is not the same as the self who suffers or takes joy in them. In the vast colony of our being there are many species of people who think and feel in different ways. At this very moment, jotting down these impressions during a break that's excusable because today there's not much work, I'm the one who is attentively writing them, I'm the one who is glad not to have to be working right now, I'm the one seeing the sky outside, invisible from in here, I'm the one thinking about all of this, I'm the one feeling my body satisfied and my hands still a bit cold. And my entire world of all these souls who don't know each other casts, like a motley but compact multitude, a single shadow – the calm, bookkeeping body with which I lean over Borges's tall desk, where I've come to get the blotter that he borrowed from me.

397

Falling between the buildings, in alternating patches of light and shadow (or of brighter and less bright light), the morning dawns over the city. It seems to come not from the sun but from the city itself, as if the sunlight emanated from the walls and rooftops – not from them physically, but because they happen to be there.

To see and feel it makes me feel a great hope, but I realize that hope is literary. Morning, spring, hope – they're linked in music by the same melodic intention; they're linked in the soul by the same memory of an identical intention. No: if I observe myself as I observe the city, I realize that all I can hope is for the day to end, like all days. Reason also sees the dawn. Whatever hope I placed in the day wasn't mine; it was of those who just live the passing hour and whose outer way of understanding I happened, for a moment, to embody.

Hope? What do I have to hope for? The day doesn't promise me more than the day, and I know it has a certain duration and an end. The light heartens but does not improve me, for I'll walk away as the same man – just a few hours older, a feeling or two happier, a thought or two sadder. When something is born, we can feel it as a birth or we can think about it having to die. Now, under the full light of the sun, the city landscape is like an open field of buildings – natural, vast and harmonious. But while seeing all this, can I forget that I exist? My consciousness of the city is, at its core, my consciousness of myself.

I suddenly remember when I was a child and saw, as today I cannot see, dawn breaking over the city. Back then it didn't break for me but for life, because back then I (not being conscious) was life. I saw dawn break and felt happy; today I see dawn break, feel happy, and become sad. The child is still there but has fallen silent. I see the way I saw, but from behind my eyes I see myself seeing, and that is enough to darken the sun, to make the green of the trees old, and to wilt the flowers before they open. Yes, I once belonged here; but today, before each landscape, no matter how fresh, I stand as a foreigner, a guest and pilgrim before it, an outsider of what I see and hear, old to myself.

I've seen everything, even what I've never seen nor will ever see. Even the memory of future landscapes flows in my blood, and my anxiety over what I'll have to see again is already monotonous to me.

And leaning on the windowsill to enjoy the day, gazing at the variegated mass of the whole city, just one thought fills my soul: that I profoundly wish to die, to cease, to see no more light shining on this city or any city, to think no more, to feel no more, to leave behind the march of time and the sun like a piece of wrapping paper, to remove like a heavy suit – next to the big bed – the involuntary effort of being.

398

I'm intuitively certain that for people like me no material circumstance can be propitious, no situation have a favourable outcome. If I already had good reasons for withdrawing from life, this is yet another one. Those courses of events that make success inevitable in an ordinary man have an unexpected, adverse effect in my case.

This observation sometimes causes me a painful impression of divine hostility. It seems that only by some conscious manipulation of events, to make them work against me, could the series of disasters that define my life have happened.

The result of all this is that I never make much of an effort. Let luck come my way, if it will. I know all too well that my greatest effort won't achieve what it would in other people. That's why I give myself up to luck, without expecting anything from it. What should I expect?

My stoicism is an organic necessity; I need to shield myself against life. Since stoicism is after all just a stringent form of Epicureanism, I try to get some amusement out of my misfortune. I don't know to what extent I achieve this. I don't know to what extent I achieve anything. I don't know to what extent anything can be achieved...

Where another man would succeed not so much by his effort as by a circumstantial inevitability, I wouldn't and couldn't succeed, whether by that inevitability or by that effort.

I seem to have been born, spiritually speaking, on a short winter day. Night fell early on my being. The only way I can live my life is in frustration and desolation.

None of this is truly stoical. It's only in words that my suffering is at all noble. I complain like a sick maid. I fret like a housewife. My life is totally futile and totally sad.

399

All I asked of life is what Diogenes* asked of Alexander: not to stand in the way of the sun. There were things I wanted, but I was denied any reason for wanting them. As for what I found, it would have been better to have found it in real life. Dreaming .....

While out walking I've formulated perfect phrases which I can't remember once I get home. I'm not sure if the ineffable poetry of these phrases belongs totally to what they were (and which I forgot), or partly to what they after all weren't.

I hesitate in everything, often without knowing why. How often I've sought – as my own version of the straight line, seeing it in my mind as the ideal straight line – the longest distance between two points. I've never had a knack for the active life. I've always taken wrong steps that no one else takes; I've always had to make an effort to do what comes naturally to other people. I've always wanted to achieve what others have achieved almost without wanting it. Between me and life there were always sheets of frosted glass that I couldn't tell were there by sight or by touch; I didn't live that life or that dimension. I was the daydream of what I wanted to be, and my dreaming began in my will: my goals were always the first fiction of what I never was.

I've never known if it was my sensibility that was too much for my intelligence, or my intelligence that was too much for my sensibility. I've always been late, I'm not sure if for the former or for the latter, or perhaps for both, or perhaps it was the third thing that was late.

The dreamers of ideals [?] – socialists, altruists, and humanitarians of whatever ilk – make me physically sick to my stomach. They're idealists with no ideal, thinkers with no thought. They're enchanted by life's surface because their destiny is to love rubbish, which floats on the water and they think it's beautiful, because scattered shells float on the water too.

400

An expensive cigar smoked with one's eyes closed – that's all it takes to be rich.

Like someone who revisits a place where he lived in his youth, with a cheap cigarette I can return – heart and soul – to the time in my life when I used to smoke them. Through the mild flavour of the smoke, the whole of the past comes back to me.

At other times it's a certain sweet. A mere piece of chocolate can shake up my nerves with the surfeit of memories it provokes. Childhood! And as my teeth sink into the dark, soft mass, I chew and savour my humble joys as the happy companion of my toy soldiers, as the knight in perfect accord with whatever stick happened to be serving as my horse. Tears well up in my eyes, and along with the flavour of the chocolate I can taste my bygone happiness, my long lost childhood, and I voluptuously bask in the sweetness of my sorrow.

This ritual of taste, however simple it may be, is as solemn as any other.

But it's cigarette smoke that most subtly, spiritually, reconstructs my past. Since it just barely grazes my awareness of taste, it evokes the moments to which I've died in a more general way, by a kind of displacement; it makes them more remotely present, more like mist when they envelop me, more ethereal when I embody them. A menthol cigarette or a cheap cigar wraps certain of my moments in a sweet softness. With what subtle plausibility – taste combined with smell – I recreate the dead stage settings and reinvest them with the colours of a past, always so eighteenth century in its weary and mischievous aloofness, always so medieval in its irreparable lostness!

401

Elevating disgrace into splendour, I created for myself a pageantry of pain and effacement. I didn't make a poem out of my pain, but I used it to make a cortège. And from the window that looks on to myself I contemplate in awe the deep-red sunsets, the wispy twilights of my sorrows without cause, where the dangers, burdens and failures of my innate incapacity for existing march by in processions of my aimlessness. The child in me that never died still watches and excitedly waves at the circus I stage for myself. He laughs at the clowns, who exist only in the circus; he fixes his eyes on the stunt men and the acrobats as if they were the whole of life. And thus all the unsuspected anguish of a human soul about to burst, all the incurable despair of a heart forsaken by God, sleeps the innocent child's sleep, without joy and yet contented, within the four walls of my room with their ugly, peeling paper.

I walk not through the streets but through my sorrow. The flanking rows of buildings are all the incomprehension that surrounds my soul; . . . . . my footsteps resound against the pavement like a ridiculous death knell, a frightful noise in the night, final like a receipt or a tomb.

Stepping back from myself, I see that I'm the bottom of a well.

The man I never was died. God forgot who I should have been. I'm just a vacant interlude.

If I were a musician, I would compose my own funeral march, and with such good reason!

402

To be reincarnated in a stone or a speck of dust – my soul weeps with this yearning.

I'm losing my taste for everything, including even my taste for finding everything tasteless.

403

I have no meaning I can fathom. . . Life weighs on me. . . Any emotion is too much for me. . . Only God knows my heart. . . What cortèges from my past cause a tedium of unremembered splendours to cradle my nostalgia? And what canopies? what starry sequences? what lilies? what pennants? what stained-glass windows?

What shady path of mystery was followed by our best fantasies, which so vividly remember this world's trickling waters, cypress trees and boxwoods, and which can find no canopies for their processions except in the fruits of abdication?

Kaleidoscope

Don't speak. . . You happen too much. . . If only I didn't see you. . . When will you be just a fond memory of mine? How many women you'll be until that happens! And my having to suppose I can see you is an old bridge no one uses. . . Yes, this is life. The others have dropped their oars. . . The cohorts have lost their discipline. . . The knights left at daybreak with the sound of their lances. . . Your castles passively waited to be deserted. . . No wind abandoned the rows of trees on the summit. . . Useless porticos, hidden silverware, prophetic signs – all of this belongs to vanquished twilights in ancient temples and not to our meeting in this present moment, for there is no reason for lindens to give shade apart from your fingers and their belated gesture. . .

All the more reason for remote territories. . . Treaties signed by stained-glass kings. . . Lilies from religious pictures. . . Whom is the retinue waiting for?. . . Where did the lost eagle go?

404

To wrap the world around our fingers, like a thread or ribbon which a woman twiddles while daydreaming at the window. . .

Everything comes down to our trying to feel tedium in such a way that it doesn't hurt.

It would be interesting to be two kings at the same time: not the one soul of them both, but two distinct, kingly souls.

405

Life, for most people, is a pain in the neck that they hardly notice, a sad affair with some happy respites, as when the watchers of a dead body tell anecdotes to get through the long, still night and their obligation to keep watch. I've always thought it futile to see life as a valley of tears; yes, it is a valley of tears, but one in which we rarely weep. Heine said that after great tragedies we always merely blow our noses. As a Jew, and therefore universal, he understood the universal nature of humanity.

Life would be unbearable if we were conscious of it. Fortunately we're not. We live as unconsciously, as uselessly and as pointlessly as animals, and if we anticipate death, which presumably (though not assuredly) they don't, we anticipate it through so many distractions, diversions and ways of forgetting that we can hardly say we think about it.

That's how we live, and it's a flimsy basis for considering ourselves superior to animals. We are distinguished from them by the purely external detail of speaking and writing, by an abstract intelligence that distracts us from concrete intelligence, and by our ability to imagine impossible things. All this, however, is incidental to our organic essence. Speaking and writing have no effect on our primordial urge to live, without knowing how or why. Our abstract intelligence serves only to elaborate systems, or ideas that are quasi-systems, which in animals corresponds to lying in the sun. And to imagine the impossible may not be exclusive to us; I've seen cats look at the moon, and it may well be that they were longing to have it.

All the world, all life, is a vast system of unconscious agents operating through individual consciousnesses. Like two gases that form a liquid when an electric current passes through them, so two consciousnesses – that of our concrete being and that of our abstract being – form a superior unconsciousness when life and the world pass through them.

Happy the man who doesn't think, for he accomplishes instinctively and through organic destiny what the rest of us must accomplish through much meandering and an inorganic or social destiny. Happy the man who most resembles the animals, for he is effortlessly what the rest of us only are by hard work; for he knows the way home, which the rest of us can reach only through byways of fiction and hazy return routes; for he is rooted like a tree, forming part of the landscape and therefore of beauty, while we are but myths who cross the stage, walk-ons of futility and oblivion dressed in real-life costumes.

406

I don't much believe in the happiness of animals, except when I want to use this conceit as a frame for highlighting a particular feeling. To be happy, it's necessary to know that one's happy. The only happiness we get from sleeping without dreaming is when we wake up and realize that we've slept without dreaming. Happiness is outside of happiness.

There's no happiness without knowledge. But the knowledge of happiness brings unhappiness, because to know that you're happy is to realize that you're experiencing a happy moment and will soon have to leave it behind. To know is to kill, in happiness as in everything else. Not to know, on the other hand, is not to exist.

Only the absolute of Hegel managed to be two things at once, but in writing. Being and non-being do not mix and meld in the sensations and laws of life; they exclude one another, by a kind of reverse synthesis.

What to do? Isolate the moment like a thing, and be happy now, in the moment we're feeling happiness, thinking of nothing but what we're feeling and completely excluding everything else. Trap all thought in our sensation . . . . .

That's what I believe this afternoon. It's not what I'll believe tomorrow morning, because tomorrow morning I'll be someone else. What kind of believer will I be tomorrow? I don't know; I would already have to be there to know. Not even God eternal, in whom today I believe, could know – today or tomorrow – anything about me tomorrow. Because today I'm I, and tomorrow it's possible that he'll have never existed.

407

God created me to be a child and willed that I remain a child. But why did he let Life beat me up, take away my toys and leave me alone during playtime, my weak hands clutching at my blue, tear-stained smock? If I couldn't live without loving care, why was this thrown out with the rubbish? Ah, every time I see a child crying in the street, left there on his own, the jolting horror of my exhausted heart grieves me even more than the child's sadness. I grieve with every pore of my emotional life, and it is my hands that wring the corner of the child's smock, my mouth that is contorted by real tears, my weakness, my loneliness. . . And all the laughs from the adult life passing by are like the flames of matches struck against the sensitive fabric* of my heart.

408

He sang, in a soft and gentle voice, a song from a faraway country. The music made the strange words familiar. It sounded like the soul's fado,* though it didn't in the least resemble fado.

Through its veiled words and human melody, the song told of things that are in the hearts of us all and that no one knows. He sang in a kind of stupor, a kind of ecstasy right there in the street, his gaze oblivious to his listeners.

The crowd that had gathered listened to him without any discernible scoffing. The song belonged to everyone, and the words sometimes spoke to us – an oriental secret of some lost race. We didn't hear the city's noises, even if we heard them, and the carts passed by so close that one of them brushed against my coat. But I only felt it; I didn't hear it. There was a rapt intensity in the stranger's song that was soothing to what in us dreams or doesn't succeed. It was a street incident, and we all noticed the policeman slowly turning the corner. He approached with the same slow gait, then stood still for a while behind the boy selling umbrellas, as if something had caught his eye. That's when the singer stopped. No one said anything. Then the policeman intervened.

409

For some reason or other, I'm alone in the office. Although this dawns on me suddenly, I had already vaguely sensed it. In some corner of my consciousness I'd felt a great sigh of relief, a deeper breathing with different lungs.

This is one of the strangest sensations that the fortuity of encounters and absences can bring: that of finding ourselves alone in a place that is normally full of people and noise, or that belongs to someone else. We suddenly have a feeling of absolute ownership, of vast and effortless dominion, and – as I said – of relief and serenity.

How good it feels to be completely alone! To be able to talk to ourselves out loud, to walk around without being looked at, to lean back in an undisturbed reverie! Every house becomes an open field, every room has the breadth of a farm.

The usual sounds are all strange, as if they belonged to a nearby but independent universe. We are kings at last. This is what we all truly long to be, and the most plebeian among us perhaps more ardently than those full of false gold. For a moment we are the universe's pensioners, recipients of a steady income, with no needs and no worries.

Ah, but in those footsteps climbing the stairs I recognize someone who's coming here, someone who will interrupt my amused solitude. My implicit empire is about to be invaded by barbarians. The footsteps don't tell me who it is that's coming; they don't recall the footsteps of anyone I know. But I have a gut instinct that I'm the destination of what for now are merely footsteps, climbing up the stairs which I suddenly see, since I'm thinking about who's climbing them. Yes, it's one of the clerks. He stops, the door opens, he enters. I see all of him. And as he enters he says: 'All alone, Senhor Soares?' And I answer: 'Yes, for some time now. . .' And then, taking off his jacket while eyeing his other, older one that's hanging up, he says: 'To be here all alone is a real bore, Senhor Soares, and not only that. . .' 'A real bore, no doubt about it,' I answer. 'It almost makes you feel like sleeping,' he says, already wearing the frayed jacket and walking towards his desk. 'It certainly does,' I agree, smiling. And reaching for my forgotten pen, I graphically re-enter the anonymous wholesomeness of normal life.

410

Whenever they can, they sit opposite a mirror. While talking to us, they look at themselves with infatuated eyes. Sometimes, as happens to people in love, they lose track of the conversation. They always liked me, because my adult aversion to my physical appearance made me automatically turn my back to whatever mirror I found. And so they treated me well, for they instinctively recognized that I was the good listener who would always let them show off and have the pulpit.

As a group they weren't so bad; as individuals, some were better and some were worse. They had tender and generous feelings that an observer of average behaviour would never expect, mean and petty attitudes that a normal human being would hardly imagine. Pathetic, envious and self-deluded – that sums them up, and the same words would sum up whatever part of this milieu has infiltrated the work of worthy men who happened to get caught for a time in its mire. (This explains the presence, in Fialho's* writings, of flagrant envy, rank vulgarity, and an abominable lack of elegance.)

Some are witty, others have nothing but wit, and still others don't exist. Café wit may be divided into jokes about those who are absent and jibes at those who are present. This kind of wittiness is known elsewhere as mere vulgarity. There's no greater proof of an impoverished mind than its inability to be witty except at other people's expense.

I passed by, I saw, and – unlike them – I conquered. Because my victory consisted in seeing. I saw that they were no different from other inferior social groups: in the house where I rent a room, I found the same squalid soul that the cafés had already revealed to me, but without – thank all the gods – any delusions of making a hit in Paris. My landlady dreams of Lisbon's newer section in her moments of imaginative fancy, but she's spared from the myth of going abroad, and my heart is touched.

From that time I spent at the tomb of human will, I remember a couple of funny jokes and otherwise being bored sick.

They're heading to the cemetery, and it seems that their past was left behind at the café, for they don't even mention it now.

. . . and posterity will never know of them, forever hidden from its view under the rotten heap of pennants they won in their verbal battles.

411

Pride is the emotional certainty of our own greatness. Vanity is the emotional certainty that others see this greatness or attribute it to us. These two sentiments don't necessarily coincide, nor do they naturally oppose each other. They're different but compatible.

Pride all by itself, unaccompanied by vanity, manifests itself in timid behaviour. One who feels he's great but isn't convinced that others recognize him as such will be afraid to pit his opinion about himself against other people's opinion.

Vanity all by itself, unaccompanied by pride, which is rare but possible, manifests itself through audacity. One who is certain that others think highly of him will fear nothing from them. Both physical courage and moral courage can exist without vanity, but audacity cannot. And by audacity I mean boldness in taking the initiative. Audacity can exist without physical or moral courage, for these character traits are of a different, incommensurable order.

412

Dolorous Interlude

I don't even have the consolation of pride. And even if I did have something I could brag about, how much more I have to be ashamed of!

I spend life lying down. And not even in my dreams can I make a move to get up, so complete is my incapacity for any and all effort.

The creators of metaphysical systems and □ of psychological explanations are still in the primary stage of suffering. What is systematizing and explaining but □ and construction? And what is all this – arranging, ordering, organizing – but achieved effort? And how deplorably this is life!

No, I'm not a pessimist. Happy those who are able to translate their suffering into a universal principle. I don't know if the world is sad or arbitrary, nor do I care, because I'm indifferent to what other people suffer. As long as they don't weep or moan, which I find bothersome and unpleasant, I don't even shrug my shoulders at their suffering. That's how deep my disdain for them runs.

I like to think of life as half light, half darkness. I'm not a pessimist. I don't complain about the horror of life; I complain about the horror of my life. The only fact I worry about is that I exist and suffer and can't even dream of being removed from my feeling of suffering.

The happy dreamers are the pessimists. They shape the world to their likeness and thus always feel at home. What grieves me the most is the disparity between the world's happy bustle and my own glum, wearisome silence.

For those who live it, life with all its sorrows and fears and jolts must be a good and happy thing, like a journey in an old stagecoach, when one is in good company (and can enjoy it).

I can't even consider my suffering a sign of Greatness. I don't know if it is or isn't. But I suffer things that are so trivial, and am hurt by things so banal, that this hypothesis – if I dared entertain it – would be an insult to the hypothesis that I might be a genius.

The splendour of a beautiful sunset saddens me with its beauty. When gazing at one I always think: what a thrill it must be for a happy man to see this!

And this book is a lament. Once written, it will replace *Alone** as the saddest book in Portugal.

Next to my pain, all other pains seem unreal or insignificant. They're the pains of people who are happy or who live life and complain. My pains are of a man who finds himself incarcerated, cut off from life. . .

Between me and life. . .

And so I see all the things which cause anguish and feel none of the things which bring joy. And I've noticed that suffering is seen more than felt, whereas happiness is felt more than seen. Because if one doesn't see or think, he will know a certain contentment, like that of the mystics and the bohemians and the riffraff. It's by the door of thought and the window of observation that suffering comes into one's house.

413

Let us live by dreams and for dreams, distractedly dismantling and recomposing the universe according to the whim of each dreaming moment. Let us do this while being consciously conscious of the uselessness and □ of doing it. Let us ignore life with every pore of our body, stray from reality with all of our senses, and abdicate from love with our whole heart. Let us fill the pitchers we take to the well with useless sand and empty them out, so as to refill and re-empty them, in utter futility.

Let us fashion garlands so that, once finished, they can be thoroughly and meticulously taken apart.

Let us mix paints on a palette without having a canvas on which to paint. Let us order stone for chiselling without having a chisel and without being sculptors. Let us make everything an absurdity and turn all our sterile hours into pure futilities. Let us play hide-and-seek with our consciousness of living.

Let us hear God* tell us we exist with a delighted and incredulous smile on our lips. Let us watch Time paint the world and find the painting not only false but also empty.

Let us think with sentences that contradict one another, speaking out loud in sounds that aren't sounds and colours that aren't colours. Let us affirm – and grasp, which would be impossible – that we are conscious of not being conscious, and that we are not what we are. Let us explain all this by way of a hidden, paradoxical meaning that things have in their divine, reverse-side dimension, and let us not believe too much in the explanation so that we won't have to give it up...

Let us sculpt in hopeless silence all our dreams of speaking. Let us make all our thoughts of action languish in torpor.

And over all of this the horror of living will hover remotely* like a blue and unbroken sky.

414

But the landscapes we dream are just shades of the landscapes we've seen, and the tedium of dreaming them is almost as great as the tedium of looking at the world.

415

Imaginary figures have more depth and truth than real ones.

My imaginary world has always been the only true world for me. I've never had loves so real and so full of verve and blood and life as the ones I've had with characters I myself created. What madness! I miss them because, like all loves, these kind also come and go. . .

416

Sometimes, in my inner dialogues on exquisite afternoons of Imagination, as I carry on weary conversations in imaginary sitting rooms at twilight, it can happen during a lull in the discussion that, finding myself alone with an interlocutor who's more I than the others, I start to wonder why our scientific age's will to understand hasn't been extended to artificial, inorganic things. And one of the questions that I most languidly ponder is why we don't develop, along with the usual psychology of human and subhuman creatures, a psychology (for surely they have one) of artificial figures and of creatures whose existence takes place only in rugs and in pictures. It's a sad view of reality that would limit it to the organic realm and not place the idea of soul in statuettes and needlework. Where there's form there's a soul.

These private deliberations aren't an idle pastime but a scientific lucubration like any other. And so, before having an answer and without knowing if I'll ever have one, I think of what's possible as if it already existed, and with inner analyses and intense concentration I envision the likely results of this actualized desideratum. As soon as I start thinking this way, scientists immediately appear in my mind, hunched over illustrations that they know to be real lives; microscopists of warp and weft emerge from the rugs, physicists emerge from the broad, swirling patterns around their borders, chemists from the idea of shapes and colours in pictures, geologists from the stratified layers in cameos, and finally (and most importantly) psychologists who record and classify – one by one – the sensations that a statuette must feel, the ideas that pass through the hazy psyche of a figure in a painting or a stained-glass window, the wild impulses, the unbridled passions, the occasional hatreds and sympathies and ☐ found in these special universes marked by death and immobility – whether in the eternal gestures of bas-reliefs or in the immortal consciousnesses of painted figures.

More than the other arts, literature and music are fertile territory for the subtleties of a psychologist. Novelistic figures, as we all know, are as real as any of us. Certain aspects of sounds have a swift, winged soul, but they are still susceptible to psychology and sociology. Let all the ignorant be informed: veritable societies exist in colours, sounds and sentences, even as regimes and revolutions, reigns, politics and ☐ exist literally, not metaphorically, in the instrumental ensembles of symphonies, in the structured wholes of novels, and in the square feet of a complex painting, where the colourful poses of warriors, lovers or symbolic figures find enjoyment, suffer, and mingle together.

When one of my Japanese teacups is broken, I imagine that the real cause was not the careless hand of a maid but the anxieties of the figures inhabiting the curves of that porcelain ☐. Their grim decision to commit suicide doesn't shock me: they used the maid as one of us might use a gun. To know this (and with what precision I know it!) is to have gone beyond modern science.

417

I know no pleasure like that of books, and I read very little. Books are introductions to dreams, and no introductions are necessary for one who freely and naturally enters into conversation with them. I've never been able to lose myself in a book; as I'm reading, the commentary of my intellect or imagination has always hindered the narrative flow. After a few minutes it's I who am writing, and what I write is nowhere to be found.

My favourite things to read are the banal books that sleep with me at my bedside. There are two that I always have close at hand: Father Figueiredo's *Rhetoric*,* and Father Freire's *Reflections on the Portuguese Language*.* I always reread these books with pleasure, and while it's true I've read them over many times, it's also true that I've read neither one straight through. I'm indebted to these books for a discipline I doubt I could ever have acquired on my own: to write with objectivity, with reason as one's constant guide.

The affected, dry, monastic style of Father Figueiredo is a discipline that delights my intellect. The nearly always undisciplined verbosity of Father Freire amuses my mind without tiring it, and teaches me without stirring up any worries. Both are learned, untroubled minds that confirm my complete lack of desire to be like them, or like anyone else.

I read and abandon myself, not to my reading but to me. I read and fall asleep, and it's as if my already dreaming eyes still followed Father Figueiredo's descriptions of the figures of speech, and it's in enchanted forests that I hear Father Freire explain that one should say 'Magdalena', because only an ignorant person says 'Madalena'.

418

I hate to read. The mere thought of unfamiliar pages bores me. I can read only what I already know. My bedside book is Father Figueiredo's *Rhetoric*, where every night I read yet again for the thousandth time, in correct and clerical Portuguese, the descriptions of various figures of speech, whose names I still haven't learned. But the language lulls me . . . . . , and I'd sleep fitfully were I to miss out on the Jesuitical words written with *c*.*

I must, however, give credit to the exaggerated purism of Father Figueiredo's book for the relative care I take – as much as I can muster – to write correctly the language in which I express myself . . . . .

And I read:
(a passage from Father Figueiredo)
– pompous, empty[?] and cold,
and this helps me forget life.
Or this:
(a passage about figures of speech),
which returns in the preface.

I'm not exaggerating a verbal smidgen: I feel all this.

As others read passages from the Bible, I read them from this *Rhetoric*. But I have two advantages: complete repose and lack of devotion.

419

The trivial things that make up life, the trifles of the ordinary and routine, like a dust that underscores – with a hideous, smudged line – the sordidness and vileness of my human existence: the Cashbook lying open before eyes that dream of countless Orients; the office manager's inoffensive joke that offends the whole universe; the could you please ask Senhor Vasques to call me, his girlfriend, Miss so-and-so, right when I was pondering the most asexual part of an aesthetic and intellectual theory.

And then there are one's friends, good fellows, good fellows, great to be with them and talk, to have lunch together, dinner together, but all of it, I don't know, so sordid and pathetic and trivial, because even on the street we remain in the fabric warehouse, even overseas we're still seated before the Cashbook, and even in infinity we still have our boss.

Everyone has an office manager with a joke that's out of place, and everyone has a soul that falls outside the normal universe. Everyone has a boss and the boss's girlfriend, and the phone call that arrives at the inevitably worst moment, when the evening is wondrously falling and girlfriends politely offer their apologies [?] or else leave messages for their lover, who we all know has gone out for a fancy tea.

All who dream – even if they don't dream in a downtown Lisbon office, bent over the accounts of a fabric warehouse – have before them a Cashbook, which may be the woman they married, or the administration of a future they've inherited, or anything at all that positively exists.

All of us who dream and think are assistant bookkeepers in a fabric warehouse or in some other business in this or another downtown. We enter amounts and lose; we add up totals and pass on; we close the books and the invisible balance is always against us.

The words I write make me smile, but my heart is ready to break – to break like things that shatter into fragments, shards and debris, hauled away in a bin on somebody's shoulders to the eternal rubbish cart of every City Council.

And everything is waiting, dressed up and expectant, for the King who will come and who is already arriving, for the dust of his retinue forms a new mist in the slowly appearing east, and the lances in the distance are already flashing with their own dawn.

420

Funeral March

Hieratic figures from mysterious hierarchies are lined up in the corridors, waiting for you. There are fair-haired boys bearing lances, young men □ with scattered flashes of naked blades, reflections glancing off helmets and brass, dark glimpses of silks and tarnished gold.

All that the imagination infects, the funereal feeling that makes pageants melancholy and even weighs on us in victories, the mysticism of nothing, the asceticism of absolute negation. . .

Not the six feet of cold earth that cover our closed eyes beneath the warm sun and next to the green grass, but the death that surpasses our life and is a life all its own – a dead presence in some god, the unknown god of the religion of my Gods.*

The Ganges also passes by the Rua dos Douradores. All eras exist in this cramped room – the mixture □ the multicoloured march of customs, the distances between cultures, and the vast variety of nations.

And right here on this very street I can wait, in ecstasy, for Death among battlements and swords.

421

Journey in the Mind

From my fourth-floor room overlooking infinity, in the viable intimacy of the falling evening, at the window before the emerging stars, my dreams – in rhythmic accord with the visible distance – are of journeys to unknown, imagined, or simply impossible countries.

422

The blond light of the golden moon shines out of the east. The shimmer it forms on the wider river opens into snakes on the sea.

423

In lavish satins and puzzled purples the empires proceeded towards death under exotic flags flanking wide roads and luxurious canopies at the stopping-places. Baldachins passed by. Roads now drab, now spruce, let the processions come through. The weapons coldly flashed in the excruciatingly slow, pointless marches. The gardens on the outskirts were forgotten, and the fountains' water was merely the continuation of what had been left behind, a distant laughter falling among memories of lights, which is not to say that the statues along the paths talked, nor did the succession of yellows stifle the autumn colours that embellished the tombs. The halberds were corners around which lay splendorous ages dressed in green-black, faded purple and garnet-coloured robes. Behind all the evasions, the squares lay empty, and never again would the flower beds where we stroll be visited by the shadows that had abandoned the aqueducts.

The drums, like thunder, drummed the tremulous hour.

424

Every day things happen in the world that can't be explained by any law of things we know. Every day they're mentioned and forgotten, and the same mystery that brought them takes them away, transforming their secret into oblivion. Such is the law by which things that can't be explained must be forgotten. The visible world goes on as usual in the broad daylight. Otherness watches us from the shadows.

425

Dreaming itself has become a torture. I've acquired such lucidity in my dreams that I see all dreamed things as real. And so all the value that they had as mere dreams has been lost.

Do I dream of being famous? Then I feel all the public exposure that comes with glory, the total loss of privacy and anonymity that makes glory painful.

426

To think of our greatest anxiety as an insignificant event, not only in the life of the universe but also in the life of our own soul, is the beginning of wisdom. To think this way right in the midst of our anxiety is the height of wisdom. While we're actually suffering, our human pain seems infinite. But human pain isn't infinite, because nothing human is infinite, and our pain has no value beyond its being a pain we feel.

How often, oppressed by a tedium that seems like insanity or by an anxiety that seems to surpass it, I stop, hesitating, before I revolt, I hesitate, stopping, before I deify myself. From among all the pains there are – the pain of not grasping the mystery of the world, the pain of not being loved, the pain of being treated unjustly, the pain of life oppressing us, suffocating and restraining us, the pain of a toothache, the pain of shoes that pinch – who can say which is the worst for himself, let alone for someone else, or for the generality of those who exist?

Some of the people I talk with consider me insensitive. But I think I'm more sensitive than the vast majority. I'm a sensitive man who knows himself, and who therefore knows sensitivity.

Ah, it's not true that life is painful, or that it's painful to think about life. What's true is that our pain is grave and serious only when we pretend it is. If we let it be, it will leave just as it came, it will die down the way it grew up. Everything is nothing, our pain included.

I'm writing this under the weight of a tedium that doesn't seem to fit inside me, or that needs more room than is in my soul; a tedium of all people and all things that strangles and deranges me; a physical feeling of being completely misunderstood that unnerves and overwhelms me. But I lift up my head to the blue sky that doesn't know me, I let my face feel the unconsciously cool breeze, I close my eyelids after having looked, and I forget my face after having felt. This doesn't make me feel better, but it makes me different. Seeing myself frees me from myself. I almost smile, not because I understand myself but because, having become another, I've stopped being able to understand myself. High in the sky, like a visible nothingness, floats a tiny white cloud left behind by the universe.

427

My dreams: In my dreams I create *friends*, with whom I then keep company. They're imperfect in a different way.

Remain pure, not in order to be noble or strong but to be yourself. To give your love is to lose love.

Abdicate from life so as not to abdicate from yourself.

Women are a good source of dreams. Don't ever touch them.

Learn to disassociate the ideas of voluptuousness and pleasure. Learn to delight in everything, not for what it is, but for the ideas and dreams it kindles. (Because nothing is what it is, but dreams are always dreams.) To accomplish this, you mustn't touch anything. As soon as you touch it, your dream will die; the touched object will occupy your capacity for feeling.

Seeing and hearing are the only noble things in life. The other senses are plebeian and carnal. The only aristocracy is never to touch. Avoid getting close – that's true nobility.

428

Aesthetics of Indifference

For each separate thing, the dreamer should strive to feel the complete indifference which it, as a thing, arouses in him.

The ability to spontaneously abstract whatever is dreamable from each object or event, leaving all of its reality as dead matter in the Exterior World – that is what the wise man should strive for.

Never to feel his own feelings sincerely, and to raise his pallid triumph to the point of regarding his own ambitions, longings and desires with indifference; to pass alongside his joys and anxieties as if passing by someone who doesn't interest him. . .

The greatest self-mastery is to be indifferent towards ourselves, to see our body and soul as merely the house and grounds where Destiny willed that we spend our life. To treat our own dreams and deepest desires with arrogance, *en grand seigneur*, politely and carefully ignoring them. To act modestly in our own presence; to realize that we are never truly alone, since we are our own witnesses, and should therefore act before ourselves as before a stranger, with a studied and serene outward manner – indifferent because it's noble, and cold because it's indifferent.

In order not to sink in our own estimation, all we have to do is quit having ambitions, passions, desires, hopes, whims or nervous disquiet. The key is to remember that we're always in our own presence – we're never so alone that we can feel at ease. With this in mind, we will overcome having passions and ambitions, for these make us vulnerable; we won't have desires or hopes, since desires and hopes are plebeian and inelegant; and we won't have whims or be disquieted, because rash behaviour is unpleasant for others to witness, and agitated behaviour is always a vulgarity.

The aristocrat is the one who never forgets that he's never alone; that's why etiquette and decorum are the privilege of aristocracies. Let's internalize the aristocrat. Let's take him out of his gardens and drawing rooms and place him in our soul and in our consciousness of existing. Let's always treat ourselves with etiquette and decorum, with studied and for-other-people gestures.

Each of us is an entire community, an entire neighbourhood of the great Mystery,* and we should at least make sure that the life of our neighbourhood is distinctive and elegant, that the feasts of our sensations are genteel and restrained, and that the banquets of our thoughts are decorous and dignified. Since other souls may build poor and filthy neighbourhoods around us, we should clearly define where our own begins and ends, and from the façades of our feelings to the alcoves of our shyness, everything should be noble and serene, sculpted in sobriety, without ostentation.

We should try to find a serene way to realize each sensation. To reduce love to the shadow of a dream of love, a pale and tremulous interval between the crests of two tiny, moonlit waves. To turn desire into a useless and innocuous thing, a kind of knowing smile in our soul; to make it into something we never dream of achieving or even expressing. To lull hatred to sleep like a captive snake, and to tell fear to give up all its outer manifestations except for anguish in our eyes, or rather, in the eyes of our soul, for only this attitude can be considered aesthetic.

429

Throughout my life, in every situation and in every social circumstance, everyone has always seen me as an intruder. Or at least as a stranger. Whether among relatives or acquaintances, I've always been regarded as an outsider. I'm not suggesting that this treatment was ever deliberate. It was due, rather, to a natural reaction in the people around me.

Everyone everywhere has always treated me kindly. Rare is the man like me, I suspect, who has caused so few to raise their voice, wrinkle their brow, or speak angrily or askance. But the kindness I've been shown has always been devoid of affection. For those who are closest to me I've always been a guest, and as such treated well, but always with the kind of attention accorded to a stranger and with the lack of affection that's normal for an intruder.

I don't doubt that this attitude in other people derives mainly from some obscure cause intrinsic to my own temperament. Perhaps I have a communicative coldness that makes others automatically reflect my unfeeling manner.

By nature I quickly strike up acquaintances. People are friendly to me right away. But I never receive affection. I've never been shown devotion. To be loved has always seemed impossible to me, like a stranger calling me by my first name.

I don't know if I should regret this, or if I should accept it as an indifferent destiny which there's no reason to regret or accept.

I've always wanted to be liked. It always grieved me that I was treated with indifference. Left an orphan by Fortune, I wanted – like all orphans – to be the object of someone's affection. This need has always been a hunger that went unsatisfied, and so thoroughly have I adapted to this inevitable hunger that I sometimes wonder if I really feel the need to eat.

Whatever be the case, life pains me.

Other people have someone who is devoted to them. I've never had anyone who even thought of being devoted to me. Others are doted on; I'm treated nicely.

I know I have the capacity to stir respect, but not affection. Unfortunately I've never done anything that would justify, for others, the respect they initially feel, and so they never come to truly respect me.

Sometimes I think I must enjoy suffering. But I know I'd really prefer something else.

I don't have the qualities of a leader or of a follower. Nor even those of a contented man, which are the ones that count when the others are missing.

Other people, less intelligent than I, are stronger. They're better at carving out their place in life; they manage their intelligence more effectively. I have all the qualities it takes to exert influence except for the knack of actually doing it, or even the will to want to do it.

Were I ever to fall in love, I wouldn't be loved back.

All I have to do is want something for it to perish. My destiny lacks the strength to be lethal in general, but it has the weakness of being lethal in whatever specifically concerns me.

430

Having seen how lucidly and logically certain madmen* justify their lunatic ideas to themselves and to others, I can never again be sure of the lucidness of my lucidity.

431

One of my life's greatest tragedies – albeit a surreptitious tragedy, of the kind that take place in the shadows – is my inability to feel anything naturally. I can love and hate like others and, like others, feel fear and enthusiasm; but neither my love nor my hate, nor my fear nor my enthusiasm, are quite like the real thing. Either they lack a certain ingredient, or they have one that doesn't belong. They are at any rate some other thing, and what I feel doesn't square with life.

In what is very aptly called a calculating personality, feelings are shaped by calculation and a kind of scrupulous self-interest to the point that they seem like something else. In what is specifically known as a scrupulous personality, the same displacement of natural instincts can be observed. In me there is a similar disturbance, a lack of clarity in my feelings, yet I am neither calculating nor scrupulous. I have no excuse for feeling things abnormally. I instinctively denature my instincts. Against my will, I will in the wrong way.

432

The slave of my own character as well as of my circumstances, offended not only by other people's indifference but also by their affection for whom they think I am – such are the human insults heaped on me by Destiny.

433

I was a foreigner in their midst, but no one realized it. I lived among them as a spy and no one, not even I, suspected it. They all took me for a relative; no one knew I'd been swapped at birth. And so I was one of their equals without anything in common, a brother to all without belonging to the family.

I had come from wondrous lands, from landscapes more enchanting than life, but only to myself did I ever mention these lands, and I said nothing about the landscapes which I saw in dreams. My feet stepped like theirs over the floorboards and the flagstones, but my heart was far away, even if it beat close by, false master of an estranged and exiled body.

No one knew me under the mask of similarity, nor ever knew that I had a mask, because no one knew that there are masked people in the world. No one imagined that at my side there was always another, who was in fact I. They always supposed I was identical to myself.

Their houses sheltered me, their hands shook mine, and they saw me walk down the street as if I were there; but the I that I am was never in their living rooms, the I whose life I live has no hands for others to shake, and the I that I know walks down no streets, unless the streets are all streets, nor is seen in them by others, unless he himself is all the others.

We all live far away and anonymous; disguised, we suffer as unknowns. For some, however, this distance between oneself and one's self is never revealed; for others it is occasionally enlightened, to their horror or grief, by a flash without limits; but for still others this is the painful daily reality of life.

To realize that who we are is not ours to know, that what we think or feel is always a translation, that what we want is not what we wanted, nor perhaps what anyone wanted – to realize all this at every moment, to feel all this in every feeling – isn't this to be foreign in one's own soul, exiled in one's own sensations?

But the mask I'd been staring at as it talked on a street corner with an unmasked man on this last night of Carnival finally held out its hand and laughingly said goodbye. The natural-faced man turned left down the street at whose corner he'd been standing. The mask – an uninteresting one – walked straight ahead, disappearing among shadows and occasional lights in a definitive farewell, extraneous to what I was thinking. Only then did I notice that there was more in the street than the glowing street lamps, and where the lamplight didn't reach there roiled a hazy moonlight, veiled and speechless and full of nothing, like life. . .

434

MOONLIGHTS

. . . damply tarnished by a lifeless brown.

. . . on the frozen avalanche of overlapping rooftops it is a greyish white, damply tarnished by a lifeless brown.

435

. . . and the whole ensemble is staggered in diverse clusters of darkness, outlined on one side by white, and dappled with blue shades of cold nacre.

436

(rain)

And finally, over the darkness of the gleaming rooftops, the cold light of the tepid morning breaks like a torment of the Apocalypse. Once again it's the vast night of increasing luminosity. Once again it's the usual horror: the day, life, fictitious purposes, inescapable activity. Once again it's my physical, visible and social personality, communicated by meaningless words and exploited by the acts and consciousness of others. Once again I'm I, exactly as I'm not. And as this light from the darkness fills with grey doubts the cracks around the shutters (far from hermetic, alas!), I begin to realize that I can no longer hold on to this refuge of staying in bed, of not sleeping but being able to, of dreaming without remembering truth and reality, of nestling between a cool warmth of clean sheets and an ignorance of my body's existence beyond its feeling of comfort. I realize that I'm losing the happy unconsciousness with which I've been enjoying my consciousness, the animal drowsiness in which I observe – as through the slowly blinking eyelids of a cat in the sun – the movements described by my free imagination's logic. I realize that the privileges of darkness are vanishing, and with them the slow rivers under the bowing trees of my glimpsed eyelashes, and the murmur of the cascades lost between the soft flowing of blood in my ears and the faint, steady rain. I'm losing myself to become alive.

I don't know if I'm sleeping or if I just feel as if I were. I'm not exactly dreaming but seem, rather, to be waking up from a sleepless slumber, for I hear the city's first sounds of life rising like floodwaters from that vague place down below, where the streets made by God run this way and that. The sounds are happy, filtered through the sadness of the rain that's falling, or that perhaps has stopped falling, for I don't hear it any more; I'm aware only of the excessive greyness it gives to the light that's advancing through the cracks, in the shadows of a clarity too faint for this time of morning, whatever time that may be. The sounds are happy, scattered, and painful to my heart,* as if they were calling me to an exam or an execution. Each new day, if I hear it break from the bed of my sweet oblivion, seems like the day of a great event in my life that I won't have the courage to face. Each new day, if I feel it rise from its bed of shadows as linens fall in the lanes and streets, comes to summon me to a court of law. Each new day, I'm going to be judged. And the man in me who is perpetually condemned clings to his bed as to the mother he lost, and fondles the pillow as if his nursemaid could protect him from people.

The happy sleep of the hulking animal shaded by trees, the balmy fatigue of the tramp lying in the tall grass, the torpor of the black man on a warm and far-away afternoon, the pleasure of the yawn that weighs in tired eyes, everything that helps us to forget and brings sleep, the peace of mind that gently closes the shutters of our soul's window, the anonymous caress of slumber. . .

To sleep, to be far away, remote without knowing it, to forget with one's very body, to have the freedom of unconsciousness like a refuge on a forgotten lake, stagnating among thick foliage in the hidden depths of forests. . .

A nothingness that breathes, a mild death from which we awaken fresh and nostalgic, a deep forgetting that massages the tissues of our soul. . .

And again I hear, like the renewed protest of one who still isn't convinced, the abrupt clamour of rain spattering the lit-up universe. I feel a chill in my imagined bones, as if I were afraid. And cowering in my insignificance, so human and alone in the last vestige of the darkness that's deserting me, I begin to weep. I weep, yes, over solitude and life, and my useless grief lies like a wheelless cart on the edge of reality, amid the dung of oblivion. I weep over everything – the loss of the lap where I once lay, the death of the hand I was given, the arms to embrace me that I never found, the shoulder to lean on that I never had. And the day that breaks definitively, the grief that breaks in me like the naked truth of day, all that I dreamed or thought or forgot – all of this, like an amalgam of shadows, fictions and regrets, blends into the wake of the passing worlds and falls among the things of life like the skeleton of a bunch of grapes, filched by young boys and eaten on the street corner.

The noise of the human day suddenly increases, like the sound of a bell that's calling. I hear, inside the building, the softly clicking latch of the first door that opens for someone to go out and live. I hear slippers in an absurd hallway leading to my heart. And with a brusque movement, as when a man finally succeeds in killing himself, I throw off the snug covers that shelter my stiff body. I've woken up. The sound of the rain fades, moving higher in the indefinite outdoors. I feel better. I've fulfilled something or other. I get up, go to the window, and open the shutters with brave determination. A day of clear rain floods my eyes with dull light. I open the window. The cool air moistens my warm skin. It's raining, yes, but although it's the same rain I'd been hearing, it's after all so much less! I want to be refreshed, to live, and I lean my neck out to life as to an enormous yoke.*

437

A rural calm sometimes visits the city. There are times in sunny Lisbon, especially at midday in summer, when the countryside invades us like a wind. And we sleep peacefully right here, on the Rua dos Douradores.

How refreshing for the soul to see a hush fall, beneath a high, steady sun, over these carts full of straw, these half-built crates, and these unhurried pedestrians who suddenly seem to be walking in a village! I myself, alone in the office and looking at them through the window, am transported: I'm in a quiet little town in the country, or stagnating in an unknown hamlet, and because I feel other, I'm happy.

I know: if I raise my eyes, I'll be confronted by the dingy row of buildings opposite, by the grimy windows of all the downtown offices, by the incongruous windows of the upper floors where people still live, and by the eternal laundry hanging in the sun between the gables at the top, among flowerpots and plants. I know this, but the golden light shining on everything is so soft, and the calm air surrounding me so devoid of sense, that even what I see is no reason to renounce my make-believe village, my rural small town whose commerce is sheer tranquillity.

I know, I know... It is indeed time for lunch, or for resting, or for doing nothing. Everything is going smoothly on the surface of life. Even I am sleeping, although my body is leaning over the balcony as over the rail of a ship sailing past an unfamiliar landscape. Even I have put my mind to rest, as if I were in the country. And suddenly something else looms before me, surrounds me, commands me: I see, behind the small town's midday, all of life in all of the small town; I see the grand stupid happiness of its domestic life, the grand stupid happiness of life in the fields, the grand stupid happiness of peaceful squalor. I see it because I see it. But I didn't see it and I wake up. I look around, smiling, and the first thing I do is shake off the dust from my unfortunately dark suit, whose sleeves had been leaning on the balcony rail which no one has ever cleaned, unaware that one day, if only for a moment, it would have to serve as a deck rail (where there could logically be no dust) of a ship on an infinite sightseeing cruise.

438

Against the blue made pale by the green of night, the cold unevenness of the buildings on the summer horizon formed a jagged, brownish-black silhouette, vaguely haloed by a yellowed grey.

In another age we mastered the physical ocean, thereby creating universal civilization; now we will master the psychological ocean, emotion, mother human nature, thereby creating intellectual civilization.

439

. . . the painful intensity of my sensations, even when they're happy ones; the blissful intensity of my sensations, even when they're sad.

I'm writing on a Sunday, the morning far advanced, on a day full of soft light in which, above the rooftops of the interrupted city, the blue of the always brand-new sky closes the mysterious existence of stars into oblivion.

In me it is also Sunday. . .

My heart is also going to a church, located it doesn't know where. It wears a child's velvet suit, and its face, made rosy by first impressions, smiles without sad eyes above the collar that's too big.

440

Every morning of that lingering summer the sky, when it woke up, was a dull green-blue, which soon changed to a blueness greyed by a silent white. In the west, however, the sky was the colour we usually ascribe to all of it.

When they feel the ground sliding beneath their feet, then how many men begin to speak the truth, to seek and find, to deny the world's illusion! And how their illustrious names mark with capital letters –

like those found on maps – the insights of sober and learned pages!

Cosmorama of things happening tomorrow that could never have ever happened! Lapis lazuli of intermittent emotions! Do you remember how many memories can spring from a false supposition, from mere imagination? And in a delirium sprinkled with certainties, the soft, brisk murmur of all the water from all parks wells up as an emotion from the depths of my self-awareness. The old benches are vacant, and all around them the paths spread their melancholy of empty streets.

Night in Heliopolis! Night in Heliopolis! Who will tell me the useless words? Who, through blood and indecision, will compensate me?

441

High in the nocturnal solitude an anonymous lamp flourishes behind a window. All else that I see in the city is dark, save where feeble reflections of light hazily ascend from the streets and cause a pallid, inverse moonlight to hover here and there. The buildings' various colours, or shades of colours, are hardly distinguishable in the blackness of the night; only vague, seemingly abstract differences break the regularity of the congested ensemble.

An invisible thread links me to the unknown owner of the lamp. It's not the mutual circumstance of us both being awake; in this there can be no reciprocity, for my window is dark, so that he cannot see me. It's something else, something all my own that's related to my feeling of isolation, that participates in the night and in the silence, and that chooses the lamp as an anchor because it's the only anchor there is. It seems to be its glowing that makes the night so dark. It seems to be the fact I'm awake, dreaming in the dark, that makes the lamp shine.

Everything that exists perhaps exists because something else exists. Nothing is, everything coexists – perhaps that's how it really is. I feel I wouldn't exist right now – or at least wouldn't exist in the way I'm existing, with this present consciousness of myself, which, because it is consciousness and present, is entirely me in this moment – if that lamp weren't shining somewhere over there, a useless lighthouse with a specious advantage of height. I feel this because I feel nothing. I think this because this is nothing. Nothing, nothing, part of the night and the silence and what I share with them of vacancy, of negativity, of in-betweenness, a gap between me and myself, something forgotten by some god or other...

442

In one of those spells of sleepless somnolence when we intelligently amuse ourselves without the intelligence, I reread some of the pages that together will form my book of random impressions. And they give off, like a familiar smell, an arid impression of monotony. Even while saying that I'm always different, I feel that I've always said the same thing; that I resemble myself more than I'd like to admit; that, when the books are balanced, I've had neither the joy of winning nor the emotion of losing. I'm the absence of a balance of myself, the lack of a natural equilibrium, and this weakens and distresses me.

Everything, all that I've written, is grey. My life, even my mental life, has been like a drizzly day in which everything is non-occurrence and haziness, empty privilege and forgotten purpose. I agonize in tattered silks. In the light and in tedium I see but don't know myself.

My humble attempt to say at least who I am, to record like a machine of nerves the slightest impressions of my subjective and ultra-sensitive life – this was all emptied like a bucket that got knocked over, and it poured across the ground like the water of everything. I fashioned myself out of false colours, and the result is an attic made out to be an empire. My heart, out of which I spun the great events of prose I lived, seems to me today – in these pages written long ago and reread now with a different soul – like a water pump on a homestead, instinctively installed and pressed into service. I shipwrecked on an unstormy sea where my feet could have touched bottom.

And I ask the conscious vestige that I still conserve, in this confused series of intervals between non-existent things, what good it did me to fill so many pages with phrases I believed in as my own, with emotions I felt as if I had thought them up, with flags and army banners that finally amount to no more than pieces of paper stuck together with spit by the daughter of the beggar who sits under the eaves.

I ask what remains of me why I bothered with these useless pages, dedicated to rubbish and dispersion, lost even before existing among Destiny's ripped up papers.

I ask but I proceed. I write down the question, wrap it up in new phrases, unravel it with new emotions. And tomorrow I'll go back to my stupid book, jotting down the daily impressions of my cold lack of conviction.

Let them keep coming. Once the dominoes are all played and the game is won or lost, the pieces are turned over and the finished game is black.

443

What Hells and Purgatories and Heavens I have inside me! But who sees me do anything that disagrees with life – me, so calm and peaceful?

I don't write in Portuguese. I write my own self.

444

Everything has become unbearable except for life. The office, my home, the streets – and even their contrary, if that were my lot – overwhelm and oppress me. Only their ensemble brings me relief. Yes, anything that comes from the whole ensemble is enough to console me: a ray of sunlight that eternally enters the dead office, a vendor's cry that flits up to the window of my room, the existence of people, the fact that there are climates and changes in weather, the world's astonishing objectivity. . .

The ray of sun suddenly entered the office for me, who suddenly saw it. . . It was actually an extremely sharp, almost colourless blade of light that sliced the dark wooden floor, quickening the old nails over which it passed, along with the furrows between the boards, black lines on non-white.

For several minutes I studied the almost imperceptible effect of the sun penetrating into the still office... Pastimes of prisons! Only the incarcerated watch the sun move this way, like someone observing a file of ants.

445

It is said that tedium is a disease of the idle, or that it attacks only those who have nothing to do. But this ailment of the soul is in fact more subtle: it attacks people who are predisposed to it, and those who work or who pretend they work (which in this case comes down to the same thing) are less apt to be spared than the truly idle.

Nothing is worse than the contrast between the natural splendour of the inner life, with its natural Indias and its unexplored lands, and the squalor (even when it's not really squalid) of life's daily routine. And tedium is more oppressive when there's not the excuse of idleness. The tedium of those who strive hard is the worst of all.

Tedium is not the disease of being bored because there's nothing to do, but the more serious disease of feeling that there's nothing worth doing. This means that the more there is to do, the more tedium one will feel.

How often, when I look up from the ledger where I enter amounts, my head is devoid of the whole world! I'd be better off remaining idle, doing nothing and having nothing to do, because that tedium, though real enough, I could at least enjoy. In my present tedium there is no rest, no nobility, and no well-being against which to feel unwell: there's a vast effacement of every act I do, rather than a potential weariness from acts I'll never do.

446

Omar Khayyám

The tedium of Khayyám isn't the tedium of those who, because they don't know how to do anything, naturally don't know what to do. This tedium belongs to those who were born dead and who understandably turn to morphine or cocaine. The tedium of the Persian sage is more noble and profound. It's the tedium of one who clearly considered and saw that everything was obscure, of one who took stock of all the religions and philosophies and said, like Solomon: 'I saw that all was vanity and vexation of spirit.' Or in the words of another king, the emperor Septimus Severus, when he said farewell to power and the world: 'Omnia fui, nihil expedit.' 'I've been everything; nothing's worth the trouble.'

Life, according to Tarde,* is the search for the impossible by way of the useless, which is what Omar Khayyám would have said, if he had said it.

That's why the Persian insists on the use of wine. 'Drink! Drink!' sums up his practical philosophy. It's not the kind of drinking inspired by happiness, which drinks to become even happier, more itself. Nor is it the drinking inspired by despair, which drinks to forget, to be less itself. Happiness adds vigour and love to the wine, and in Khayyám we find no note of energy, no words of love. The wispy, gracile figure of Sáki appears only occasionally in the *Rubáiyát*, and she is merely 'the girl who serves the wine'. The poet appreciates her elegant shape as he appreciated the shape of the amphora containing the wine.

Dean Aldrich* is an example of how happiness speaks of wine:

> If all be true that I do think,
> There are five reasons we should drink;
> Good wine – a friend – or being dry –
> Or lest we should be by and by –
> Or any other reason why.

The practical philosophy of Khayyám is essentially a mild form of Epicureanism, with only a slight trace of desire for pleasure. To see roses and drink wine is enough for him. A gentle breeze, a conversation without point or purpose, a cup of wine, flowers – in this, and in nothing else, the Persian sage places his highest desire. Love agitates and wearies, action dissipates and comes to nothing, no one knows how to know, and to think muddles everything. Better to cease from desire and hope, from the futile pretension of explaining the world, and from the foolish ambition of improving or governing it. Everything is nothing, or, as recorded in The Greek Anthology, 'All that exists comes from unreason.' And it was a Greek,* hence a rational soul, who said it.

447

We are ultimately indifferent to the truth or falseness of all religions, all philosophies, and all the uselessly verifiable hypotheses we call sciences. Nor are we really concerned about the fate of so-called humanity, or about what as a whole it does or doesn't suffer. Charity, yes, for our 'neighbour', as the Gospel says, and not for man, of whom it says nothing. And we all feel this way to a certain extent. How much does a massacre in China really disturb even the most noble of us? It's more heart-rending, even for the most sensitively imaginative, to see a child in the street get slapped for no apparent reason.

Charity for all, intimacy with none. Thus FitzGerald, in one of his notes, interprets a certain aspect of Khayyám's ethics.

The Gospel recommends love towards our neighbour; it doesn't mention love towards man or towards humanity, which no one can help or improve.

Some may wonder if I myself subscribe to the philosophy of Khayyám as restated and interpreted here (with fair accuracy, I believe). I would have to say that I don't know. On certain days it seems to me the best, and even the only, practical philosophy there is. On other days it strikes me as void, dead and useless, like an empty glass. Because I think, I don't know myself. And so I don't know what I really think. If I had faith, I would be different, but I would also be different if I were crazy. I would be different, yes, if I were different.

Besides these lessons from the profane world, there are, of course, the secret teachings of esoteric orders, the mysteries that are freely acknowledged but kept strictly secret, and the veiled mysteries embodied in public rites. There are things hidden, or half hidden, in great universal rites such as the Marian Ritual of the Roman Church, or the Freemasons' Ceremony of the Spirit.

But who's to say that the initiate, having entered the inner sanctum of mystery, isn't merely the eager prey of a new facet of our illusion? What certainty can he have, if a madman is even more certain of his mad ideas? Spencer compared our knowledge to a sphere which, as it expands, touches more and more on all that we don't know. And I also remember, with respect to secret initiations and what they can offer us, the terrible words of a Grand Wizard: 'I have seen Isis and touched Isis, but I do not know if she exists.'

448

Omar Khayyám

Omar had a personality; I, for better or worse, have none. In an hour I'll have strayed from what I am at this moment; tomorrow I'll have forgotten what I am today. Those who are who they are, like Omar, live in just one world, the external one. Those who aren't who they are, like me, live not only in the external world but also in a diversified, ever-changing inner world. Try as we might, we could never have the same philosophy as Omar's. I harbour in me, like unwanted souls, the very philosophies I criticize. Omar could reject them all, for they were all external to him, but I can't reject them, because they're me.

449

There are inner sufferings so subtle and so diffuse that we can't tell whether they belong to the body or the soul, whether they're an anxiety that comes from our feeling that life is futile or an indisposition originating in some organic abyss such as the stomach, liver or brain. How often my normal self-awareness becomes turbid with the stirred dregs of an anguished stagnation! How often it hurts me to exist, with a nausea so indefinite I'm not sure if it's tedium or a warning that I'm about to vomit! How often. . .

Today my soul is sad unto my body. All of me hurts: memory, eyes and arms. It's like a rheumatism in all that I am. My being isn't touched by the day's limpid brightness, by the sheer blue sky, by this unabating high tide of diffuse light. I'm not soothed by the soft cool breeze – autumnal but reminiscent of summer – which gives the air personality. Nothing touches me. I'm sad, but not with a definite sadness, nor even with an indefinite sadness. I'm sad down there, on the street littered with packing crates.

These expressions don't exactly translate what I feel, for surely nothing can exactly translate what one feels. But I try to convey at least some impression of what I feel, a blend of various views of me and of the street, which is also, since I see it, a part of me in some profound way I can't fathom.

I'd like to live a different life in far-off lands. I'd like to die as someone else among unfamiliar flags. I'd like to be acclaimed emperor in other eras, better today because they're not of today, and we see them as hazy, colourful, enigmatic novelties. I'd like to have all that could make what I am ridiculous, and precisely because it would make what I am ridiculous. I'd like, I'd like. . . But there's always the sun when the sun is shining and the night when the night falls. There's always grief when grief troubles us and dreams when dreams lull us. There's always what there is, and never what there should be, not for being better or worse but for being different. There's always. . .

The loaders are clearing the crates off the street. Amid jokes and laughter they place the crates one by one on to wagons. I'm looking down at them from my office window, with sluggish eyes whose eyelids are sleeping. And something subtle and inscrutable links what I feel to the freight that's being loaded; some strange sensation makes a crate out of all my tedium, or anxiety, or nausea, which is hoisted on the shoulders of someone who's loudly joking and then loaded on to a wagon that's not there. And in the narrow street, the ever serene daylight diagonally shines on where they're hoisting the crates – not on the crates themselves, which are in the shade, but on the far corner where the delivery boys are occupied in doing nothing, indeterminately.

450

Something still more portentous, like a black expectation, now hovered in the air, so that even the rain seemed intimidated; a speechless darkness fell over the atmosphere. And suddenly, like a scream, a dreadful day shattered. The light of a cold hell swept through the contents of all things, filling minds and crannies. Everything gaped in awe, and then heaved a sigh of relief, for the strike had passed. The almost human sound* of the sad rain was happy. Hearts automatically pounded hard, and thinking made one dizzy. A vague religion formed in the office. No one was himself, and Senhor Vasques appeared at the door of his office to say he didn't quite know what. Moreira smiled, the fringes of his face still yellow from the sudden fright, and his smile was no doubt saying that the next bolt of thunder would strike further away. A swift wagon loudly broke in on the usual noises from the street. The telephone shivered uncontrollably. Instead of retreating to his private office, Vasques stepped towards the phone in the common office. There was a respite, a silence, and the rain fell like a nightmare. Vasques forgot about the phone, which had stopped ringing. The office boy fidgeted in the back of the office like a bothersome object.

An enormous joy, full of deliverance and peace of mind, disconcerted us all. We returned to our work a bit light-headed, becoming spontaneously sociable and pleasant with each other. Without being told to, the office boy opened wide the windows. The fragrance of something fresh entered with the damp air into the office. The now gentle rain fell humbly. The sounds from the street, which were the same as before, were different. We could hear the voices of the wagoners, and they were really people. The clear-ringing bells of the trams a block over participated in our sociability. A lone child's burst of laughter was like a canary in the limpid atmosphere. The gentle rain tapered off.

It was six o'clock. The office was closing. Through the half-open door of his private office Senhor Vasques said, 'You can all go now,' pronouncing the words like a business benediction. I immediately stood up, closed the ledger and put it away. I returned my pen with a deliberate gesture to its place in the inkstand, walked towards Moreira while pronouncing a 'See you tomorrow' full of hope, and then shook his hand as if he'd done me a big favour.

451

Travel? One need only exist to travel. I go from day to day, as from station to station, in the train of my body or my destiny, leaning out over the streets and squares, over people's faces and gestures, always the same and always different, just like scenery.

If I imagine, I see. What more do I do when I travel? Only extreme poverty of the imagination justifies having to travel to feel.

'Any road, this simple Entepfuhl road, will lead you to the end of the World.'* But the end of the world, when we go around it full circle, is the same Entepfuhl from which we started out. The end of the world, like the beginning, is in fact our concept of the world. It is in us that the scenery is scenic. If I imagine it, I create it; if I create it, it exists; if it exists, then I see it like any other scenery. So why travel? In Madrid, Berlin, Persia, China, and at the North or South Pole, where would I be but in myself, and in my particular type of sensations?

Life is what we make of it. Travel is the traveller. What we see isn't what we see but what we are.

452

The only real traveller with soul that I've known was an office boy at another firm where I was once employed. This young fellow collected promotional brochures for cities, countries and transportation companies; he had maps that he'd torn out of journals or that he'd asked for here and there; he had illustrations of landscapes, prints of exotic costumes, and pictures of boats and ships that he'd clipped out of newspapers and magazines. He would go to travel agencies in the name of some imaginary office, or perhaps in the name of a real office, perhaps even the one where he worked, and he would ask for brochures about trips to Italy, brochures about excursions to India, brochures listing the boat connections between Portugal and Australia.

He was not only the greatest – because truest – traveller I've known, he was also one of the happiest people I've had the privilege to meet. I regret not knowing what's become of him, or rather, I pretend I should regret it; in fact I don't, because by now, ten years or more after the brief period when I knew him, he must be a grown-up, a responsible idiot who fulfils his duties, perhaps as a married man, somebody's provider – dead, that is, while still alive. And maybe he has even travelled in body, he who travelled so well in his soul.

I just remembered: he knew the exact route of the train from Paris to Bucharest as well as the routes of all the trains in England, and as he mispronounced the strange names, I could see the glowing certainty of his greatness of soul. Today, yes, he probably exists as a dead man, but perhaps one day, in his old age, he will remember how it's not only better but also truer to dream of Bordeaux than to actually go there.

Then too, all of this may have some other explanation: he may just have been imitating someone. Or. . . Yes, I sometimes think, given the appalling difference between the intelligence of children and the stupidity of adults, that in childhood we're accompanied by a guardian spirit who lends us his own astral intelligence, and that later, perhaps with regret but compelled by a higher law, he abandons us – like animal mothers after they've nursed their young – to our destiny as fattened pigs.

453

From the terrace of this café I look at life with tremulous eyes. I see just a little of its vast diversity concentrated in this square that's all mine. A slight daze like the beginning of drunkenness reveals to me the soul of things. Visible, unanimous life proceeds outside me in the clear and distinct steps of passing pedestrians, in the regulated fury of all their motions. In this moment when my feelings are but a lucid and confused mistake, when my senses have stagnated and everything seems like something else, I spread my wings without moving, like an imaginary condor.

Man of ideals that I am, perhaps my greatest ambition is really no more than to keep sitting at this table in this café.

Everything is futile, like stirring dead ashes, and hazy like the moment before dawn breaks.

And the light strikes things so perfectly and serenely, gilding them with sadly smiling reality! All the world's mystery descends until I see it take shape as banality and street.

Ah, the mysteries grazed by ordinary things in our very midst! To think that right here, on the sunlit surface of our complex human life, Time smiles uncertainly on the lips of Mystery! How modern all this sounds! And yet how ancient, how hidden, how full of some other meaning besides the one we see glowing all around us!

454

Reading the newspaper is always unpleasant from an aesthetic point of view, and often from a moral point of view as well, even for those who don't worry much about morality.

Reading about the effects of wars and revolutions – there's always one or the other in the news* – doesn't make us feel horror but tedium. What really disturbs our soul isn't the cruel fate of all the dead and wounded, the sacrifice of all who die in action or who die without seeing action, but the stupidity that sacrifices lives and property to some inevitably futile cause. All ideals and all ambitions are a hysteria of prattling women posing as men. No empire justifies breaking a child's doll. No ideal is worth the sacrifice of a toy train. What empire is useful or what ideal profitable? It's all humanity, and humanity is always the same – variable but unimprovable, with fluctuations but unprogressive. *Vis-à-vis* the intransigent march of all things, the life that we were given without knowing why and that we'll lose we don't know when, the ten thousand chess games that constitute our life in common and in conflict, the tedium of uselessly contemplating what we'll never accomplish . . . . . – *vis-à-vis* all that, what can the wise man do but ask to retire, to be excused from having to think about life (since living it is already burdensome enough), to have a little sun and fresh air and at least the dream that there's peace on the other side of the hills?

455

All those unfortunate occasions in life when we've been ridiculous or boorish or woefully late should be seen, in the light of our inner serenity, as the vicissitudes of travel. We are but tourists in this world, travelling willingly or unwillingly between nothing and nothing or between everything and everything, and we shouldn't worry too much about the bumps along the way and the mishaps of the journey. I take comfort in this thought, either because there's something in it that's comforting, or simply because I take comfort in it. But fictitious comfort, if I don't think about it, is real enough.

And there are so many things that comfort! There's the blue sky above, clear and calm, where odd-shaped clouds are always floating. There's the light breeze, which in the country shakes the thick branches of trees, while in the city it whips the laundry hanging from the fourth and fifth floors. There's warmth when it's warm, and coolness when it's cool, and always a memory with its nostalgia, its hope, and a magic smile at the window of the world, and what we want knocking on the door of what we are, like beggars who are the Christ.

456

How long since I last wrote something! In the past few days I've lived through centuries of wavering renunciation. I've stagnated, like a forsaken pond, among landscapes that don't exist.

Meanwhile I've been going through the varied monotony of every day, the never-equal succession of the equal hours, life. Everything has been going well. If I'd been sleeping, it wouldn't have gone any differently. I've stagnated, like a pond that doesn't exist, among forsaken landscapes.

It often happens that I don't know myself, which is typical in those who know themselves. I look at myself in the various disguises that make me alive. Of all that changes, I possess whatever remains the same; of all that is accomplished, whatever amounts to nothing.

I remember far-off inside me, as if I were journeying within, the monotony of that old house in the country, so different from the monotony I feel now... I spent my childhood in that house, but I couldn't say (if I ever wanted to) whether it was happier or sadder than my life today. It was a different self that lived back then. That life and this one are different, diverse, incomparable. The same monotonies that link them on the outside are undoubtedly different on the inside. They're not just two monotonies, but two lives.

Why do I bother to remember? Weariness. Remembering is a repose, for it means not doing. For even greater repose, I sometimes remember what never was, and my memories of the countryside where I really lived can't begin to compare, in sharpness and nostalgia, to my memories that inhabit – floorboard by creaking floorboard – the vast rooms of yesteryear that I never inhabited.

I've become so entirely the fiction of myself that any natural feeling I may have is immediately transformed, as soon as it's born, into an imaginary feeling. Memories turn into dreams, dreams into my forgetting what I dreamed, and knowing myself into not thinking of myself.

I've so stripped myself of my own being that existence consists of dressing up. I'm only myself when disguised. And all around me expiring, unknown sunsets gild the landscapes I'll never see.

457

Modern things include

(1) the development of mirrors;
(2) wardrobes.

We evolved, body and soul, into clothed creatures. Since the soul always conforms to the body, it developed an intangible suit. We advanced to having a soul that's basically clothed, in the same way that we advanced – as physical humans – to the category of clothed animals.

The point isn't just that our suit has become an integral part of us; it's the complexity of this suit and the curious lack of any real relationship between it and the features that make our body and our body's movements naturally elegant.

Were I asked to discuss the social causes responsible for my soul's condition, I would speechlessly point to a mirror, a clothes hanger, and a pen.

458

In the light morning fog of mid-spring, the downtown area wakes up groggy and the sun rises as if sluggishly. There's a calm joy in the slightly cold air, a kind of non-breeze softly blows, and life vaguely shivers from the cold that has ceased – not from the bit of cold that lingers but from the memory of the cold; not from today's weather but in comparison with the approaching summer.

The shops are still closed except for the cafés and dairy bars, but the stillness isn't one of torpor, like on Sundays – it's just stillness. A blond tinge streaks the air that's emerging from the night, and through the dissipating fog the blueness lightly blushes. The first signs of movement dot the streets, with each pedestrian standing out distinctly, while up above hazy figures can be seen stirring in the few open windows. The clanging trams trace their yellow, numbered furrows in mid-air. Little by little the streets begin to undesert.

I drift without thoughts or emotions, just sense impressions. I woke up early and came out to the street without preconceptions. I observe as if in a reverie. I see as if deep in thought. And a gentle mist of emotion absurdly rises up in me. The fog that's disappearing outside seems to be seeping into me.

I realize that I've been inadvertently thinking about my life. I hadn't noticed, but that's what I was doing. I thought I was no more in my leisurely stroll than a reflector of given images, a blank screen on which reality projects colours and light instead of shadows. But I was unwittingly more than that. I was also my self-denying soul, and even my abstract observing was a denial.

As the mist diminishes, the air darkens, imbued by a pale light that seems to have incorporated the mist. I suddenly notice that it's much noisier and that many more people exist. The steps of the now more numerous pedestrians are less hurried. And then, breaking in on everyone else's lesser haste, the sprightly fishwives pop into view, bakers come swaying under their monstrously large breadbaskets, and the diverse sameness of the street vendors is only demonotonized by the contents of their baskets, in which the colours vary more than the actual objects. The unequal cans of the milkmen jangle like absurd hollow keys. The policemen stand stock-still in the intersections, like civilization's uniformed denial of the invisibly rising day.

How I would love right now to be able to see all this as somebody whose only relation to it was visual – to view everything as an adult traveller who has just arrived at the surface of life! To not have learned from birth to attach predetermined meanings to all these things. To be able to see them in their natural self-expression, irrespective of the expressions that have been imposed on them. To be able to recognize the fishwife in her human reality, independent of her being called a fishwife and my knowing that she exists and sells fish. To see the policeman as God sees him. To notice everything for the first time, not as apocalyptic revelations of life's Mystery, but as direct manifestations of Reality.

Bells or a large clock strike what, without counting, I know must be eight o'clock. I awaken from myself because of the banality of measured time, that cloister which society imposes on time's continuity, a border to contain the abstract, a boundary around the unknown. I see that the mist which has completely quit the sky (except for the quasi-blue that still lingers in the blueness) has indeed penetrated into my soul, and has likewise penetrated to the depths of things where they have contact with my soul. I've lost the vision of what I was seeing. My eyes see, but I am blind. I've begun to perceive things with the banality of knowledge. What I see is no longer Reality, it's just Life.

. . . Yes, the life to which I also belong, and which also belongs to me; and no longer Reality, which belongs only to God or to itself, which contains neither mystery nor truth, and which – since it is real or pretends to be real – exists somewhere invariably, free from having to be temporal or eternal, an absolute image, the external equivalent to the idea of a soul.

I turn and walk slowly, though faster than I think, to the door that will lead me back up to my rented room. But I don't enter; I hesitate; I keep going. Praça da Figueira,* gaping with variously coloured wares and filling up with customers, blocks the horizon from my view. I advance slowly, lifelessly, and my vision is no longer mine, it's no longer anything: it's merely the vision of a human animal that inexorably inherited Greek culture, Roman order, Christian morality, and all the other illusions that form the civilization in which I feel and perceive.

Where are the living?

459

I'd like to be in the country to be able to like being in the city. I like being in the city in any case, but I'd like it twice over if I were in the country.

460

The greater the sensibility and the subtler its capacity for feeling, the more absurdly it shivers and shudders over little things. It takes extraordinary intelligence to feel anxiety because of an overcast day. Humanity, basically insensitive, doesn't get anxious over the weather, because there's always weather; humanity doesn't feel the rain unless it's falling on its head.

The hazy, torpid day humidly swelters. Alone in the office, I review my life, and what I see is like the day that oppresses and afflicts me. I see myself as a child happy for no reason, as an adolescent full of ambition, as a full-grown man without happiness or ambition. And it all happened in a haze and a torpor, like this day that makes me see or remember it.

Who among us, looking back down the path of no return, can say they followed it in the right way?

461

Knowing how easily the littlest things can torture me, I deliberately avoid contact with the littlest things. If I suffer when a cloud passes in front of the sun, how will I not suffer from the darkness of the forever overcast day that's my life?

My isolation isn't a search for happiness (which my soul wouldn't know how to feel), nor for tranquillity (which no one obtains unless he never really lost it), but for sleep, for effacement, for a modest renunciation.

The four walls of my squalid room are at once a cell and a wilderness, a bed and a coffin. My happiest moments are those when I think nothing, want nothing and dream nothing, being lost in a torpor like some accidental plant, like mere moss growing on life's surface. I savour without bitterness this absurd awareness of being nothing, this foretaste of death and extinction.

I've never had anyone I could call 'Master'. No Christ died for me. No Buddha showed me the way. No Apollo or Athena, in my loftiest dreams, ever appeared to enlighten my soul.

462

But my self-imposed exile from life's actions and objectives and my attempt to break off all contact with things led precisely to what I tried to escape. I didn't want to feel life or to touch anything real, for the experience of my temperament in contact with the world had taught me that the sensation of life was always painful to me. But in isolating myself to avoid that contact, I exacerbated my already overwrought sensibility. If it were possible to cut off completely all contact with things, then my sensibility would pose no problem. But this total isolation cannot be achieved. However little I do, I still breathe; however little I act, I still move. And so, having exacerbated my sensibility through isolation, I found that the tiniest things, which even for me had been perfectly innocuous, began to wrack me like catastrophes. I chose the wrong method of escape. I fled via an uncomfortable and roundabout route to end up at the same place I'd started from, with the fatigue of my journey added to the horror of living there.

I've never seen suicide as a solution, because my hatred of life is due to my love of life. It took me a long time to be convinced of this unfortunate mistake in how I live with myself. Convinced of it, I felt frustrated, which is what I always feel when I convince myself of something, since for me each new conviction means another lost illusion.

I killed my will by analysing it. If only I could return to my childhood before analysis, even if it would have to be before I had a will!

My parks are all a dead slumber, their pools stagnating under the midday sun, when the drone of insects swells and life oppresses me, not like a grief but like a persistent physical pain.

Far-away palaces, pensive parks, narrow paths in the distance, the dead charm of stone benches where no one sits any more – perished splendours, vanished charm, lost glitter. O my forgotten yearning, if I could only recover the grief with which I dreamed you!

463

Peace at last. All that was dross and residue vanishes from my soul as if it had never been. I'm alone and calm. It's like the moment when I could theoretically convert to a religion. But although I'm no longer attracted to anything down here, I'm also not attracted to anything up above. I feel free, as if I'd ceased to exist and were conscious of that fact.

Peace, yes, peace. A great calm, gentle like something superfluous, descends on me to the depths of my being. The pages I read, the tasks I complete, the motions and vicissitudes of life – all has become for me a faint penumbra, a scarcely visible halo circling something tranquil that I can't identify. The exertion in which I've sometimes forgotten my soul, and the contemplation in which I've sometimes forgotten all action – both come back to me as a kind of tenderness without emotion, a paltry, empty compassion.

It's not the mild and languidly cloudy day. It's not the feeble, almost non-existent breeze, hardly more perceptible than the still air. It's not the anonymous colour of the faintly and spottily blue sky. It's none of this, because I feel none of it. I see without wanting to see, helplessly. I attentively watch the non-spectacle. I don't feel my soul, just peace. External things, all of them distinct and now perfectly still, even if they're moving, are to me as the world must have been to Christ when, looking down at everything, Satan tempted him. They are nothing, and I can understand why Christ wasn't tempted. They are nothing, and I can't understand why clever old Satan thought they would be tempting.

Go swiftly by, life that's not felt, a stream flowing silently under forgotten trees! Go gently by, soul that's not known, an unseen rustle beyond large fallen branches! Go uselessly by, pointlessly by, consciousness conscious of nothing, a hazy flash in the distance amid clearings in the leaves, coming from and going to we don't know where! Go, go, and let me forget!

Faint breath of what never dared live, dull sigh of what failed to feel, useless murmur of what refused to think, go slowly, go slackly, go in the eddies you have to have and in the dips you're given, go to the shadow or to the light, brother of the world, go to glory or to the abyss, son of Chaos and of the Night, but remember in some obscure part of you that the Gods came later and that they will also pass.

464

Whoever has read the pages of this book will by now surely have concluded that I'm a dreamer. And he will have concluded wrongly. I lack the money to be a dreamer.

Great melancholies and sorrows full of tedium can exist only in an atmosphere of comfort and solemn luxury. That's why Poe's Egaeus,* pathologically absorbed in thought for hours on end, lives in an ancient, ancestral castle where, beyond the doors of the lifeless drawing room, invisible butlers administer the house and prepare the meals.

Great dreams require special social circumstances. One day, when the doleful cadence of a certain passage I'd written made me excitedly think of Chateaubriand, it didn't take me long to remember that I'm not a viscount, nor even a Breton. On another occasion, when I'd written something whose content seemed to recall Rousseau, it likewise didn't take long for me to realize that, besides not being the noble lord of a castle, I also lack the privilege of being a wanderer from Switzerland.

But there is also the universe of the Rua dos Douradores. Here God also grants that the enigma of life knows no bounds. My dreams may be poor, like the landscape of carts and crates from among whose wheels and boards I conceive them, but they're what I have and am able to have.

The sunsets, to be sure, are somewhere else. But even from this fourth-floor room that looks out over the city, it's possible to contemplate infinity. An infinity with warehouses down below, it's true, but with stars up above... This is what occurs to me as I look out my high window at the close of day, with the dissatisfaction of the bourgeois that I'm not, and with the sadness of the poet that I can never be.

465

The advent of summer makes me sad. It seems that summer's luminosity, though harsh, should comfort those who don't know who they are, but it doesn't comfort me. There's too sharp a contrast between the teeming life outside me and the forever unburied corpse of my sensations – what I feel and think, without knowing how to feel or think. In this borderless country known as the universe, I feel like I'm living under a political tyranny that doesn't oppress me directly but that still offends some secret principle of my soul. And then I'm slowly, softly seized by an absurd nostalgia for some future, impossible exile.

What I mostly feel is slumber. Not a slumber that latently brings – like all other slumbers, even those caused by sickness – the privilege of physical rest. Not a slumber that, because it's going to forget life and perhaps bring dreams, bears the soothing gifts of a grand renunciation on the platter with which it approaches our soul. No: this is a slumber that's unable to sleep, that weighs on the eyelids without closing them, that purses the corners of one's disbelieving lips into what feels like a stupid and repulsive expression. It's the kind of sleepiness that uselessly overwhelms the body when one's soul is suffering from acute insomnia.

Only when night comes do I feel, not happiness, but a kind of repose which, since other reposes are pleasant, seems pleasant by way of analogy. Then my sleepiness goes away, and the confusing mental dusk brought on by the sleepiness begins to fade and to clear until it almost glows. For a moment there's the hope of other things. But the hope is short-lived. What comes next is a hopeless, sleepless tedium, the unpleasant waking up of one who never fell asleep. And from the window of my room I gaze with my wretched soul and exhausted body at the countless stars – countless stars, nothing, nothingness, but countless stars. . .

466

Man shouldn't be able to see his own face – there's nothing more sinister. Nature gave him the gift of not being able to see it, and of not being able to stare into his own eyes.

Only in the water of rivers and ponds could he look at his face. And the very posture he had to assume was symbolic. He had to bend over, stoop down, to commit the ignominy of beholding himself.

The inventor of the mirror poisoned the human heart.

467

He listened to me read my verses – which I read well that day, for I was relaxed – and said to me with the simplicity of a natural law: 'If you could always be like that but with a different face, you'd be a charmer.' The word 'face' – more than what it referred to – yanked me out of myself by the collar of my self-ignorance. I looked at the mirror in my room and saw the poor, pathetic face of an unpoor beggar; and then the mirror turned away, and the spectre of the Rua dos Douradores opened up before me like a postman's nirvana.

The acuity of my sensations is like a disease that's foreign to me. It afflicts someone else, of whom I'm just the sick part, for I'm convinced that I must depend on some greater capacity for feeling. I'm like a special tissue, or a mere cell, that bears the brunt of responsibility for an entire organism.

When I think, it's because I'm drifting; when I dream, it's because I'm awake. Everything I am is tangled up in myself, such that no part of me knows how to be.

468

When we constantly live in the abstract, be it the abstraction of thought itself or of thought sensations, then quite against our own sentiment or will the things of the real world soon become phantoms – even those things which, given our particular personality, we should feel most keenly.

However much and however sincerely I may be someone's friend, the news that he is sick or that he died produces in me only a vague, indefinite, dull impression, which it embarrasses me to feel. Only direct contact, the actual scene, would kindle my emotion. When we live by the imagination, we exhaust our capacity for imagining, and especially for imagining what's real. Mentally living off what doesn't and can never exist, we lose our ability to ponder what can exist.

I found out today that an old friend, one I haven't seen for a long time but whom I always sincerely remember with what I suppose is nostalgia, has just entered the hospital for an operation. The only clear and definite sensation that this news aroused in me was weariness at the thought of my having to visit him, with the ironic alternative of forgoing the visit and feeling guilty about it.

That's all. . . From dealing so much with shadows, I myself have become a shadow – in what I think and feel and am. My being's substance consists of nostalgia for the normal person I never was. That, and only that, is what I feel. I don't really feel sorry for my friend who's going to be operated on. I don't really feel sorry for anyone who's going to be operated on or who suffers and grieves in this world. I only feel sorry for not being a person who can feel sorrow.

And all at once I'm helplessly thinking of something else, impelled by I don't know what force. And as if I were hallucinating, everything I was never able to feel or be gets mixed up with a rustling of trees, a trickling of water into pools, a non-existent farm. . . I try to feel, but I no longer know how. I've become my own shadow, as if I'd surrendered my being to it. Contrary to Peter Schlemihl* of the German story, I sold not my shadow but my substance to the Devil. I suffer from not suffering, from not knowing how to suffer. Am I alive or do I just pretend to be? Am I asleep or awake? A slight breeze that coolly emerges from the daytime heat makes me forget everything. My eyelids are pleasantly heavy. . . It occurs to me that this same sun is shining on fields where I neither am nor wish to be. . . From the midst of the city's din a vast silence emerges. . . How soft it is! But how much softer, perhaps, if I could feel!. . .

469

Even writing has lost its appeal. To express emotions in words and to produce well-wrought sentences has become so banal it's like eating or drinking, something I do with greater or lesser interest but always with a certain detachment, and without real enthusiasm or brilliance.

470

To speak is to show too much consideration for others. It's when they open their mouths that fish, and Oscar Wilde, are fatally hooked.

471

Once we're able to see this world as an illusion and a phantasm, then we can see everything that happens to us as a dream, as something that pretended to exist while we were sleeping. And we will become subtly and profoundly indifferent towards all of life's setbacks and calamities. Those who die turned a corner, which is why we've stopped seeing them; those who suffer pass before us like a nightmare, if we feel, or like an unpleasant daydream, if we think. And even our own suffering won't be more than this nothingness. In this world we sleep on our left side, hearing even in our dreams the heart's oppressed existence.

Nothing else. . . A little sunlight, a slight breeze, a few trees framing the distance, the desire to be happy, regret over time's passing, our always doubtful science, and the always undiscovered truth. . . That's all, nothing else. . . No, nothing else. . .

472

To attain the satisfactions of the mystic state without having to endure its rigours; to be the ecstatic follower of no god, the mystic or epopt* with no initiation; to pass the days meditating on a paradise you don't believe in – all of this tastes good to the soul that knows it knows nothing.

The silent clouds drift high above me, a body inside a shadow; the hidden truths drift high above me, a soul imprisoned in a body. . . Everything drifts high above. . . And everything high above passes on, just like everything down below, with no cloud leaving behind more than rain, no truth leaving behind more than sorrow. . . Yes, everything that's lofty passes high above, and passes on; everything that's desirable is in the distance and distantly passes on. . . Yes, everything attracts, everything remains foreign, and everything passes on.

What's the point of knowing that in the sun or in the rain, as a body or a soul, I will also pass on? No point – just the hope that everything is nothing and nothing, therefore, everything.

473

Every sound mind believes in God. No sound mind believes in a definite God. There is some being, both real and impossible, who reigns over all things and whose person (if he has one) cannot be defined, and whose purposes (if he has any) cannot be fathomed. By calling this being God we say everything, since the word God – having no precise meaning – affirms him without saying anything. The attributes of infinite, eternal, omnipotent, all-just or all-loving that we sometimes attach to him fall off by themselves, like all unnecessary adjectives when the noun suffices. And He who, being indefinite, cannot have attributes, is for that very reason the absolute noun.

The same certainty and the same obscurity exist with respect to the soul's survival. We all know that we die; we all feel that we won't die. It's not just a desire or hope that brings us this shadowy intuition that death is a misunderstanding; it's a visceral logic that rejects . . . . .

474

A Day

Instead of eating lunch – a necessity I have to talk myself into every day – I walked down to the Tagus, and I wandered back along the streets without even pretending that it did me good to see it. Even so. . .

Living isn't worth our while. Only seeing is. To be able to see without living would bring happiness, but this is impossible, like virtually everything we dream. How great would be the ecstasy that didn't include life!

To create at least a new pessimism, a new negativity, so that we can have the illusion that something of us – albeit something bad – will remain!

475

'What are you laughing about?' the voice of Moreira harmlessly wondered beyond the two bookshelves that mark the boundary of my pinnacle.

'I mixed up some names,' I answered, and my lungs calmed.

'Oh,' he said quickly, and dusty silence fell once more over the office and over me.

The Viscount of Chateaubriand doing the books! Professor Amiel* sitting here on a high royal stool! Count Alfred de Vigny debiting

Grandela Department Store! Senancour on the Rua dos Douradores!

Not even poor miserable Bourget, whose books are as tiresome as a building without an elevator. . . I turn and lean out the window to look once more at my Boulevard Saint Germain, and precisely at that moment the ranch owner's partner is spitting from the next window over.

And between thinking about this and smoking, and not connecting one thing to the other, my mental laughter finds the smoke, gets tangled in my throat, and expands into a mild attack of audible laughter.

476

It will seem to many that my diary, written just for me, is too artificial. But it's only natural for me to be artificial. How else can I amuse myself except by carefully recording these mental notes? Though I'm not very careful about how I record them. In fact I jot them down in no particular order and with no special care. The refined language of my prose is the language in which I naturally think.

For me the outer world is an inner reality. I feel this not in some metaphysical way but with the senses normally used to grasp reality.

Yesterday's frivolity is a nostalgia that gnaws at my life today.

There are cloisters in this moment. Night has fallen on all our evasions. A final despair in the blue eyes of the pools reflects the dying sun. We were so many things in the parks of old! We were so voluptuously embodied in the presence of the statues and in the English layout of the paths. The costumes, the foils, the wigs, the graceful motions and the processions were so much a part of the substance of our spirit! But who does 'our' refer to? Just the fountain's winged water in the deserted garden, shooting less high than it used to in its sad attempt to fly.

477

. . . and lilies on the banks of remote rivers, cold and solemn, on a never-ending close of day in the heart of real continents.

With nothing else, and yet utterly real.

478

(lunar scene)

The entire landscape is in no place at all.

479

Far below, sloping down in a tumult of shadows from the heights where I gaze, the icy city sleeps in the moonlight.

An anxiety for being me, forever trapped in myself, floods my whole being without finding a way out, shaping me into tenderness, fear, sorrow and desolation.

An inexplicable surfeit of absurd grief, a sorrow so lonely, so bereft, so metaphysically mine . . . . .

480

The silent, hazy city spreads out before my wistful eyes.

The buildings, all different, form a confused, self-contained mass, whose dead projections are arrested in the pearly, uncertain moonlight. There are rooftops and shadows, windows and middle ages, but nothing around which to have outskirts. There's a glimmer of the far away in everything I see. Above where I'm standing there are black branches of trees, and all of the city's sleepiness fills my disenchanted heart. Lisbon by moonlight and my weariness because of tomorrow!

What a night! It pleased whoever fashioned the world's details that for me there should be no better melody or occasion than these solitary moonlit moments when I no longer know the self I've always known.

No breeze, no person interrupts what I'm not thinking. I'm sleepy in the same way that I'm alive. But there is feeling in my eyelids, as if something were making them heavy. I hear my breathing. Am I asleep or awake?

To drag my feet homeward weighs like lead on my senses. The caress of extinction, the flower proffered by futility, my name never pronounced, my disquiet like a river contained between its banks, the privilege of abandoned duties, and – around the last bend in the ancestral park – that other century, like a rose garden. . .

481

I went into the barbershop as usual, with the pleasant sensation of entering a familiar place, easily and naturally. New things are distressing to my sensibility; I'm at ease only in places where I've already been.

After I'd sat down in the chair, I happened to ask the young barber, occupied in fastening a clean, cool cloth around my neck, about his older colleague from the chair to the right, a spry fellow who had been sick. I didn't ask this because I felt obliged to ask something; it was the place and my memory that sparked the question. 'He passed away yesterday,' flatly answered the barber's voice behind me and the linen cloth as his fingers withdrew from the final tuck of the cloth in between my shirt collar and my neck. The whole of my irrational good mood abruptly died, like the eternally missing barber from the adjacent chair. A chill swept over all my thoughts. I said nothing.

Nostalgia! I even feel it for people and things that were nothing to me, because time's fleeing is for me an anguish, and life's mystery is a torture. Faces I habitually see on my habitual streets – if I stop seeing them I become sad. And they were nothing to me, except perhaps the symbol of all of life.

The nondescript old man with dirty gaiters who often crossed my path at nine-thirty in the morning. . . The crippled seller of lottery tickets who would pester me in vain. . . The round and ruddy old man smoking a cigar at the door of the tobacco shop. . . The pale tobacco shop owner. . . What has happened to them all, who because I regularly saw them were a part of my life? Tomorrow I too will vanish from the Rua da Prata, the Rua dos Douradores, the Rua dos Fanqueiros. Tomorrow I too – I this soul that feels and thinks, this universe I am for myself – yes, tomorrow I too will be the one who no longer walks these streets, whom others will vaguely evoke with a 'What's become of him?'. And everything I've done, everything I've felt and everything I've lived will amount merely to one less passer-by on the everyday streets of some city or other.

A Disquiet Anthology

Pessoa, in a note on how to organize The Book of Disquiet *(in Appendix III), considered publishing some of the passages with titles in a separate volume. The titled texts included in this section all date from the 1910s and have been ordered alphabetically. Roman numerals have been used to distinguish among the separate fragments that Pessoa left for certain texts, such as 'Advice to Unhappily Married Women'.*

Advice to Unhappily Married Women (I)

(Unhappily married women include all who are married and some who are single)

Beware, above all else, of cultivating humanitarian sentiments. Humanitarianism is a vulgarity. I write coldly, rationally, thinking of your own good, you poor unhappily married women.

The essence of all art, all freedom, is to submit one's spirit as little as possible, letting the body be submitted instead.

Immoral behaviour is inadvisable, for it demeans your personality in the eyes of others and makes it banal. But to be inwardly immoral while being held in high esteem by everyone around you, to be a dedicated and corporally chaste wife and mother while at the same time mysteriously catching diseases from all the men in the neighbourhood, from the grocers to □ – this is the height of gratification for anyone who really wants to enjoy and expand her individuality without stooping to the base method of naturally base housemaids or else falling into the rigid virtuousness of profoundly stupid women, whose virtue is merely the offspring of self-interest.

According to your superiority, female souls who read me, will you be able to grasp what I write. All pleasure is in the mind; all crimes that occur are committed in dreams and in dreams alone! I remember a beautiful, authentic crime. It never happened. The beautiful crimes aren't the ones we know. Borgia committed beautiful crimes? Believe me that he didn't. The one who committed beautiful, lavish, fruitful crimes was our dream of Borgia, the idea we have of Borgia. I'm certain that the Cesare Borgia* who existed was banal and stupid. He must have been, because to exist is always stupid and banal.

I offer you this advice disinterestedly, applying my method to a case which doesn't personally interest me. My dreams are of empire and glory, with nothing sensual about them. But I'd like to be useful to you, if for no other reason than to annoy myself, because I hate what's useful. I'm an altruist in my own way.

Advice to Unhappily Married Women (II)

I will now teach you how to cheat on your husbands in your imagination.

Make no mistake: only an ordinary woman really and truly cheats on her husband. Modesty is a *sine qua non* for sexual pleasure, and to yield to more than one man destroys modesty.

I grant that female inferiority requires the male species, but I think that each woman should limit herself to just one male, making him, if necessary, the centre of an expanding circle of imaginary males.

The best time for doing this is in the days immediately preceding menstruation.

Like so:

Picture your husband with a whiter body. If you're good at this, you'll feel his whiteness on top of you.

Refrain from excessively sensual gestures. Kiss the husband on top of your body and replace him in your imagination – remember the man who lies on top of you in your soul.

The essence of pleasure is in multiplication. Open your shutters to the Feline in you.

How to upset your husband...

It's important that your husband gets angry now and then.

Learn to feel attracted to repulsive things without relaxing your outward discipline. The greatest inward unruliness combined with the greatest outward discipline makes for perfect sensuality. Every gesture that realizes a dream or desire unrealizes it in reality.

Substitution is less difficult than you think. By substitution I mean the practice of imagining an orgasm with man A while copulating with man B.

Advice to Unhappily Married Women (III)

My wish for you, my dear disciples, is that by faithfully following my advice you'll experience vastly multiplied sensual pleasures *with*, not in the *acts of*, the male animal to whom Church and State have tied you by your womb and a last name.

It's by digging its feet in the ground that the bird takes off in flight. May this image, daughters, serve as a perpetual reminder of the only spiritual commandment there is.

The height of sensuality, if you can achieve it, is to be the lewdest slut imaginable and yet never unfaithful to your husband, not even with your eyes.

To be a slut *on the inside*, to be unfaithful to your husband *on the inside*, to cheat on him as you hug him, to kiss him with kisses that aren't for him – that is sensuality, O superior women, O my mysterious and cerebral disciples.

Why don't I give the same advice to men? Because the man is a different kind of creature. If he's inferior, I recommend that he seduce as many women as he can, resorting to my contempt when . . . . . The superior man doesn't need women. He can have sensuality without sexual possession. This is something a woman, even a superior one, could never accept. The woman is a fundamentally sexual creature.

Apocalyptic Feeling

Since every step I took in life brought me into horrifying contact with the New, and since every new person I met was a new living fragment of the unknown that I placed on my desk for my frightful daily meditation, I decided to abstain from everything, to go forward in nothing, to reduce action to a minimum, to make it hard for people and events to find me, to perfect the art of abstinence, and to take abdication to unprecedented heights. That's how badly life terrifies and tortures me.

To make a decision, to finalize something, to emerge from the realm of doubt and obscurity – these are things that seem to me like catastrophes or universal cataclysms.

Life, as I know it, is cataclysms and apocalypses. With each passing day I feel that much more incompetent even to trace gestures or to conceive myself in clearly real situations.

With each passing day the presence of others – which my soul always receives like a rude surprise – becomes more painful and distressing. To talk with people makes my skin crawl. If they show an interest in me, I run. If they look at me, I shudder. If . . . . .

I'm forever on the defensive. I suffer from life and from other people. I can't look at reality face to face. Even the sun discourages and depresses me. Only at night and all alone, withdrawn, forgotten and lost, with no connection to anything real or useful – only then do I find myself and feel comforted.

Life makes me cold. My existence is all damp cellars and lightless catacombs. I'm the disastrous defeat of the last army that sustained the last empire. Yes, I feel as if I were at the end of an ancient ruling civilization. I, who was used to commanding others, am now alone and forsaken. I, who always had advisers to guide me, now have no friend or guide.

Something in me is always begging for compassion, and it weeps over itself as over a dead god whose altars were all destroyed when the white wave of young barbarians stormed the borders and life came and demanded to know what the empire had done with happiness.

I'm always afraid others might talk about me. I've failed in everything. I didn't dare think of being something; I didn't even dream of thinking about being something, because even in my dreams – in my visionary state as a mere dreamer – I realized I was unfit for life.

No feeling in the world can lift my head from the pillow where I've let it sink in desperation, unable to deal with my body or with the idea that I'm alive, or even with the abstract idea of life.

I don't speak the language of any reality, and I stagger among the things of life like a sick man who finally got up after being bedridden for months. Only in bed do I feel like part of normal life. It pleases me to get a fever, since it seems perfectly natural □ to my recumbent state. Like a flame in the wind I flutter and get dizzy. Only in the dead air of closed rooms do I breathe the normality of my life.

I don't even miss the ocean breeze. I've become resigned to having my soul for a cloister and to being no more to myself than an autumn in an arid expanse, with only a glimmer of living life, as of a light which expires in the canopied darkness of pools, with no energy and colour but that of the violet splendour of exile when the sun dips behind the hills. . .

I have no other real pleasure besides the analysis of my pain, nor any other sensual delight besides the morbid dribbling of sensations when they crumble and rot – light footsteps in the murky shadows, and we don't even turn around to find out whose they are; faint songs in the distance, the words of which we don't try to catch, for we are lulled more by the vagueness of what they're saying and by the mystery of where they come from; hazy secrets of pallid waters, filling the □ and nocturnal spaces with ethereal far-aways; bells of distant carriages, and who knows where they're returning from or what laughs and gaiety they contain, because from here they're just distant, drowsy carriages in the dull torpor of an afternoon in which summer is giving way to autumn. . .

The flowers in the garden have died and withered to become other flowers – older and more noble, their dead yellow more compatible with mystery, silence and solitude. The water bubbles that surface in the pools have their place in dreams. The distant croaking of frogs! O lifeless countryside within me! O rustic peacefulness of dreams! O my life, futile as that of a shiftless vagabond who sleeps on the side of the road, in a fresh and transparent slumber, with the fragrance of the meadows entering his soul like a mist, profound and full of eternity like everything that's not linked to anything, nocturnal, anonymous, nomadic and weary beneath the stars' cold compassion.

I follow wherever my dreams lead, making the images into steps that lead to other images; I unfold – like a fan – each chance metaphor into a large, inwardly visible picture; I cast off my life like a suit that's too tight. I hide among trees, far away from the roads. I lose myself. And for a few tenuous moments I'm able to forget my taste for life, to bury the thought of daylight and bustle, and to consciously, absurdly terminate in my sensations, with an empire in agonizing ruins but also with a grand entrance amid victory banners and drums into a glorious final city where I would weep over nothing and desire nothing, asking no one – not even myself – for so much as the right to exist.

It's me who suffers from the sickly surfaces of the pools I've created in dreams. Mine is the paleness of the moon I envision over wooded landscapes. Mine is the weariness of the stagnant autumn skies that I remember but have never seen. All of my dead life, all my flawed dreams and all that I had that wasn't mine oppresses me in the blue of my inner skies, in the visible rippling of my soul's rivers, and in the vast, restless serenity of the wheat on the plains which I see but don't see.

A cup of coffee, a bit of tobacco whose aroma passes through me when I smoke it, my eyes half shut in a half-dark room – this, and my dreams, are all I want from life. If it doesn't seem to me like too little? I don't know. How should I know what's a little and what's a lot?

O summer afternoon outside, how I'd like to be utterly different... I open the window. Everything outside is soft, but it cuts me like an indefinite pain, like a vague feeling of dissatisfaction.

And one last thing cuts me, tears me, rips my soul to pieces. It's that I, in this moment and at this window, thinking these sad and soft things, ought to be an attractive, aesthetic figure, like a figure in a painting – and I'm not even that...

Let the moment pass and be forgotten... Let the night come, let it grow, let it fall over everything and never lift back up. Let this soul be my tomb for ever, and □ become sheer darkness, and may I never be able to live again without feelings and desires.

The Art of Effective Dreaming (I)

Make sure, first of all, that you respect nothing, believe nothing, □ nothing. But while showing disrespect, you should hold on to the desire to respect something; while despising what you don't love, you should retain the painful longing to love someone; and while disdaining life, you should preserve the idea that it must be wonderful to live and cherish it. Having done this, you'll have laid the foundations for the edifice of your dreams.

Remember that you're embarking on the loftiest task of all. To dream is to find ourselves. You're going to be the Columbus of your soul. You're going to set out to discover your own landscapes. Make sure you're on the right track and that your instruments can't mislead you.

The art of dreaming is difficult, because it's an art of passivity, in which we concentrate our efforts on avoiding all effort. If there were an art of sleeping, it would no doubt be somewhat similar.

Note that the art of dreaming is not the art of directing our dreams. To direct is to act. The true dreamer surrenders to himself, is possessed by himself.

Avoid all material stimulants. In the beginning you'll be tempted to masturbate, to consume alcohol, to smoke opium ..... This is all effort and seeking. To be a good dreamer, you have to be nothing but a dreamer. Opium and morphine are purchased in pharmacies – how can you expect to dream through them? Masturbation is a physical thing – how can you expect .....

Now if you dream about masturbating, all fine and good. If you dream about smoking opium or taking morphine, and become intoxicated from the idea of the opium, □ of the morphine of your dreams, then you deserve to be praised: you are performing like a perfect dreamer.

Always think of yourself as sadder and more miserable than you are. There's no harm in it. It even serves as a kind of trick ladder to the world of dreams.

The Art of Effective Dreaming (II)

§ Postpone everything. Never do today what you can leave for tomorrow.* In fact you need not do anything at all, tomorrow or today.

§ Never think about what you're going to do. Don't do it.

§ Live your life. Don't be lived by it. Right or wrong, happy or sad, be your own self. You can do this only by dreaming, because your real life, your human life, is the one that doesn't belong to you but to others. You must replace your life with your dreaming, concentrating only on dreaming perfectly. In all the acts of your real life, from that of being born to that of dying, you don't act – you're acted; you don't live – you're merely lived.

Become an inscrutable sphinx to others. Shut yourself in your ivory tower, but without slamming the door. Your ivory tower is you.

And if someone tells you this is false and absurd, don't believe it. But don't believe in what I say either, because one ought not believe in anything.

§ Disdain everything, but in such a way that your disdain doesn't disturb you. Don't think you're superior because you disdain. This is the key to the art of noble disdain.

The Art of Effective Dreaming (III)

By virtue of dreaming everything, everything in life will make you suffer more . . . . .

That's the cross you will have to bear.

The Art of Effective Dreaming for Metaphysical Minds

Reason, □ – everything is easy and □, because everything for me is a dream. I decide to dream something and I dream it. Sometimes I create in myself a philosopher, who methodically expounds philosophies while I, a young page, pay court to his daughter, whose soul I am, outside the window of her house.

I'm limited, of course, by what I know. I can't create a mathematician. But I'm content with what I have, which already allows for infinite combinations and countless dreams. And perhaps, through dreaming, I'll achieve still more. Though it's not really worth the bother. I'm already quite satisfied.

Pulverization of the personality: I don't know what my ideas are, nor my feelings or my character. . . When I feel something, I feel it only vaguely, in the visualized person of some being or other that appears in me. *I've replaced my own self with my dreams.* Each person is merely his own dream of himself. I'm not even that.

Never read a book to the end, nor in sequence and without skipping.

I've never known what I felt. Whenever people spoke to me of such and such emotion and described it, I always felt they were describing something in my soul, but when I thought about it later, I always doubted. I never know if what I feel I am is what I really am or merely what I think I am. I'm a character of* my own plays.

Effort is useless but entertains. Reason is sterile but amusing. To love is tiresome but is perhaps preferable to not loving. Dreaming, however, substitutes for everything. In dreams I can have the impression of effort without actual effort. I can enter battles without the risk of getting scared or being wounded. I can reason without aiming to arrive at some truth (which I would never arrive at in any case), without trying to solve some problem (which I know I would never solve) . . . . . I can love without worrying about being rejected or cheated on, and without getting bored. I can change my sweetheart and she'll always be the same. And should I wish to be cheated on or spurned, I can make it happen, and always in the way I want, always in the way that gives me pleasure. In dreams I can experience the worst anxieties, the harshest torments, the greatest victories. I can experience all of it as if it happened in life; it depends only on my ability to make my dreams vivid, sharp, real. This requires study and inner patience.

There are various ways of dreaming. One is to surrender completely to your dreams, without trying to make them clear and sharp, letting yourself go in the hazy twilight of the sensations they arouse. This is an inferior, tiresome form of dreaming, for it's monotonous, always the same. Rather different is the clear and *directed* dream, but the effort expended on directing it makes the dream too obviously artificial. The supreme artist – the kind of dreamer I am – expends only the effort of *wanting* his dream to be such and such, in accord with his whims, and it unfolds before him exactly as he would have desired but could never have conceived, because the mental effort would have worn him out. I want to dream of myself as a king. I decide all of a sudden that this is what I want, and lo and behold I'm the king of some country. Which one and what kind, the dream will tell me. For I've so triumphed over my dreams that they always unexpectedly bring me what I want. By focusing more sharply, I can perfect those scenes of life that come to me as only vague impressions. I would be utterly incapable of consciously picturing the various Middle Ages of diverse eras on diverse Earths that I've experienced in dreams. I'm amazed at the wealth of imagination that I never realized was in me. I let my dreams go their own way... They've become so pure that they always surpass my expectations. They're always even more beautiful than what I wanted. But only the most advanced dreamer can hope to reach this point. I've spent years dreamingly striving for this, and today I achieve it without effort.

The best way to start dreaming is through books. Novels are especially helpful for the beginner. The first step is to learn to give in completely to your reading, to live totally with the characters of a novel. You'll know you're making progress when your own family and its troubles seem insipid and loathsome by comparison. It's best to avoid reading literary novels, which tend to divert our attention to the formal structure.

I'm not ashamed to admit that this is how I started. Strangely enough, detective novels, □ are what I □ instinctively read. I was never able to read romantic novels in any sustained way, but this is for personal reasons, I being romantically disinclined even in my dreams. Let each man cultivate his particular inclination. Let us never forget that to dream is to explore ourselves. Sensual souls, for their reading matter, should choose the opposite of what I read.

When the dreamer experiences *physical* sensation – when a novel about combat, flights and battles leaves his body *really* exhausted and his legs worn out – then he has passed beyond the first stage of dreaming. In the case of the sensual soul, he should be able – without any masturbation except in his mind – to experience an ejaculation at the appropriate moment during the novel.

Next, the dreamer should try to transfer all of this to the mental plane. The dreamed ejaculation (which I choose as the most violent and striking example) *should be felt without actually happening*. The fatigue will be greater, but the pleasure will be incomparably more intense.

In the third stage all sensation becomes mental. This increases the feeling of pleasure and also of fatigue, but the body no longer feels anything; instead of weary limbs, it's our mind, will and emotions that become slack and sluggish... Having arrived this far, it's time to advance to the supreme stage of dreaming.

The second stage is to construct novels for your own enjoyment. This should be attempted only once dreaming has become perfectly mentalized, as described above. Otherwise, the effort to set a novel in motion will hinder the smooth mentalization of pleasure.

Third stage: Once our imagination has been trained, it will fashion dreams all by itself whenever we want.

At this point there's hardly even any mental fatigue. The dissolution of personality is total. We are mere ashes endowed with a soul but no form – not even that of water, which adopts the shape of the vessel that holds it.

With this □ thoroughly established, complete and autonomous plays can unfold in us line by line. We may no longer have the energy to write them, but that won't be necessary. We'll be able to create secondhand; we can imagine one poet writing in us in one way, while another poet will write in a different way. I, having refined this skill to a considerable degree, can write in countlessly different ways, all of them original.

The highest stage of dreaming is when, having created a picture with various figures whose lives we live all at the same time, *we are jointly and interactively all of those souls*. This leads to an incredible degree of depersonalization and the reduction of our spirit to ashes, and it is hard, I admit, not to feel a general weariness throughout one's entire being. But what triumph!

This is the only final asceticism. It's an asceticism without faith, and without any God.

God am I.

Cascade

Children know that the doll isn't real, but they treat it as if it were, to the point of crying with grief when it breaks. The art of children is in non-realization. How blessed is that deluded age, when life is negated* by the absence of sex, and reality is negated by the act of playing, unreal things standing in for real ones!

If I could only go back to being a child and remain one for ever, oblivious to the values that men attach to things and the relations they establish between them! When I was little, I often stood my toy soldiers on their heads. And what convincing argument of logic can prove to me that real soldiers shouldn't march head downward?

Gold is worth no more than glass to a child. And is gold's value truly any greater? The child obscurely senses the absurdity of the wraths, passions and fears he sees sculpted in adult gestures. And aren't all our fears, hatreds and loves truly vain and absurd?

O divinely absurd intuition of children! True vision of things, which we always dress with conventions, however nakedly we see them, and always blur with our ideas, however directly we look at them!

Might not God be an enormous child? Doesn't the whole universe seem like a game, like the prank of a mischievous child? So unreal, so . . . . .

I laughingly threw out this idea for consideration, and only now, seeing it from a distance, do I realize how ghastly it is. (Who's to say it isn't true?) And it falls to the ground at my feet, shattering into shards of mystery and pulverized horror. . .

I wake up to make sure I exist. . .

An immense, indefinite tedium gurgles with a deceptively fresh sound in the cascades past the beehives, at the stupid far end of the yard.

Cenotaph

No surviving widow or son placed the obol in his mouth to pay Charon. We'll never know with what eyes he crossed the Styx and saw his face – forever veiled to us – reflected nine times in the waters of the underworld. The name of his shadow, which now wanders on the banks of the gloomy rivers, is for us but another shadow.

He died for his Country, without knowing how or why. His sacrifice had the glory of going unrecognized. He gave his life with his whole heart and soul: out of instinct, not duty; because he loved his Country, not because he was conscious of it. He defended it as a man defends his mother, whose son he is by birth rather than by logic. Faithful to the primeval secret, he didn't think about or wish for his death but instinctively lived it, as he had lived his life. The shadow he now inhabits is brother to the shadows that fell at Thermopylae, faithful in their flesh to the pledge made at their birth.

He died for his Country the way the sun daily rises. He was already, by nature, what Death would make of him.

He did not fall on behalf of some zealous faith, nor was he killed in the vile struggle for some great ideal. Unsullied by faith or humanitarianism, he did not die in defence of a political idea, the future of humanity, or a new religion. Having no faith in another world, with which the credulous of Mohammed and the followers of Christ deceive themselves, he saw death arrive without hoping for life in it; he saw life leave him without hoping for a better one.

He passed on naturally, like the wind and the day, taking with him the soul that had made him different. He plunged into the shadows the way a man, arriving at a door, walks through it. He died for his Country, the only thing above us that we can know and grasp. Neither the paradise of Moslems and Christians nor the transcendental oblivion of Buddhists was reflected in his eyes when in their depths the flame of his earthly life went out.

If we don't know who he is, neither did he know who he was. He did his duty without knowing what he'd done. He was guided by what makes the roses bloom and the death of leaves beautiful. Life has no better purpose, nor death a better reward.

Now, according as the gods allow, he visits the lightless regions, passing by the laments of Cocytus and the fire of Phlegethon, and hearing in the night the slow flowing of the livid, Lethean current.

He is anonymous like the instinct that killed him. He didn't think he would die for his Country; he died for it. He didn't decide to do his duty; he just did it. Since his soul bore no name, it is only right that we not ask what name defined his body. He was Portuguese, but not this or that Portuguese, and so he stands as the universal Portuguese.

His place is not next to the creators of Portugal, who have a different stature and a different consciousness. He doesn't belong in the company of our demigods, whose daring extended the routes of the sea and brought within our reach more land than could be had.

Let no statue or stone commemorate this soul who was all of us. Since he was the entire people, for a tomb he should have this entire land. We should bury him in his own memory, with only his example for a stone.

Declaration of Difference

The things of city and state have no power over us. It doesn't matter that the ministers and their courtiers shamelessly mishandle the nation's affairs. All of this occurs outside, like mud on a rainy day. We have nothing to do with it, however much it may have to do with us.

We are likewise indifferent to great convulsions such as war and crises around the world. As long as they don't come to our house, we don't care on whose door they knock. This attitude would appear to be founded on a profound contempt for others, but its real basis is merely a sceptical view of ourselves.

We're not kind or charitable. Not because we're the opposite, but because we're neither one way nor the other. Kindness is the form of delicacy that belongs to crude souls. It interests us as a phenomenon that takes place in other people, who have other ways of thinking. We observe without approving or disapproving. Our vocation is to be nothing.

We would be anarchists if we had been born in the classes which call themselves underprivileged, or in any of the others from which one can move up or down. But we are for the most part individuals born in the cracks between classes and social divisions – nearly always in that decadent space between the aristocracy and the upper-middle class, the social niche of geniuses and lunatics with whom it's possible to get along.

Action disconcerts us, partly because of our physical incompetence, but mainly because it offends our moral sensibility. We consider it immoral to act. It seems to us that every thought is debased when expressed in words, which transform the thought into the property of others, making it understandable to anyone who can understand it.

We're sympathetic towards the occult and the secret arts. We are not occultists, however. We weren't born with the kind of will it takes, let alone the patience to educate and develop such a will into the perfect instrument of a wizard or hypnotist. But we sympathize with occultism, especially since it tends to express itself in ways that many who read and even think they understand it don't understand a thing. Its arcane attitude is arrogantly superior. It is, in addition, a rich source of mysterious and terrifying sensations: astral larvae, the strange beings with strange bodies evoked in its temples by ritual magic, and the immaterial presences that hover all around our unperceiving senses, in the physical silence of inner sound – all of this comforts us in darkness and distress with the caress of its sticky, horrid hand.

But we don't sympathize with occultists when they act as apostles and champions of humanity; this strips them of their mystery. The only valid reason for an occultist to operate in the astral realm is for the sake of a higher aesthetic, not for the insidious purpose of doing good to others.

Almost unawares we harbour an ancestral sympathy for black magic, for the forbidden forms of transcendental science, and for the Lords of Power who sold themselves to Condemnation and a degenerate Reincarnation. The eyes of our weak, vacillating souls lose themselves – like a bitch in heat – in the theory of inverse degrees, in corrupted rites, and in the sinister curve of the descendent, infernal hierarchy.

Like it or not, Satan exerts an attraction on us like a male on a female. The serpent of Material Intelligence has wound around our heart, as around the symbolic caduceus of the God who communicates: Mercury, lord of Understanding.

Those of us who aren't homosexuals wish we had the courage to be. Our distaste for action can't help but feminize us. We missed our true calling as housewives and idle chatelaines because of a sexual mix-up in our current incarnation. Although we don't believe this one bit, to act as though we do smacks of irony's very blood.

None of this is out of meanness, just weakness. In private we adore the Bad, not because it's bad, but because it's stronger and more intense than the Good, and all that is strong and intense is attractive to nerves that should have belonged to a woman. *Pecca fortiter* can't apply to us, for we have no force, not even the force of intelligence, which is the only one we could ever claim. To think of sinning forcefully – that's the most we can do with this severe dictum. But even this is not always possible, for our inner life has its own reality which we sometimes find painful just because it is a reality. The existence of laws governing the association of ideas (along with all other mental operations) is insulting to our inherent lack of discipline.

Divine Envy

Whenever I experience an agreeable sensation in the company of others, I begrudge the part they had in the sensation. It strikes me as an indecency that they should feel the same thing I do, that they should penetrate my soul through their own concordantly feeling soul.

How can I take pride in the landscapes I contemplate, when the painful truth is that someone else has no doubt contemplated them for the same reasons I do? At other times and on other days, to be sure, but to call attention to such differences would be a pedantic consolation that's beneath me. I know all too well that these differences are petty and that other people, with the same spirit of contemplation, have seen the landscape in a way not identical, but similar, to my own.

That's why I constantly strive to alter what I see, thereby making it indisputably mine – to alter the mountains' profile while making it every bit as beautiful, and beautiful in the exact same way; to replace certain trees and flowers with others that are vastly and very differently the same; to see other colours that produce an identical effect in the sunset. In this way I create, thanks to my experience and my habit of spontaneously *seeing* when I look, an inner version of the outer world.

And this is but the lowest level of replacing the visible. In my best and most intense moments of dreaming, I alter and create much more.

I cause the landscape to affect me like music and to evoke visual images for my viewing pleasure – a peculiar and difficult ecstasy to achieve, since the evocative agent is of the same order as the sensations it evokes. My greatest triumph of this sort occurred when, during a moment of hazy light and atmosphere, I looked at the square at Cais do Sodré* and clearly *saw* it as a Chinese pagoda with odd bells hanging like absurd hats from the tips of its roof-tiles – a strange Chinese pagoda *painted* in space, painted I don't know how on this satin-like space that endures in the abominable third dimension. And the moment smelled to me just like a cloth dragging somewhere far away, highly envious of reality. . .

Funeral March

What does anyone do that can disturb or change the world? Isn't there always, for every man of worth, another man just as worthy? One ordinary man is worth another; a man of action is worth the force he interprets; the man of thought is worth what he creates.

Whatever you've created for humanity is at the mercy of the Earth's cooling down. Whatever you've left for posterity is so characteristic of you that no one else will understand it, or it belongs only to your age and won't be understood by future ages, or it speaks to all ages but won't be understood by the final abyss into which all ages will fall.

We are but windows, making gestures in the shadows, while behind us Mystery . . . . .

We are all mortal, with a given duration – never longer or shorter. Some die as soon as they die, while others live on for a time in the memory of those who knew and loved them; others survive in the memory of the nation that bore them; still others enter into the memory of the civilization they were part of; and some very few are able to span the contrary tendencies of differing civilizations. But all of us are surrounded by the abyss of time, in which we will ultimately vanish; the hunger of the abyss will swallow us all . . . . .

Durability is just a wish, and eternity an illusion.

Death is what we are and what we live. We are born dead, we deadly exist, and we are already dead when we enter Death.

Whatever lives, lives because it changes; it changes because it passes; and, because it passes, it dies. Whatever lives is constantly transforming into something else – it continually denies itself, it perpetually evades life.

Life is thus an interval, a link, a relation, but a relation between what has passed and what will pass, a dead interval between Death and Death.

. . . intelligence, an errant fiction of the surface.

Material life is either pure dream or a mere ensemble of atoms, oblivious to our rational conclusions and our emotional motivations. And so the essence of life is an illusion, an appearance, which is either pure being or non-being, and the illusion or appearance that it's nothing must belong to non-being – life is death.

How vain is all our striving to create, under the spell of the illusion of not dying! 'Eternal poem,' we say, or 'Words that will never die.' But the material cooling down of earth will carry off not only the living who cover it, but also . . . .

A Homer or a Milton can do no more than a comet that strikes the earth.

Funeral March for Ludwig II, King of Bavaria*

Today Death, tarrying longer than ever, came to sell at my doorstep. Slower than ever, she unfolded before me the rugs, silks and linens of her oblivion and her consolation. She smiled with satisfaction at the things she showed, without caring that I saw her smile. But as soon as I felt tempted to buy them, she said they weren't for sale. She hadn't come to make me want the things she showed but, through those things, to make me want her. The rugs, she said, were the kind that graced her far-away palace; the silks were the same ones worn in her castle of darkness; and even better linens than what she had showed me draped the altarpieces of her abode in the nether world.

She gently unravelled the ties that held me to my native, unadorned home. 'Your fireplace,' she said, 'has no fire, so why do you want a fireplace?' 'Your table,' she said, 'has no bread, so what is your table for?' 'Your life,' she said, 'has no friend or companion, so why does your life charm you?'

She said, 'I am the fire of cold fireplaces, the bread of bare tables, the faithful companion of the lonely and the misunderstood. The glory that's missing in this world is the pride of my black domain. In my kingdom love doesn't weary, for it doesn't long to possess; nor does it suffer from the frustration of never having possessed. My hand lightly rests on the hair of those who think, and they forget; those who have waited in vain lean against my breast, and finally come to trust.

'The love that souls have for me is free of the passion that consumes, of the jealousy that deranges, of the forgetfulness that tarnishes. To love me is as calm as a summer night, when beggars sleep in the open air and look like rocks on the side of the road. My lips utter no song like the sirens' nor any melody like that of the trees and fountains, but my silence welcomes like a faint music, and my stillness soothes like the torpor of a breeze.

'What do you have,' she said, 'that binds you to life? Love doesn't follow you, glory doesn't seek you, and power doesn't find you. The house that you inherited was in ruins. The lands you received had already lost their first fruits to frost, and the sun had withered their promises. You have never found water in your farm's well. And before you ever saw them, the leaves had all rotted in your pools; weeds covered the paths and walkways where your feet had never trod.

'But in my domain, where only the night reigns, you will be consoled, for your hopes will have ceased; you'll be able to forget, for your desire will have died; you will finally rest, for you'll have no life.'

And she showed me the futility of hoping for better days when one isn't born with a soul that can know better days. She showed me how dreaming never consoles, for life hurts all the more when we wake up. She showed me how sleep gives no rest, for it is haunted by phantoms, shadows of things, ghosts of gestures, stillborn desires, the flotsam from the shipwreck of living.

And as she spoke, she slowly folded up – more slowly than ever – her rugs which tempted my eyes, her silks which my soul coveted, and the linens of her altarpieces, where my tears were already falling.

'Why try to be like others if you're condemned to being yourself? Why laugh if, when you laugh, even your genuine happiness is false, since it is born of forgetting who you are? Why cry if you feel it's of no use, and if you cry not because tears console you but because it grieves you that they don't?

'If you're happy when you laugh, then when you laugh I've triumphed; if you're happy, because you don't remember who you are, then think how much happier you'll be with me, where you won't remember anything! If you rest perfectly on those rare occasions when you sleep without dreaming, then think how you'll rest in my bed, where sleep never has dreams! If you sometimes feel exalted because, seeing Beauty, you forget yourself and Life, then how much more you'll feel exalted in my palace, whose nocturnal beauty is always harmonious and never ages or decays; in my halls, where no wind ruffles the curtains, no dust covers the chairs, no light slowly fades the velvets and the silks, and no time yellows the vacant whiteness of the walls!

'Come to my affection, which never changes, and to my love, which has no end! Drink from my inexhaustible chalice the supreme nectar which doesn't jade or taste bitter, which doesn't nauseate or inebriate! Look out the window of my castle and contemplate not the moonlight and the sea, which are beautiful and thus imperfect things, but the vast, maternal night, the undivided splendour of the bottomless abyss!

'In my arms you will forget even the painful road that brought you to them. Against my breast you won't even feel the love that prompted you to come and seek it. Sit next to me on my throne and you will for ever be the undethronable emperor of the Mystery and the Grail, you will coexist with the gods and with all destinies, and like them you'll be nothing, you'll have no here or hereafter, and you won't need what you abound in, nor what you lack, nor even what suffices you.

'I will be your maternal wife, the twin sister you've at long last recovered. And with all your anxieties married to me, with all that you vainly sought in yourself now entrusted to me, you yourself will become lost in my mystic substance, in my forsworn existence, in my breast where things smother, in my breast where souls drown, in my breast where the gods vanish.'

◆

Sovereign King of Detachment and Renunciation, Emperor of Death and Shipwreck, living dream that grandly wanders among the world's ruins and wastes!

Sovereign King of Despair amid splendours, grieving lord of palaces that don't satisfy, master of processions and pageants that never succeed in blotting out life!

Sovereign King risen up from the tombs, who came in the night by the light of the moon to tell your life to the living, royal page of lilies that have lost their petals, imperial herald of the coldness of ivory!

Sovereign King Shepherd of the Watches, knight errant of Anxieties travelling on moonlit roads without glory and without even a lady to serve, lord in the forests and on the slopes, a silent silhouette with visor drawn shut, passing through valleys, misunderstood in villages, ridiculed in towns, scorned in cities!

Sovereign King consecrated by Death to be her own, pale and absurd, forgotten and unrecognized, reigning amid worn-out velvets and tarnished marble on his throne at the limits of the Possible, surrounded by the shadows of his unreal court and guarded by the fantasy of his mysterious, soldierless army.

Bring the goblets, platters and garlands, all you pages and damsels and servants! Bring them for the feast which Death will host! Bring them and come dressed in black, with your heads crowned by myrtle.

Bring mandrake in the goblets, □ on your platters, and make your garlands from □ violets, from all the flowers that evoke sadness.

The King is going to dine with Death in her ancient palace next to the lake, up in the mountains and far from life, cut off from the world.

Let the orchestras rehearsing for the feast be made up of strange instruments, whose mere sound prompts tears. Let the servants be clad in sober liveries of unknown colours; let them be lavish yet simple, like the catafalques of heroes.*

And before the feast begins, let the long medieval cortège of dead purple robes promenade in a grandly silent ritual on the tree-lined paths of vast parks, like beauty passing through a nightmare.

Death is Life's triumph!

It is by death that we live, because we exist today only for having died to yesterday. It is by death that we hope, for we can believe in tomorrow only because we're sure today will die. It is by death that we live when we dream, since to dream is to deny life. It is by death that we die when we live, since to live is to deny eternity! Death guides us, death seeks us, death accompanies us. All that we have is death, all that we want is death, and death is all that we care to want.

A breeze of attention sweeps through the wings.

Here he comes, escorted by Death, whom no one sees, and by □, who never arrives.

Heralds, sound your horns! Attention!

Your love for things dreamed was your contempt for things lived.

Virgin King who disdained love,
Shadow King who despised light,
Dream King who denied life!

Amid the muffled racket of cymbals and drums, Darkness acclaims you Emperor!

Imperial Legend

My Imagination is a city in the Orient. The entire substance of its spatial reality has the surface sensuality of a plush and luxurious rug. The tents and stalls that brightly colour the streets stand out against a strange background that doesn't match, like red or yellow embroidery on light-blue satin. The entire history of this city circles around the light bulb of my dream like a scarcely audible moth in the penumbra of my room. My fantasy once lived amid splendours and received time-tarnished jewels from the hands of queens. Intimate velvets carpeted the beaches of my non-existence, and seaweeds like shadowy puffs floated in plain view on my rivers. And so I was porticos from lost civilizations, feverish arabesques in dead friezes, the blackening of eternity in the twists of broken columns, lonely masts of remote shipwrecks, the stone steps of toppled thrones, veils veiling nothing but seeming to veil shadows, phantoms risen up from the ground like smoke from dashed censers. My reign was gloomy, and constant wars in the border regions tainted the imperial peace of my palace. Always the vague sound of parties in the distance, always a procession that was supposed to pass beneath my windows, but no golden red fish in my pools, and no apples in the green stillness of my orchard; and not even the smoke from beyond the trees, rising from the chimneys of poor huts with happy people, ever lulled to sleep with their ballads of simplicity the restless mystery* of my self-awareness.*

In the Forest of Estrangement

I know I have woken up and still sleep. My ancient body, exhausted from living, tells me it is still very early... I feel distantly feverish. I weigh on myself, without knowing why...

Half awake and half asleep, I stagnate in a lucid, heavily immaterial torpor, in a dream that is a shadow of dreaming. My attention floats between two worlds, blindly seeing the depths of an ocean and the depths of a sky; and these depths blend, they interpenetrate, and I don't know where I am or what I'm dreaming.

A gust of shadows blows ashes of dead intentions over the part of me that's awake. A warm dew of tedium falls from an unknown firmament. An enormous, inert anxiety sifts through my soul and unwittingly changes me, as the breeze changes the line formed by the tops of the trees.

In my warm, languid alcove, the imminent dawn is just a shadowy glow. I'm overwhelmed by a quiet confusion... Why must a new day break?... It weighs on me to know it will break, as if I had to do something to make it happen.

Slowly, as if in a daze, I grow calm, then numb. I hover in the air, neither awake nor asleep, and find myself engulfed by another sort of reality, appearing from I don't know where...

This new reality – that of a strange forest – makes its appearance without effacing the reality of my warm alcove. The two realities coexist in my captivated attention, like two mingled vapours.

And that tremulous, transparent landscape clearly belongs to them both!...

And who is this woman who joins me in clothing, with her gaze, that forest of otherness? Why do I stop to ask myself?... I don't even know how to want to know...

The hazy alcove is a dark glass through which I consciously view that landscape... And I've known that landscape for a long time, and for a long time I've walked with this woman I don't know, wandering as a different reality through her unreality. I can feel, deep down, all the centuries through which I've known those trees, those flowers and those straying paths, as well as the me that wanders there, ancient and visible to my gaze – a gaze that's shadowed by my awareness of being in this alcove.

Sometimes in that forest, where from afar I see and feel myself, a light breeze spreads a mist, and that mist is the dark, clear vision of the alcove where I exist in reality, among these hazy pieces of furniture and drapes and nocturnal torpor. Then the breeze subsides and the landscape of that other world returns to being completely and exclusively itself...

At other times this small room is but an ashen whiff of fog on the horizon of that so different land... And there are times when this tangible alcove is the ground we tread in that other land...

I dream and lose myself, doubly so, in me and the woman... I'm consumed by the black fire of an overwhelming fatigue... I'm constricted by the false life of an enormous, passive yearning...

O tarnished happiness!... Eternal hesitation at the crossroads!... I dream, and behind my consciousness someone is dreaming with me... And perhaps I'm no more than a dream of that Someone who doesn't exist...

The dawn outside is so far away! and the forest so near to those other eyes of mine!

When I'm far from the forest, I almost forget it, but when I have it I feel nostalgia for it, and roaming through it makes me weep and yearn for it...

The trees! the flowers! the paths hidden among the brush!...

We sometimes strolled arm in arm under the cedars and redbuds, and neither of us thought about living. Our flesh was a wispy fragrance and our life the echo of a trickling fountain. We held hands and our gazes wondered what it would be like to be sensual and to try to live out the illusion of love in the flesh...

Our garden had flowers endowed with every kind of beauty: roses with ruffled edges, yellowish-white lilies, poppies that would remain hidden if their deep red didn't betray them, violets towards the verdant borders of the flower beds, delicate forget-me-nots, camellias with no scent... And above the tall grasses, the startled eyes of solitary sunflowers stared at us intently.

Our souls, which were pure vision, stroked the visible coolness of the mosses, and passing by the palm trees we vaguely intuited other lands... And tears welled up at the thought, for not even here were we happy when happy...

Oak trees full of knotty centuries made our feet trip over the dead tentacles of their roots... The plane trees stood perfectly still... And through the nearby trees we could see, in the distance, blackish clusters of grapes hanging in the silence of trellised vines...

Our dream of living went ahead of us, on wings, and we both smiled at it with the same detached smile, agreed upon in our souls without looking at each other, unaware of each other except for the felt presence of one person's arm supporting the other's.

Our life had no inner dimension. We were outer and other. We no longer knew ourselves. It was as if we had arrived back at our souls after a journey through dreams...

We had forgotten time, and the immensity of space had become tiny in our eyes. Besides the nearby trees and the distant grape vines and the last hills on the horizon, was there anything real, anything worthy of the rapt attention paid to things that exist?...

In the clepsydra of our imperfection, steady drops of dreaming marked the unreal hours... Nothing is worth our while, O my faraway love, except to know how sweet it is to know that nothing is worth our while...

The static motion of the trees; the troubled quiet of the fountains; the indefinable breathing of the saps' deep pulsing; the slow arrival of dusk, which seems not to fall over things but to come from inside them and to reach its spiritually kindred hand up to that distant sorrow (so close to our soul) of the heavens' lofty silence; the steady and futile falling of leaves, drops of estrangement in which the landscape comes to exist only in our hearing, and it becomes sad in us like a remembered homeland – all of this girded us uncertainly, like a belt coming undone.

There we lived in a time that couldn't possibly flow, in a space one could never even dream of measuring. A flowing that occurred outside of Time, an expanse that didn't respect the norms of spatial reality...

All those hours we spent there, O useless soulmate of my tedium! All those hours of joyful disquiet that pretended to be ours!. . . All those hours of spiritual ashes, days of spatial nostalgia, inner centuries of outer landscape. . . And we didn't ask what it was all for, because we revelled in knowing that it was for nothing.

There we knew, by an intuition that was surely not ours, that this sorrowful world in which we were two was situated – if it existed – beyond the farthest line where the mountains were only hazy shapes, and we knew that beyond that line there was nothing. And it was this contradiction that made the time we spent there dark like a cave in a superstitious country, and our awareness of the contradiction was eerie, like the silhouette of a Moorish city against an autumn sky at twilight. . .

On the horizon of our hearing, unknown seas lapped beaches we would never be able to see, and it was a joy to hear – and to see in ourselves – that sea on which caravels no doubt sailed, and for other ends besides the useful ones that reign on Earth.

We suddenly realized, as when someone realizes he's alive, that the air was full of birdsong and that we were imbued by the loud rustle of leaves – like satin by an ancient perfume – even more than by our consciousness of hearing it.

And so the warbling of the birds, the whispering of the trees and the monotonous, forgotten depths of the eternal sea circled our abandoned life with a halo of no longer knowing that life. There we slept away waking days, glad of being nothing, of having no desires or hopes, of having forgotten the colour of loves and the taste of hatreds. We thought we were immortal. . .

There we lived hours that we felt in a new way, hours of an empty imperfection that were therefore perfect, perfectly diagonal to life's rectangular certainty. . . Deposed imperial hours, hours clad in fraying purple robes, hours fallen into this world from another world, one that boasts of having more dismantled anxieties. . .

And to enjoy all of that was painful, truly painful. . . For in spite of the peaceful exile it afforded us, the landscape smacked of our belonging to this world, it was steeped in the pomp of a vague tedium, sad and vast and perverse like the decadence of some unknown empire. . .

In the curtains of our alcove the morning is a shadow of light. My lips, which I know are pale, taste to each other like they don't wish to live.

The air of our neutral room is as heavy as a drape across a doorway. Our drowsy attention to the mystery of all this is limp like the train of a robe dragged across the ground during a ceremony at twilight.

None of our yearnings has any reason to exist. Our attentive gaze is an absurdity allowed by our winged inertia.

I don't know what penumbral oils anoint the idea we have of our body. The fatigue we feel is the shadow of a fatigue. It comes from far away, like the idea that our life exists...

Neither of us has a plausible existence or name. If we could be noisy to the point of imagining ourselves laughing, we would doubtless laugh at our belief that we live. The warmed-up coolness of the bed sheet caresses (surely for you as well as for me) our two feet that nakedly touch each other.

Let us stop being deluded about life and its ways. Let us flee, my love, from being ourselves... Let us never remove from our finger the magic ring that summons, when turned, the fairies of silence and the elves of darkness and the gnomes of oblivion...

And just as we were thinking of mentioning the forest, it looms once more before us, as dense as ever but now more anguished with our anguish, and sadder with our sadness. Our idea of the real world flees in its presence like a dissipating fog, and once more I possess myself in my wandering dream, set in that mysterious forest...

The flowers, ah, the flowers I lived there! Flowers that our eyes recognized and translated into their names... Flowers whose fragrance was gathered by our soul – gathered not from the flowers but from the melody of their names... Flowers whose names, repeated in sequence, were orchestras of resonant perfumes... Trees whose green sensuality gave cool shade to their names... Fruits whose names were a sinking of teeth into the soul of their pulp... Shadows that were relics of happy yesteryears... Clearings, bright clearings, that were broad smiles of the landscape, and after each smile it yawned... O multicoloured hours!... Moments like flowers, minutes like trees, O time frozen in space, time dead from space and covered by flowers, by the fragrance of flowers, and by the fragrance of the names of flowers!...

Dreamed madness in that estranging silence!...

Our life was all of life... Our love was love's perfume... We lived impossible hours, full of being ourselves... And all because we knew, with every scrap of our flesh, that we were not a reality...

We were impersonal, devoid of self, something else altogether... We were that landscape dissipated in its self-awareness... And just as it was two landscapes, in the reality it was and in its illusion, so we were obscurely two, neither of us knowing for sure if we weren't actually the other, or if the uncertain other even lived...

When suddenly we came out to the stagnation of the ponds, we felt like weeping... There the landscape had eyes brimming with water, eyes perfectly still, full of the endless tedium of being, full of the tedium of having to be something, reality or illusion – and that tedium had its homeland and its voice in the speechless exile of those ponds... And although we kept walking, without realizing it or wanting to, it seemed we still lingered at the edge of those ponds, so much of us staying and abiding there with them, symbolized and absorbed...

And what a fresh and happy horror that there was nobody there! Not even we, who walked there, were there... For we were nobody. We were nothing at all... We had no life for Death to have to kill. We were so tenuous and slight that the wind's passing left us prostrate, and time's passage caressed us like a breeze grazing the top of a palm.

We belonged to no age and had no purpose. For us the ultimate purpose of all beings and things had remained at the door of that paradise of absence. The souls all around us, so as to feel us feel them, had become perfectly still: from the woody soul of branches to the reaching soul of their leaves, from the nubile soul of flowers to the dangling soul of fruits...

And thus we died our life, so individually intent on dying it that we never noticed that we were only one, that we were each an illusion of the other, and that each of us – as a separate self – was nothing on the inside but an echo of that self...

A fly buzzes, uncertain and minute...

Faint and dispersed but definite sounds dawn in my awareness, filling my consciousness of our room with the fact day has broken... Our room? Mine and who else's, if I'm here alone? I don't know. Everything blends and all that remains is a fleeting mist of reality in which my uncertainty founders and my self-awareness is lulled to sleep by opiums...

Morning has broken, as if it had fallen from the pallid summit of Time...

The embers of our dreams have died out, my love, in the hearth of our life...

Let us give up the illusion of hope, which betrays; of love, which wearies; of life, which surfeits but never satisfies; and even of death, which brings more than we want and less than we hope for.

Let us give up, O Veiled One, even our tedium, which wears out its own self and dares not to be all the anxiety that it is.

Let us not weep, nor hate, nor desire...

Let us cover with a sheet of fine linen, O Silent Soulmate, the dead, stiff profile of our Imperfection...

The Lake of Possession (I)

I see possession as an absurd lake – very large, very dark, and very shallow. The water only seems deep because it's dirty.

Death? But death is part of life. Do I die completely? I know nothing about life. Do I survive myself? I keep on living.

Dreaming? But dreaming is part of life. Do we live our dreams? We live. Do we only dream them? We die. And death is part of life.

Life pursues us like our own shadow. And that shadow disappears only when there's nothing but shadow. Only when we surrender to it does life stop pursuing us.

The most painful thing about dreaming is our not existing. In reality, we cannot dream.

What does it mean to possess? We don't know. So how is it possible to possess anything? You will say that we don't know what life is, and yet we live... But do we really live? To live without knowing what life is – is that living?

The Lake of Possession (II)

Be it atoms or souls, nothing interpenetrates, which is why possession is impossible. From truth to a handkerchief – nothing is possessable. Property isn't a theft: it's nothing.*

A Letter (I)

For some indefinite number of months you've seen me looking at you, constantly looking at you, always with the same hesitant and solicitous gaze. I know you've noticed this. And since you've noticed, you must have thought it strange that this gaze, which can't really be called shy, has never intimated a meaning. Always attentive, vague and unchanging, as if satisfied to be only the sadness of all this. . . Nothing else. . . And when you've thought about this – regardless of what you feel when you think about me – you must have considered my possible intentions. You must have reasoned, without being too convinced, that I'm either an eccentric version of the shy type or else something on the order of a madman.

I can assure you, Madam, with respect to my habit of looking at you, that I am not merely bashful nor positively mad. I am, first and foremost, something else, as I shall explain, without much hope you'll believe me. How often I've whispered to my dream of you: 'Do your duty as a useless amphora; fulfil your calling as a mere vessel.'

What nostalgia I felt for the idea I wanted to have of you when I learned, one day, that you were married! What a tragic day in my life that was! I wasn't jealous of your husband. It had never even occurred to me to wonder if you had one. I simply felt nostalgia for my idea of you. Were I to learn the absurd fact that a woman in a painting – yes, a painting – was married, I would feel just as sorry.

Possess you? I don't know how that might be done. And even if I had the human stain of knowing how, what a disgrace I would be to myself, what a flagrant insult to my own greatness were I even to think of putting myself on a par with your husband!

Possess you? One evening when you happen to be alone on a dark street, an attacker can subdue and possess you. He can even fertilize you, leaving behind a trace of himself in your womb. If possessing you means to possess your body, what good is that?

The attacker doesn't possess your soul? But how is a soul possessed? And is there a lover clever enough to be able to possess your 'soul' . . . . . ? I leave the job to your husband. Or do you expect me to stoop to his level?

How many hours I've spent in secret company with my idea of you! How much we've loved each other in my dreams! But I swear that even there I've never dreamed of possessing you. I'm a courteous and chaste man, even in my dreams. I have respect for the mere idea of a beautiful woman.

◆

I wouldn't know how to make my soul interested in having my body possess yours. The very idea makes me trip in myself over unseen obstacles, and I get all tangled up in obscure inner webs. Imagine what would happen to me if I really wanted to possess you!

I would, I repeat, be incapable of trying to do it. I can't even make myself dream of doing it.

These, Madam, are the words I have to write in response to your involuntarily interrogative glance. It is in this book that you'll first read this letter to you. If you don't realize it's for you, it won't matter. I write to entertain myself more than to tell you anything. Only business letters are addressed to other people. The rest of one's letters, at least for a superior soul, should be exclusively from and to oneself.

I have nothing else to say to you. Be assured that I esteem you as much as I can. I should be pleased if you sometimes think of me.

A Letter (II)

Ah, if only you understood your duty to be merely a dreamer's dream. To be nothing but the censer in the cathedral of reveries. To trace your gestures like dreams, like mere windows opening on to new landscapes in your soul. To model your body so perfectly after dreams that no one could look at you without thinking of something else, since you would call to mind everything in the world but you, and to see you would be to hear music and to sleepwalk across vast landscapes with stagnant ponds, through hazy and quiet forests lost in the depths of ages past, where other invisible couples experience feelings we don't have.

The only thing I'd ever want you for is to not have you. If I were dreaming and you appeared, I'd want to be able to imagine I was still dreaming, perhaps without even seeing you, though perhaps noticing that the moonlight had filled the stagnant ponds with □ and that echoes of songs were suddenly rippling through the great inexplicit forest, lost in impossible ages.

My vision of you would be the bed where my soul would lie down and sleep, like a sick child, to dream once more of other skies. If you could talk? Yes, but only if hearing you wouldn't be hearing you but seeing great bridges joining the two dark shores of a moonlit river leading to the ancient sea where the caravels are forever ours.

You smile? I hadn't realized, but the stars were coursing my inner skies. You call me in my sleep. I hadn't noticed, but from that far-flung boat whose dreamed sail was cutting the moonlight, I can see distant coasts.

Lucid Diary

My life: a tragedy booed off stage by the gods,* never getting beyond the first act.

Friends: not one. Just a few acquaintances who imagine they feel something for me and who might be sorry if a train ran over me and the funeral was on a rainy day.

The logical reward of my detachment from life is the incapacity I've created in others to feel anything for me. There's an aureole of indifference, an icy halo, that surrounds me and repels others. I still haven't succeeded in not suffering from my solitude. It's hard to achieve that distinction of spirit whereby isolation becomes a repose without anguish.

I put no faith in the friendship I was shown, and I wouldn't have put any in love had I been shown love, which wouldn't even have been possible. Although I never harboured illusions about those who claimed to be my friends, I inevitably managed to feel disillusioned with them – such is my complex and subtle destiny of suffering.

I never doubted that everyone would let me down, and I was always dumbfounded when they did. When the thing I was expecting happened, it always hit me like something unexpected.

Having never discovered qualities in myself that might attract someone else, I could never believe that anyone felt attracted to me. This opinion of myself would be stupidly modest, if facts on facts – those unexpected facts I expected – didn't always confirm it.

I can't even imagine receiving affection out of pity, for although physically ungainly and unappealing, I'm not organically malformed enough to enter the sphere of those who deserve the world's pity, nor do I have the winsomeness that attracts pity even when it's not clearly deserved; and what in me deserves pity can't have it, for there is no pity for the lame in spirit. So I fell into the centre of gravity of the world's disdain, in which I tend towards the fellow feeling of nobody.

My entire life has been a struggle to adapt to this circumstance without being overwhelmed by its cruelty and humiliation.

It takes a certain intellectual courage for a man to frankly recognize that he's nothing more than a human tatter, an abortion that survived, a madman not mad enough to be committed; and once he recognizes this, it takes even more moral courage to devise a way of adapting to his destiny, to accept without protest and without resignation, without any gesture or hint of a gesture, the organic curse imposed on him by Nature. To want not to suffer from this is to want too much, for it's beyond human capacity to accept what's obviously bad as if it were something good; and if we accept it as the bad thing it is, then we can't help but suffer.

To conceive of myself from the outside was my ruin – the ruin of my happiness. I saw myself as others see me, and I despised myself – not because I had character traits that made me worthy of contempt, but because I saw myself through the eyes of others, and felt the contempt they feel towards me. I experienced the humiliation of knowing myself. Since there's nothing noble about this calvary, and no resurrection three days later, I couldn't help but suffer from its disgrace.

I realized that nobody could love me unless he were completely lacking in aesthetic sensibility, in which case I would then despise him; and even a fond feeling towards me couldn't be any more than a whim of someone's basic indifference.

To see clearly into ourselves and into how others see us! To stare into the face of that truth! And in the end the cry of Christ on Calvary, when he stared into the face of *his* truth: 'My God, my God, why have you forsaken me?'

The Major

There's nothing that so intimately reveals and so perfectly conveys the substance of my innate misfortune as the type of daydream I most cherish, the personal balsam I most often choose to allay the anxiety I feel for existing. The essence of what I desire is simply this: to sleep away life. I love life too much to want it to be over; I love not living too much to have an active craving for life.

That's why, of all my dreams, the one I'm about to write down is my favourite. Sometimes at night, when the house is still because the landlords have gone out or fallen silent, I close my window and its heavy shutters; wearing an old suit, I sink down in my easy chair, and I slide into this dream in which I'm a retired major in a small-town hotel, hanging on after dinner in the company of several other guests who are more sober than I – the lingering major, sitting there for no reason.

I imagine myself born that way. I'm not interested in the boyhood of the retired major, nor in the military ranks through which he ascended to arrive at the place I yearn for. Independent of Time and of Life, the major I imagine myself to be doesn't have any kind of past life, nor does he or did he ever have relatives; he exists externally in the life he lives at the small-town hotel, already weary of the jokes and the talk of the other guests who linger there with him.

Maxims

§ To have sure and definite opinions, instincts, passions, and a dependable, recognizable character – all of this leads to the horror of transforming our soul into a fact, into a material and external thing. To live in a sweet, fluid state of ignorance about things and about oneself is the only lifestyle that suits a wise man and makes him warm.

§ To be adept at constantly standing between ourselves and external things is the highest degree of wisdom and prudence.

§ Our personality should be inscrutable, even to ourselves. That's why we should always dream, making sure that we're included in our dreams so that we won't be able to have opinions about ourselves.

And we should especially protect our personality against being invaded by others. All outside interest in us is a flagrant disrespect. What saves the banal greeting 'How are you?' from being an inexcusable vulgarity is the fact that it's usually completely empty and insincere.

§ To love is to tire of being alone; it is therefore a cowardice, a betrayal of ourselves. (It's exceedingly important that we not love.)

§ To give good advice is to disdain the faculty of erring that God gave to others. Not only that, we should be glad that other people don't act like us. It makes sense only to *ask* for advice from others, so that we can be sure – by doing just the opposite – that we are totally ourselves, in complete disagreement with all Otherness.

§ The only advantage of studying is to take delight in all the things that other people haven't said.

§ Art is an isolation. Every artist should seek to isolate others, to fill their souls with a desire to be alone. The supreme triumph for the artist who writes is when his readers, on reading his works, prefer just to have them and not read them. This doesn't necessarily happen to celebrated writers, but it is the greatest tribute . . . . .

§ To be lucid is to be out of sorts with oneself. The right state of mind for looking inside ourselves is that □ of someone looking at nerves and indecisions.

§ The only intellectual attitude worthy of a superior creature is that of a calm and cold compassion for everything that isn't himself. Not that this attitude has a grain of legitimacy or truth, but it's so enviable that he must adopt it.

Milky Way

. . . with twisting phrases that have a poisonous spirituality. . .

. . . rituals clothed in tattered purples, mysterious ceremonial rites from the time of no one*. . .

. . . sequestered sensations felt in a body that is not our physical body and yet is physical in its own way, with subtleties that fall between the complex and the simple. . .

. . . lakes where a pellucid hint of muted gold hovers, hazily divested of ever having been materialized, and no doubt through tortuous refinements, a lily in sheer white hands. . .

. . . pacts between torpor and anguish – dull green-black and looking terribly weary between their sentries of tedium. . .

. . . nacre of useless consequences, alabaster of many macerations – the welcome distraction of violet gold sunsets with fringes, but no boats leading to better shores, nor bridges to better twilights. . .

. . . nor even to the edge of the idea of pools, lots of pools, in the distance amid poplar trees or perhaps cypresses, depending on the syllables employed by the wistful moment to utter their name. . .

. . . hence windows opening on to wharfs, a continual pounding of waves against docks, a mad and enraptured retinue like a confusion of opals in which amaranths and terebinths write with lucid insomnias on the dark stone walls of being able to hear. . .

. . . strands of fine silver, ties made from the thread of unravelled robes, futile feelings beneath linden trees, ancient couples on quiet paths lined by hedges, sudden fans, vague gestures, and no doubt better gardens awaiting the placid weariness of nothing but paths and promenades. . .

. . . bowers, trees in quincunxes, artificial grottoes, sculpted flower beds, fountains, all the art that survives from the dead masters whose dissatisfaction duelled with the visible, and they authored whole processions of things made for dreams along the narrow streets of the ancient villages of sensations. . .

. . . melodies that resound against the marble of distant palaces, reminiscences that place their hands on ours, sunsets in fateful skies like fortuitous glances of uncertainty, giving way to starlit nights over silently decaying empires. . .

———

To reduce sensation to a science, to make psychological analysis into a microscopically precise method – that's the goal that occupies, like a steady thirst, the hub of my life's will.

It's between my sensations and my consciousness of them that all of my life's great tragedies occur. It's there in that murky, indefinite region of nothing but woods and every kind of water sound, where not even the commotion of our wars is felt, that my true being – which I try in vain to see clearly – takes place.

I lay down my life. (My sensations are a long-drawn-out epitaph* on top of my dead life.) I subsist in death and dusk. The most I can sculpt is my tomb of inner beauty.

The gates of my seclusion open on to parks of infinity, but no one passes through them, not even in my dreams – and yet they are open eternally on to the useless, they are eternally of iron opening on to the unreal. . .

I pluck the petals of private glories in the gardens of my inner splendours, and between dreamed hedges my feet loudly tread the paths that lead to the Confused.

I've pitched my Empires in the Confused, at the edge of silences, in the tawny war that will do away with the Exact.

———

The man of science realizes that the only reality for him is his own self, and that the only real world is the world as his sensations give it to him. That's why, instead of following the fallacious path of adapting his sensations to other people's, he uses objective science to try to achieve a perfect knowledge of his world and his personality. There's nothing more objective than his dreams, and nothing more infallibly his than his self-awareness. Around these two realities he refines his science. It's very different from the one practised by the old scientists, who, rather than studying the laws of their own personality and the organization of their dreams, sought the laws of the 'outside' and the organization of what they called 'Nature'.

◆

What's primordial in me are my habit of dreaming and my knack for dreaming. The circumstances of my life, solitary and quiet since my childhood, and perhaps forces that go further back, moulding me to their sinister specifications through the obscure action of heredity, have made my mind an endless stream of daydreams. Everything I am comes down to this, and even what seems farthest in me from the dreamer belongs unequivocally to the soul of one who only dreams, with his soul as elevated as it can be.

For the sake of my own pleasure in self-analysis, I would like to express in words, as far as I'm able, the mental processes which in me are really just one process – that of a life devoted to dreaming, of a soul that knows only how to dream.

Seeing myself from the outside (as I almost always do), I'm unfit for action, flustered when I have to take a step or make a move, tongue-tied when I have to talk to someone, lacking the inner lucidity needed to enjoy things that require mental effort, and without the physical stamina to entertain myself through some merely mechanical labour.

It's only natural that I'm this way. A dreamer is expected to be this way. All reality disconcerts me. Other people's speech throws me into a state of great anguish. The reality of other souls always astounds me. The vast network of unconscious behaviours responsible for all the action I see strikes me as an absurd illusion, without any plausible coherence, nothing.

But should someone imagine that I'm ignorant of the workings of other people's psychology, that I'm not clearly aware of their motives and private thoughts, then he'll be quite mistaken about what I am.

For I'm not just a dreamer, I'm exclusively a dreamer. My sole habit – to dream – has endowed me with an extraordinarily keen inner eyesight. I not only see the figures and stage sets of my dreams with astounding and startling clarity, I see just as clearly my abstract ideas, my human feelings (what's left of them), my secret urges and my psychological attitudes towards myself. I even see, inside myself, my own abstract ideas; I see them in an internal space, with my veritable inner eyesight. And thus their meanders are visible to me in every detail.

I therefore know myself completely and, knowing myself completely, I know all of humanity completely. There is no base impulse or noble intention that hasn't been a flash in my soul, and I know the tell-tale gestures of each one. Beneath the masks of goodness or indifference that wicked thoughts wear, even within us, I recognize them for what they are by their gestures. I know what strives, inside us, to delude us. And thus I know most people better than they know themselves. I often probe them at some length, for in that way I make them mine. I conquer every psyche I fathom, because for me to dream is to possess. And so it's only natural that I, dreamer that I am, should be the analyst I profess to be.

That's why plays count among the few things I occasionally enjoy reading. Plays are performed in me every day, and I know exactly how souls are laid out flat, in a Mercator projection. But this doesn't really amuse me much, because playwrights are always making the same trite and glaring errors. No play ever satisfied me. Knowing human psychology with a lightning precision that probes every cranny with a single glance, I find the crude analysis and construction of playwrights offensive, and the little that I read in this genre annoys me like a blot of ink on a handwritten page.

Things are the raw material of my dreams; that's why I apply a distractedly hyperattentive attention to certain details of the Outside.

To give contours and relief to my dreams, I have to understand how life's characters and reality's landscapes appear to us with contours and relief. Because the dreamer's eyesight is not like the eyesight we use to see actual things. In dreams we do not, as in reality, focus equally on the important and unimportant aspects of an object. The dreamer sees only what's important. An object's true reality is only a portion of what it is; the rest is the heavy tribute it pays to physical matter for the right to exist in space. In like manner, certain phenomena that are palpably real in dreams have no reality in space. A real sunset is imponderable and transitory. A dreamed sunset is fixed and eternal. Those who can write are those who know how to see their dreams with sharp clarity (and do so) and to see life as they see dreams, to see life immaterially, taking pictures of it with reverie's camera, which is insensible to the rays of what's heavy, useful and circumscribed, such things yielding nothing but a black blur on the photographic plate of the soul.

This attitude, engrafted into me from so much dreaming, makes me always see the dream side of reality. My eyesight suppresses those aspects of an object that my dreams can't use. And so I always live in dreams, even when I live in life. To look at a sunset inside me or at a sunset on the Outside is all the same to me, for I see them in the same way, my eyesight registering the same thing in both cases.

It will therefore seem to many that I have a distorted view of myself. In a certain way it is distorted. But I dream myself and choose those parts of me that are dreamable, constructing and reconstructing myself in every way possible until what I am and what I am not conform to my ideal. Sometimes the best way to see an object is to delete it, because it subsists in a way I can't quite explain, consisting of the substance of its negation and deletion; this is what I do with vast areas of my real-life being, which, after they're deleted from my picture of myself, transfigure my true being, the one that's real for me.

How do I keep from deceiving myself in these processes of illusion applied to my own person? Well, the process that thrusts a certain aspect of the world or the figure of a dream into a more-than-real reality also thrusts emotions and thoughts into the more-than-real sphere, stripping them of all the false trappings (and only rarely are they not false) of nobility and purity. It should be noted that my objectivity couldn't be more absolute, for I create each object absolute, with absolute qualities in its concrete form. I haven't really fled from life, in the sense of seeking a softer bed for my soul; I've merely changed lives, finding in my dreams the same objectivity that I found in life. My dreams – I discuss this in another passage – take shape independently of my will, and they frequently shock and offend me. The things I discover in myself very often make me feel dismayed, ashamed (perhaps due to some vestige of humanity in me – what is shame?), and alarmed.

In me ceaseless daydreaming has replaced attention. Over everything I see, including things seen in dreams, I've taken to superimposing other dreams I have inside me. I'm already sufficiently inattentive to be adept at what I've dubbed 'the dream view' of things. Even so, since this inattentiveness was motivated by a perpetual daydreaming and by a preoccupation (likewise not overly attentive) with the course of my dreams, I superimpose what I dream on the dreams I see in the real world around me, intersecting reality already stripped of its physical matter with an absolute immateriality.

This explains the ability I've acquired to focus on various ideas at the same time, to observe certain things while at the same time dreaming other, very different things, to dream simultaneously of a real sunset over the real Tagus River and a dreamed morning on an inner Pacific Ocean; and the two dreamed things crisscross without blending, without anything getting mixed up besides the different emotional states induced by each. It's as if I saw a number of people walking down a street and felt all their souls inside me (which could occur only in a unity of feeling) at the same time that I saw their various bodies (these I could see only separately) crossing paths on the street full of legs in motion.

Millimetres

(the sensation of slight things)

The present is ancient, because everything from the past was in the present when it existed, and so I have an antique dealer's fondness for things precisely because they belong to the present, and I have the wrath of an outrivalled collector for anyone who tries to replace my mistaken notions about things with plausible and even provable, scientifically based arguments.

The various points that a butterfly successively occupies in space are various things which, to my astonished eyes, remain visible in space. My recollections are so intense that . . . . .

But it is only the subtlest sensations of the slightest things that I live intensely. Perhaps this is due to my love of futility. Or maybe it's because of my concern for detail. But I'm inclined to believe – I can't say I know, for these are things I never bother to analyse – that it's because slight things, having absolutely no social or practical importance, are for that very reason absolutely free of sordid associations with reality. Slight things smack to me of unreality. The useless is beautiful because it's less real than the useful, which continues and extends, whereas the marvellously futile and the gloriously minuscule stay where and as they are, living freely and independently. The useless and the futile open up humbly aesthetic interludes in our real lives. What dreams and fond delights are stirred in my soul by the puny existence of a pin in a ribbon! What a pity for those who don't realize how important this is!

Among the sensations that inwardly torture us to the point of becoming pleasurable, the disquiet provoked by the world's mystery is one of the most common and complex. And that mystery is never more evident than when we contemplate tiny things, which don't move and are therefore perfectly translucent, allowing their mystery to show through. It's harder to feel mystery when contemplating a battle (and yet to meditate on the absurdity of there being people and societies and conflicts between them is what can most unfurl in our minds the flag of triumph over mystery) than when contemplating a small stone on the road which, since it brings to mind no idea beyond that of its existence, will naturally and necessarily lead us – if we keep thinking about it – to consider the mystery of its existence.

Blessed be instants and millimetres and the shadows of tiny things, which are even more humble than the things themselves! Instants . . . . . Millimetres – how astonished I am by their audacity to exist side by side and so close together on a tape measure. Sometimes these things make me suffer or rejoice, and then I feel a kind of gut pride.

I'm an ultrasensitive photographic plate. All details are engraved in me out of all proportion to any possible whole. The plate fills up with nothing but me. The outer world that I see is pure sensation. I never forget that I feel.

Our Lady of Silence

Sometimes, when I feel discouraged and depressed, even my ability to dream loses its leaves and shrivels, and the only kind of dreaming I can have is to muse on my dreams, and so I leaf through them, like a book one leafs through over and over, finding nothing but inevitable words. And then I ask myself who you are, you this figure who traverses all my languid visions of unknown landscapes and ancient interiors and splendid pageants of silence. In all of my dreams you appear, in dream form, or you accompany me as a false reality. With you I visit regions that are perhaps dreams of yours, lands that are perhaps your bodies of absence and inhumanity, your essential body dissolved into the shape of a tranquil plain and a stark hill on the grounds of some secret place. Perhaps I have no dream but you. Perhaps it is in your eyes, when my face leans into yours, that I read these impossible landscapes, these unreal tediums, these feelings that inhabit the shadows of my weariness and the caves of my disquiet. Perhaps the landscapes of my dreams are my way of not dreaming about you. I don't know who you are, but do I know for certain who I am? Do I really know what it means to dream, such that I can know what it means to call you my dream? How do I know that you're not a part of me, perhaps the real and essential part? And how do I know it's not I who am the dream and you the reality, I who am your dream instead of you being mine?

What sort of life do you have? By what manner of seeing do I see you? Your profile? It's never the same, yet it never changes. And I say this because I know it, without knowing that I know it. Your body? It's the same whether naked or dressed, and in the same position whether seated or standing or lying down. What is the meaning of this that means nothing?

◆

My life is so sad, and I don't even think of weeping over it; my days are so false, and I don't even dream of trying to change them.

How can I possibly not dream of you? Lady of the Passing Hours, Madonna of stagnant waters and rotting seaweed, Tutelary Goddess of the sprawling deserts and the black landscapes of barren cliffs – deliver me from my youth.

Consoler of the disconsolate, Tears of those who never weep, Hour that never strikes – deliver me from joy and happiness.

Opium of all silences, unplucked Lyre, Stained-Glass Window of distance and exile – make me hated by men and scorned by women.

Cymbal of Extreme Unction, Caress that doesn't touch, Dove lying dead in the shade, Oil of hours spent dreaming – deliver me from religion, for it is sweet, and from unbelief, for it is strong.

Lily drooping in the afternoon, Keepsake Box of wilted roses. Silence between prayers – fill me with loathing for being alive, with resentment for being healthy, and with contempt for my youth.

Make me useless and sterile, O Shelter of all hazy dreams; make me pure for no reason, and indifferently false, O Running Water of Sad Experience; let my mouth be a frozen landscape, my eyes two dead ponds, and my gestures the slow withering of decrepit trees, O Litany of Disquiet, O Royal Mass of Weariness, O Corolla, O Holy Fluid, O Ascension!

What a pity I must pray to you as to a woman and cannot love you □ as one loves a man, nor feast my dream's eyes on you as the Dawn-in-Reverse of the unreal sex of those angels who never entered heaven!

◆

In my prayer to you I offer my love, because my love is itself a prayer, but I don't think of you as my beloved nor hold you up before me as a saint.

May your acts be the statue of renunciation, your gestures the pedestal of indifference, and your words the stained-glass windows of denial.

◆

Splendour of nothing, name from the abyss, peace from the Beyond. . .

Eternal virgin, who existed before the gods, before the gods' fathers, and before the fathers of the gods' fathers, barren Virgin of all the worlds, sterile Virgin of all souls. . .

To you we lift up all days and all beings; the stars are votive offerings in your temple; and the weariness of the gods returns to your breast like the bird to the nest it built without knowing how.

From the height of anguish may we see the day come into view! And if we see no day come, then let that be the day that comes into view!

Shine, absence of sun! Glow, fading moon!. . .

Only you, unshining sun, light up the caves, for the caves are your daughters. Only you, unreal moon, give □ to the caverns, for the caverns . . . . .

◆

Your sex is that of dreamed forms, the sterile sex of □ figures. Now a vague profile, now a mere stance, and sometimes just a languid gesture – you are moments and stances which, spiritualized, become mine.

My dreaming of you implies no fascination with your sex, with what lies beneath your ethereal robe, O Madonna of inner silences. Your breasts are not the kind one would imagine kissing. Your body is all soulish flesh, and yet it is body, not soul. The substance of your flesh isn't spiritual, it's spirituality. You are the woman before the Fall, still a sculpture made from that clay that □ paradise.

My horror of real women endowed with sex is the road that brought me to you. How can one love the women of earth, who must endure the shifting weight of a man to be □? How can one's love not wither in the foreglimpse of the pleasure that serves [. . .] sex? Who can honour the Wife without being assaulted by the thought that she's a woman who copulates? Who can help but despise having a mother by whom he was so vulvally, loathsomely born?* How can we not despise ourselves when we think of the carnal origin of our soul, of that restless, bodily □ that brings our flesh into the world? And however lovely that flesh may be, it's ugly by virtue of its origin, loathsome because it was born.

False, real-life idealists dedicate poems to the Wife and kneel to the idea of the Mother. . . Their idealism is a cloak that disguises, not a dream that creates.

You alone are pure, Lady of Dreams, whom I can conceive as a lover without conceiving any stain, for you are unreal. I can conceive of you as a mother and adore you, for you were never defiled by the horror of being fertilized or the horror of giving birth.

How not adore you when you alone are adorable? How not love you when you alone are worthy of love?

Perhaps by dreaming you I create you, real in some other reality; perhaps it is there that you are mine, in a different, pure world where we love each other without tangible bodies, with another kind of embrace and other, ideal forms of possessing. Perhaps I didn't create you; perhaps you already existed and I merely saw you with a different kind of vision – pure and inner – in another, perfect world. Perhaps my dreaming of you was simply my finding you, and my loving you merely my thinking of you. Perhaps my contempt for the flesh and my loathing of love were the obscure desire with which, unaware of your existence, I waited for you; perhaps they were my uncertain hope by which, without knowing you, I already loved you.

It could even be that I already loved you in some vague wherever, and that my nostalgia for that love makes everything in my present life a tedium. Perhaps you are just my nostalgia for something, an embodiment of some absence, the presence of some Distance, female for reasons that don't have to do with being a female.

I can think of you as both a virgin and a mother, for you are not of this world. The child you hold in your arms was never any younger that you could have defiled him by carrying him in your womb. You were never other than who you are, so how could you not be a virgin? I can both love and adore you, for my love doesn't possess you and my adoration doesn't put you at a distance.

Be the Eternal Day and let my sunsets be made of your sun's rays, inseparable from you.

Be the Invisible Twilight, with my disquiet and my yearnings as the shades of your indecision, the colours of your uncertainty.

Be the Absolute Night, the Sole Night, in which I totally lose and forget myself, with my dreams glowing as stars on your body of distance and negation. . .

Let me be the folds of your robe, the jewels of your tiara, and the strange gold in the rings on your fingers.

Let me be ashes from your fireplace, because so what if I'm dust? Or a window in your room, because so what if I'm mere space? Or an □ hour in your clepsydra, because so what if I pass on but remain yours, if I die but live on as yours, if I lose you but by losing you find you?

Mistress of absurdities, Votary of nonsense phrases,* may your silence cradle me and your □ lull me. May your pure being caress and soothe and comfort me, O heraldic Lady from the Beyond, O Empress of Absence, Virgin Mother of all silences, Hearthstone of cold souls, Guardian Angel of the forlorn, O unreal and human Landscape of sad, eternal Perfection.

◆

You aren't a woman. Not even within me do you evoke anything that feels feminine to me. It's only when I speak of you that the words call you female and the phrases outline a woman's profile. For I can't help but speak of you with tenderness and dreamy affection, and words find a voice for this only by addressing you as a woman.

But you, in your vague substance, are nothing. You have no reality, not even a reality that belongs only to you. Strictly speaking, I don't see you or even feel you. You're like a feeling whose object is its own self, contained entirely in the heart of its being. You're always the landscape that I was just about to lay eyes on, the hem of the robe that I just missed seeing, lost in an eternal Now beyond the bend in the road. Your profile is your nothingness, and the contour of your unreal body tears apart, into separate pearls, the necklace of the very idea of contour. You've already passed, you've already gone, and I've already loved you – this is what I feel when I feel your presence.

You occupy the blanks in my thoughts and the gaps in my sensations, which is why I neither think of you nor feel you. But my thoughts are vaulted with the feeling of you, and my feelings are gothic with your lofty evocation.

Moon of lost memories over the black, vividly empty landscape of my imperfection's self-awareness. My being feels you vaguely, as if it were one of your belts that feels you. I lean over your white face that flutters in the nocturnal waters of my disquiet, knowing that you are the moon in my sky that causes it, or a strange underwater moon that somehow feigns it.

If only someone could create New Eyes through which to see you, New Thoughts and Feelings by which to think and feel you!

When I go to touch your robe, my expressions grow weary from the effort to stretch out their hands, and a stiff, painful fatigue freezes in my words. And so the flight of a bird circles around what I wished to say about you, seeming to come nearer but never arriving, for the substance of my phrases cannot imitate the substance of your footsteps' soft thudding, or of your glance's slow sweeping, or of the sad, empty colour traced by the gestures you never made.

◆

And should I speak with someone far away, and should you who today are a cloud of the possible fall tomorrow as rain of reality over the earth, don't ever forget your divine origin as my dream. Let whatever you are in real life serve as the dream of a loner, never as a lover's refuge. Do your duty as a mere vessel. Fulfil your calling as a useless amphora. Let no one ever say of you what the river's soul might say of its banks: that they exist to confine it. It were better not to flow in life, better to let the dream dry up.

May your essence consist in being superfluous, and may your life be the art of gazing at your life, of being gazed at, never identical. Don't ever be anything more.

Today you are but a profile, created out of this book, a moment made incarnate and separated from other moments. If I were sure that's what you are, I would found a religion on the dream of loving you.

You're what everything is lacking. You're what's missing in each thing that would allow us to love it for ever. Lost key to the doors of the Temple, secret pathway to the Palace, distant Island forever hidden from view by the fog. . .

Pedro's Pastoral

I don't know where or when I saw you. I don't know if it was in a picture or in the actual countryside, with real grass and trees growing around your body; but perhaps it was in a picture, so idyllic and legible is my memory of you. And although I don't know when this happened or if it really did happen (for it may be that I didn't even see you in a picture), I know with all my mind's feeling that it was the most peaceful moment of my life.

You calmly came down the wide stretch of road, a graceful herdswoman with a huge, gentle ox. I seem to remember seeing you from afar, and you came towards me and passed on by. You didn't seem to notice me. You walked slowly and unmindful of the large ox. Your gaze had forgotten all memory, and it revealed a vast clearing in your inner life: your consciousness of self had abandoned you. In that moment you were nothing more than a . . . . .

Seeing you, I remembered that cities change but the fields are eternal. If we call rocks and mountains 'biblical', it's because they're surely just like the ones from biblical times.

It's in the fleeting image of your anonymous figure that I place all that the country evokes for me, and all the peace that I've never known fills my soul when I think of you. You walked with a light swing, a vague swaying, and a bird alighted* on each of your gestures; invisible vines wound around the □ of your chest. Your silence – the day was sinking down, and jingling flocks bleated their weariness on the greying slopes – your silence was the song of the last shepherd, who was left out of an eclogue that Virgil never wrote and thus remained forever unsung, forever a wandering silhouette in the fields. It's possible you were smiling – to yourself, to your soul, seeing yourself smile in your mind – but your lips were as still as the outline of the mountains, and the gesture (which I don't remember) of your rustic hands was garlanded with flowers from the fields.

Yes, it was in a picture that I saw you. But where did I get this idea that I saw you approach and pass by me while I just kept going, never once turning around, since I could still see you, then and always? Time suddenly stops to let you pass, and I get you all wrong when I try to put you into life, or into its semblance.

PERISTYLE

It was in the silence of my disquiet, at the hour of day when the landscape is a halo of Life and dreaming is mere dreaming, my love, that I raised up this strange book like the open doors of an abandoned house.*

I gathered every flower's soul to write it, and from the fleeting moments of every song of every bird I wove eternity and stagnation. A steady weaver □, I sat at the window of my life and forgot that I lived there and existed, shrouding my tedium in the chaste linens I wove for the altars of my silence . . . . .

And I offer you this book because I know it is beautiful and useless. It teaches nothing, inspires no faith, and stirs no feeling. A mere stream that flows towards an abyss of ashes scattered by the wind, neither helping nor harming the soil . . . . . I put my whole soul into making it, but without thinking about it as I made it, for I thought only of me, who am sad, and of you, who aren't anyone.

And because this book is absurd, I love it; because it is useless, I want to give it away; and because it serves no purpose to want to give it to you, I give it to you. . .

Pray for me by reading it, bless me by loving it, and forget it as today's sun forgets yesterday's, as I forget the women from my dreams that I was never very good at dreaming. . .

Tower of Silence of my yearnings, may this book be the moonlight that transformed you on the night of the Ancient Mystery!

River of painful Imperfection, may this book be the boat that drifts with your waters until it ends in the dreamed sea.

Landscape of Estrangement and Exile, may this book be yours like your very Hour, and not be limited by you or by the Hour of false purples.

◆

Eternal rivers flow beneath the window of my silence. I never stop seeing the far shore, and I don't know why I don't dream of being there, different and happy. Perhaps because you alone console, you alone lull, and you alone anoint and officiate.

What white Mass do you interrupt to give me the blessing of showing me you exist? At what whirling moment of the dance do you halt, and Time with you, making your sudden halt into a bridge to my soul, and your smile into the royal purple of my splendour?

Swan of rhythmic disquiet, lyre of immortal hours, faint harp of mythic sorrows – you are both the Awaited and the Departed, the one who soothes and also wounds, who gilds joys with sadness and crowns griefs with roses.

What God created you, what God who must be hated by the God who created the world?

You don't know, you don't know you don't know, you don't want to know or not know. You've stripped all purpose from your life, you've haloed your appearing with unreality, you've clothed yourself with perfection and intangibility so that the Hours won't kiss you, nor the Days smile at you, nor the Nights come and place the moon, like a lily, in your hands.

Shower me, my love, with the petals of better roses, of lovelier lilies, of □ chrysanthemums scented with the melody of their name.

And I will die my life in you,* O Virgin for whom no arms are waiting, whom no kisses seek, and whom no thought deflowers.

Foyer of all hopes, Threshold of all desires, Window to all dreams . . . . .

Belvedere that looks out on to all landscapes of nocturnal forests with far-off rivers shimmering in the bright moonlight. . .

Poems and prose that were never meant to be written, just dreamed. . .

◆

I know full well that you don't exist, but do I know for certain that I exist? Do I, who make you exist in me, have more real life than you, than this dead life* that lives you?

Flame transformed into halo, absent presence, rhythmic and female silence, twilight of wispy flesh, goblet that was left out of the banquet, stained-glass window of some painter-dream from the Middle Ages of another Earth.

Chastely elegant chalice and host, abandoned altar of a still living saint, corolla of a dreamed lily in a garden no one has ever entered. . .

You're the only form that never brings tedium, for you always change according to our feelings, kissing our joy as well as lulling our pain and our weariness. You're the opium that soothes, the sleep that refreshes, and the death that crosses and joins our hands.

Angel □, of what substance does your winged matter consist? What life holds you to what earth – you who are the never rising flight, a stagnant ascension, a gesture of rapture and of rest?

◆

My dreaming of you will be my strength, and when my sentences tell your Beauty they will have melodies of form, curves of stanzas, and the sudden splendours of immortal verses.

Let us create, O Mine Alone, an art like no other, founded on the wonder of you existing and on my seeing you exist.

May I be able to extract the soul of new verses from the useless amphora that's your body! And in your slow and quiet, wave-like rhythm, may my trembling fingers find the perfidious lines of a prose still virgin to human ears!

May your fading, melodious smile be for me a symbol – the visible emblem of the whole world's choked sob when it realizes it is error and imperfection.

May your harpist's hands pull my eyelids shut when I die from having given my life to making you. And you who are nobody will be forever, O Supreme One, the cherished art of the gods who never were, and the sterile, virgin mother of the gods who will never be.

Random Diary

Every day I'm mistreated by Matter. My sensibility is a wind-whipped flame.

Walking down a street I see, in those who pass by me, not the facial expressions that they really have but the expressions that they would have if they knew what I'm like and the kind of life I lead, if my face and my gestures betrayed the shy and ridiculous abnormality of my soul. In eyes that don't even look at me I suspect there are smirks (which I consider only natural) directed at the awkward exception I embody in a world of people who know how to act and to enjoy life; and the passing physiognomies, informed by an awareness that I myself have interposed and superimposed, seem to snicker out loud at my life's timid gesticulations. Reflecting on all this, I try to convince myself that the smirks and mild reproach I feel come from me, and me alone, but once the image of me looking ridiculous has been objectified in others, I can no longer say it's just mine. I suddenly feel myself suffocating and vacillating in a hothouse of mockery and hostility. All point their finger at me from the depths of their souls. All who pass by pelt me with their mirthful and contemptuous taunts. I walk among fiendish phantoms that my sick imagination has invented and placed in real people. Everything slaps me in the face and makes fun of me. And sometimes in the middle of the street – where in fact no one even notices me – I suddenly stop and look around me, as if searching for a new dimension, a door leading to the inside of space, to the other side of space, where I could run away from my awareness of other people, from my overly objectified intuition of the reality that belongs to other living souls.

Does this habit of placing myself in the souls of others really lead me to see myself as others see me or would see me, if they took notice of me? Yes. And as soon as I realize how they would feel about me if they knew me, it's as if they really did feel that way, as if right at that moment they were feeling exactly that, and expressing what they feel. To associate with others is sheer torture for me. And the others are in me. I'm forced to associate with them even when they're nowhere near. All alone, I'm surrounded by multitudes. There's no escape possible, unless I were to escape from myself.

O magnificent hills at twilight, O narrowish streets in the moonlight, if only I had your □ unconsciousness, your spirituality that's nothing but Matter, with no inner dimension, no sensibility, and no place for feelings, thoughts, or disquiet of the spirit! Trees so completely and only trees, with your greenness so pleasant to look at, so foreign to my troubles and concerns, so soothing to my anxieties precisely because you don't have eyes with which to see them nor a soul which, seeing through those eyes, might misunderstand and make fun of them! Stones on the road, logs here and there, anonymous dirt of the ground that's everywhere, my sister because your unawareness of my soul is a cosy and peaceful repose... Sunlit or moonlit things of Earth, my mother, so tenderly my mother, who can't even criticize me like my own human mother, for you lack the soul that would instinctively analyse me, nor do you have swift glances which would betray thoughts about me that you'd never even confess to yourself... Vast ocean, my roaring childhood companion that soothes and lulls me, because your voice isn't human and thus can never whisper my weaknesses and shortcomings into human ears... Broad and blue sky so close to the mystery of the angels ....., you do not look at me with deceitful green eyes, and if you hold the Sun against your chest you don't do it to seduce me, nor when you [cover yourself] with stars are you trying to show me that you're superior... Universal peace of Nature, maternal because you don't know me; aloof tranquillity of atoms and systems, so brotherly in your complete ignorance of me... I'd like to pray to your vastness and your calm, as a sign of my gratitude for having you and being able to love you without any doubts or qualms; I'd like to give ears to your inability to hear despite your always hearing us, to give eyes to your sublime blindness with which you always see us, and to be the object of your attentions via these imaginary ears and eyes, to feel the comfort of being noticed by your Nothingness, as if it were a definitive death, far far away, beyond any hope for another life, beyond any God and the possibility of other beings, voluptuously nil, with the spiritual colour of all matter...

The River of Possession

That all of us are different is an axiom of our true nature.* We only look like each other from a distance – to the extent, therefore, that we are not ourselves. That's why life is for the indefinite; the only people who get along well are those who never define themselves, those who are equally nobody.

Each of us is two, and when two people meet, come into contact or join together, it's rare that the four of them can agree. If the man who dreams in the man who acts is so frequently at odds with him, how can he help but be at odds with the man who acts and the man who dreams in the Other?

Each life, because it's life, is a distinct force, and each of us naturally tends towards himself, stopping at other people along the way. If we have enough self-respect to find ourselves interesting . . . . . Every coming together is a conflict. The other is always an obstacle for those who seek. Only those who don't seek are happy, because only those who don't seek find; since they seek nothing, they already have it, and to already have – whatever it may be – is to be happy, just as not to think is the best part of being rich.

Within me I look at you, imagined bride, and we start to clash even before you exist. My habit of dreaming things vividly gives me an accurate notion of reality. Whoever dreams to excess must give reality to his dreams. Whoever gives reality to his dreams must give them the equilibrium of reality. Whoever gives the equilibrium of reality to his dreams will suffer from the reality of dreaming as much as from the reality of life, and from the unreality of his dreams as much as from his feeling that life is unreal.

I'm waiting for you, in a state of reverie, in our bedroom that has two doors; I dream I hear you coming, and in my dream you enter by the door on the right. If, when you actually enter, it's by the door on the left, there will already be a difference between you and my dream. The whole of the human tragedy is summed up in this tiny example of how the people we think about are never the people we think they are.

Love demands identification with something different, which isn't even possible in logic, much less in real life. Love wants to possess. It wants to make into its own that which must remain outside it; otherwise the distinction between what it *is* in itself and what it *makes* into itself will be lost. Love is surrender. The greater the surrender, the greater the love. But total surrender also surrenders its consciousness of the other. The greatest love is therefore death, or forgetting, or renunciation – all forms of love that make love an absurdity.

On the ancient terrace of the seaside palace, we will meditate in silence on the difference between us. I was the prince and you the princess, on the terrace by the sea. Our love was born in our meeting, the way beauty was born when the moon met the waves.

Love wants to possess, but it doesn't know what possession is. If I'm not my own, how can I be yours, or you mine? If I don't possess my own being, how can I possess an extraneous being? If I'm even different from my own identical self, how can I be identical to a completely different self?

Love is a mysticism that wants to be materialized, an impossibility that our dreams always insist must be possible.

I'm talking metaphysics? But all of life is a metaphysics in the darkness, with a vague murmur of the gods and only one way to follow, which is our ignorance of the right way.

The most insidious aspect of my decadence is my love of health and clarity. I've always felt that a handsome body and the carefree rhythm of a youthful stride were more useful in the world than all the dreams that exist in me. It's with a joy of the old in spirit that I sometimes observe, without envy or desire, the casual couples that the afternoon brings together and that walk arm-in-arm towards the unconscious consciousness of youth. I enjoy them as I enjoy a truth, without considering whether it applies to me. If I compare them to myself, I still enjoy them, but as one who enjoys a truth that hurts, the pain of the hurt being compensated by the pride of having understood the gods.

I'm the opposite of the Platonic* symbolists, for whom every being and every event is the shadow and only the shadow of a reality. Everything for me, rather than a point of arrival, is a point of departure. For the occultist everything ends in everything; for me everything begins in everything.

I proceed, as they do, by way of analogy and suggestion, but the small garden that to them suggests the soul's order and beauty, to me suggests merely the larger garden where, far away from humans, this unhappy life perhaps could be happy. Each thing suggests to me not the reality of which it is the shadow, but the reality for which it is the path.

The garden of Estrela,* in late afternoon, suggests to me a park from olden times, in the centuries before the soul became disenchanted.

Self-Examination

One who lives life falsely, in dreams, is still living life. Renunciation is an act. Dreaming is a confession of one's need to live, with real life simply being replaced by unreal life, to compensate for the irrepressible urge to live.

What does all this amount to but the search for happiness? And does anyone search for anything else?

Have constant daydreaming and endless analysis given me anything *essentially* different from what life would have given me?

Withdrawing from people didn't help me find myself, nor . . . . .

This book is a single state of soul, analysed from all sides, investigated in all directions.

Has this attitude at least brought me something new? Not even this consolation is mine. Everything was already said long ago, by Heraclitus and Ecclesiastes: *Life is a child's game in the sand. . . vanity and vexation of spirit. . .* And in that single phrase of poor Job: *My soul is weary of my life.*

I listen to myself dream. I lull myself with the sound of my images. Strange melodies inside me spell out □.

A phrase that resonates with images is worth so many gestures! A metaphor can make up for so many things!

I listen to myself. . . Inside me there are ceremonies, cortèges. . . Spangles in my tedium. . . Masked balls. . . I observe my soul with astonishment. . .

Kaleidoscope of fragmented sequences . . . . .

Splendour of intensely experienced sensations. . . Royal beds in deserted castles, jewels of dead princesses, sea coves seen through castle loopholes. . . Honour and power will doubtless come, and the happiest souls will have cortèges in their exile. . . Sleeping orchestras, □ threads embroidering silks. . .

In Pascal:

In Vigny: In you . . . . .

In Amiel,* so completely in Amiel:. . . *(certain phrases)*. . .

In Verlaine and the symbolists:

I feel so sick inside, and without even a little originality in my sickness... I do what countless others have done before me... I suffer what's old and hackneyed... Why do I even think these things, when so many have already thought and suffered them?...

And yet I have after all introduced something new, although I'm not responsible for it. It came from the Night and glows in me like a star... All of my effort couldn't have produced it or snuffed it out... I'm a bridge between two mysteries, with no idea of how I got built.

THE SENSATIONIST

In this twilight of spiritual disciplines, with beliefs dying out and the old cults gathering dust, our sensations are the only reality we have left. The only scruples we have at this point, and the only science that satisfies, are those of our sensations.

I'm more convinced than ever that inferior adornment is the highest and most enlightened destiny we can confer on our souls. If my life could be lived in tapestries of the spirit, I'd have no depths of despair to bemoan.

I belong to a generation – or rather, to part of a generation – that lost all respect for the past and all belief or hope in the future. And so we live off the present with the hunger and eagerness of those who have no other home. And since it is in our sensations, and particularly in the useless sensations of our dreams, that we find a present which remembers neither past nor future, we smile indulgently at our inner life while yawning with disdain at the quantitative reality of things.

Perhaps we are not all that different from those who, in real life, think only of amusing themselves. But the sun of our egoistic concern is setting, and it's in colours of twilight and contradiction that our hedonism is slowly cooling.

We're convalescents. Most of us are people who never learned an art or a trade, not even the art of enjoying life. Since we're basically averse to prolonged social contact, even the greatest of friends tend to bore us after half an hour; we long to see them only when we think about seeing them, and the best moments we spend with them occur in our dreams. I don't know if this is indicative of superficial friendship.

Perhaps not. What I do know is that the things we love, or think we love, have their full weight and worth only when simply dreamed.

We don't care for shows. We despise actors and dancers. Every show is a coarse imitation of what should have been only dreamed.

We're indifferent to other people's opinion – not innately, but because of an education of our sentiments that has generally been forced on us by various painful experiences. But we treat others courteously and even like them, with an indifferent sort of interest, because everyone is interesting and convertible into dreams and into other people . . . . .

With no aptitude for loving, we are wearied by the mere thought of the words we would have to say in order to be loved. Besides, who among us wants to be loved? The '*on le fatigait en l'aimant*'* apropos René is not quite the right motto for us. The very idea of being loved wearies us, and to the point of panic.

My life is an unrelenting fever, an unquenchable thirst. Real life afflicts me like a hot day, and there's something mean about the way it afflicts me.

Sentimental Education

For those who choose to make dreams their life, and to make a religion and politics out of cultivating sensations like plants in a hothouse, the sign that they've successfully taken the first step is when they feel the tiniest things in an extraordinary and extravagant way. That's all there is to the first step. To know how to sip a cup of tea with the extreme voluptuousness that the normal man experiences only when overcome by joy at seeing his ambition suddenly fulfilled or himself suddenly cured of a terrible nostalgia, or when he's in the final, carnal acts of love; to be able to achieve in the vision of a sunset or in the contemplation of a decorative detail that intensity of feeling which generally can't occur through sight or hearing but only by way of the carnal senses – touch, taste and smell – when they sculpt the object of sensation on our consciousness; to be able to convert our interior vision, the hearing in our dreams, and all imagined senses and the senses of the imagination into tangible receptors like the five senses that receive the outside world: these are some of the sensations (and similar examples can be imagined) that the trained cultivator of his own feelings is able to experience with a convulsive fervour, and I mention them so as to give a rough but concrete idea of what I'm trying to convey.

Arriving at this degree of sensation, however, causes the lover of sensations to feel griefs – both from the outside and from inside himself – with the same conscious intensity. It is when he realizes, and because he realizes, that to feel in the extreme can mean not only extreme pleasure but also acute suffering that the dreamer is led to take the second step in his self-ascension.

I'll leave aside the step that he might or might not take and that, if he can and does take it, will determine certain of his attitudes and affect the general way he proceeds – I mean the step of completely isolating himself from the real world, which of course he can take only if he's rich. For I suppose it's clear by reading between the lines that the dreamer, depending on his relative possibility of isolation and self-dedication, should with greater or lesser intensity concentrate on his work of pathologically stimulating his sensitivity to things and dreams. The man who must actively live and associate with people – and even in this case it's possible to reduce intimacy with others to a minimum (intimacy with people, and not mere contact, is what's detrimental) – will have to freeze the entire surface of his social self, so that every fraternal and friendly gesture he receives will slide off and not enter or make a lasting impression. This seems hard to do but isn't. People are easy to drive away: all we have to do is not go near them. Anyway, I'll pass over this point and return to what I was explaining.

The creation of an automatically heightened and complex awareness of the simplest and commonest sensations leads not only to a vast increase in the enjoyment we get from feeling but also, as I've said, to a tremendous upsurge in the amount of pain we experience. The second step for the dreamer should therefore be to avoid pain. He shouldn't avoid it like the Stoics or the early Epicureans, by abandoning the nest, for that will harden him against pleasure as well as against pain. He should, instead, seek pleasure in pain, and then learn how to feel pain falsely – to feel some kind of pleasure, that is, whenever he feels pain. There are various paths for reaching this goal. One is to hyperanalyse our pain (but only after we've first trained ourselves to react to pleasure by exclusively feeling it, with no analysis). This is an easier technique than it seems, at least for superior souls. To analyse pain and to get in the habit of submitting all pains to analysis, until we do it automatically, by instinct, will endow every pain imaginable with the pleasure of analysing it. Once our ability and instinct to analyse grow large enough, our practice of it will absorb everything, and there will be nothing left of pain but an indefinite substance for analysis.

Another method, more subtle and more difficult, is to develop the habit of incarnating the pain in an ideal figure. First we must create another I, charged with suffering – in and for us – everything we suffer. Next we need to create an inner sadism, completely masochistic, that enjoys its suffering as if it were someone else's. This method, which on first reading seems impossible, isn't easy, but it is eminently attainable, presenting no special difficulties for those who are well versed in lying to themselves. Once this is achieved, pain and suffering acquire an absolutely tantalizing flavour of blood and disease, an incredibly exotic pungency of decadent gratification! The feeling of pain resembles the anguished, troubled height of convulsions, and suffering – the long and slow kind – has the intimate yellow which colours the vague bliss of a profoundly felt convalescence. And an exquisite exhaustion tinged with disquiet and melancholy evokes the complex sensation of anguish that our pleasures arouse, in the thought that they will vanish, as well as the melancholy pre-weariness we feel in our sensual delights, when we think of the weariness they'll bring.

There is a third method for subtilizing pains into pleasures and for making doubts and worries into a soft bed. It consists in intensely concentrating on our anxieties and sufferings, making them so fiercely felt that by their very excess they bring the pleasure of excess, while by their violence they suggest the pleasure that hurts for being so pleasurable and the gratification that smacks of blood for having wounded us. This can only happen, of course, in souls dedicated to pleasure by habit and by education. And when, as in me – refiner that I am of fallacious refinements, an architect dedicated to building myself out of sensations subtilized through the intellect, through abdication from life, through analysis and through pain itself –, all three methods are employed simultaneously, when every felt pain (felt so quickly there's no time for the soul to plan any defence) is automatically analysed to the core, ruthlessly foisted on an extraneous I, and buried in me to the utmost height of pain, then I truly feel like a victor and a hero. Then life stops for me, and art grovels at my feet.

Everything I've been describing is just the second step that the dreamer must take to reach his dream.

Who besides me has been able to take the third step, which leads to the sumptuous threshold of the Temple? This is the step which is indeed hard to take, for it requires an inward effort vastly greater than any effort we make in life, but it also rewards us to the heights and depths of our soul in a way that life never could. This step is – once everything else has been completely and simultaneously carried out, the three subtle methods having been applied to exhaustion – to immediately pass the sensation through pure intelligence, filtering it through a higher analysis that shapes it into a literary form with its own substance and character. Then I have completely fixed the sensation. Then I have made the unreal real and have given the unattainable an eternal pedestal. Then, within myself, I have been crowned Emperor.

Don't imagine that I write to publish, or merely to write, or to produce art. I write because this is the final goal, the supreme refinement, the organically illogical refinement, □ of my cultivation of the states of soul. If I take one of my sensations and unravel it so as to use it to weave the inner reality I call 'The Forest of Estrangement' or 'A Voyage I Never Made', you can be sure I don't do it for the sake of a lucid and shimmering prose, nor even for the sake of the pleasure I get from that prose – though I'm quite glad to have it as an additional final touch, like a splendidly falling curtain over my dreamed stage settings – but to give complete exteriority to what is interior, thereby enabling me to realize the unrealizable, to conjoin the contradictory and, having exteriorized my dream, to give it its most powerful expression as pure dream. Yes, this is my role as a stagnator of life, chiseller of inaccuracies, sick pageboy of my soul and Queen, reading to her at twilight not the poems from the book of my Life that lies open on my knees, but the poems that I invent and pretend to read, and that she pretends to hear, while somewhere and somehow the

Evening is softening – over this metaphor raised up in me into Absolute Reality – the last hazy light of a mysterious spiritual day.

Symphony of the Restless Night

The twilights of ancient cities, with lost traditions inscribed in the black stones of their massive buildings; tremulous dawns over inundated fields, swampy and damp like the air before the sun comes out; the narrow lanes where anything could happen; the heavy chests in age-old sitting rooms; the well behind the farmhouse on a moonlit night; the letter dating from when our grandmother whom we never met was first in love; the mildew in the rooms where the past is stored; the rifle no one knows how to use any more; the fever of hot afternoons next to the window; not a soul on the road; fitful slumber; the blight in the vineyards; church bells; the cloistral grief of living. . . Hour of blessings: your soft, frail hands. . . The caress never comes, the stone in your ring bleeds in the growing darkness. . . Religious celebrations with no belief in our soul: the material beauty of the ugly, roughhewn saints, romantic passions lived in the mind, the smell of the sea as night falls on the docks of the city made damp by the chilling air. . .

Your slender hands hover, like wings, over someone whom life sequesters. Long corridors and cracks around the windows, open even when closed, the floor as cold as tombstones, the nostalgia for love like a trip yet to be made to incomplete lands. . . Names of ancient queens. . . Stained-glass windows depicting stalwart counts. . . The vaguely scattered morning light, like a cold incense filling the air of the church and concentrated in the darkness of the impenetrable ground. . . Dry hands pressed one against the other.

The scruples of the monk when he discovers the teachings of occult masters in the strange ciphers of an ancient book, and the steps of Initiation in the book's decorative prints.

A beach in the sun – fever in me. . . The sea that shimmers in the anxiety that chokes me. . . The sails in the distance and how they sail in my fever. . . The steps leading down to the beach in my fever. . . Warmth in the cool breeze from across the sea, *mare vorax*, *minax*, *mare tenebrosum* – the dark, far-away night of the argonauts,* and my forehead burning with their primitive ships...

Everything belongs to others except my grief for not having any of it.

Give me the needle... Today the house is missing the sound of her soft footsteps, and I miss not knowing where she might be and what she might be making with pleats, with colours, with pins... Today her sewing, locked for ever in the drawers of the chest, is superfluous, and there is no warmth of dreamed arms clasping round my mother's neck.

The Visual Lover (I)

*Anteros**

I have a decorative and superficial concept of profound love and its usefulness. I prefer visual passions, keeping my heart intact for the sake of more unreal destinies.

I don't remember having ever loved more than the 'painting' in someone, the pure exterior, in which the soul's only role is to animate and enliven it, making it different from a painting done on canvas.

This is how I love: I fix my attention on a beautiful or attractive or otherwise lovable figure, whether of a woman or a man (where there's no desire, there's no sexual preference), and that figure captivates, obsesses, possesses me. But I want only to see it, and nothing would horrify me more than the prospect of meeting and speaking to the real person whom the figure visibly manifests.

I love with my gaze, and not even with fantasy. Because there's nothing I fantasize about the figure that captivates me. I don't imagine myself linked to it in any other way, because my decorative love has no psychological depth. I'm not interested in knowing the identity, activities or opinions of the human creature whose outward appearance I see.

The vast succession of persons and things that make up the world is for me an endless gallery of paintings, whose inner dimension doesn't interest me. It doesn't interest me, because the soul is monotonous and always the same in everybody; only its personal manifestations change, and the best part of the soul spills over into dreams, behaviour and gestures, thereby entering the painting which captivates me and in which I see faces that are faithful to my affection.

A human creature, as far as I'm concerned, has no soul. The soul is his own affair.

It is thus in pure vision that I experience the animated exterior of things and beings, indifferent – like a god from another world – to their spirit content. I delve into their being by exploring the surface; when I want depth, I look for it in myself and in my concept of things.

What can I gain from personal acquaintance with people I love merely as décor? Not disillusion, since I harbour no fantasies and love only their appearance, which won't be affected by their stupidity or mediocrity; I hoped for nothing from them but their appearance, which was already there and which persists. But personal acquaintance is harmful because it's useless; materially useless things are always harmful. What's the point of knowing the person's name? And yet it's inevitably the first thing I'm told when we're introduced.

Personal acquaintance should also mean the freedom to contemplate, which is my way of loving. But we can't freely regard or contemplate someone we know personally.

From the artist's viewpoint, anything extra counts as a deficit, for it interferes with and thus diminishes the desired effect.

My natural destiny is to be a visual lover of nature's shapes and forms, an objectifier of dreams, a passionate and indefinite contemplator of appearances and the manifestations of things .....

It's not a case of what psychiatrists call psychic onanism, nor is it what they term erotomania. I don't fantasize, as in psychic onanism; I don't imagine myself as a carnal lover or even as a casual friend of the person I gaze at and remember. Nor, as in erotomania, do I idealize and remove the person from the concretely aesthetic sphere; I don't think about or desire anything more from the person than what I receive from my eyes and from the pure, direct memory of what my eyes have seen.

The Visual Lover (II)

And I avoid spinning webs of fantasy around the figures I contemplate to entertain myself. I see them, and their value for me consists only in their being seen. Anything I might add to them would only diminish them, for it would diminish their 'visibility'.

Whatever I might fantasize about them would instantly hit me with its obvious falseness; and while dreamed things please me, false things disgust me. I'm enchanted by pure dreams, those which have no relation to reality nor even any point of contact with it. But imperfect dreams, which have their basis in life, fill me with loathing, or would fill me with loathing were I to indulge in them.

I see humanity as a vast decorative motif that lives through our eyes and ears, as well as through psychological emotion. All I want from life is to observe humanity. All I want from myself is to observe life.

I'm like a being from another existence who passes, with a certain amount of interest, through this one. I'm alien to it in every way. There's a kind of glass sheet between me and it. I want the glass to be perfectly clear, so that it will in no way hinder my examination of what's behind it, but I always want the glass.

For every scientifically minded spirit, to see in something more than what's there is to see it less. Materially adding to it spiritually diminishes it.

This attitude is no doubt responsible for my aversion to museums. The only museum for me is the whole of life, in which the picture is always absolutely accurate, with any inaccuracy being due to the spectator's imperfection. I do what I can to reduce that imperfection, and if I can't do anything, then I rest content with the way it is, because, like everything else, it can't be any other way.

A Voyage I Never Made (I)

It was at a vaguely autumnal twilight hour that I set out on the voyage I never made.

The sky, as I impossibly remember, was tinged by a purplish remnant of sad gold, and the clear, agonizing line of the hills was wrapped by a deathly-coloured glow that penetrated and softened the accuracy of its contours. On the other side of the ship (the night was colder and farther advanced under that side of the deck awning) lay the open ocean, trembling all the way out to where the eastern horizon was growing sad and where a darker air, placing shadows of early night on the obscure liquid line of the sea's visible limit, hovered like haze on a hot day.

The sea, I remember, had shadowy hues mixed in with wavy patches of faint light – and it was all mysterious like a sad idea in a happy hour, portending I don't know what.

I didn't set out from any port I knew. Even today I don't know what port it was, for I've still never been there. And besides, the ritual purpose of my journey was to go in search of non-existent ports – ports that would be merely a putting-in at ports; forgotten inlets of rivers, straits running through irreproachably unreal cities. You will doubtless think, on reading me, that my words are absurd. That's because you've never journeyed like I have.

I set out? I wouldn't swear to you that I set out. I found myself in other lands, in other ports, and I passed through cities that were not the one I started from, which, like all the others, was no city at all. I can't swear to you that it was I who set out and not the landscape, that it was I who visited other lands and not they that visited me. Not knowing what life is, nor if I'm the one living it rather than it living me (whatever the hollow verb 'live' may mean), I'm not about to swear anything.

I made a voyage. I presume it's not necessary to explain that my voyage didn't last for months or for days or for any other quantity of measurable time. I journeyed in time, to be sure, but not on this side of time, which we count by hours, days and months. My voyage took place on the other side of time, where it cannot be counted or measured but where it nevertheless flows, and it would seem to be faster than the time that has lived us. You are no doubt asking me, within yourselves, what meaning these sentences have. Don't make that mistake. Say goodbye to the childish error of asking words and things what they mean. Nothing means anything.

On what ship did I make this voyage? On the steamer *Whichever*. You laugh. Me too, and perhaps at you. How do you (or even I) know that I'm not writing symbols for the gods alone to understand?

No matter. I set out at twilight. In my ears I can still hear the clanging iron of the anchor being pulled up. In the corner of my memory's eye I can still see the arms of the crane – which some hours before sailing had tortured my vision with countless crates and barrels – slowly moving until at last they enter their position of rest. These crates and barrels, secured by a chain, would suddenly appear over the gunwale, after first hitting against it and making a scraping sound; then, swaying, they were pushed along to the hatchway, where they abruptly descended . . . . . , until with a dull wooden, crashing thud they arrived at some invisible place in the hold. From below came the sound of them being untied, and then the chain would rise up by itself, jingling, and everything would start over in seeming futility.

Why am I telling you this? Because it's absurd to be telling you this, after having said I would talk about my voyages.

I visited New Europes and was greeted by different Constantinoples as I sailed into the ports of pseudo-Bosporuses. It baffles you that I sailed in? You read me right. The steamer in which I set out came into port as a sailboat [. . .]. That's impossible, you say. That's why it happened to me.

Other steamboats brought us news of imaginary wars in impossible Indias. And when we heard about those lands, we felt an annoying nostalgia for our own land, but only, of course, because it was no land at all.*

A Voyage I Never Made (II)

I hide behind the door, so that Reality won't see me when it enters. I hide under the table, from where I can jump out and give Possibility a scare. Thus I cast off, like the two arms of an embrace, the two huge tediums that squeeze me – the tedium of being able to live only the Real, and the tedium of being able to conceive only the Possible.

In this way I triumph over all reality. You say my triumphs are castles of sand?. . . And what divine substance constitutes the castles which are not of sand?

How do you know that my kind of voyaging doesn't rejuvenate me in some obscure way?

Child of absurdity, I relive my early years, playing with ideas of things as with toy soldiers, which in my infant hands did things that went against the very notion of a soldier.

Drunk on errors, for a little while I stray and quit feeling myself live.

A Voyage I Never Made (III)

Shipwrecks? No, I never suffered any. But I have the impression that I shipwrecked all my voyages, and that my salvation lay in interspaces of unconsciousness.

Hazy dreams, blurry lights, confused landscapes – that's all that remains in my soul from all the travelling I did.

I have the impression that I've known hours of every colour, loves of every flavour, yearnings of every size. Throughout my life I lived to excess, and I was never enough for myself, not even in my dreams.

I must explain to you that I really did travel. But everything seems to indicate that I travelled without living. From one end to the other, from north to south and from east to west, I bore the weariness of having had a past, the disquiet of living the present, and the tedium of having to have a future. But I strive so hard that I remain completely in the present, killing inside me both past and future.

I strolled along the banks of rivers whose names I suddenly realized I didn't know. At the tables of cafés in foreign cities, it would dawn on me that everything had a hazy, dreamy air about it. Sometimes I even wondered if I weren't still seated at the table of our old house, staring into space and dazed by dreams! I can't be sure that this isn't actually the case, that I'm not still there, that all of this – including this conversation with you – isn't a pure sham. Who are you anyway? The equally absurd fact is that you can't explain. . .

A Voyage I Never Made (IV)

To sail without ever landing doesn't have a landing-place. To never arrive implies never arriving ever.

Appendix I: Texts Citing the Name of Vicente Guedes

As explained in the Introduction, Vicente Guedes was for many years the fictional author of The Book of Disquiet, *until he was replaced by (and absorbed into) Bernardo Soares. Perhaps to avoid confusion, Pessoa excluded the following three passages from the large envelope where he left material for* Disquiet.

AP- I

It was entirely by chance that I got to know Vicente Guedes. We often ate at the same quiet, inexpensive restaurant. Since we knew each other by sight, we naturally began to exchange silent greetings. One day we happened to be seated at the same table and we traded several remarks. A conversation ensued. We began to meet there every day, both for lunch and dinner. Sometimes we would leave together after dinner and stroll around for a while, talking.

Vicente Guedes endured his utterly grey life with the indifference of a master. A stoicism for the weak formed the basis of his entire mental outlook.

His natural temperament had condemned him to have every conceivable yearning; his destiny had led him to give them all up. I've never known another soul that startled me more. Without any kind of asceticism to spur him on, this man had renounced all the goals to which his nature had predisposed him. Born to be ambitious, he took languid pleasure in having no ambition at all.

AP- 2

. . . this gentle book.

This is all that remains and will remain of one of the most subtly passive souls and one of the purest, most profligate dreamers that the world has ever known. I doubt that any outwardly human creature has lived their consciousness of self in a more complex fashion. A dandy in spirit, he promenaded the art of dreaming through the randomness of existing.

This book is the autobiography of a man who never existed.*

No one knows who Vicente Guedes was or what he did or . . . . .

This book is not by him: it is him. But let us always remember that, behind whatever these pages tell us, mystery slithers in the shadows.

For Vicente Guedes, to be conscious of himself was an art and a morality; to dream was a religion.

He was the definitive creator of inner aristocracy – that posture of soul which most resembles the bodily posture of a full-fledged aristocrat.

AP- 3

The anguish of a man afflicted by life's tedium on the terrace of his opulent villa is one thing; quite another is the anguish of someone like me, who must contemplate the scenery from my fourth-floor rented room in downtown Lisbon, unable to forget that I'm an assistant bookkeeper.

'Tout notaire a rêvé des sultanes'* . . .

Every time I'm obliged by some official act to state my profession, I smile to myself at the irony of the undeserved ridicule when I declare 'Office clerk' and no one finds it all strange. I don't know how it got there, but that's how my name appears in the *Professional Register*.

Epigraph to the Diary:
Guedes (Vicente), office clerk, Rua dos Retroseiros,
17, fourth floor.
Professional Register of Portugal

Appendix II: Two Letters

Pessoa planned to insert phrases and ideas from the following letters in The Book of Disquiet. *This intention is clearly stated in the second letter, while the first letter – or rather, Pessoa's typed copy of it – was marked* B. of D. *at the top.*

AP- 4

Letter to his Mother

5 June 1914

My health has been good and my state of mind, oddly enough, has improved. Even so, I'm tortured by a vague anxiety that I don't know what to call but an intellectual itch, as if my soul had chicken-pox. It's only in this absurd language that I can describe what I feel. But what I'm feeling isn't the same as those sad moods I sometimes tell you about, in which the sadness has no cause. My present mood has a definite cause. Everything around me is either departing or crumbling. I don't use these two verbs with gloomy intent. I simply mean that the people I associate with are or will be going through changes, marking an end to particular phases of their lives, and all of this suggests to me – as when an old man, because he sees his childhood companions dying all around him, feels his time must be near – that in some mysterious way my life likewise should and will change. Not that I think this change will be for the worse. On the contrary. But it's a change, and for me a change – to pass from one state to another – is a partial death; something in us dies, and the sadness of its dying and its passing on cannot help but touch our soul.

Tomorrow my best and closest friend* is leaving for Paris – not for a visit but to live there. And Aunt Anica (see her letter) will probably leave soon for Switzerland with her daughter, who will be married by then. Another good friend is going off to Galicia for a long while. Still another fellow, my next best friend after the first one I mentioned, is going to Oporto to live. Thus everything in my human circle is coming together (or apart) to force me either into isolation or else on to a new, uncertain path. Even the circumstance of publishing my first book will alter my life. *I'll lose something: my unpublished status.* To change for the better, because change is bad, is *always* to change for the worse. And to lose something negative – be it a personal defect or deficiency, or the fact of being rejected – *is still a loss.* Imagine, Mother, how someone who feels this way must live, overwhelmed by such painful daily sensations!

What will I be ten years from now, or even five? My friends say I'll be one of the greatest contemporary poets – they say this based on what I've already written, not what I may yet write (otherwise I wouldn't mention what they say. . .). But even if this is true, I have no idea what it will mean. I have no idea *how it will taste.* Perhaps glory tastes like death and futility, and triumph smells of rottenness.

AP- 5

Letter to Mário de Sá-Carneiro*

14 March 1916

I'm writing to you today out of an emotional necessity – an anguished longing to talk to you. I have, in other words, nothing special to say. Except this: that today I'm at the bottom of a bottomless depression. The absurdity of the sentence speaks for me.

This is one of those days *in which I've never had a future.* There's just a static present, surrounded by a wall of anxiety. The other side of the river, as long as it's the other side, is not this side; that is the root cause of all my suffering. There are many boats destined for many ports, but no boat for life to stop hurting, nor a landing-place where we can forget everything. All of this occurred a long time ago, but my grief is even older.

On days of the soul like today I feel, in my awareness of every bodily pore, like the sad child who was beaten up by life. I was put in a corner, from where I can hear everyone else playing. In my hands I can feel the shoddy, broken toy I was given out of some shoddy irony. Today, the fourteenth of March, at ten after nine in the evening, this seems to be all my life is worth.

In the park that's visible from the silent windows of my confinement, all the swings have been wrapped high around the branches from where they hang, so that not even my fantasy of an escaped me can forget this moment by swinging in my imagination.

This, but with no literary style, is more or less my present mood. Like the watching woman of *The Mariner*,* my eyes sting from having thought about crying. Life pains me little by little, by sips, in the cracks. All of this is printed in tiny letters in a book whose binding is falling apart.

If I weren't writing to you, I would have to swear that this letter is sincere, that its hysterical associations of ideas have flowed spontaneously from what I feel. But you know all too well that this unstageable tragedy is as real as a teacup or a coat hanger – full of the here and now, and passing through my soul like the green in a tree's leaves.

That's why the Prince never ruled. This sentence is totally absurd. But right now I feel that absurd sentences make me want to cry.

If I don't post this letter today, then perhaps tomorrow, on rereading it, I'll take the time to make a typed copy, so as to include some of its sentences and grimaces in *The Book of Disquiet*. But that won't take away from all the sincerity I've put into writing it, nor from the painful inevitability of the feeling behind it.

There you have the latest news. There is also the state of war with Germany, but pain caused suffering long before that. On the other side of Life, this must be the caption of some political cartoon.

What I'm feeling isn't true madness, but madness no doubt results in a similar abandon to the very causes of one's suffering, a shrewd delight in the soul's lurches and jolts.

What, I wonder, is the colour of feeling?
Thousands of hugs from your very own

Fernando Pessoa

P.S. – I wrote this letter in one go. Rereading it I see that, yes, I'll definitely make a copy before posting it to you tomorrow. Rarely have I so completely expressed my psychology, with all of its emotional and intellectual attitudes, with all of its fundamentally depressive bent, with all the so characteristic corners and crossroads of its self-awareness...

Don't you agree?

Appendix III: Reflections on The Book of Disquiet *from Pessoa's Writings*

A. TWO NOTES

Note concerning the actual editions

(AND WHICH CAN BE USED IN THE PREFACE)

Collect later on, in a separate book, the various poems I had mistakenly thought to include in *The Book of Disquiet*; this book of poems should have a title indicating that it contains something like refuse or marginalia – something suggestive of detachment.

This book, furthermore, could form part of a definitive collection of dregs, the published depository of the unpublishable – allowed to survive as a sad example. It would be somewhat analogous to a book of unfinished poems by a poet who died young, or the letters of a great writer. But the book I have in mind would include material that is not only inferior but also different, and it is this difference that would justify its publication, which obviously couldn't be justified by the fact it shouldn't be published.

B. of D.

(NOTE)

The organization of the book should be based on a highly rigorous selection from among the various kinds of texts written, adapting the older ones – which lack the psychology of Bernardo Soares – to that true psychology as it has now emerged. In addition, an overall revision of the style needs to be made, but without giving up the dreaminess and logical disjointedness of its intimate expression.

It must also be decided whether to include the large texts with grandiose titles, such as the 'Funeral March for Ludwig II, King of Bavaria' or 'Symphony of the Restless Night'. The 'Funeral March' could be left as it is, or it could be made part of another book, one that would gather together all the Large Texts.

B. EXCERPTS FROM LETTERS

To João de Lebre e Lima – 3 May 1914*

The subject of tedium reminds me of something I wanted to ask you. . . Did you happen to see, in an issue of *A Águia* that came out last year, a piece by me titled 'In the Forest of Estrangement'? If not, let me know. I'll send it to you. I'd very much like you to read it. It's my only published text in which I make tedium – and the sterile dream that wearies of itself even before it starts dreaming – a motif and the central theme. I don't know if you'll like the style in which it's written. It's a style quite my own, which various friends jokingly call 'the estranged style', since it made its first appearance in that text. And they talk of 'estranged writing', 'estranged speech', etc.

That piece belongs to a book of mine for which I've written other, still unpublished passages, but I have a long way to go before finishing it. The book is called *The Book of Disquiet*, since restlessness and uncertainty are the dominant note. This is evident in the one published passage. What is apparently the narration of a mere dream, or daydream, is actually – and the reader feels this at the outset and should, if I've been successful, feel it throughout his entire reading – a dreamed confession of the painful, sterile rage and utter uselessness of dreaming.

To Armando Cortes-Rodrigues – 2 September 1914*

. . . I haven't written anything worth sending along. Ricardo Reis and futurist Álvaro have been silent. Caeiro has perpetrated a few lines that will perhaps find refuge in some future book. . . What I've mainly written is sociology and disquiet. The last word, as you'll have guessed, refers to the 'book' of the same name. I have, in fact, written a number of pages for that pathological production, which thus continues to go complexly and tortuously forward.

To Armando Cortes-Rodrigues – 4 October 1914

Nor am I sending you any of the other little things I've written in recent days. Some of them aren't worth sending; others are incomplete; the rest are broken, disconnected pieces of *The Book of Disquiet*.

. . . . .

My present state of mind is of a deep and calm depression. For some days now I've been at the level of *The Book of Disquiet*. Just today I wrote almost an entire chapter.

To Armando Cortes-Rodrigues – 19 November 1914

My state of mind compels me to work hard, against my will, on *The Book of Disquiet*. But it's all fragments, fragments, fragments.

To João Gaspar Simões – 28 July 1932*

My original intention was to begin the publication of my works with three books, in the following order: (1) *Portugal*,* a small book of poems (41 in all) whose second part is 'Portuguese Sea' (published in *Contemporânea* 4); (2) *The Book of Disquiet* (by Bernardo Soares, but only secondarily, since B.S. is not a heteronym but a literary personality); (3) *Complete Poems of Alberto Caeiro* (with a preface by Ricardo Reis and, at the end of the volume, Álvaro de Campos's 'Notes for the Memory of my Master Caeiro'). A year after the publication of these books, I planned to bring out, either by itself or with another volume, *Songbook* (or some other equally inexpressive title), which would have included (in Books I–III or I–V) a number of my many miscellaneous poems, which are too diverse to be classified except in that inexpressive way.

But there is much to be revised and restructured in *The Book of Disquiet*, and I can't honestly expect that it will take me less than a year to do the job. And as for Caeiro, I'm undecided...

To Adolfo Casais Monteiro – 13 January 1935*

How do I write in the name of these three? Caeiro, through sheer and unexpected inspiration, without knowing or even suspecting that I'm going to write in his name. Ricardo Reis, after an abstract meditation which suddenly takes concrete shape in an ode. Campos, when I feel a sudden impulse to write and don't know what. (My semi-heteronym Bernardo Soares, who in many ways resembles Álvaro de Campos, always appears when I'm sleepy or drowsy, so that my qualities of inhibition and rational thought are suspended; his prose is an endless reverie. He's a semi-heteronym because his personality, although not my own, doesn't differ from my own but is a mere mutilation of it. He's me without my rationalism and emotions. His prose is the same as mine, except for a certain formal restraint that reason imposes on my own writing, and his Portuguese is exactly the same – whereas Caeiro writes bad Portuguese, Campos writes it reasonably well but with mistakes such as 'me myself' instead of 'I myself', etc., and Reis writes better than I, but with a purism I find excessive...)

C. FROM THE UNFINISHED PREFACE TO FICTIONS OF THE INTERLUDE

I place certain of my literary characters in stories, or in the subtitles of books, signing my name to what they say; others I project totally, with my only signature being the acknowledgement that I created them. The two types of characters may be distinguished as follows: in those that stand absolutely apart, the very style in which they write is different from my own and, when the case warrants, even contrary to it; in the characters whose works I sign my name to, the style differs from mine only in those inevitable details that serve to distinguish them from each other.

I will compare some of these characters to show, through example, what these differences involve. The assistant bookkeeper Bernardo Soares and the Baron of Teive – both are me-ishly extraneous characters – write with the same basic style, the same grammar, and the same careful diction. In other words, they both write with the style that, good or bad, is my own. I compare them because they are two instances of the very same phenomenon – an inability to adapt to real life – motivated by the very same causes. But although the Portuguese is the same in the Baron of Teive and in Bernardo Soares, their styles differ. That of the aristocrat is intellectual, without images, a bit – how shall I put it? – stiff and constrained, while that of his middle-class counterpart is fluid, participating in music and painting but not very architectural. The nobleman thinks clearly, writes clearly, and controls his emotions, though not his feelings; the bookkeeper controls neither emotions nor feelings, and what he thinks depends on what he feels.

There are also notable similarities between Bernardo Soares and Álvaro de Campos. But in Álvaro de Campos we are immediately struck by the carelessness of his Portuguese and by his exaggerated use of images, more instinctive and less purposeful than in Soares.

In my efforts to distinguish one from another, there are lapses that weigh on my sense of psychological discernment. When I try to distinguish, for example, between a musical passage of Bernardo Soares and a similar passage of my own. . .

Sometimes I can do it automatically, with a perfection that astonishes me; and there's no vanity in my astonishment, since, not believing in even a smidgen of human freedom, I'm no more astonished by what happens in me than I would be by what happens in someone else – both are perfect strangers.

Only a formidable intuition can serve as a compass on the vast expanses of the soul. Only with a sensibility that freely uses the intelligence without being contaminated by it, although the two function together as one, is it possible to distinguish the separate realities of these imaginary characters.

◆

These derivative personalities or, rather, these different inventions of personalities, fall into two categories or degrees, which the attentive reader will easily be able to identify by their distinctive characteristics. In the first category, the personality is distinguished by feelings and ideas which I don't share. At the lower level within this category, the personality is distinguished only by ideas, which are placed in rational exposition or argument and are clearly not my own, at least not so far as I know. 'The Anarchist Banker'* is an example of this lower level; *The Book of Disquiet*, and the character Bernardo Soares, represent the higher level.

The reader will note that, although I'm publishing *The Book of Disquiet* under the name of a certain Bernardo Soares, assistant bookkeeper in the city of Lisbon, I have not included it in these *Fictions of the Interlude*. This is because Bernardo Soares, while differing from me in his ideas, his feelings, and his way of seeing and understanding, expresses himself in the same way I do. His is a different personality, but expressed through my natural style, with the only distinguishing feature being the particular tone that inevitably results from the particularity of his emotions.

In the authors of *Fictions of the Interlude*, it's not only their ideas and feelings that differ from mine; their technique of composition, their very style, is also different from mine. Each of these authors is not just conceived differently but created as a wholly different entity. That's why poetry predominates here. In prose it is harder to other oneself.

Notes

Before his death Pessoa gathered together several hundred texts into a large envelope labelled Livro do Desassossego *(*Book of Disquiet*), and these take up the first five envelopes of the Pessoa Archives, housed at the National Library in Lisbon, but there are several hundred additional texts – scattered throughout the rest of the author's papers – that are specifically labelled* L. do D. *In the notes that follow, the manuscripts for the Portuguese texts are designated, in square brackets, by their official archival reference numbers (with the envelope number appearing before the slash) and identified as typed, handwritten ('ms.'), or partly typed, partly handwritten ('mixed'). Those texts that were not actually identified by Pessoa as belonging to* The Book of Disquiet *(and whose inclusion in* The Book *is therefore conjectural) are marked by a †. The manuscripts contain over 600 alternate wordings in the margins and between the lines, but only the most significant ones are cited in these notes, where the main concern has been to elucidate literary, historical and geographical references.*

Preface

[6/1–2, typed; 7/21, ms.] Pessoa wrote various prefatory texts for *The Book of Disquiet*, two of which appear here. Both were no doubt written in the 1910s, but the second text describes a fictional author who lived in two rented rooms, not one, and who seemed rather more prosperous than the assistant bookkeeper described elsewhere. Perhaps the author/narrator, who in *The Book*'s early days was called Vicente Guedes (see Introduction), was still not clearly delineated in Pessoa's mind, though there is a first-person text (AP-3) in which Guedes refers to his fourth-floor rented room (singular) and to his profession as an assistant bookkeeper. Two other prefatory passages that mention Guedes by name appear in Appendix I (AP-1 and AP-2), while several others – written from the narrator's point of view, not from Pessoa's

– have been incorporated into the section titled 'A Factless Autobiography'. *Orpheu* was founded by Fernando Pessoa, Mário de Sá-Carneiro and Luís de Montalvor in 1915. Although only two issues were published, the review was pivotal for the development of twentieth-century Portuguese literature.

A Factless Autobiography

1 [4/38–9, typed] Dated 29 March 1930. Marked *beginning passage*.
Vigny: Alfred de Vigny (1797–1863), French author of poems, essays, plays and a novel. Disillusioned in love, unsuccessful in politics, and unenthusiastically received by the French Academy, he withdrew from society and became increasingly pessimistic in his writings, which recommended stoical resignation as the only noble response to the suffering life condemns us to.
2 [5/29, ms.] Marked *B. of D. (Preface?)*.
3 [1/88, mixed] The first three paragraphs were published in *Solução Editora*, no. 2, 1929. The last two paragraphs were handwritten on the original typescript.
Cesário Verde (1855–86) may be considered the father of modern Portuguese poetry. The vivid images and exuberance of his verses, often set in the streets of downtown Lisbon, find echoes in the poetry of Pessoa's heteronym Álvaro de Campos.
4 [1/59, ms.]
5 [2/7, typed] Published in *Solução Editora*, no. 4, 1929.
6 [1/79, ms.]
7 [2/12–13, typed]
8 [1/73, typed]
9 [2/4, typed]
fourth-floor room: The original reads 'second-floor', presumably a slip, since all other references situate Soares's rented room on the fourth floor.
10 [1/58, typed]
11 [9/34, ms.]
12 [3/17, typed]
13 [2/90, ms.]
14 [1/22, typed]
15† [28/21, ms.] Marked *Preface*, but with no explicit indication that it pertains to *The Book of Disquiet*.
16 [2/53, typed]
Cascais and *Estoril*: Beach towns south-west of Lisbon.

Cais do Sodré: One of Lisbon's wharfs and the site of the railway station that serves the Cascais line.

17† [9/52, ms.]

18 [2/39–41, ms.]

delivery boy: In Pessoa's time these were a regular presence on many downtown Lisbon street corners. Self-employed, they would deliver or fetch objects large and small as well as run errands.

19 [1/76, typed] Dated 22 March 1929.

Moorish ladies of folklore: Since the Moorish occupation of Iberia, legends of enchanted Moorish ladies have abounded in Portuguese and Spanish folklore. The typical lady is a ravishing beauty, good-hearted, often a princess, and an inhabitant of nature, sometimes haunting a cave or a well.

20† [28/7, typed] Marked *Preface*, but with no explicit indication that it pertains to *The Book of Disquiet.*

21† [15B³/86] Dated 24 March 1929.

22† [94/75, ms.]

23 [7/44, ms.]

24 [1/64, ms.]

25 [1/15, typed]

26 [4/44, ms.]

27 [2/70, typed]

28 [2/66, ms.]

29 [3/18, typed] Dated 25 December 1929.

30 [4/29, ms.]

Vieira: Father António Vieira (1608–97), a Jesuit who spent much of his life in Brazil, is one of the great Portuguese prose stylists. His enormous output includes about 200 sermons and over 500 letters.

31 [3/21, typed]

32 [3/6, ms.] The manuscript evidence indicates that this passage was written during *The Book*'s last phase. The section titled 'A Disquiet Anthology' contains a 'Symphony of the Restless Night', written during the first phase.

tomb of God: 'tomb of the world'/'tomb of everything' (alternate versions)

33 [3/22, typed]

34 [2/67–8, ms.]

35 [7/4, ms.]

36 [3/26, typed] Dated 5 February 1930.

Vieira: See note for Text 30.

Sousa: Frei Luís de Sousa (1555–1632), a Portuguese Dominican whose biographies of religious figures are admired for the limpid elegance of their prose.

dignity of my soul: 'divinity of my soul'/'detachment of my soul' (alternate versions)

37 [9/24, ms.]

38 [5/79, ms.]

39 [2/74, mixed] Dated 21 February 1930.

40 [3/67, typed]

41 [3/15, typed] Dated 14 March 1930.

42 [1/81–2, mixed]

on the surface of never changing: 'on its surface, which is all it consists of' (alternate version)

43 [3/13, ms.] Dated 23 March 1930.

44 [1/77, typed]

45 [9/9, typed]

46 [4/34, typed] Dated 24 March 1930.

Caeiro: Alberto Caeiro, one of Pessoa's poetic heteronyms, supposedly lived in the country. The cited verses are from the seventh poem of *The Keeper of Sheep*.

47 [1/24, typed]

48 [1/32, ms.]

49 [1/34, typed]

50 [2/45, mixed]

Graça or São Pedro de Alcântara: Two look-out points on either side of downtown Lisbon.

51 [4/42, typed] Dated 4 April 1930.

52 [1/72, ms.]

53 [7/16, ms.] Marked *B. of D. (preface)*.

54 [2/9–10, mixed]

55 [3/64, typed] Dated 5 April 1930.

Vieira's prose: See note for Text 30.

56 [3/66, typed] Dated 5 April 1930.

a sphinx from the stationer's: This might refer to a paperweight in the form of a miniature sphinx.

57 [3/62, ms.] Dated 5 April 1930.

58 [3/59–61, ms.] Dated 6 April 1930.

59 [1/65, mixed]

60 [$144D^2$/45, ms.]

61 [9/25, ms.]

62 [3/57, mixed] Dated 10 April 1930.

63 [3/54–5, ms.] Dated 10 April 1930.

64† [23/28, ms.]

65† [94/13, ms.]
66 [1/57, typed]
67 [3/56, typed] Dated 12 April 1930.
68 [1/88, ms.]
69 [5/2, ms.]
70 [1/30, typed]
71 [3/58, ms.] Dated 13 April 1930.
Vieira: See note for Text 30.
72 [1/53, typed] Published in *Revolução*, 6 June 1932.
Amiel: Henri-Frédéric Amiel (1821–81), a Swiss professor of aesthetics and philosophy, gained posthumous fame for his *Fragments d'un journal intime*, which in certain respects resembles *The Book of Disquiet*.
São Pedro de Alcântara: See note for Text 50.
Poço do Bispo: A dock area in north-east Lisbon.
73 [3/51–3, ms.] Dated 14 April 1930.
74 [3/30–31, ms.]
75 [7/12, ms.]
76† [8/11–12, typed]
77 [5/67, ms.]
78 [3/46, typed] Dated 21 April 1930.
79 [3/47, typed] Dated 21 April 1930.
80 [9/36, 36a, ms.]
81 [2/63, ms.]
82 [3/45, ms.] Dated 23 April 1930.
83 [3/40–41, typed] Dated 25 April 1930.
Vieira: See note for Text 30.
Frei Luís de Sousa: See note for Text 36. The biography alluded to, published in 1619, tells the life of Frei Bartolomeu dos Mártires, a Portuguese archbishop.
offspring of the stiff furniture: 'offspring of dead things' (alternate version)
84 [3/42, typed] 25 April 1930.
Sigismund, King of Rome: The Holy Roman Emperor from 1411 to 1437.
The title is royal, and the reason for it is imperial: 'The title isn't bad, and it belongs to the man who can "is himself"' (alternate version)
85 [2/3, typed]
86 [2/3, ms.]
the Romanization of Hellenism through Judaism: 'the Judaization of Hellenism through Rome' (alternate version)
our age – senile and carcinogenic: 'our age – an illiterate's bibliophilia' (alternate version)

gave rise to all the negations we use to affirm ourselves: 'gave rise to the era that brought their fall' (alternate version)
with sociologies such as these?: 'with all these civilizations?' (alternate version)
87 [3/39, ms.] Dated 6 May 1930.
thereby shoving it up against the wall: 'thereby letting it flow like a river, the slave of its own bed' (alternate version)
88 [5/60, ms.]
89† [133F/95, ms.]
90 [3/34, typed] Dated 14 May 1930.
91 [3/35, typed] Dated 15 May 1930.
92 [5/42–4, ms.] The text carries the following heading, in English: *(our childhood's playing with cotton reels, etc.)*
my inner life: 'my inner stage setting' (alternate version)
window on to the street of my dreams: 'window that looks inside me' (alternate version)
93 [5/19, ms.]
94 [3/33, ms.] Dated 18 May 1930.
95 [2/78, typed] Dated 18 May 1930. Published in *Presença*, June–July 1930.
96 [3/16, typed]
97 [4/84, ms.]
98 [1/56, typed]
99 [3/32, typed] Dated 12 June 1930.
100 [3/29, ms.] Dated 13 June 1930.
101 [5/1, ms.]
102 [3/27, typed] Dated 27 June 1930.
103 [144X/29, ms.]
104† [133F/79, typed]
105† [20/50, typed]
106 [1/89, typed]
Cesário Verde: See note for Text 3.
107 [7/14, ms.]
Terreiro do Paço: 'Palace Square', so called because of the royal palace that stood there from the sixteenth to the eighteenth centuries. When the palace was destroyed by the 1755 earthquake, the large and elegantly redesigned square was renamed Praça do Comércio.
108 [2/80, typed] Dated 16 July 1930.
the poet: José de Espronceda (1808–42). The two verses, taken from a long narrative poem titled *El Estudiante de Salamanca*, were cited by Pessoa in the original: *languidez, mareo / y angustioso afán*. Pessoa left an incomplete English translation of the work, which he titled *The Student of Salamanca*

and credited to heteronym Charles James Search, brother of Alexander.
109 [2/16, typed] The parenthetical heading is in English in the original.
110 [2/29, typed] Dated 20 July 1930.
111 [5/49, typed]
112 [2/83, ms.] Dated 25 July 1930.
113 [5/78, ms.]
114 [4/85, ms.]
115 [4/82, ms.]
116 [7/30, typed]
117 [2/82, typed] Dated 27 July 1930.
118 [3/2, ms.]
119 [5/46, ms.]
Amiel's diary: See the note for Text 72.
Scherer: Edmond Scherer (1815–89), a well-known French literary critic, was a friend of Amiel's and wrote the Preface to his posthumously published *Fragments d'un journal intime*. Pessoa's memory of the passage alluded to was inaccurate. The journal records that Scherer, in a conversation, spoke of '*l'intelligence de la conscience*'; it was Amiel himself who spoke of '*la conscience de la conscience*'.
120 [4/67, typed]
121 [1/16a, ms.]
122 [2/50, ms.]
I live, all of it equally condemned to change: 'I live which, because it moves, is passing' (alternate version)
cross the river. . . from the Terreiro do Paço to Cacilhas: Ferries still make frequent crossings from several points in Lisbon to the former fishing village of Cacilhas, from where many buses proceed to surrounding towns. See note for Text 107.
123 [4/40, typed]
Santa Justa Lift: Built in 1902, it connects the lower and upper parts of Lisbon's centre.
124 [7/20, typed] The parenthetical heading is in English in the original.
The argonauts said: Pessoa often used the word 'argonauts' to mean ancient navigators in general (cf. Text 125 and 'Symphony of the Restless Night'), and the phrase he cites was in fact not the motto of the Argonauts led by Jason. It was uttered, according to Plutarch, by Pompey the Great when, in spite of a heavy storm, he ordered his ships to set sail for Rome with the grain they had loaded in Sicily, Sardinia and North Africa.
125† [28/12, ms.]
argonauts: See note for Text 124.

126 [2/84, typed] Dated 10 December 1930.

127† [8/9, ms.]

128 [3/49, ms.]

129 [3/14, ms.]

130 [3/44, typed]

Cesário Verde: See the note for Text 3.

131 [3/12, ms.]

Vieira: See note for Text 30.

like the Fate of us all: 'like this note I've been writing' (alternate version)

132 [5/30, typed]

133]2/58–9, mixed]

134 [5/41, ms.]

135 [2/21, ms.]

136 [3/48, ms.]

137 [4/21, typed]

138 [4/37, typed]

Benfica: Once an outlying suburb and now a fully integrated neighbourhood of Lisbon.

'Any road,' said Carlyle: In Thomas Carlyle's *Sartor Resartus: The Life and Opinions of Herr Teufelsdröckh*.

Condillac begins his celebrated book: Etienne de Condillac (1715–80) begins his *Essai sur l'origine des connaissances humaines* (1746) not by saying that we never escape our sensations but that we never escape our own selves (which is also what Pessoa says in his next sentence, after the inaccurate citation). Further on in the *Essai*, however, Condillac affirms that everything we know depends on our sensations. Pessoa seems to have crunched several ideas into one, without after all being unfaithful to the French philosopher's thought.

139 [2/87, typed] Dated 8 January 1931.

140 [2/1, mixed]

141 [7/31, ms.]

142 [1/17, typed]

143 [1/33, typed]

144 [3/7, ms.] Dated 1 February 1931. The manuscript ends with the following paragraph, crossed out by the author: *What do I know? What do I seek? What do I feel? What would I ask for if I had to ask?*

145 [4/12, typed] Dated 2 February 1931.

146 [3/1, ms.]

147 [1/70, typed]

148 [9/17, ms.]

149 [3/87–8, typed] Dated 3 March 1931. Published in *Presença*, November 1931–February 1932.

Haeckel: Ernst Heinrich Haeckel (1834–1919), a German biologist and philosopher. Pessoa had four books by Haeckel in his personal library (in French translations), including *Riddle of the Universe* (1899), which propounds a materialist view of the world.

Loures: Located about ten miles north-west of Lisbon.

Sanches: Francisco Sanches (1551–1623) was a Portuguese doctor and philosopher who spent most of his life in France. His most important work, *Quod nihil scitur* (1581), systematically employs doubt to argue that nothing can be known with certainty.

150 [1/67, typed]

151 [6/14, typed]

152 [1/14, typed]

153 [6/9, typed]

154 [2/65, ms.]

155 [4/30, typed] Dated 10 March 1931.

156 [7/15, ms.]

157 [5/52, typed]

158 [4/20, ms.] In a letter sent from Pisa to John Gisborne on 22 October 1821, Shelley wrote: 'You are right about Antigone; how sublime a picture of a woman! (.) Some of us have, in a prior existence, been in love with an Antigone, and that makes us find no full content in any mortal tie'

159 [5/50, typed]

160 [2/33, typed] Dated 8 April 1931.

to be beyond repair: 'to lack the soul to be' (alternate version)

161 [2/46, typed]

162 [2/24, ms.]

Horace said: In the third ode of his third book of odes.

163 [2/38, ms.]

164 [7/28–28a, ms.]

165 [1/12, typed]

166 [2/54, typed] Dated 18 June 1931.

167 [2/56, typed] Dated 20 June 1931.

168 [1/35, typed]

who timidly hate life, fear death with fascination: 'between life which I grudgingly love and death which I fear with fascination' (alternate version)

169 [2/64, typed]

170 [2/55, typed] Dated 30 June 1931.

171 [1/74–5, typed]

Rotunda: refers to the Praça Marquês de Pombal, a large roundabout.
Benfica: See note for Text 138.
Sintra: Located north-west of Lisbon, this ancient town has long been famous for its agreeable climate, its setting among lush green hills, and the various palaces built by Moorish and Portuguese kings.
His reality won't let him feel: 'won't let him exist' (alternate version)
172 [4/44a, ms.]
173 [15^1/73, ms.]
174 [2/35, typed] Dated 2 July 1931.
175 [5/36, typed] Preceded by the heading *1st article* (in English).
176† [183A/27, ms.]
177† [15^5/13, typed]
178 [2/60, mixed]
179 [7/2, ms.]
180 [1/60, typed]
181 [2/37, typed] Dated 13 July 1931.
182 [138A/5, ms.]
183 [1/50, typed]
Benfica: See note for Text 138.
the Avenida: Presumably the Avenida da Liberdade, in central Lisbon.
184 [2/36, mixed] Dated 22 August 1931.
what nostalgia for the future: 'what regret that I'm not someone else' (alternate version)
incipient self-unawareness: 'incipient impatience with myself' (alternate version)
185 [9/27, ms.]
186† [94/100, ms.]
187 [1/83–4, mixed]
188 [1/43, typed]
189 [5/62, ms.]
190 [1/51, typed]
191 [2/20, ms.]
192 [2/28/ typed]
193 [2/42, typed] Dated 2 September 1931.
194† [94/83, ms.]
195 [5/66, ms.]
196 [2/43, typed] Dated 3 September 1931.
197 [5/76–7, ms.]
198 [1/55, typed]
199 [7/11, typed]
200 [3/23, typed]

201 [4/10, mixed] Dated 10–11 September 1931. Notation at the top of the text: *(alternate passages like these with the longer ones?).*
202 [4/11, typed] Dated 14 September 1931.
203 [4/31, typed] Dated 15 September 1931.
204 [4/8, typed] Dated 15 September 1931. Published in *Descobrimento. Revista de Cultura*, no. 3, 1931.
205 [4/32, typed] Dated 16 September 1931.
206 [3/50, ms.] This text seems to refer to 'In the Forest of Estrangement', where an alcove is mentioned.
207 [6/12, typed] At the top of the text: *B. of D. (or Teive?).* See the Introduction for information about the Baron of Teive, Pessoa's aristocratic heteronym.
fiction of the interlude: See note for Text 325.
208 [4/17–18, typed] Dated 18 September 1931. Published in *Descobrimento. Revista de Cultura*, no. 3, 1931.
209 First published by António de Pina Coelho in his book *Os Fundamentos Filosóficos da Obra de Fernando Pessoa* (Lisbon, 1971), where it was identified as a passage belonging to *The Book of Disquiet*. The whereabouts of the original manuscript is unknown.
210† [15^2/89, ms.] Alternate title in the manuscript: *Ethics of Discouragement.*
211 [7/42, ms.]
212† [133F/87, typed]
213 [2/76, typed]
214 [2/75, typed]
215† [$144D^2$/44–5, ms.]
216 [2/44, typed] Dated 7 October 1931.
217 [3/24, typed]
218† [8/6, ms.]
219† [28/9–10, typed] *Scotus Erigena*: John Scotus Erigena (810–77) was an Irish Neoplatonist philosopher and theologian.
220 [9/23, ms.]
221 [4/13, typed] Dated 16 October 1931.
Pessanha: Camilo Pessanha (1867–1926) was an important Portuguese Symbolist poet who influenced the poetry of Pessoa.
The Gold Lion: Located in downtown Lisbon, this restaurant (*Leão d'Ouro* in Portuguese) first opened its doors in 1885.
I know because I imagine: 'I know or imagine' (alternate version)
222 [1/48, ms.]
Almada: A town near Lisbon, located on the other side of the Tagus River.
223 [4/41, typed]

224 [2/89, ms.]
225 [4/15–16, typed] Dated 16–17 October 1931. Published in *Descobrimento. Revista de Cultura*, no. 3, 1931.
Terreiro do Paco: See note for Text 107.
226† [14^{2}/55, ms.]
227 [4/3, typed] Dated 18 October 1931. Published in *Descobrimento. Revista de Cultura*, no. 3, 1931.
228 [4/4, ms.]
229† [$144D^{2}$/137, ms.]
230 [1/1, typed] The manuscript carries the heading *A. de C. (?) or B. of D. (or something else)*.
231 [5/57, typed]
gladiolated: After a neologism in the original. This might mean that Soares's foreglimpse of dissatisfaction is surrounded by gladioli, perhaps to suggest a funeral (cf. the 'truth that needs no flowers to show it's dead' of Text 193). Or it might refer to the structure of the plant, whose horizontal spikes create a kind of louvred effect; Soares, then, would be glimpsing the future as if through a set of louvres.
232 [2/88, typed]
233 [2/91, ms.]
234 [9/7, ms.]
235 [2/5, typed]
236 [2/69, ms.]
237† [94/98, typed]
238† [15^{5}/14, typed]
Tarde: Gabriel Tarde (1843–1904) was a French sociologist and criminologist. (The quote reappears in Text 446.)
239† [138/87, typed]
240 [5/34, ms.]
241 [8/11, typed]
242 [1/18, typed]
243 [3/19–20, typed] Dated 4 November 1931.
244 [5/47, ms.]
245 [5/28, ms.]
246† [114^{1}/77, ms.]
247† [7/34, typed]
248 [9/3, ms.]
249† [9/18–22, ms.]
250 [7/18, ms.]
251 [7/4, 8/5, 8/7, ms.]

252 [9/1, ms.]
253 [2/8, typed]
254 [1/44–5, typed]
255 [4/26–8, typed] Dated 29 November 1931.
256 [2/49, typed]
257 [1/87, typed]
258 [9/2, ms.] On the same manuscript sheet, Pessoa wrote in English: 'Your poems are of interest to mankind; your liver isn't. Drink till you write well and feel sick. Bless your poems and be damned to you.'
259 [4/5–6, typed] Published in *Descobrimento. Revista de Cultura*, no. 3, 1931.
Fialho: José Valentim Fialho de Almeida (1857–1911) was a Portuguese writer of stories and social commentary. Initially informed by naturalism but later embodying Decadent ideals, his writing became increasingly concerned to force the limits of language, using it impressionistically to represent feelings and sensations not conveyed by traditional diction and syntax.
Vieira: See note for Text 30.
phonetic rather than etymological spelling: Literally, 'simplified spelling'. In 1911, one year after Portugal became a republic, an Orthographic Reform introduced sweeping changes into the spelling of Portuguese, with *y* being replaced by *i*, *ph* by *f*, and most silent letters being dropped. Pessoa, who never accepted or adopted most of these changes, was a strong defender of etymological orthography ('Graeco-Roman transliteration'), both theoretically and in his actual practice.
260 [3/84, typed] Dated 1 December 1931.
261 [2/25, ms.]
262 [4/2, typed] Dated 1 December 1931.
infinitudinous: A neologism formed from the words *infinito* and *múltiplo* is employed in the original.
263 [4/1, typed] Dated 1 December 1931.
the man that sold his shadow: Peter Schlemihl, protagonist of a novel by Adelbert von Chamisso (see note for Text 468).
264† [28/24, ms.]
265 [1/41, typed]
266 [4/22, mixed] Dated 3 December 1931.
Vieira: See note for Text 30.
267 [9/10, typed] At the bottom of the manuscript, in English: *(transformation of Sherlock Holmes article – should it be done?).*
268 [2/81, typed]
Cesário: See note for Text 3.
269 [7/41, ms.]

270 [3/3, typed]
271 [3/4, typed]
272 [3/5, typed]
273 [1/86, typed]
274 [1/63, typed]
275 [1/3, typed]
276† [133B/39, ms.]
277 [1/19, 21, typed]
Chiado: A fashionable neighbourhood of central Lisbon, much frequented by writers and intellectuals in Pessoa's time.
278 [1/69, mixed]
'Most people are other people': From *De Profundis*. The passage cited by Pessoa continues: 'Their thoughts are someone else's opinions, their lives a mimicry, their passions a quotation.'
Antero de Quental: A Portuguese poet and thinker (1842–91) much admired by Pessoa. Quental's chronic pessimism, coupled with mental instability, worsened with age, until he finally committed suicide.
279 [3/82, typed] Dated 16 December 1931.
280† [9/33, ms.]
281 [1/66, ms.]
interexist: After a neologism in the original.
282 [2/48, typed] Preceded by this notation: *(written in spells, and with much to revise)*.
283 [7/40, typed]
284 [9/42, ms.]
285 [4/23, typed] Dated 20 December 1931.
286 [2/86, typed]
287 [1/28, ms.]
288† [144D^2/123, ms.]
289 [5/51, typed]
the scattered traits of its various parts!: This translation presupposes a typographical error in the manuscript, *duas* in lieu of *suas*. Not assuming an error, the translation could be 'the scattered traits of the two parts!'.
290 [2/21, ms.]
Horaces: 'Verlaines' (alternate version)
291 [1/62, ms.]
292 [9/30, ms.]
293 [138/21, ms.]
294 [9/34a, ms.]
295 [9/35, 35a, ms.]

296 [7/17, ms.]
animal happiness: 'animal spirits' (alternate version, written in English)
297† [28/96, ms.]
298 [4/33, typed]
299 [5/74, ms.]
Cascais: See note for Text 16.
300 [94/87, ms.]
301 [5/7a, 9a, ms.]
302 [2/62, mixed]
303 [4/24–5, typed] Dated 17 January 1932.
fooling himself with a double personality, plays against his own person: 'cheating on the score with a double personality, plays against himself' (alternate version)
304 [Sinais 3, ms.]
305† [8/4, ms.] The first two manuscript pages of this passage are missing. In the portion of the text that has survived, the end of the first sentence literally translates as 'obstacles to doing this constantly', where 'this' presumably refers to something from the previous (now lost) paragraph.
ubiquitize: After a similar neologism in the original.
306 [6/13, typed] The translation reflects, as far as possible, the peculiar shifts from third-person plural to first that occur in the last four paragraphs.
argonauts' adventurous precept: See note for Text 124.
307 [5/80 ms.]
308† [9/33a, ms.]
309 [9/51, ms.]
310 [4/68, ms.]
311 [3/9, typed]
312 [1/36, typed]
313 [1/25, mixed]
314 [144D^2/43–4, ms.]
Island of the superiors: 'City of the superiors' (alternate version)
315 [5/39, ms.]
316 [144G/38, ms.]
317 [3/81, mixed] Dated 26 January 1932.
318 [3/83, ms.]
319 [5/45, 45a, ms.]
320 [3/69, mixed] Dated 29 January 1932.
321 [4/36, ms.]
322 [5/63–4, ms.]
Waters: 'Metals'/'Seaweed' (alternate versions)

323 [1/52, typed]
324† [144D²/19, ms.]
325 [4/54, typed]
Fictions of the interlude: This phrase was supposed to serve as the general title for Pessoa's heteronymic work, which he planned to bring out in various volumes (see the excerpted Preface to *Fictions of the Interlude* in Appendix III), and actually did serve as a title for a group of five poems signed by his own name and published in 1917. The last two paragraphs of Text 348 elucidate its meaning.
326† [9/46, ms.]
327 [2/57, typed]
328 [4/86, ms.] At the bottom of the manuscript sheet, written upside-down: *Nobody achieves anything. . . Nothing's worth doing.*
329 [4/87, ms.]
330 [5/25–6, ms.]
331 [3/71, typed] Dated 5 February 1932.
332 [5/73, ms.]
333 [144D²/135, ms.] Dated 18 July 1916.
334 [3/68, typed] Dated 16 March 1932.
335 [144X/36, ms.]
336 [3/80, typed]
337 [3/70, typed]
338 [1/31, typed]
Pays du Tendre: An allegorical *Carte du Tendre*, or map of the country called 'Tender', was published in the first volume (1654) of *Clélie*, a novel of love and courtship written by Madeleine de Scudéry (1607–1701). 'Tender', the country of love, is traversed by the River of Affections, includes a Lake of Indifference towards the east, and has numerous towns with such names as Sincerity, Tenderness, Thoughtlessness and Spite. Many other examples of 'amorous geography' circulated in France during the second half of the seventeenth century.
339 [3/75, typed] Dated 28 March 1932.
340 [2/61, ms.]
Amiel's: See note for Text 72.
341 [2/72–3, typed]
342 [3/72, typed] Dated 2 May 1932.
343 [7/43, ms.]
344 [4/70, ms.]
perverse: 'sublime' (alternate version)
345 [4/69, ms.]

chaste like dead lips: 'chaste like hermits' (alternate version)
346† [94/93, ms.]
like our souls: 'like our idea of them'/'like our seeing' (alternate versions)
347 [9/14, ms.]
348 [3/74, typed] Dated 15 May 1932.
349 [7/19, ms.]
350 [3/73, typed] Dated 23 May 1932.
351 [7/17, ms.]
352 [3/78, typed] Dated 31 May 1932.
353† [94/4, typed]
354 [4/43, typed]
355 [3/63, typed]
the light of all hells: 'an infinite day'/'a mighty day' (alternate versions)
the hard veil of the abyss: 'silks/fabrics from the abyss' (alternate versions)
356 [4/45, typed] Dated 11 June 1932.
357 [3/79, typed]
358 [2/77, typed]
359 [3/77, ms.] Dated 14 June 1932.
the poet: Matthew Arnold, in his poem 'To Marguerite – Continued'.
master of St Martha: Pessoa might be referring to the scene, recorded in the Gospel of Luke, where Jesus chides Martha for worrying too much about serving the meal instead of enjoying his company, like her sister Mary, and/or he might have in mind the Gospel of John, where Jesus is reported to have defended Mary's 'wasteful' gesture of anointing his feet with costly spikenard.
360 [1/23, typed]
361 [3/10, typed]
362 [5/37, ms.]
363 [9/37–8, ms.] Marked *B. of D. or Stamp Collector*. 'The Stamp Collector' was one of many short stories that Pessoa never finished.
364† [9/29, 94/76, ms.] Alternate version of first paragraph: 'Our sensations pass, so how can we possess them, let alone what they make known to us? Can anyone possess a river that flows? Does the wind that blows past us belong to anyone?'
365† [94/89, ms.]
366 [9/50, ms.]
367 [7/41, ms.]
368† [15B[1]/58, ms.]
never lingers at the windows of an attitude: 'never assumes a definite stance' (alternate version)
369 [7/1, ms.] The manuscript also contains the title of a projected passage,

'Love with a Chinese Woman on a Porcelain Teacup', for which just one sentence was written: 'Our love took place peacefully, the way she wanted it, in just two dimensions.'

370 [7/5–10, ms.]

wouldn't have wanted to say: 'couldn't have helped having finally said' (alternate version)

371 [28/98, ms.]

372 [133/10, ms.]

373 [3/76, typed] Dated 23 June 1932.

English poet: Edmund Gosse (1849–1928), in a poem titled 'Lying in the Grass'.

374 [4/46, typed] Dated 2 July 1932. Published in *A Revista*, no. 1, 1932.

Benfica: See note for Text 138.

375 [7/38, ms.]

376 [5/61, ms.]

377 [3/65, typed] Dated 16 July 1932.

the nerves: 'the mind' (alternate version)

378 [2/15, typed] Dated 25 July 1932.

379 [138/21, ms.]

380 [4/49, typed] Dated 28 September 1932.

381 [4/50–51, typed] Dated 28 September 1932.

382 [2/26, ms.]

383 [9/48, ms.]

384 [5/38, ms.]

385 [4/48, ms.] Dated 2 November 1932.

386 [2/22, typed] Dated 28 November 1932.

387 [3/25, typed]

388 [9/13, ms.]

389 [5/40, ms.]

390† [8/2, ms.]

391 [2/23, typed] Dated 13 December 1932.

392† [138A/10, typed]

393 [1/68, mixed]

since Mystery plays a part in these: 'and our very life denies itself' (alternate version)

fado: Portugal's plaintive national folksong, whose name also means 'fate'.

the same watered-down life: 'the same sensation/consciousness of life' (alternate versions)

394 [144D^{2}/37, ms.]

395† [8/13, typed]

396 [2/27, typed] Dated 30 December 1932.

397 [2/14, ms.]

398 [5/48, ms.]

399 [2/32, ms.]

Diogenes: Plutarch reports that when Alexander the Great was declared general of the Greeks, everyone came to congratulate him except Diogenes the Cynic. Alexander went with his entourage to Diogenes, whom he found lying in the sun. Distracted by the bustle of people, Diogenes looked up at Alexander, who asked him if he wanted anything. 'Yes,' answered the philosopher, 'I would like you to stand a little out of my sun.' Alexander, impressed with this answer, went away saying that, if he weren't Alexander, he would choose to be Diogenes.

400 [9/6, ms.]

401† [138A/41, ms.]

402† [133C/59, ms.]

403† [94/2, typed]

404 [144D^2/43, ms.]

405 [1/13, typed] Dated 23 March 1933.

406 [2/85, typed] The following, isolated phrase appears between the last two paragraphs: *the bright maternal smile of the brimming earth, the hermetic splendour of the darkness on high . . . . .*

407 [1/37, typed]

sensitive fabric: 'wrinkled/rough/outer fabric' (alternate versions)

408 [1/61, typed]

fado: See note for Text 393.

409 [2/30, typed] Dated 29 March 1933.

410 [1/20, typed]

Fialho's: See note for Text 259.

411 [1/6, typed]

412 [9/43–6, ms.]

Alone: A much-admired book of rueful poems (titled *Só* in the original) by António Nobre (1867–1900).

413 [9/26, ms.]

hear God: 'hear the hours' (alternate version)

And over all of this the horror of living will hover remotely: 'And may the horror of living hover remotely over all of this' (alternate version)

414 [9/26, ms.]

415 [7/11, ms.]

416 [5/55, mixed]

417 [1/46, typed]

Father Figueiredo: António Cardoso Borges de Figueiredo (1792–1878), a priest who wrote a number of instructional books for use in schools. Pessoa's surviving personal library contains a well-worn copy of Figueiredo's *Rhetoric*, with notes on the flyleaves and even several poems.
Father Freire: Francisco José Freire (1719–73), better known by his pen-name, Cândido Lusitano, was a founding member of Arcadia, an influential Portuguese literary academy.
418 [1/16, ms.]
written with c: Father Figueiredo's *Rhetoric* contains no specific lists of 'words written with *c*'. Pessoa is no doubt referring to the fact that the Jesuit's orthography, reflecting the conventions of the eighteenth century, employed *c* in various words from which it later dropped out (because it was silent) or in which it was replaced by *s* or *ss*.
419 [1/71, 71a, mixed]
420 [114[1]/18, ms.]
the unknown god of the religion of my Gods: 'the unknown god whom perhaps the Gods remember' (alternate version)
421 [1/71, ms.]
422 [1/80, typed]
423† [94/13, 13a, ms.]
424 [5/23, ms.]
425 [144X/99, ms.]
426 [2/17, typed] Dated 5 April 1933.
427 [9/4, ms.] The passage is followed by two proverbs (incorporated into a group of 300 Portuguese proverbs that Pessoa collected and translated in the 1910s for an English publisher, who did not finally publish the projected volume, due to economic difficulties):

> *The sun rises for everyone.*
> *God is good, but the devil isn't bad.*

The proverbs are followed by this random note: *Its faults notwithstanding, the Romantic equilibrium is better than that of the 17th century in France.*
428 [4/82–3, ms.]
neighbourhood of the great Mystery: 'neighbourhood of God' (alternate version)
429 [5/31–2, ms.] Dated 18 September 1917.
430 [5/27, ms.]
certain madmen: 'systematized lunatics' (alternate version)
431 [1/47, typed]
432 [3/43, ms.]

433 [2/29, typed] Dated 7 April 1933.
434 [4/35, typed]
435 [1/27, typed]
436 [1/38–40, mixed]
painful to my heart: 'painful to my consciousness' (alternate version)
to life as to an enormous yoke: 'to life, to the abstract yoke of God'/'to life, stretching it across the window as across a guillotine' (alternate versions)
437 [2/18, typed] Dated 29 August 1933.
438† [94/16, ms.]
439 [1/29, ms.]
440 [3/28, typed]
441 [2/19, typed] 8 September 1933.
442 [2/71, typed]
443 [5/8a, ms.]
444 [2/34, ms.]
445 [4/53, typed] 18 September 1933.
446 [1/5, typed] This and the next two passages were found in the large envelope where Pessoa placed material for *The Book of Disquiet*, but they undoubtedly belonged to his projected essay on Omar Khayyám, for which various other passages were written. Perhaps Pessoa, giving up on the fragmentary essay, decided to include parts of it in *The Book of Disquiet.*
Tarde: See note for Text 238.
Dean Aldrich: Henry Aldrich (1647–1710), the Dean of Christ Church in Oxford, was a humanist of many vocations, from theology to architecture. Pessoa did not record Aldrich's epigram, 'Reasons for Drinking', on the manuscript copy of this passage about Khayyám, but he evidently meant to fill in the blank space later with his own translation of the verses into Portuguese, found elsewhere among the thousands of papers he left.
it was a Greek: Glykon.
447 [1/4, mixed] The following epithet appears at the end of the passage: *The Persian poet, Master of disconsolation and disillusion.*
448 [1/2, typed]
449 [4/52, typed] Dated 2 November 1933.
450 [1/49, typed]
almost human sound: 'harsh and humble sound' (alternate version)
451 [2/51, typed]
'Any road, this simple Entepfuhl road. . . World': From Thomas Carlyle, cf. Text 138.
452 [2/52, typed]
453† [9/41, ms.]

454 [1/85, typed]
in the news: 'in progress' (alternate version)
455 [4/55, ms.] Dated 23 December 1933.
456 [4/56–7, ms.] Dated 31 March 1934.
457 [7/3, ms.]
458 [2/11, typed]
Praça da Figueira: One of Lisbon's downtown squares, which in Pessoa's day was taken up by a public market.
459 [2/2, ms.]
460 [2/47, typed]
461 [5/59, ms.]
462 [5/10, typed]
463 [7/39, typed] Dated 5 June 1934.
464 [6/16, typed]
Poe's Egaeus: From the short story 'Berenice'.
465 [6/15, typed] Dated 9 June 1934.
466 [5/35, ms.]
467 [28/26, ms.]
468 [5/12, typed] Dated 19 June 1934.
Peter Schlemihl: The protagonist of *Peter Schlemihls wundersame Geschichte*, published in 1814 by Adelbert von Chamisso (1781–1838).
469 [9/11, ms.]
470 [144Y/52, ms.]
471 [5/33, typed] Dated 21 June 1934.
472 [7/49, ms.] Dated 29 June 1934.
epopt: An initiate in the highest order of the Eleusinian mysteries.
473 [7/50, ms.] Dated 26 July 1934.
474 [112/9, ms.]
475 [133G/30, ms.]
Amiel: See note for Text 72.
476 [5/69, ms.]
477 [3/8, ms.]
478 [1/26, ms.] The parenthetical heading is in English in the original.
479 [2/31, ms.]
480 [1/78, ms.]
481 [6/17, typed]

A Disquiet Anthology

ADVICE TO UNHAPPILY MARRIED WOMEN (I) [5/65, ms.]
Cesare Borgia: Cited by Machiavelli as a prime example of the modern 'prince', Cesare (*c.*1475–1507) was one of the most notorious members of the politically ruthless Borgia clan.
ADVICE TO UNHAPPILY MARRIED WOMEN (II) [5/8a, ms.]
ADVICE TO UNHAPPILY MARRIED WOMEN (III) [114^1/97, ms.] No title appears on the manuscript, but Pessoa almost certainly had his 'Advice' to unhappy wives in mind.
APOCALYPTIC FEELING [7/23–7, ms.]
THE ART OF EFFECTIVE DREAMING (I) [$15B^1$/96, ms.]
THE ART OF EFFECTIVE DREAMING (II) [5/5, ms.]
you can leave for tomorrow: 'you can likewise not do tomorrow' (alternate version)
THE ART OF EFFECTIVE DREAMING (III) [9/23a, ms.]
THE ART OF EFFECTIVE DREAMING FOR METAPHYSICAL MINDS [$144D^2$/46–50, ms.]
I'm a character of: 'I'm bits of characters from' (alternate version)
CASCADE [5/6, ms.]
when life is negated: 'when love is negated' (alternate version)
CENOTAPH [5/15–16, typed] The sixth paragraph is followed by two incomplete phrases, which Pessoa presumably thought of incorporating into a revised version of this text:

> *– of simple heroism, with no heaven to win through martyrdom, nor humanity to save through struggle; of the old pagan race that belongs to the City and outside of which all are barbarians and enemies.*
>
> *– but with the emotion of the son who loves his mother because she is his mother and not because he is her son.*

DECLARATION OF DIFFERENCE [5/56, typed]
DIVINE ENVY [4/65–6, ms.]
Cais do Sodré: See note for Text 16.
FUNERAL MARCH† [138A/33–4, ms.]
FUNERAL MARCH FOR LUDWIG II, KING OF BAVARIA [4/59–63, 138A/56, ms.] The following phrases, which Pessoa perhaps meant to incorporate into a revised version of this text (along with several other fragmentary passages that have turned up in his archives), appear at the end of the manuscript copy:

. . . and in the background Death. . .

Your coming glows in the sunset, in the regions where Death reigns.

They have crowned you with mysterious flowers of unknown colours, an absurd garland worthy of a deposed god.

. . . your purple devotion to dreaming, splendour of Death's antechamber.

. . . impossible hetairas of the abyss. . .

Sound your horns, heralds, from the tops of the battlements, in salute of this great dawn! The King of Death is about to enter his domain!

Flowers from the abyss, black roses, moon-white carnations, radiant red poppies.

Ludwig II, King of Bavaria: This whimsical German monarch was born in 1845, came to the throne in 1864, and died in 1886, on 13 June, exactly two years before Pessoa was born. A fervent admirer and supporter of Richard Wagner, Ludwig had little interest in government affairs but preferred to spend his time and the state's money building mock-Gothic castles and sponsoring lavish performances of plays, concerts and operas for his own private enjoyment. His exasperated ministers finally declared him mentally unfit to rule and sent him to his castle-turned-asylum at Berg, where the next day his drowned corpse was found in Lake Starnberg, but whether he committed suicide or was the victim of foul play remains a mystery. This would perhaps please the so-called Dream King, who once wrote: 'I want to remain an eternal enigma, both to myself and to others.'
catalfalques of heroes: 'catafalques of suicides' (alternate version)
IMPERIAL LEGEND [5/75, ms.]
restless mystery: 'congenital mystery' (alternate version)
my self-awareness: 'my soul' (alternate version)
IN THE FOREST OF ESTRANGEMENT Published in *A Águia*, July–December 1913, as a passage from *The Book of Disquiet* and signed by Fernando Pessoa. The whereabouts of the original manuscript is unknown.
THE LAKE OF POSSESSION (I) [9/47, ms.]
THE LAKE OF POSSESSION (II) [5/5, ms.]
Property isn't a theft: it's nothing: This statement refutes, or relativizes, the notion of Proudhon. But in a note written in English [15^4/15], Pessoa agreed with the author of *Qu'est-ce que la propriété?*: 'The true word on the case was first spoken by Proudhon. "Property," he said, "is a theft." And the words were truer than he himself believed, for property, in truth, is a theft and had its origin in robbery.'
A LETTER (I) [4/74, 5/9, ms.]
A LETTER (II)† [114^1/75, ms.]

LUCID DIARY [5/17, typed]
by the gods: 'by the angels' (alternate version)
THE MAJOR [9/5, ms.] Dated 8 October 1919.
MAXIMS [7/32–3, ms.]
MILKY WAY [7/37, 7/35–6, typed]
rites from the time of no one: 'rites contemporaneous to no one's understanding' (alternate version)
long-drawn-out epitaph: 'Gongoristic epitaph' (alternate version)
MILLIMETRES [9/49, typed]
OUR LADY OF SILENCE [4/75–7, 9/28, 94/80, 4/78–9, 4/73, 4/72, ms.]
so loathsomely born?: 'so loathsomely expelled into the world?/into the light?' (alternate versions)
Votary of nonsense phrases: 'Votary of sexless phrases' (alternate version)
PEDRO'S PASTORAL [8/8, ms.] Alternate title in the manuscript: *Pedro's Eclogue*.
a bird alighted: 'the idea of a bird alighted' (alternate version)
PERISTYLE [9/39, 31, 32, 40, ms.]
like the open doors of an abandoned house: 'like open gates at the end of a tree-lined drive' (alternate version)
my life in you: 'your life in me' (alternate version)
than this dead life: 'than this very life' (alternate version)
RANDOM DIARY [5/68, ms.]
THE RIVER OF POSSESSION [5/70–72, ms.]
our true nature: 'our true humanity'/'our maturity' (alternate versions)
Platonic: 'spiritualist' (alternate version)
garden of Estrela: A large public garden in Lisbon.
SELF-EXAMINATION [94/88, 88a, ms.]
Amiel: See note for Text 72.
THE SENSATIONIST [144D^2/82–4, ms.]
'on le fatigait en l'aimant': From Chateaubriand. See Text 235.
SENTIMENTAL EDUCATION [5/53–4, typed]
SYMPHONY OF THE RESTLESS NIGHT [94/3, mixed]
argonauts: See note for Text 124.
THE VISUAL LOVER (I) [7/45–7, ms.]
Anteros: According to some mythological accounts, when young Eros (called Cupid by the Romans) complained to his mother that he was lonely, Aphrodite gave him a brother, Anteros, to be his playmate. A symbol of reciprocal affection, this Anteros was known as the god of unrequited love, punishing those who didn't return the affection they were shown. But Pessoa, in an unpublished text from his archives [107/23–5], follows another ancient line

of thought, which understood Anteros as an anti-Cupid. According to Pessoa, Eros represented instinctive love, motivated by sensual attraction, whereas Anteros represented love founded on reason and the intelligence.

'Anteros' was also the title for the last in a projected cycle of five poems that would have traced the history of love in the Western world. Pessoa wrote and published the first two poems in English: 'Antinoüs' (which he linked to Greece) and 'Epithalamium' (Rome). The third poem, 'Prayer to a Woman's Body', would have represented the Christian era, and the fourth poem, 'Pan-Eros', the modern era. 'Anteros' was supposed to tell the future of love, and although no trace of such a poem has been uncovered, Pessoa did leave various (still unpublished) prose fragments in English for an essay likewise titled 'Anteros', into which he probably thought of incorporating 'The Visual Lover'. The content of these various prose pieces confirms that Anteros, for Pessoa, opposes and transcends carnal love.

THE VISUAL LOVER (II) [5/58, typed]

A VOYAGE I NEVER MADE (I) [4/80–81, ms.]

our own land, but only, of course, because it was no land at all: 'our own, which we'd left so far behind, who knows whether in that same world' (alternate version)

A VOYAGE I NEVER MADE (II) [5/4, ms.]

A VOYAGE I NEVER MADE (III) [5/3, ms.] No title appears on the manuscript, but it seems to have been written for Pessoa's unrealized 'Voyage'.

A VOYAGE I NEVER MADE (IV) [5/24, ms.] No title appears on the manuscript.

Appendix I: Texts Citing the Name of Vincent Guedes

AP-1 [6/3, ms.] Marked *Preface*, this passage contains elements incorporated by Pessoa into the (presumably subsequent) Preface placed at the front of this edition.

AP-2 [8/3, ms.]

autobiography of a man who never existed: 'biography of a man who never lived' (alternate version)

AP-3 [7/17, ms.]

'Tout notaire a rêvé des sultanes': 'Every notary has dreamed of sultanas' (from Flaubert).

Appendix II: Two Letters

AP-4 [7/48, typed] The typescript carries the heading: *(Copy of a letter to Pretoria)*. In 1896 Pessoa's mother, widowed and remarried, had moved with young Fernando to Durban, South Africa, where her new husband served as the Portuguese consul. Pessoa returned to Lisbon in 1905, his mother (with the children from her second marriage) in 1920, once more a widow.
my best and closest friend: Mário de Sá-Carneiro. See note below.
AP-5 *Mário de Sá-Carneiro*: A close friend (1890–1916) and collaborator of Pessoa, was one of Portugal's most important Modernist poets as well as a notable writer of fiction. The theme of all but his earliest work was the torment he felt for not living up – in his flesh, in his writing, and even in his imagination – to an ideal of beauty he could only intuit, not define, though it was clearly informed by a Decadent, post-Symbolist aesthetic. Pessoa posted this letter to Paris, where one month later Sá-Carneiro committed suicide in his room at the Hôtel de Nice.
The Mariner: Pessoa's only complete play (*O Marinheiro*), which he classified as a 'static drama'. It was published in 1915, in the first issue of *Orpheu* (see note to Pessoa's 'Preface' at the beginning of this volume).

Appendix III: Reflections on The Book of Disquiet *from Pessoa's Writings*

B. Excerpts from letters
João de Lebre e Lima: A little-known poet (1889–1959).
Armando Cortes-Rodrigues: Azorean poet (1891–1971) who actively collaborated with Pessoa and other Portuguese Modernists in the 1910s.
João Gaspar Simões: A major critic (1903–87) of twentieth-century Portuguese literature and a co-founder of *Presença* (published from 1927 to 1940), the Coimbra-based literary magazine that recognized Pessoa's extreme originality and actively promoted his work when it was still not well known. Gaspar Simões published, in 1950, the first biography of Pessoa.
Portugal: This long work in progress was finally published in 1934 under a different title, *Mensagem (Message)*, and with forty-four poems instead of forty-one. It was the only volume of Pessoa's Portuguese poetry to see print in his lifetime.
Adolfo Casais Monteiro: Poet and critic (1908–72) who was an editor of

Presença (see note on João Gaspar Simões) and an important advocate of Pessoa's work.

C. From the Unfinished Preface to *Fictions of the Interlude*

These are just two of various passages written by Pessoa for his Preface-in-progress to the *Fictions*, which would have brought together the work of his major poetic heteronyms. (See note for Text 325.)

'The Anarchist Banker': A lengthy short story (*'O Banqueiro Anarquista'*) that really amounts to a Socratic dialogue, published by Pessoa in 1922.

Table of Heteronyms

Pessoa referred to the many names under which he wrote prose and poetry as 'heteronyms' rather than pseudonyms, since they were not merely false names but belonged to invented others, to fictional writers with points of view and literary styles that were different from Pessoa's. The three main poetic heteronyms – Alberto Caeiro, Ricardo Reis and Álvaro de Campos – came into existence in 1914, but Pessoa wrote under some seventy-five names, the first of which go back to his childhood. Some, such as Maria José, were shooting stars who authored a single work; others, such as Vicente Guedes, shifted position and shone now brightly, now dimly, before eventually fading from view; and a very few, such as Campos, were permanent (though never static) bodies in Pessoa's cosmography. The following is a list of the most significant names, along with some curious, lesser lights. They are presented in their approximate, sometimes conjectural order of appearance in Pessoa's writing.

Chevalier de Pas Identified by Pessoa as 'my first heteronym, or rather, my first non-existent acquaintance', this friendly knight reportedly wrote letters to and through Pessoa when he was just six years old, perhaps in French, a language that both his parents spoke fluently.

Charles Robert Anon First full-fledged heteronym, created by Pessoa when still a teenager in South Africa, probably in 1903. His poetry and prose, written in English, are concerned with philosophical problems such as being vs. non-being and free will vs. determinism, and with the personal anxieties of a young man (himself? Pessoa?) on the threshold of becoming an adult. C. R. Anon, as he often signed himself, was basically anti-Christian and sometimes quite violently so, as in his 'Epitaph of the Catholic Church' and his prose piece that decreed a 'sentence of excommunication on all priests and all sectarians of all religions in the world'.

Alexander Search Pessoa even had calling cards printed up for this English heteronym, who was born in Lisbon on the same day as his maker: 13 June

1888. Most of his close to two hundred poems were written in the three years immediately following Pessoa's return to Lisbon in 1905, though a few date as late as 1910, while others go back to 1903–4 (at least some of these earlier poems were only credited to Search retroactively, however). His poems cannot compare, as literary creations, to the Portuguese verses written in the names of Caeiro, Campos and Reis, but they contain all the major themes subsequently developed by the illustrious trio. Search also wrote prose, including a macabre story titled 'A Very Original Dinner', in which the unsuspecting diners feast on human flesh.

Charles James Search Born on 18 April 1886, Alexander's brother was a full-time translator of (mostly) Portuguese literature into English. The majority of his projects, such as a translation of Eça de Queiroz's *The Mandarin*, never got off the ground, but he did produce many English versions of sonnets by the philosophically inclined Antero de Quental (1842–91). He also left a partial translation of a long Spanish verse play, *The Student of Salamanca*, by José de Espronceda (1808–42).

Jean Seul de Méluret Pessoa's French heteronym, born on 1 August 1885, seems to have dawned on Pessoa's imagination some time around 1907. Besides writing poetry, Jean Seul left two unfinished essays: 'Des cas d'exhibitionnisme', concerned with the phenomenon of young women who perform half naked in Paris music halls, and a moral satire titled 'La France en 1950' (or, alternatively, 'La France à l'an 2000'), in which the futuristic narrator observes such oddities as a certain 'Monsieur Sleeps-in-the-bed-of-four-women Giraud' being hauled off to prison for 'the crime of refusing to commit incest'.

Vicente Guedes The first large-scale heteronym to write in Portuguese probably came into existence in 1907 or 1908. Besides poetry, stories, translations and diaristic writings, Guedes was for a time in charge of *The Book of Disquiet* (see the Introduction). His biographical details – assistant bookkeeper and solitary bachelor living in a rented fourth-floor room in Lisbon – exactly match those of Bernardo Soares, who seems to have been his reincarnation.

Alberto Caeiro Recognized as their master by Álvaro de Campos, by Ricardo Reis and by Pessoa himself, Alberto Caeiro da Silva was born in Lisbon on 16 April 1889, lived most of his life with an old aunt in the country, and died in Lisbon in 1915, the victim of tuberculosis. He continued, however, to write poems through Pessoa until at least 1930. Billed as 'Nature's poet', this supposed shepherd admitted in his very first poem that 'I've never kept sheep,/ But it's as if I did.' Conceived in 1914, Caeiro was originally destined to be a highly eclectic vanguardist, responsible not only for the apparently naïve, anti-metaphysical poems of *The Keeper of Sheep* but also for the long Futurist odes that came to be written by Campos and for some Cubist-inspired poems that were ultimately attributed to Pessoa himself. Divested of these more self-consciously literary modes, Caeiro retreated to the country with no other ambition than to see things as things, without philosophy.

Álvaro de Campos Pessoa's most vociferous heteronym was born in Tavira, the Algarve, on 15 October 1890, studied naval engineering in Glasgow, interrupted his studies to make a voyage to the Orient, lived for a time in London, and eventually settled in Lisbon. A dandy who used an in-those-days stylish monocle, smoked opium, drank absinthe, and was as readily attracted to young men as to young women, Campos the writer initially produced loud and long 'Sensationist' odes reminiscent of Walt Whitman, but as the years wore on his poems became shorter and more melancholy. He never stopped being mischievous, however, meddling at frequent intervals in his creator's real-world life. To the ire and chagrin of Pessoa's friends, the naval engineer sometimes showed up in his stead at appointments, and in 1929 Campos took it upon himself to write to Ophelia Queiroz, Pessoa's one sweetheart, exhorting her to flush all thought of her beloved 'down the toilet'.

Ricardo Reis Born 19 September 1887 in Oporto, this classicist and trained physician was hazily revealed to Pessoa in 1912 but did not heteronymically affirm himself until two years later. A monarchist sympathizer (Portugal's last king abdicated in 1910, whereupon a republic was formed), he supposedly moved to Brazil in 1919, though Pessoa elsewhere reports that he was a 'Latin teacher in an important American high school', and the archives contain an address for a Dr Ricardo Sequeira Reis in Peru. Characterized by Pessoa as 'a Greek Horace who writes in Portuguese', Reis composed short odes that advocated a stoic acceptance of life with its small and fleeting pleasures, its inevitable sorrow, and its lack of any discoverable meaning.

Frederico Reis Ricardo's brother, of whom we know only that he lived abroad, wrote a pamphlet about the so-called Lisbon School of poetry (whose key practitioners were Alberto Caeiro, Álvaro de Campos and Ricardo Reis), defending it as Portugal's only truly cosmopolitan literary movement. He was also a sympathetic critic of his brother's 'profoundly sad' poetry, which he described as 'a lucid and disciplined attempt to obtain a measure of calm'.

Thomas Crosse Responsible for taking Portuguese culture to the English-speaking world, this essayist and translator was especially committed to promoting the work of Alberto Caeiro. 'Strange and terribly, appallingly new' is how he characterized Caeiro in an Introduction he wrote for an edition of the pseudo-shepherd's *Complete Poems*, which he was supposed to translate into English. But this worthy project, like so many plans announced by Pessoa and his fictional collaborators, never amounted to more than a good intention.

I. I. Crosse This probable brother of Thomas Crosse wrote critical pieces in praise of Caeiro (for his 'mysticism of objectivity') and Campos ('the greatest rhythmist that there has ever been').

A. A. Crosse This third Mr Crosse competed for cash prizes in the puzzle and word games published in the pages of English newspapers.

António Mora As the chief theoretician of Neopaganism, a movement designed to replace an ailing and decadent Christianity, Mora passionately elucidated the genius of Caeiro and Reis, whom he regarded as direct poetic expressions of paganism. He also left dozens and dozens of typed and handwritten passages belonging to ambitious works-in-progress with titles such as *Return of the Gods* (co-authored by Ricardo Reis), *Prolegomena to a Reformation of Paganism* and *The Foundations of Paganism* (billed as a 'rebuttal of Kant's *Critique of Pure Reason*, and an attempt to reconstruct pagan Objectivism').

Raphael Baldaya Identified in a letter by Pessoa as an astrologer with a long beard, Baldaya was conceived in late 1915. In addition to horoscopes and his writings on the stars, he produced several philosophical texts, including a 'Treatise on Negation', in which he affirmed that being is 'essentially Illusion and Falsehood. God is the Supreme Lie'.

Bernardo Soares The ultimate fictional author of *The Book of Disquiet* seems to have taken on this job in 1928, presumably the same year he moved to the Rua dos Douradores, but he was originally cast in the role of a short-story writer. Pessoa's strong kinship with Soares – whom he called a semi-heteronym, since his was not a different personality but a mutilated version of Fernando's – is reflected in their names, 'Bernardo' and 'Soares' containing almost the same letters as 'Fernando' and 'Pessoa'.

Maria José Pessoa's only known female persona was the author of a single, long and pathetic love letter to Senhor António, a handsome metalworker who passed by her window on his way to and from work each day. Hunchbacked, virtually crippled, and dying of TB, Maria José had no intention of ever sending her desperate letter. 'My days are numbered,' she explained in one of its last paragraphs, 'and I'm only writing this letter to hold it against my chest as if you'd written it to me instead of me to you.'

Baron of Teive Conceived in 1928, the Baron may have been Pessoa's last invented author. Similar in many respects to Bernardo Soares (Pessoa compares the two in his Preface to *Fictions of the Interlude* – in Appendix III), Teive may likewise be classified as a semi-heteronym, as a mutilated or distorted copy of Pessoa. Endowed with Pessoa's ultra-rationalist bent, he also incarnated his creator's aristocratic pretensions (Pessoa was rather proud of the vaguely blue blood that trickled on his father's side). Haunted, like Pessoa, by a helpless inability to finish any of his writing projects, the Baron finally took the rational, logical step of committing suicide. His creator, perhaps with a giggle, kept on writing.

FOR MORE FROM FERNANDO PESSOA, LOOK FOR THE 

A Little Larger Than the Entire Universe
Selected Poems

Translated and Edited with an Introduction and Notes by Richard Zenith

Writing obsessively in French, English, and Portuguese, Fernando Pessoa left a prodigious body of work, much of it under "heteronyms"—fully fleshed alter egos with startlingly different styles and points of view. Offering a unique sampling of all his most famous voices, this collection features poems that have never before been translated alongside many originally composed in English. In addition to such major works as "Maritime Ode" and his Goethe-inspired "Faust," written in blank verse, there are several stunning poems that have only recently come to light. Selected and translated by leading Pessoa scholar Richard Zenith, this is a fine introduction to the breadth of Pessoa's genius.

ISBN 978-0-14-303955-6

THE STORY OF PENGUIN CLASSICS

Before 1946 . . . "Classics" are mainly the domain of academics and students; readable editions for everyone else are almost unheard of. This all changes when a little-known classicist, E. V. Rieu, presents Penguin founder Allen Lane with the translation of Homer's *Odyssey* that he has been working on in his spare time.

1946 Penguin Classics debuts with *The Odyssey,* which promptly sells three million copies. Suddenly, classics are no longer for the privileged few.

1950s Rieu, now series editor, turns to professional writers for the best modern, readable translations, including Dorothy L. Sayers's *Inferno* and Robert Graves's unexpurgated *Twelve Caesars*.

1960s The Classics are given the distinctive black covers that have remained a constant throughout the life of the series. Rieu retires in 1964, hailing the Penguin Classics list as "the greatest educative force of the twentieth century."

1970s A new generation of translators swells the Penguin Classics ranks, introducing readers of English to classics of world literature from more than twenty languages. The list grows to encompass more history, philosophy, science, religion, and politics.

1980s The Penguin American Library launches with titles such as *Uncle Tom's Cabin,* and joins forces with Penguin Classics to provide the most comprehensive library of world literature available from any paperback publisher.

1990s The launch of Penguin Audiobooks brings the classics to a listening audience for the first time, and in 1999 the worldwide launch of the Penguin Classics website extends their reach to the global online community.

The 21st Century Penguin Classics are completely redesigned for the first time in nearly twenty years. This world-famous series now consists of more than 1300 titles, making the widest range of the best books ever written available to millions—and constantly redefining what makes a "classic."

The Odyssey continues . . .